Mamie and the Root Woman

Elizabeth Bowles

Outskirts Press, Inc.
Denver, Colorado

Outskirts Press
http://www.outskirtspress.com

ISBN-10: 1-59800-481-6
ISBN-13: 978-1-59800-481-6

Library of Congress Control Number: 2006927307

Printed in the United States of America

Dedication

This book is dedicated to all my teachers, mentors, friends and family who inspired a love for words, reading and writing. Without them, this book would not have come to fruition. My heartfelt thanks to all of you.

Acknowledgments

I give special thanks to L. Gray Bailey, my friend and editor and one who always encouraged me. Thanks also have to go to Liz Jameson, my teacher and first rough draft editor. I thank my son, Michael, who helped with computer problems and to Chadwick Teate for building my web site.

Prologue

After the Civil War, in December of 1865, six Confederate Veterans formed a little club. Soon the *club* became America's first organized terrorist group—the Ku Klux Klan.

Southerners, recently defeated, passed laws known as the Black Codes to suppress the civil rights of the newly freed slaves. Reconstruction followed. Vigilante law—a carryover of law in the frontier west, quickly emerged in answer to the Reconstruction policy of the federal government.

In April, 1867, all dens and chapters of the Klan throughout the south were asked to send a representative to Nashville, Tennessee to plan Klan response to the new federal Reconstruction policy. What had begun as a mischief-making group of local hoodlums, soon became a group of violent night riders—The Ku Klux Klan. They terrorized, tortured, and lynched those they deemed in violation of White supremacy ideals.

Members of the Klan were called Ghouls. Draped in white sheets, with grotesque masks and tall pointed white hats, they struck fear into the hearts of blacks.

1868: Balters, South Carolina.

Mamie, aged four, played in the loft where she and her mother, Lizzye Managault, had lived with another colored family since first moving to Balters.

"Mama, what you and Miz Alice talkin' 'bout?" asked Mamie. "What is *night riders*?"

"Men who ride in the night and scare the colored folk," Lizzye answered.

"How they do that?" Mamie asked. Recently coming to Balters from the sheltered life of Creole society in New Orleans, Mamie knew nothing of the Klan.

"Sweetheart," Lizzye answered, giving her daughter a hug, "they dress up in silly white sheets and try to scare people. Let's get ready for bed now. Mama starts teaching tomorrow at the Freedman's school."

In the backwaters of the south, violence against the blacks occurred on an almost daily basis. In Balters, South Carolina, a black town, on the outskirts of Kingstree, South Carolina, these night-riding *ghouls* played tricks on the colored community.

What seemed like fun to the white vigilantes reminded the blacks of the prewar slave patrols, and the patter rollers, hired thugs who tried to catch (and sometimes mutilated or murdered those they caught) runaway slaves.

1872: Balters, South Carolina.

"Mama, I want to go back to live in New Orleans. Them night riders scare me," Mamie said, coming in from the area outside the one-room school.

Lizzye jumped up from her desk and rushed to the window. Looking out, she saw a few children playing, and a few adult students, standing under a clump of live oak, talking.

"What happened? Did you see something that upset you?" she asked.

"No, ma'ma," Mamie answered, "but Lula Belle say the Klan ride into her yard last night. A ghost man asked for a whole bucket o' water. Gulp it down, ask for another one. Drink it down, too. Drink the third bucket o' water, and—"

"Oh, child, it's a trick. They sometimes do that to scare people into thinking they are truly ghosts," Lizzye said, kneeling down and taking the trembling child into her arms. "They pour the water into funnels attached to a hose and running to a small barrel on their saddles. They are not drinking that water!" Now Lizzye, too, trembled. She trembled from a different kind of fear.

Though I look white, teach school, and speak proper English, I am nevertheless colored. Yet, to the whites, I don't fit the image the have of how colored people should look, dress, behave. I live alone with my young daughter in my own house on my own land. I know I must be a target. Perhaps I'll speak to Root Woman about my fears.

"Well, daughter, you and Mamie can always hide out in the swamp with me," Saylee said.

"Saylee, I can't do that. But maybe we should move back to New Orleans. What do you think?"

"Can't say. That have to be your decision," Root Woman said as she gathered her parcels and prepared to leave.

From silly pranks such as appearing to drink gallons of water, to more and more violent acts, the terror of the Ku Klux Klan was spreading throughout the south. As the lenient policies of the federal government under Johnson gave way to the harsher Reconstruction era, the mischievous silliness was turning ugly and life threatening.

Lynchings, and a punishment called tarring and feathering, would soon become commonplace in and around Balters as the 1870's progressed. Most attributed to the Klan.

1875: Balters, South Carolina.

"Mama, I was standing over on the road that goes up past the old Rodenburg pond, talking to that white boy own the vegetable and fruit stand. He nice. His name is Isaiah. We been knowin' each other for about a month," Mamie paused to catch her breath. Her eyes rolled. Lizzye offered her a dipper of the cold well water she had just drawn.

"Mamie, what happened? Catch your breath first," Lizzye said.

She speaks more and more like her playmates. Maybe that will help to protect her, though.

Mamie gulped some water, wiped her forehead, and continued.

"A man ride up and get off his horse real fast. He say, 'You mighty friendly with this here colored girl, boy. You want the night riders to pay you a visit, or what?' I take off running so I ain't hear what that white boy say back to that man. Mama, that man on the horse must be one of the Klan!"

"Mamie, stay away from the white community. That boy may very well be *nice,* as you say, but, you never know who sees you. Please!"

Mamie is so likable and outgoing. A Klan rider in broad daylight?

They're getting bold. And mean! Well, I'm not going back to New Orleans. Not yet, anyway.

"Mamie, promise me you will be more careful. Promise?"

"Yessum," Mamie mumbled, just barely understanding the danger.

Mamie's fifteenth birthday on January 1, 1879, dawned bright and cold. Her mother, with permission from the Freedman's Bureau, had closed the school for that day. Now she and Mamie worked side by side preparing for the late afternoon party.

"Mama, Rosco coming to my birthday party, you know."

"Well, of course, I know. I invited him. Why you ask?"

"I likes him *special*," Mamie said, as she continued to peel the shrimp for the gumbo.

"You're too young to be liking a boy. Besides, Rosco must be eighteen or nineteen years old. You're still a child. Be sure to get the black vein out of the shrimp," Lizzye added.

"Mama?" Mamie changed the subject, "Why so many white people talk about the Ku Klux Klan like they some kinda good peoples? They ain't!"

"How do you know about what the white community talks about?"

"I hear talk sometimes when I in the general store over in Brio."

"I thought I told you to stay away from that boy. Especially now that you are older. His little old vegetable stand is a general store now?"

"Well, sort of. I go in there to buy penny candy when I get the chance," she said as she cut her eyes at her mama. "Sometimes I look at the bolts of pretty cloth in the back. The store not much morn' a shed, but I like to go there. Isaiah and me talks when nobody else is around."

"I told you not to be hanging around that boy. Go in there, buy what you need, and leave," Lizzye said.

"When they is other people in the store, I just listens to them talk. I hear old Miz Clayton, the judge's wife, say that the Klan does a powerful lot of good, protectin' the virtues of the white womens."

"You are fifteen years old as of today. Leave the whites alone! The Klan is dangerous!" Lizzye grabbed Mamie by the shoulders and shook her slightly. "Leave all whites alone."

The Ku Klux Klan was openly active from 1866 until 1879; underground, but still active, from 1879 until about 1915. It then became, for many years, openly hostile and extremely active against Blacks, Jews, Catholics, and any other group against whom it chose to vent its ire. It has had several periods in its infamous history. In November of 1879, the Ku Klux Klan rode again. One of the last overt, violent acts of the 1800's Klan involved Mamie, her mother and Root Woman. This then, is their story.

Chapter 1

Rosco

Deep in the swamp for a deed most vile
Done by Klansmen to a little child
Voodoo Queen step out of the night
Curse the men with all her might
Give them death, grief, and strife
For pain they cause in this child's life . . . .

On a bitterly cold night in November, 1879, Rosco ran deeper and deeper into the swamp. In the twilight, barely able to see, he fled for his life. His heart pounded in his chest. Through water, then back onto higher ground, his feet thudded on the spongy, moss-covered swamp floor. His shoes squished with cold swamp water.

Where them train tracks is? I not sure I has to leave town, but Mama say go, so I gone. New York, here I come.

An owl flew from a low branch. The young man stopped, but, more afraid of his mother's ire than an evil omen, he headed again in what he hoped was the direction of the tracks.

He splashed through water, expecting to hear bloodhounds, all the while scanning nervously for alligators. Whenever the fear of the scaly monsters got the best of him, he jumped back onto higher ground. Thinking he heard the baying of bloodhounds in the distance, Rosco moved back into the knee deep water. In the deepening gloom of the night, his eyes strained to see any sign of the cold, steel rails.

Just as panic gripped him, he came upon the raised bed of steel and cross ties. He followed the rails deeper into the Congaree Swamp. Just before the big bend in the tracks, he stepped onto the gnarled roots of an old oak tree. He climbed up, sat in a fork, and thought about what had gotten him into trouble in the first place.

Silly, old, fat white woman! What she think she got I want?

He slapped at the back of his neck, imagining something crawling.

Wonder what Mama doin' right now? She sho Lawd got the scares for me. Say theys a lynch mob commin'. Can't even say 'boo' to no white woman.

Rosco stared at the deepening night sky. He hugged himself and tried to control his shivering by rubbing his arms and legs. Unable to fathom the immensity of the change about to come into his life, he nevertheless sensed that nothing would ever be the same.

Aw, Mamie. What's we gonna do now? Some people think that little yellow gal is ugly, but to me she pretty as *a puppy dog. I wisht I hadda gone by her house. Didn't even get to say good-bye. She gonna be mad at me. Mama so scared of the Klan. She so bossy. Boss me around like I's a chil.! I come home and Mama was all over me. She say...*

"Hurry Rosco. They's commin. You got to high-tail it outta here. Summey overhear them Klan's people talkin' about teachin' you a lesson." Callie put her finger to her lips. She looked out of the small window listening as she peered into the late afternoon gloom. Nothing. Turning again toward Rosco, she snapped, "Hurry up. Is you through—"

"Maw," Rosco repeated, "all I said to Miz Thompson was, 'This un's mine.' She reached for the sack of cracked corn on the other side of that aisle after I done grabbed it from my side. I said, as politely as ever you heard, 'Scuse me, but this un's mine.' I didn't mess with that woman. Drinkin' or not, I know not to do that."

"Boy, time is all you got between you and a noose," Callie said. She continued cooking the sparse meal for him. Though it was cold, her bare feet slapped the boards of the floor as she walked from stove to table.

"Maw, did you hear what I just—"

"Rosco, you done tole me that ten times. You can't say nothin' to no white woman. 'Specially if you been drinkin'. Is you crazy? I guess you is!" She rolled her eyes in exasperation when he just stared at her with his mouth open.

"Put on two pairs of pants. Go get that old coat you wore last winter. It hangin' on a peg over by the back door. Hurry."

She ran to the window and peered out again. Turning back, she saw that he still stood looking at her.

"Take this heah five dollar gold piece give to me on Freedom Day. And here's a few nickels and dimes from my egg money. I wish I had more to give you. Git on a train headin' north. Don't let nobody see you."

When he continued to stand there, she slapped him hard, then gasped and pulled him to her ample bosom in a hug. Her wet face pressed against his cheek. He kissed his maw on the cheek and tasted salt.

Jolted by the slap, he jumped from foot to foot in his hurry to get the extra pair of pants on. He stumbled and almost fell. She shoved the poke into his hands as soon as he regained his balance.

"Write to me at your Aunt Mary's over in Jackson County. Is you know the address?"

"You better write it down for me."

"You knows I can't write. Here, write it down on this brown paper sack. 'Mary Lincoln, Post Office, Greely Corners'. Stick it way down in the bottom of your poke and don't lose it. Write to me. I get somebody to read me yo letter. I send you word when all this boils out and it safe to come back." She watched him write the address on the brown paper sack, then turned to the window once again.

"I ain't know for sure where the train tracks is," Rosco shoved the address down into his poke. Neither he nor Callie saw it follow his hand out of the sack and drop to the kitchen floor where it slid, unnoticed, under the table.

"I ain't never been as far as the tracks—"

"Rosco, just try. You go far enough into the swamp, you bound to come up on the tracks. And hurry. Hide alongside the tracks 'til you hear the train. After it pass, jump out and run. It slow down some 'cause of the swamp mists from what I hear. But you still gots to be fast. Pay attention. You hear me?"

Callie took the corn pone and fried fat back and wrapped them in a red bandanna. She stuck a little jug of molasses down in the croaker sack, then shoved her son, with all his worldly goods, out the door.

Callie stood in the street and watched Rosco as he ran toward the swamp. He never looked back. When she could no longer see him, she turned and went back into the cabin. She hurriedly packed her own things and those of Rosco's younger sister, Bessie, ignoring the young girl's frantic questions.

"Mama, what Rosco done? Why he leave so quick? Where we goin?"

Twenty minutes later, Callie slipped out, pulling the girl by the hand. She and Bessie walked the five miles to her sister's house in Greely Corners, cutting through back yards and woods, and avoiding main roads whenever they could.

"Mama, where we goin'? Where Rosco go?" Bessie asked.

"Bessie, honey, Rosco not but three years old when slavery ended," Callie said.

"Yessum, but where we headed and where Rosco—"

"He so head-strong," Callie hurried on. "Why he have to go in there all likkered up? Maybe this all boil over, and we kin get back to livin' a normal life."

"Yessum, what'd he do?"

"I sho hope he catch that train," Callie ignored her daughter. "Cold out here tonight, ain't it?"

Robert Norris watched as his son combed his dark curly hair and tried to get a straight center part.

"You don't want to go fooling around with this Ku Klux Klan group, Isaiah. They're up to no good, I tell you."

"Aw, Paw, we're just going to mess with that uppity nigger who scared Mrs. Thompson 'most to death. I'll be back before you know I'm gone." He eyed his reflection in the mirror one more time, frowned, and walked out of the room.

"Bye, Paw. Bye, Maw," he called over his shoulder.

Judge Clayton stood six feet tall; his long, black riding coat reached his boots. At Clayton's barn, six men milled about speaking in hushed tones. Isaiah rode into the yard on an old sorrel. The boy hitched the horse to a post, walked into the barn, and joined the group. There were seven of them including the judge.

When the judge cleared his throat, the men drew near. Claude, first to join the Klan, cradled his white robe in the crook of one arm. His hand caressed the carefully stitched cross. He lifted his hand from its red satin and motioned for the others to be quiet.

"Okay, men," the judge said, "Let's get started. You all know about that nigger, Rosco, insulting Mrs. Thompson—"

"I hear he was dead drunk, stumbled into her and then rubbed his crotch right in front of her." Clem said.

The judge's face contorted in an angry scowl. Thrusting and bobbing, his gray goatee on his long, thin face took on a life of its own. His eyes narrowed to slits.

"Well, it's for sure he came into the feed and seed store all likkered up and took liberties with Mrs. Thompson. Joseph said he looked her up and down and mumbled some kind of insult." The judge paused as he surveyed the group. "We need to teach that boy a lesson."

Claude hopped from foot to foot and raised his hand. Judge Clayton nodded in his direction.

"I think he tried to feel her up. That's what I heard somebody say over to Joe's Feed and Seed."

"He may have," the judge shook his head. "He may have. But, when we get through with him, he'll think twice before messing around with our womenfolk. If any of you don't yet have your robes made, see my wife. She's got some white sheets in the kitchen. Now, let's sheet up and ride out."

Isaiah cleared his throat. Moving through to the front of the men, he asked, "Uh, Judge Clayton, what are we going to do to him when we find him? When Clem came by my store today, he said you wanted us to ride out to the nigger settlement and burn a cross."

Judge Clayton pointed to a pack horse with a long creosote pole tied to each side of her. "See those poles? They burn nice and bright on a cold November night"

"We not going to do nothing but burn a cross, are we?"

Judge Clayton looked at Isaiah through narrowed eyes.

"You getting cold feet?" Clayton asked. "'Cause if you are, you might as well ride on out of here right now. No telling what we gonna do. Maybe just burn a cross, maybe catch us a nigger in a noose."

The others laughed and looked at the young man. Isaiah swallowed hard.

The three men who didn't yet have Klan robes draped sheets over their heads with holes cut out for the eyes.

Isaiah sheeted up with the rest.

Half an hour after leaving the judge's kitchen, the group of seven rode their white draped horses into the dead quiet of the Negro settlement. Each rider turned in his saddle, looking around. Nobody in the settlement stirred, not a dog barked.

They checked the house they thought was rented out to Callie and her two children. Empty. Isaiah, the last to leave, saw a brown paper sack on the floor under the table. He picked it up and shoved it into his pocket, saying nothing to the men. They moved on to the other houses. The second house. Empty.

In the third shack, they found an old man, apparently sick. He huddled in a narrow bed, sweat drenched his feverish skin.

Claude pulled the old man to his feet questioning him as to the whereabouts of the rest of the colored folk in the settlement. He was incoherent.

As the others tried to question the old man, Isaiah slipped the paper sack out of his pocket and read: 'Aunt Mary, Post office Grely Corner'. He shoved the bag back into his pocket before anyone could see.

"Leave him be," ordered the judge.

Claude turned the man loose, and he crumpled in a heap on the floor. They left him where he had fallen.

The other houses were deserted, too.

"Judge," Isaiah said, "I know where Rosco's girlfriend lives. I was on the old Tamarack road and got behind Rosco driving a wagon. That old mule was clippety-clopping along at a snail's pace. I couldn't go around them 'cause the road is so narrow, so I just sat back and watched them two spooning in the moonlight."

The men all laughed. Isaiah turned in his saddle and grinned at them.

"That girl is so ugly." he said. "I saw them turn into a yard. I bet I could find the house again. They live just over in Balters."

"You'll be a real asset to the Klan, boy," Judge Clayton slapped Isaiah on the back. "Let's go."

It was a half-hour ride to Balters. For the first time, the men included Isaiah in some of their banter. Isaiah, for the most part, rode in silence, grinning from time to time at something one of them said. He positioned his horse next to the judge again.

"Maybe I can't find her house. It's been several months since I saw them two. Maybe we should just go on back."

"I'm sure you'll be able to find the place. Don't worry so. We're just gonna scare that boy. We can't scare him if we can't find him. You done good to speak up."

The judge spurred his horse and sprinted away before Isaiah could answer.

Lizzye heard the hoof beats of many horses rush into her front yard. She sat by the window wearing a gray dress that reached her ankles.

I w*ish I had heeded my instinct to hide in the swamp at Saylee's. Too late now. God, protect my child!*

Lizzye forced herself to breathe deeply and to walk slowly as she answered the pounding on the door, stopping only to light the kerosene lamp on her way.

"Good evening, gentlemen. Won't you come in?"

Her white collar gleamed in the light of the moon and the kerosene lamp. Her skin was almost as white.

"The girl," Judge Clayton said without preliminary. "Mamie. We want to question the girl. Get her."

They stood just inside the parlor, with the door wide open. Lizzye shivered as a cold wind whipped into the room. The fire in her fireplace, almost burned out, flared up with new life.

"Perhaps I can help. My child is fast asleep and has to be rested for school tomorrow."

Judge Clayton slapped the woman across the head, knocking her to the floor. He motioned toward the back of the house, but Lizzye was quicker than the man who started toward the bedroom door.

"I'm sorry. I misspoke. I'll bring her out straight away. One moment, please," she said, wiping a thin trickle of blood from her mouth with the corner of her apron.

"Mamie, wake up. Wake up. Don't be afraid."

Pulling the sleeping girl from her bed, she dressed her with shaking hands in the warm clothing already laid out. Lizzye then buttoned her into a long, hooded coat.

"Mama, I don't want to wear that."

"Wear this, and be quiet. I don't want those prying eyes to see any more of you than your face." she whispered.

"I dressed her warmly because the house is cold," she said as she came out with the sleepy girl.

"Where's Rosco?" asked Judge Clayton.

Mamie blinked, "I don't know. At his house, I guess. He stay over in—"

"I know where the boy lives. What do you take me for, a fool?" He crossed the room in two strides and put his face in hers, "By God, tell me where that bastard is."

"Suh," Mamie said, "I don't know where he is."

"I know you're trying to protect that low-life. Tell me where he's hiding, or so help me, I'll beat it out of you." he shouted.

"Oh, Judge," Lizzye cried as she stepped between her child and the angry man, "She don't know. She really—"

Before his fist struck her temple, she realized the mistake she had made.

"You impudent white nigger! You dare call me 'Judge'?"

Lizzye flew three feet across the room, where her head struck the corner of the mantle with a resounding crack. She slid down the wall, her eyes locked on her daughter. With her mouth open as though to speak, she slipped to the floor, leaving a wide smear of blood from the mantle to the bottom of the fireplace.

Mamie ran toward her mother, but Lem stuck out his foot and

tripped her. She fell within inches of Lizzye.

"Mama, Mama."

"Get the girl," Judge Clayton motioned toward the door, "and let's go. I've got a plan. We haven't burned the cross yet, and I know how we can get her to talk."

Lem carried the girl over his left shoulder like a sack of potatoes. He walked out of the house with Mamie crying and begging them to get help for her mama. He slung her across his horse.

"Pull the hood of the coat down over her head and face to muffle that squalling," the judge called over his shoulder as they rode out of the yard. "Girl, you know what's good for you, you'll shut up that yammering."

Lizzye's neighbors came running as soon as the Klan were out of sight. Caroline was the first one in the door. The black woman let out a thin, high-pitched wail as she knelt by Lizzye's side with the others crowding close.

Lizzye's eyes fluttered open.

"My child," she whispered, "they took Mamie. Get Root Woman. If she lives, she will need—"

Lizzye died in Caroline's arms, a three-inch piece of skull embedded in her brain.

"Oh, Miz Lizzye. Miz Lizzye." Caroline cried. "She gone."She turned to the assembled group. "Go get Root Woman. If they don't kill the child, they shore to hurt her bad the mood they's in."

The men left Lizzye's house and stood in the front yard deciding the best way to proceed. Three men started out at a run for the swamp and Root Woman.

Saylee set off in the direction of Balters. She sensed an urgent need, but couldn't yet get a clear vision.

Something to do with my friend, Lizzye. What? What goin' on?

Just then, she heard a screech owl high overhead. She knew. She retraced her steps to her cabin for the exact medicines she would need.

This the child of my vision. No. Not my friend Lizzye's child.

Nearing her cabin, she stared at the full moon and saw a splash of blood across its face. As she ran, she heard her friend cry out.

"My baby. They got my Mamie."

Now I know what that old vision meant. Mamie is the child. This the child I saw even before she was born! Can I change the vision like I did so long ago when I saw my mama trip and break her neck? I don't think so. No legs? No legs? But who do this? And where she be? Aw, God. Please not let this be. Hurry. I need powerful magic. Dambala, help me. Help me, now.

Back in her cabin now, she hurried with preparations.

I need elderberry root, willow bark and yarrow. Come magic healing potions. Come together for Saylee, Root Woman, descended from long line of medicine women of The Chicora and my papa's line from the land of Africa. Big trouble brewing. Big magic needed. Willow bark tea for the pain. Fine yellow yarrow powder mixed with lard and just a little coal tar for the—Please don't let it be.

She set off again with the ointment and willow bark tea tucked in with sundry herbs and roots which she always carried. As she neared the edge of the swamp, she heard the excited voices of three men as they approached. She stepped off the path and into the trees. Hiding behind a clump of cypress, she listened.

"I's scared goin' so deep into the swamp. And at night, too."

"Yeah, me too. 'Specially so late at night," came another voice.

"You right. Let's turn back. We don't know where Root Woman live. We don't know where the Klan done take Mamie, and poor Lizzye dead anyway." said the first man in a voice high-pitched with dread.

"Lizzye dead, you right 'bout that," answered a new voice, "but we owe it to Mamie to try to find Root Woman. I think I know where her cabin is."

Root Woman turned back again and headed off at a trot without making a sound.

Aw, no. Poor Lizzye. Poor Mamie. Gotta hurry now.

A bone-chilling mist had risen in the swamp so that it was impossible to see more than a few feet away. Rosco sat hunched, worried that he might not see the train in time, or that he would be too cold to run along the tracks and grab hold.

The loud clank of wheels on steel echoed down the track along with the screech of brakes. The screaming brakes drowned the sound of the terrified child, Mamie, crying to be home with her mama, and the yelling of a young man, Isaiah.

It slowing down. It stopping so the mens can search fo me! Oh Lordy. Gotta get on board and hide.

He scampered down from his perch in the oak tree and hid in the bushes by the tracks. Now, he saw the lights from the engine. He heard the squeal of the brakes and then felt a whoosh of wind that nearly sucked him into the train's path. The noise was deafening. Even though the train had slowed considerably, it still hammered down the tracks at a good clip, shooting off steam and kicking up cinders.

After the lights of the train passed him, Rosco jumped up from his hiding place. He ran along side the train. He threw himself at some handholds, nearly slipped, and barely grabbed onto just one. He hung on as the behemoth slammed him like a rag-doll against its side. He scrabbled with his other hand to reach the handhold, managing finally to fling himself around so that he could catch hold with both hands. He hung for a moment with all the breath knocked out of him. As he slowly began his climb into the boxcar, he heard the scream of the train whistle and the screech of brakes again. With strength he didn't know he possessed, he scrambled into the car and wondered if this was the dreaded moment when they would find him.

The men continued on, picking their way through the swamp, never suspecting that they had been within five feet of the famed, old healer.

When Saylee reached her cabin, she got out her live lightning bugs.

I hates having to sacrifice you little critters, but I needs you! After smearing the bug juice all over, she glowed with an eerie phosphorescent green. She grabbed twine, scissors, sulfur powder, and the supplies she had earlier prepared. She left her cabin long before the hesitant men found their way there. She headed off in the direction of the railroad tracks, knowing that's where the Klan had taken the girl.

Root Woman saw the burning cross long before reaching the tracks. She heard a child screaming. Then the screaming stopped. In the silence, Saylee's skin prickled. When she got to the clearing, she stayed out of sight, watching to size up the situation. Mamie, tied across the tracks, seemed dead. Mamie's coat was pulled up and the hood completely covered her face. Her dress was up around her waist, and her long bloomers had been cut off exposing her privates.

"Go on Clem, get you some of that yellow stuff."

Clem poked a finger into the girl's vagina, then straightened up and said, "Naw, too ugly for me. You go right ahead."

They all laughed, except for Isaiah, who stood with tears streaming down his face. He shouted to the judge and others to leave the girl alone.

"She don't know. She don't. Leave her be. Cut her loose. Untie her. What if a train was to come —"

Judge Clayton, ignoring the actions of Clem and Claude, turned to Isaiah.

"Shut up," he ordered. Turning back to Mamie, he shouted at her to tell him where Rosco was hiding.

Isaiah grabbed the man's sleeve.

"Judge, stop. Please stop. Maybe she really don't know. She's just a child. God."

Judge Clayton spun around, staring at Isaiah.

"Go stand over there by that tree. These damn darkies know plenty. Time they're this age they've already dropped two or three little pickaninnies. I know how their grapevine works. She knows. And, by God, I intend to find out what she knows." he yelled.

Standing just inside the door, Rosco leaned out and saw the burning cross and the sheeted horses and men.

They done flag down the train so they can search fo me wid bloodhounds. Looka dem pointed hats, dem white robes. Gawd A'mighty, there's the burning cross I done been hearing 'bout. Aw, Lordy. I done for. Mama you was right 'bout this.

Where to hide? Where? Where I gonna hide?

Looking around the inside of the boxcar, he saw the steel side of a tall silo. He shinnied up the ten-feet-tall round drum by placing his back against the metal corn crib and his feet against the wall of the car. When he got to the top, he turned, clutched the edge of the drum and swung his feet and legs over the top.

When he flopped about two feet down onto shelled corn, a wharf rat bit his thumb. Rosco's cold fingers closed around the animal's neck. He squeezed until he heard a crack. Still holding the dead rat, he got to his feet and peered over the top of the silo, and out of the open door of the car. Only the sight of the burning cross was visible to him. He heard the shrill of the brakes and a jumble of voices.

Isaiah did as he was ordered. Clouds rushed briefly over the moon. He stood with eyes downcast. Just then, Root Woman stepped from the shadows.

"Untie the child." she thundered.

Isaiah's head snapped up and he stared open-mouthed at the apparition. The men gasped. Before them appeared an old woman glowing green in the moonlight, even her silver hair streaming over her shoulders and down her back had a greenish glow. She stood tall and straight. Her high cheek bones defined in the half light.

She stared and then threw something down. A yellowish color blended with the swamp mists giving off an odor of sulfur as it rose all around her. It swirled up in long writhing trails. In her hand she carried a snake coiled around a long pole. The snake, seen through the wisps of yellowish mists, seemed to coil and uncoil around the pole.

"Dambala!" she shook the pole at them. "Dambala curse the lives of all. Pain, sickness, sorrow, misery-y-y."

Four of the men mounted their horses and took off at a gallop.

"Yellow-bellied, white devils, ride out, but you can not outrun the curse of Dambala. Foot. Leg. Mind and heart."

Judge Clayton took a step back, stumbled, and almost fell.

"You d-don't scare me with your cheap mumbo-jumbo," he said.

Root Woman turned toward him. She held her arms out, and with fingers spread uttered another Voodoo curse.

"Untie the girl, now!" she intoned. "By your actions tonight, you have sealed your fates. You, man named Clayton, will die friendless and all alone after years of sickness and misfortune. I have said it. It is done."

As she uttered the curse, she walked toward the tracks. Her voice grew louder and deeper as she emerged from the trees.

It was then they heard the train. They heard the screech of brakes and the piercing whistle before they saw the steel monster clanking and thundering down the tracks. Judge Clayton stood as though frozen.

Isaiah whirled around to face the judge.

"Give me a knife. Damn it, move." When the judge stood as though turned to stone, Isaiah turned toward the other man. "Do you have a knife?"

Both the judge and Clem shook their heads no. Isaiah knelt on the tracks to untie the girl, but the knots held fast. Root Woman ran toward him from a distance of thirty feet with a knife in her outstretched hand, but it was too late.

The light from the burning cross, the full moon and the bright beams of the train illuminated the tracks like day. As the train thundered down the track, the engineer saw something on the tracks. In one blinding moment, he viewed the group of white-sheeted men, and understood. He tried in vain to stop the train as steel screamed against steel.

Isaiah and Root Woman jumped clear of the track in the last possible moment. Their faces grimaced in horror. Then, the screeching of the train's brakes stopped along with the train. Listening, Rosco heard a voice yelling at the 'dumb bastards dressed up in bed sheets.' He strained to hear, holding his breath.

"Mamie. Is she dead? She's under the wheels. Her legs. Oh God, pull her out." a young man screamed.

Rosco, thinking he heard, "Mamie is dead", fell backwards in a dead faint onto the corn in the silo.

After pulling the girl out from under the train, the engineer became aware of the tall, thin woman.

"Give me the child," she said.

Blood poured from the severed legs. Root Woman knelt and tied strong twine around each leg. Picking up the girl, she pulled the hood off her face with one deft movement, and took the barely conscious Mamie over to the burning cross.

The men watched. Mamie, roused to full consciousness by the cauterizing of both legs, let out a blood-curdling howl. The smell of charred flesh penetrated the swamp as Mamie collapsed back against Root Woman.

Saylee knelt, smeared an ointment on the limp girl's stumps, and cradled the child in her arms like a baby. She left without a word, disappearing into the swamp.

When Rosco came to, the train moved along at a steady pace with a gentle rocking motion. He still clutched the dead rat. He threw it over the side of the container. With his other hand, he wiped tears from his face and sat slumped over, moaning.

Deep into the swamp, Saylee trotted with the girl. An owl screeched. She heard the bellow of a bull alligator and the cry of night-birds as she passed along the familiar trail. The fecund smell of swamp rot surrounded her as she ran with the unconscious girl. Root Woman sang a healing song as she jogged through the swamp. She sang a song that would, one day, bring Mamie back to life and to pain.

Chapter 2

Root Woman's Roots

The dark swamp welcomed Mamie
There Root Woman worked her charm
For years she kept the girl from the world
Soothing body and soul away from all harm
Hidden deep in the swamp, Mamie's healing began
As Isaiah grew from a boy to a man

At Root Woman's cabin, she made a bed for the girl. She worked for three days and slept only in snatches.

On the fourth day, Mamie bolted upright.

"Mama, help me. Aiy-e-e-e-e, the cross, the burning cross . . .Ow-w-w, burn me, Mama . . . Jesus burned me with his . . . cross . . . Oh, I dying . . .". Mamie's eyes searched the cabin. Sweat beaded her forehead. "Mama is dead . . . Ow-w-w aiy-e-e-e . . . Untie me . . . Train commin'. . . let me loose . . .Please . . . Help me, please." She sank back against Saylee's chest. Exhausted, the girl slept.

The next day, Mamie continued to babble, rambling day and night. When, after three weeks, her fever broke, she fell silent.

"I know there's terror bottled up inside, Girl. *Talk. Please talk.*" Saylee said. "*Talk . . . Scream.*" But still Mamie lay mute.

During that long, hard winter of 1882, Mamie didn't speak. She didn't even cry out when Saylee scraped the suppurating flesh away from the bone and dressed the wounds.

After the first few weeks, Root Woman began a course of 'talking magic' even while Mamie slept.

"Mamie talk today? I sing you a song to make you better." Saylee said each day, rocking the limp bundle that was Mamie. When awake, the girl stared into Saylee's eyes as if trying to find the words she had once known. Over and over, Saylee told Mamie what had happened. To her. To her mama. To the members of the Klan, now living with a curse hanging over their heads. She talked to Mamie about Isaiah, 'the good boy'. Mamie stared but said nothing.

Spring arrived and Root Woman took Mamie to a Voodoo ceremony in a clearing in the swamp. The very night Mamie's legs had been severed, Saylee had slipped out and gotten Mamie's clothes and her drum from Lizzye's house. She placed a protective spell over the house. She then gathered Mamie's limbs. The next morning, Saylee laid the legs and feet outside in a weighted, wire cage, singing a chant over them. Now, the bones were ready to be used for Mamie's healing.

Saylee met with a group of initiates near where the horrid events of that night in November had taken place.

Mamie, near comatose from drugs, slept on a travois propped against a large boulder. Flowers, feathers, bones and gris-gris--little cotton sacks filled with graveyard dirt and herbs--were placed in a semi-circle around her.

The mambo began the ceremony with chanting. Drumming came next, and dancing. The hougnan, a voodoo priest, caught Saylee when she swooned from the dance. Saylee performed this mad whirling in order to become possessed by the serpent god, Dambala.

As she came back to her senses, the hougnan gave her some of his own gris-gris.

The bones from the toes of Mamie's severed limbs, picked clean over the winter by the scavenger beetles, would become part of her powerful voodoo gris-gris.

The Mambo joined them.

The hougan left to attend to others.

The Mambo and Root Woman rested under a large oak tree. "Tell me" the mambo asked, "how you come to be powerful healing woman?"

"I not sure I is a powerful woman. I is Saylee, daughter of Pali, Medicine woman of the Chicora Tribe and Germahl, son of African chief. They long dead now."

"Tell me about your papa."

"This," Root Woman began, "is what I remember of my papa's dying . . . ."

"Pali, my mama, stand in the doorway—I see her from my bed. She breathing in the cool night air. She hear my papa groan, and leaving the door open, she tiptoe back to the sleeping place. He asleep, drenched in sweat. She go back to the door, and stand staring out toward the old slave cemetery..

"Hearing the screech of an owl, she jump and let out a shriek. Papa groan in his sleep, but didn't wake up.

"Mama dig through her medicine bag until she find the dried leg bone of a rooster. She take off at a dead run for the cemetery. I sneak and follow her. I hide. She bury the bone in the ground by the oldest grave in the plot and wait.

"She say, 'Let it be that hateful old man, Sinclair,'. She gaze at the moon, so I do, too. A cloud pass over the moon, and, in that moment, I hear the wind whisper my papa's name —"

"So. Even as a child you knew things?" the mambo asked.

"Yes, always. I knew my papa was dying. We tended old Zeke, and then Tacie Farmer, who was having a baby soon."

"That winter of 1821—"

"So. You must be seventy-two years old now?" the voodoo priestess asked, passing Saylee the corncob pipe.

"Yes, I born in 1809. Anyway, that winter, the cold hit in November and not let up. It now the end of March and still below freezing most nights. Tacie get the same rations of cornmeal, fatback and molasses the other nine slaves get, even though she expectin' her tenth child—most likely Sinclair's baby.

"Mama share her own roots and herbs as best she can, but supplies is almost gone. She barely have plants for medicine.

"Mama attend her; She birth that baby. Wrapping the infant in an old shirt, she lay it on Tacie's breast.

"Mama and me hurry home to Papa. He still breathing, but wheezing so he fill our cabin with the sound of his struggle. Mama send for Aunt Mindy. The old woman come.

"Musta' been hard for a little girl like you was to see all that suffering," the Mambo said, shaking her head over her corn cob pipe, and then passing it to Saylee.

Saylee nodded her head as she took a whiff of the woman's pipe. The Voodoo drums beat softly now and people rested against tree trunks in the clearing. Mamie still slept a drugged sleep.

"Papa open his eyes and call for Mama. She knelt by his cot and lay a cool rag on his forehead. He grabbed her other hand, too.

"'Pali,' he say, 'I wish I could stay with you and Saylee'".

"He took one shuddering breath, breathing my name! 'No, don't go', I cried. 'I can't go with you! I don't want you to go. Papa, Papa—'" The Mambo patted Saylee's shoulder.

"Then my mama says, 'Let him go, Child. He stay close to you. For awhile anyway. Till he find his way. You remember the story he tell you? How the spirit of the person who die stay close by? Then, by and by—'

"I cry, my arms wrapped around my daddy's chest. Then my mama's voice continue,'. . . in a happy land, Africa Land, deep under the sea.'

"My mama say this without a tear, but her voice is strained and she rock back and forth, holding me close.

"My papa lay there, thin, gaunt, his skin a dull grayish color.

"I hear my mama say, 'His skin not the beautiful black I remember from the first time I ever see him. I was bathing in the old natural spring pond over by the stone outcropping where the apple and plum trees grow'.

"She say to Aunt Mindy—they forget I in the room—she say, 'I can't remember now if he was the first black man I ever seen or not. I motion for him to come into the water.'

"Then, Aunt Mindy touched her shoulder. She say, 'He gone. We best be gettin' him washed and dressed. I got some tallow to grease his skin. Come now, Saylee, don't you want to cry? Cryin' good for you.'"

"You seen," the Mambo said, "the death and them fixin' him for his burial, too?"

"Naw, they sent me out to stay with the family next door. Aunt Mindy went with me.

"She say, 'Your daddy too young to die, but he did. Now you got to be a big girl and help your mama all you can. She not always have it easy round heah. Some folks treat her worse than a slave.'

"Yessum," I ask. "Who does?"

"Aunt Mindy say, 'Masta Sinclair, for one! I seen the way he look at her. You too. I gonna speak to your mama tonight 'bout some things I know. You gonna be all right by and by. Come along now. I tells the folks next door what happen. When we finish, I come and get you.'

"I only half listen to the old woman, because I don't know what Aunt Mindy was talking about and don't know if she know either, but I never let on that I think she on the wrong side of sensible. I just say, 'Yessum,' as though I agree with every word she say."

The two women laughed and Mamie stirred in her sleep.

"Mamie be much better now," the mambo said. "You was too young to understand what the old cook signified, eh? But you knows now! Yes."

"Well, yes, the old man Sinclair was a scoundrel. I sneak out of that cabin and crouch under the open window. I spy through a crack in the cabin wall. When Aunt Mindy return, she found my mama sitting by the bed crooning to Papa, and still holding his hand.

"Mama look up. She say to Aunt Mindy, 'Do you believe you can love someone from the first? I had gathered plums that day. I was in the pond swimming when I looked up and saw this black, black boy. I thought, 'He good to look at, so black. Black like the night sky.' I beckon for him to come to me.'

"When Aunt Mindy only nodded, she continued: 'He strip off his clothes and we swim. When we get out, I give him a plum to eat and teach him the Chicora word for plum, *phutti*. We swim all that summer. Then one day in late summer, he touch my breast. He kiss my lips. I tell my mama. She know I don't like the brave my papa say I must marry in the tenth moon of the year. We break camp soon. Big ceremony for many young girls and braves. The brave my papa promised me to is old, ugly, mean!"

"You got powerful voodoo magic from both your mama and your papa, eh?" the voodoo priestess said, nodding. We talk more, eh? I come tomorrow night to your cabin. You tell me more, eh?" With that, she sprang to her feet, and, not waiting for an answer, disappeared into the swamp.

Spring passed, and still Mamie didn't talk. Once in the summer, she mouthed the word 'Mama,' but no sound came out.

On the anniversary of Mamie's horrid experience, she lapsed into a coma. Saylee sat with the child, singing the chant that seemed to soothe her, "Na-na-na-na-nay. Na-na-na-na-nay," until the old healer was hoarse and could sing no more.

.

The voodoo Mambo, true to her word, came all through that summer for more of Saylee's history, saying little about herself. Saylee enjoyed the companionship of this strange woman.

"Tell me about your mama and daddy's courtship," the mambo said as Salye sat, holding the sleeping Mamie.

Root Woman began . . . .

"She say to Aunt Mindy the day my Papa die, 'My mama'

"—that would be my Chicora grandma—"she help me run away to be with Germahl."

"How she do that?" the mambo asked.

Saylee heaved a sigh and explained that Pali's mother tore the young girl's clothes, "tear with bear claw, smear with blood and say that all she find." Saylee shrugged and shook her head. "My mama's Papa believed my grandma."

"Then what happened?" the mambo asked with a grin.

"Mama say my papa, Germahl, take her to a cave close by the pond on far side of where rocks stick up out of ground. Mouth of cave hidden by heavy brush. She say, 'We live all that cold winter with no fire, but we happy. When I big with Saylee—'

"'O, child', Aunt Mindy say, 'I remember. Pali come to the door of my kitchen. Look like she ready to have that baby. Masta Sinclair take her in 'cause she say she good at doctoring'.

"That all she tell of courtship that day," Root Woman said. "My mama started keening, got onto her knees, and began to rock back and forth by the side of my Papa. Aunt Mindy busied herself with tidying up the cabin, sitting when she had finished. She rocked and watched my mama."

Root Woman stood and walked to her cabin door.

"Finally, my mama stopped wailing and they begin to strip the body and the bed.

"Aunt Mindy," Saylee began again, turning back from the door to her cabin, "said, 'Pali, you got to put a hex on Masta Sinclair 'cause he up to no good. He got the hot blood for you and for Saylee.'"

"Naw, girl you remember all that?" the voodoo queen asked, laughing and slapping her thigh.

"My mama say, 'I already do that.' Then I hear the funniest story!" My mama say, 'I seen that look. What with white men? They women not satisfy them? They mixed chidden on every plantation in these parts. I think it's this Queen on the other side of the ocean. A Queen Victoria! I hear women talking bout how this 'Queen Victoria set a high standard for the whole wide world'. I not know the word 'standard,' but I think it have to do with mens and womens lovin.' My mama say, 'I was birthing a white baby and they wanted me to reach my arms up under sheet. Not look! Can you imagine? I tell them—'

"Aunt Mindy say, 'Aw, naw. How a body supposed to birth—'

"Then Mama say, 'I tell them I do no such thing. If they want the child to come out alive, I need to see what I doin'. They finally reckoned I could see 'tween her fat thighs, seeing as how I was a woman. If they all like them womens, I believe they don't like to pleasure they menfolk '

"Slaves musta' had plenty to talk about in that line," said the mambo, laughing uproariously. Saylee joined in the laugh as they sat and rocked.

Root Woman looked closely at her friend.

She older than me. Wonder was she a slave?

"So, go on wid your story, child," the mambo said.

"Well," Saylee said, "Mama say, 'Old man Sinclair gonna get himself killed. Soon now.'

"I knew mama had made a doll and had one pin stuck in the doll. I had wanted to stick more pins in, but Mama say, 'Don't take but one, if you know what you doin'. One!'

Root Woman gazed into the fire and remembered.

"Mama say it was for the night of the full moon. I remember thinking . . . ."

Tomorrow night be the night of the full moon.

"I knew," Saylee said, "about the way he looked at Mama, but didn't know he looked at me in that way, too. I was twelve and knew about love making. In the slave cabins, a child would have to be deef and blind not to know. I remember how my thinking ran that night . . . ."

Maybe Mama will want that hateful Sinclair now that Papa is dead.

"At the thought of my papa lying cold and dead, I begin to wail. Both women jump. Aunt Mindy say, 'What that noise? Somebody cryin', or what? Hope it ain no haint!"

"'Haint, Mama asked?'

"'Yeah' Aunt Mindy said, 'A haint. A ghost.'

"Mama look outside the cabin and find me crouched by the side of the shanty, crying.

"Mama pick me up and say, 'Oh, child. Oh, Saylee, I sorry. I sad, too. Come inside. Come. Cry if you want to. It ain't goin' to bring him back, but I understands.'

"So! Your Papa dead. When you bury him? On the night of the full moon?" the mambo asked.

Root Woman nodded.

"At daybreak, word sent to hurry to Tacie. Aunt Mindy and Mama double the white cotton sheet back up over Papa and go to the Farmer cabin, taking me with them. The baby lay cold and lifeless in his mama's arms. Mama say, 'Tacie? Let me take the baby now. He dead.'

"Tacie hold fast to that po' lifeless baby. 'He not dead. He too little to cry, that all.'

"My mama and Aunt Mindy look at each other. Aunt Mindy try next. 'Tacie, you sad for losing this little one. I know. I done lost one myself. It was years ago, but I remembers! He in a warm, good place up in the sky. Heaven where he is.' She said all this while gently tugging at Tacie's arms, trying to get her to turn the baby loose.

"'He not dead,' Tacie scream. 'Now leave me be. I gone nurse him. He hungry, that all that wrong with this baby.'

"Mama stepped closer to the bed and thunder, 'No! Give me the child. Now. Right now!'

"Slowly, Tacie released her hold on the tiny infant's body. She turn her face to the wall, emitting a thin inhuman sound like the mewing of a kitten. Mama hand the lifeless body to Aunt Mindy and climb into bed with the woman. She cradle the thin, cold woman in her arms, chanting one of her healing songs. She ask for more blankets. 'Pile 'em on' she say.

"Mindy got crackin'. She went to the big house, creeping in to steal supplies for a soup. She got fat back, meal, potatoes, onions that she had dried the year before, and a whole jar of jam. She wrapped it all in a heavy old quilt. Nobody stirred in the house.

"Tacie's baby," Root Woman continued, "born too soon, was laid to rest later that same morning. Wrapped in a crude feed sack, he was placed in a grave dug by Tacie's man. The slaves sang an old spiritual.

"The Sinclairs didn't come to the burial although they had been told of both deaths. The death of Germahl the night before, and of the baby's death that morning.

"Aunt Mindy went back with us to our cabin.

"Mama say, 'You best be gettin' on up to the big house. The sun is far up in the sky. They be wantin' breakfast.'

"Aunt Mindy roll her eyes and say, 'Yes Lawd! Can't keep the Masta and Missus waitin' fo they brekfast. Two deaths, but breakfast more important to them!'

"She say, 'Deaths come in threes. Who next?'

"Mama ain't answer her. Aunt Mindy say 'I goin' now. When you want to bury Germahl?'

"Mama say, 'Tonight, by the light of the full moon. Tell slaves to bring rattles and drums.'

"About half way to the house, I hear her start singing, 'Jimmy crack corn, and I don't care, Jimmy crack corn, and I don't care, Jimmy crack corn, and I don't care—the masta's goin' away! I knew then that she had made the connection 'bout old man Sinclair goin' to be the third death.

"We seen the lights shining through all the windows in the big house as we walk in the funeral procession late that night. They were still on as we come home later.

"I remember thinking that he would die this night. And so he did. Shot through the heart for trying to cheat at cards."

"Well, child, I gotta go. You take good care of yourself and Mamie in case I never see you again," the mambo said.

"Wait," Root Woman called, but the mambo slipped away through the swamp, never to be seen again.

Mamie did, however, start to crawl that summer.

On a beautiful summer day, a bird flew into an open window. Mamie's eyes rolled, and she looked around the cabin, but she did not convulse. The slightest noise set off the trembling, the uncontrollable shaking, that caused her teeth to clamp shut, her head to jerk back, and the inevitable convulsions. Those upsets always led to unconsciousness.

Sometimes she started and screamed, eyes rolled back in her head, body tense, then she lapsed into the coma again. Saylee kept her drugged most of the time, now.

Mamie remained comatose for three months. Saylee fed her a rich broth, spoonful by spoonful. It took over an hour to get one feeding down. Root Woman fed her every three hours around the clock.

When an early spring made its appearance toward the end of February, Saylee rigged a travois and took Mamie to a quiet pool. She sat with Mamie in her lap in the warm sunshine in mid-afternoon, enjoying the sun and the sound of birds singing. Mamie opened her eyes and looked around.

"Bird," Mamie said in a voice cracked from disuse.

"Yes, 'bird'," Saylee said. "Bird singing to you, Mamie. Do you like the bird?"

Mamie did not reply, but nodded her head, and stared through solemn eyes first at the bird, then at Saylee. From then on, Mamie talked a little almost every day.

A fighter, the child is a fighter. Good!

"Do a penny . . . ?" Mamie asked. When Saylee simply nodded, she continued, "Mens now come why? No. White horse, no, no. Go way bad cross. Bad mens . . .. Burning Jesus cross a-lot-ty-no."

Mamie garbled her speech with strange words, strung together without rhyme or reason. Occasionally she made sense.

The mambo must have known that we would not see her again. Did she die? I miss her.

In September of the following year, 1884, Saylee heard a knock at the door.

"Root Woman? You in there?" Isaiah called.

She opened the door, holding the sleeping child, cradled like a baby.

"Come in, I been expecting you for some time, now," she said.

"I . . . I brought some supplies from my store. I'll just lay them here, if that's all right?" the boy asked.

He stood just inside the cabin, squinting. Mamie, covered by a big shawl that hid her wasted body and the stumps of her legs, didn't move.

"Is that Mamie? Well, of course it is. I'm sorry. I'm so sorry for my part in . . . ."

Saylee stood, holding the child, staring straight at the young man. Not helping. The silence lay between them thick as swamp fog. He began again.

"My maw and pa tried to tell me, but I wouldn't listen. I didn't know. *I didn't know*. I . . . I better go. I—"

"Stay. Sit down," Saylee said.

She indicated a straight-backed, chair. An intricately carved chair with a red, upholstered seat. Isaiah Norris sat on the edge of the seat. Sliding further back in the chair, he crossed one leg, then the other, then sat with both feet on the floor. He glanced around the dimly-lit cabin. When Saylee finally spoke, he jumped.

"I heard what you said to that Clayton man. I know you not one of them. Why you go with them?"

"I don't know," Isaiah said. "I . . . I . . . it's all my fault!"

This last, he blurted out in almost a shout. Mamie stirred in Root Woman's arms.

"Sh, sh-h-h, it's all right," she said to the sleeping girl.

"How," Saylee asked, "is it your fault? You just a boy. You tried to help Mamie. I heard what you said before the train came."

"If it hadn't been for me, they would never have taken her. Me and my big mouth! I told them where Mamie lived."

Isaiah sat with arms resting on his knees, holding his head.

"Look at me," Root Woman commanded. When Isaiah continued to look down at his feet, she repeated, "Look at me!"

He looked up and held her gaze.

"You did not know. You did not do. You foolish, but not evil. What they did *was* evil! They pay. Some with health, some with wealth, some with life. One with all three! I do left-handed Voodoo on them. Not on you."

"Left-handed Voodoo? What," Isaiah asked, "is—"

"Is Voodoo that hurts or kills!" Then, Saylee smiled at him. "What you bring this old woman?"

She handed the sleeping child over to Isaiah as easily as if she were handing him a book. She walked over to the box he had set down just inside the door.

Isaiah sat, not moving, with Mamie in his lap. She continued to doze while Root Woman examined each can of food, the sacks of floor, grits, and sugar, the cured ham, and the home-made sausage. She walked back over, patted his shoulder, and took Mamie from him.

"She's a good girl and about your age, too. She a good girl and you a good boy. Just foolish."

"How is Mamie? Can she walk at all?"

"No. She crawl. Sometimes. She don't talk much. Her mind locked up with the terror of that night."

"I'm so sorry," Isaiah said.

"I know," Saylee said, holding his gaze with a tender look.

Isaiah looked closely at Root Woman. Although obviously old, she looked ageless. The preparation of medicines sometimes called for the biting and chewing of fibrous roots, but despite this, her teeth gleamed in her dark face. The young white boy and the ancient black woman sat in awkward silence, occasionally talking, but mostly just staring at each other.

I wonder how old she is?

"You do a good thing today," Saylee said. "This go a long way toward helping you shake off your guilt, and remember what I say. Don't hang on to your guilt like it is some kind of trophy you has won! Let it go!"

Isaiah nodded.

Back home, Isaiah sat high up in the barn.

Mamie lay light as a feather when I held her back at Root Woman's cabin. Wish I could have seen her legs! *Not legs,* he thought, *stumps*. He cringed and dropped his head.

Why did Root Woman plop Mamie into my arms like that?

He lay back on the cool boards of the barn loft.

How different things would be if I had not ridden with the Klan, or even, if I had just kept my mouth shut. But no, I had to prove myself. I remember thinking 'this is fun.' I thought we would just ride around and scare people. Even that is wrong.

But I'll try not to blame those men. I was the one who told Judge Clayton where Mamie lived. Nobody twisted my arm! I blabbed.

Isaiah's pa found him at the barn.

"You been cryin', Son? What's wrong?"

Robert listened as Isaiah poured out his anguish and confusion over his part in Mamie's ordeal. Half sitting on the edge of the water trough, Robert's arms folded across his chest, he nodded his head. After a long pause, he straightened his lean frame and stepped over to Isaiah.

"Now you listen to me, Son," he said, putting his hands on the boy's shoulders, "you were sixteen years old when that happened. A mere boy. Your being there was an accident. A foolish, bull-headed mistake. No one is blaming you for your part in it." Robert stared at his son.

His father turned to go, but Isaiah stepped in front of him.

"Pa, I have tried to 'let it go.' God knows, I've tried, but I can't. I can't shake it. I took some groceries out there. The Root Woman—she was a little spooky at first. She put Mamie in my lap, I think for a reason. More than just wanting to look at what was in the box I had brought her. I didn't like holding her, but I'm glad I did."

"How so, Son?"

Isaiah looked at his pa, and shook his head.

"I . . . I don't know exactly," he said. "Holding her somehow—helped. Oh, by the way, Root Woman said I was to give you . . .. "

He walked over to where he had slung his saddle bag and dug out the little bottle of medicine.

". . . this. She said to give you this for 'the misery in your hands and fingers'. Did you ever tell her about your arthritis, Pa?"

"Must be twenty years since I even seen the woman everybody calls Root Woman." He turned toward the house, holding the bottle of medicine close to his face. "No, let's see, it was right after the war between the states. Must have been in sixty-seven, maybe sixty-eight. Folks got to sayin' her ghost haunted the old place. Her ghost! Legend sure has grown up around that woman."

He said all this while turning the bottle in his hands, holding it up in the fast-fading sunlight.

"She say how I was to take this?"

He sniffed the concoction after uncorking it.

"Never mind!" he exclaimed. "I guess I'm supposed to rub it in, not drink it. Well, that makes sense. I'll try it."

He put a little in his palm, rubbing it onto his hands and fingers. Robert worked as a blacksmith. Lately, he could hardly hold a hammer, let alone pound red-hot iron on the anvil when his arthritis acted up.

He worked his hands and fingers as they walked back to the house.

"I think I feel a difference already."

He fished the bottle out of his pocket and smelled it again.

"It's hot enough. Wonder what she puts in it?"

They walked into the kitchen just as Sadie began setting out their dinner of fresh vegetables.

"What in the world is that smell? Horse liniment?" Sadie asked, wrinkling up her nose. Robert smiled and nodded his head.

She bustled back and forth from the stove to the table, her long, full skirt brushing the bare wooden floor. Her face was flushed from the heat of the wood stove, and several curls clung to her forehead. One played about her cheeks.

"Once a whole wagon-load of relatives from another state pulled up in our yard when she was way on along toward having you." Robert poked Isaiah in the ribs and winked, as he continued bragging in a low voice. "She had just started to make Sunday dinner for our seven younguns and the two of us when they pulled up.

"Oh Robert, he don't care to hear that old story! Shucks! He's heard it before, I bet!" Sadie said, grinning from ear to ear.

"Yes, I do! Tell it, Papa!" Isaiah said, laughing.

"Well, your mama picked more of everything. She washed,

chopped, stirred, and seasoned like a spinning top. No time to kill and dress more chickens."

Sadie listened to 'The Surprise Company for Sunday Dinner' story.

Watching them laugh, Robert sniffed his hands. He shook them and blew on them.

"This shore heats up a body's hands and fingers." Robert said. "It's strong enough to be horse liniment. Root Woman sent this to me."

"Root Woman? Who brought it?" Sadie asked. "I didn't know anybody knew how to find her place. It's way out in the swamp, ain't it?"

"I went to see her this afternoon, Ma," Isaiah said. "I took her some groceries from the store. She sent the medicine back by me."

"Why'd you do a thing like that? I hear tell she's a voodoo queen, like they have in New Orleans. One of the ladies in the sewing circle at the church said she didn't know much about such stuff, but that her cousin had actually gone to a voodoo ceremony. It was held way out in the countryside outside of New Orleans." Sadie's face, flushed from working over a wood stove, turned a deeper red.

"Them people dance around to the beating of drums until they get themselves possessed by devils. She said her cousin told her that they can lift people and throw 'em like they was match sticks clear cross the clearing." She shivered, a spasm shaking her small body.

"She said Root Woman is just another name for voodoo queen. I want you to stay away from her, ya hear?" Sadie demanded with hands on her hips.

Robert put his arms around Sadie as she spun around from confronting Isaiah.

"Now, Love, that's just hearsay. I don't imagine she is an evil person. She takes care of that colored girl who got her legs cut off. If Isaiah wants to help them, I don't see any harm. Um-m-m?"

He smiled down at his wife of twenty-seven years. His hands caressed her back. She studied his face, started to say something, changed her mind, brushed his cheek with the back of her hand, and nodded in agreement. Isaiah looked away, embarrassed by the hunger he saw in their eyes.

"Well, you two better wash up for dinner. It's ready. And Isaiah? Be careful going out there in the swamp," Sadie said.

The family sat down and began to eat supper.

"So tell me about her cabin, Isaiah. And that poor little colored girl. Can she walk now? I don't imagine she can. From what I heard, her legs were cut plumb off. That Judge Clayton should have been shot. They didn't even have a trial!"

Seeing the stricken look on her son's face, she quickly added.

"Not that you knew. You didn't know they was goin' to kill her mama and kidnap the poor child. And then cause her legs . . . . You were just a boy, for goodness sake!"

"Yeah, I was just a stubborn, foolish boy! But I should have known better. Anyway, Ma, to answer your questions, the cabin is real dark. I sat on a straight-backed chair when I held Mamie."

"You *held* Mamie?" Sadie asked. "What, you had to hold her down?"

"No, Ma! She was asleep, and Root Woman was rocking her. She wanted to see what I had brought them, so she put the sleeping child on my lap."

Isaiah grinned, remembering the way Saylee had so casually placed the child in his lap.

"The child? I thought the girl was about the same age as you? Say, has anyone ever seen that boy—Rosco was his name, I think—has he ever come back into these parts again?"

"She seems like a child. Always little. I remember when she used to come into my store. Now she's . . . ." He trailed off, then said, "No, her boyfriend never returned. I heard from some colored men that he never even wrote a letter to his mama. He lost her address, I think."

"Well, that's all very sad," Sadie said, "and I wish it had never happened, but it did. He probably got himself killed somewhere way off from here."

"Papa," Isaiah said, turning to his pa, "tell me what you know about Root Woman. How old is she? Was she a slave? Is she part Indian?"

"Son, I don't know too much about her directly. Just the legends that have grown up around her. Yes, I do believe she is part Indian. Seems I heard her mama was a pure Indian and her daddy came over here as a slave from Africa."

"Wow! Where did she live before she started living in the swamp? She said she used to live close to our place."

"Back during slavery, the Rodenburg place was called the Sinclair Plantation. Mean man if ever one lived. Got himself killed, and the Rodenburgs bought the place when it went on the auction block," Robert said.

"Well, you sure are taken with this Root Woman," Sadie said, "better leave her alone is what I think!" She got up from the table. "Time to get this kitchen cleaned up."

Isaiah helped clear the table, started to leave, but came back into the kitchen.

"Pa? I'm thinking of buying a parcel of land. There's a few acres on that road that cuts across the road the Rodenburg place is on. It would be a good location for my general store."

Robert looked at his son for a long moment before he answered him.

"Yes, I agree. State Road Fifty-two seems to be the road everybody goes up and down on. You got that kind of money saved up? Enough for buying acreage? How much they asking for it?"

Sadie, cleaning the kitchen, listened to every word as they talked about acreage and price.

"What's the rush to build your store?" she asked. "You got a store right next door. It's doing a right smart amount of business, ain't it? You ain't studying on getting married, are you? You ain't even seeing no one that I know about."

Isaiah looked at his mother as though she had dropped in from another world. He was always amazed at how she could jump to such wild conclusions. Women's intuition, she called it.

"No, Ma. I ain't got no girl, and I ain't gettin' married no time soon, but I want to build me a real honest-to-God general store."

The *store* next door was little more than a roofed packing shed.

Sadie dropped her dishrag, and, was right in front of Isaiah, hands on her hips, and eyes flashing.

"Don't you go using that kind of language in my kitchen. Taking

God's name in vain is a sin, and I won't stand for it!"

Isaiah smiled his sweetest smile.

"I'm sorry, Ma. Didn't mean it in that way. I just want to build one with an old pot-bellied stove smack in the middle, and chairs with a table for playin' checkers, and a barrel for garlic pickles. I want a store big enough to offer anything a body might want. How does 'Ike's General Emporium'sound to you?"

Satisfied her boy was not headed straight for Hell, Sadie rewarded him with a big smile.

"Sounds mighty highfalutin' to me," she said, pinching his cheek as she passed. "What's wrong with 'Ike's General Store'?"

Robert stood by the door, leaning against the wall, arms folded across his chest, a tolerant smile on his face. Father and son's eyes met. Robert winked at Isaiah. Isaiah ducked his head in silent acknowledgment that he'd had a close call with his mother.

"If you want," Robert said, "I'll ride over with you to see the land tomorrow. Who has it for sale? Let's walk out for a spell."

This was a time-honored custom among men in the family to give themselves a little privacy. They used this break to get a snort of whiskey or to smoke a cigarette or pipe.

Father and son walked out by the well. Robert, tall and lean with white hair, rolled a cigarette and lit it with a kitchen match. Taking a puff, he held the smoke in his lungs for a long time and then blew smoke rings. Isaiah had tried a cigarette a few months back and knew that he would never smoke.

A full moon sailed in a cloudless sky. Stars looked like they were close enough to touch.

"Ah, just look at all this beauty!" Robert said.

An autumn breeze blew silvered foliage to the ground. Leaves danced like argent jewels above their heads in the shaking branches of the trees.

"Yeah, it's beautiful out here in the country!" Isaiah said, drawing in a deep breath.

The apple tree, heavy with almost-ripe fruit, sent a delicate fragrance their way.

"This," said Robert, "is a night for lovers. You ain't met no one you could fall in love with, Son? I was just a little older than you are right now when your ma and me got married. That firecracker of a woman . . . . Ah, she was just a child when we married. She looks as young today as she did back then—well almost as young. She shore ain't all gray like me."

"Aw, Papa, you ain't—"

"But," Robert said, "gettin' back to the subject. Have you met your true love yet?

I could say Lacy LaFont, the new school teacher at the Freedman's school. But, nothing will ever come of it. She looks as white as me, but she's colored . . . .

"So," Isaiah said, "you think you'd like to ride over there to see the piece of land. How much do you reckon it would take to get the store built? And up and running? Remember, I'll have to buy inventory. Of course, I have the inventory from my store here, but I'll need lots more."

Robert walked over to the apple tree and leaned against it before replying.

"But you didn't answer—oh, uh, I see." Robert said. "Um, as for the cost for your store, I don't know. Depends on how big you plan to make it. If I knew the square footage, I could pretty much figure the cost of the lumber. You plannin' on doing the work yourself, or hiring it done?"

Isaiah started backing toward the house.

"Wait right here," he said, "I got a drawing in my room. Be right back."

Isaiah's voice rang with excitement. He covered the distance from the apple tree to the house, his long legs pumping, in just a few minutes. Robert smiled.

Isaiah ran back. He was out of breath and clutched a sheet of lined ledger paper. Robert could see the drawing in the bright light of the moon.

"Here, towards the back of the store," Isaiah gulped, "will be tools. The pot-bellied stove will sit right up here next to a table and chairs for the men to play checkers."

Father and son talked. They modified the plan, making changes here and corrections there. For over an hour, they worked on the project

They walked into the house laughing about something one of them had said. Sadie sat in the rocking chair in which she had rocked each child. When she heard them come in, she closed the Bible and asked if they would like some warm milk or hot cocoa.

"Yes Ma'am," Isaiah said, "but let me make it. Hot cocoa for me. Do you want a cup, too? How about you, Pa?"

Isaiah fixed hot cocoa for them all while his pa and ma sat talking at the kitchen table. His pa spread the plans out and showed Sadie the changes they had made.

"Mighty ambitious plans for so young a whipper-snapper, but if you've set your heart on it, I'm sure you will be able to do it." Sadie said. She smiled at him.

Isaiah came around the table and hugged her. After finishing the hot cocoa, the two men continued going over the plans and talking long after Sadie went to bed.

Later that night, Isaiah sat by his open window, gazing out to the apple tree, and above to the moon.

Mamie was so little. Wish I could have seen her legs. Just look at that moon. Lacy wants me to take her to see Mamie. She wants to ask Root Woman if she can live in Lizzye's house. We'll go together. *I wish we could go to one of the church socials.*

The moon seemed to mock him with its mouth open as if saying, "Oh? You're in love with who?" He pulled out his journal and began to write. It was after midnight when he went to bed.

When he finally got to sleep, he dreamed. He heard the awful pleas for mercy, and he saw the burning cross and smelled the charred flesh. In his dream he saw Root Woman.

"Why," she screamed at him. "Why did you tell them how to find the poor child? Why? Why?"

She walked toward him, green, and glowing like an apparition. Her finger pointed at him, and she cursed him with a curse he couldn't hear. Then the dream changed.

"Leave," said his pa and his ma in unison. "Leave, you have disgraced us."

"Leave!" said people in the community as they advanced upon him with outstretched arms. "Go away! No store for you! We won't buy from the likes of you!"

He woke up in a sweat, his heart thrumming in his chest. He got up and stood by the open window. The moon was behind a thick cloud, but cast a bright outline around one side of it. The dream bothered him. And for some reason he thought again of the strange words of Root Woman, 'guilt can be a kind of pride.' He recorded the dream along with this remark in his journal which still lay open on the table beside his bed.

He padded downstairs to the kitchen for a glass of water.

His pa sat at the kitchen table in the dark with his head in his hands. His shoulders jerked and sounds like some kind of crazy hiccups escaped his throat.

Puzzled, Isaiah sat down.

"Pa? he asked, "you all right?"

His father jumped. He looked up, as though confused.

"Isaiah? Son," Robert gasped. He made a gagging sound. "Your ma—she,

She's . . . ."

Isaiah tore up the stairs two at a time. He ran to his ma's bedside. She lay there as though asleep. Dropping to his knees, he touched her hand. It lay on her chest outside the covers. Cold. Leaning over, he kissed her forehead. Cold.

No. No. You can't be dead.

He knelt for a long time by her bed. Softly, he cried.

Isaiah lifted his head and felt again his mother's cold face and hand. Then, burying his head once more, he thought.

Seth left home last year and the twins left only last month. Oh, Mama. You're too young to just up and die! I wanted you to have time to enjoy life without the work of us kids! Why did you die?

He walked to the window and looked out. The moon was out from behind the cloud. He heard a cock crow, though it was still dark. Way off in the distance he heard the scream of a panther coming from the direction of the swamp. He found himself wondering if Root Woman heard it, too. Remembering his pa, he returned to the kitchen.

His father still sat, head buried in his hands. Isaiah observed him closely. His pa looked suddenly old.

Isaiah sat at the table with his pa. Robert looked at his son, his face worked, his lips and mouth moved, but no sound came out.

"Pa, why? What happened? Was Ma sick?"

His father shook his head and shrugged his shoulders, a puzzled look on his face.

"I didn't think so. She, she . . . . "

He got up, patted Isaiah absent-mindedly on the shoulder, and went up to sit by his wife's body. The only sound in the house was the occasional, strangled noise of a man not used to crying.

Each sat, trying to cope with his feelings of loss and grief. To somehow make sense of a life cut short. Isaiah remembered her last words to him and the unconditional love she had given him.

Given to all of us. How will we manage without you, Ma?

He remained at the kitchen table all the rest of that lonely, awful night, and when the dawn broke, he made breakfast for the two of them.

Chapter 3

Germahl

Africa Land down under the sea
Spirit land for you and me
We will be together again
In that place with no more pain

"Yep, lost a field hand today," Robert Sinclair said as he brought out a deck of cards. He shuffled the cards, and added, "Them darkies plan to bury him at midnight."

"Hm-m-m, midnight you say?" Buster Clayton asked.

"Well," Johnny Carlton said, "midnight or not, let's see that deck of cards you got there, Mister."

"I been suspectin' he trying to cheat," Buster said, jumping up with gun drawn, "ever since we let him start playin' poker with us."

"Plantation owner," Johnny said, jumping up and knocking over his chair. "Thinks he's better'n us poor dirt farmers." Phewt! He shot a stream of tobacco juice straight into the jar on the floor.

Buster was thirty-two and still lived with his mother and father in a shack that was falling down around them. His hand shook as he trained it on Sinclair.

"Put away the gun." Sinclair stood. His face blanched white. "If this is a marked deck, I sure don't know anything about it!"

He handed the deck to Johnny.

"I gotta get on back home anyway. Matilda's not feeling well. See you boys."

He reached the door, but turned back toward the kitchen table. Buster shot him in the heart. One shot. Just one.

Buster collapsed into a chair.

"My God, is he dead?" he asked. "Maw will kill me. She's always sayin' we ain't nothing but white trash."

After Sinclair was killed, Matilda, his wife, couldn't raise a thin dime. The plantation and slaves were auctioned off by the end of April.

The Rodenburgs bought the plantation, keeping all nine slaves. The community, astir over the shooting, now turned their attention on the new owners.

"Jews on a plantation? Ridiculous," Otis Hemingway said. He owned the barber shop.

"Well," Thomas Clayton said into the mirror, "we at Union Trust Bank are supposed to look out for the place, but that New York Jew must be some kind of dumb! I don't have time to drive out there to oversee a plantation. Puny little place though it may be!"

"Bought it at auction, sight unseen I hear," Cyrus Gant said.

"Sight unseen," Clayton agreed.

"What's the new owner's name, anyway?" Otis asked.

"Rodenburg," snorted Clayton.

"Well, Rodenburg, the Jew, will find out that some of his property done stole away in the night, carrying anything they kin tote!" Cyrus said, shaking his newspaper as he turned the page.

Pali sat and rocked for long hours. Saylee tried to talk with her mother, but she found Pali's eyes vacant most of the time. More and more Saylee talked with her departed father. She heard his voice whispering to her in the trees at night as she lay half asleep.

I hear him now, his words like music, spelling out the magic for me.

"*Snake is powerful, powerful. In Africa, Dambala is the Serpent God for our religion. Dambala do wonderful things.*"

She saw her father as he stood in the swamp in the moonlight, lifting his mighty arms high to honor the spirit world.

He was so strong. Why he die so young? A beautiful, strong man.

Pali stirred as though waking from a long sleep. "Saylee, what is it? You crying. What's wrong?"

Saylee ran to her mama and said, "I missing Papa. You gone most of the time, too. Sometimes I get scared. Why he die so soon? I not ready for him to die!" She burst into tears.

"We talk more from now on," Pali said. "I not go away no more. I stay and we talk together about your papa. He was a good man." Pali sat with her daughter until late in the night telling her stories about Gerhmal. After that, Pali grieved, but managed to stay present for Saylee. She related much about Gerhmal and her own people.

The Rodenburgs finally moved into the big house a couple of months after the auction. All nine slaves were there.

One day Ira Rodenburg sent for Pali to come up to the big house as soon as she could. This was unusual in itself. In the few instances in which she had been summoned, it was: 'Come' . . . 'Now' . . . 'Hurry'.

She came in the kitchen door with raised eyebrows and asked Aunt Mindy what was afoot. Aunt Mindy, just as silently, answered that she didn't know.

Pali stood by the kitchen doorway and studied the woman doing needle work.

"Oh," Rose Rodenburg said, looking up, "you must be the Indian girl, Pali?" Pali nodded and bowed slightly. "Mr. Rodenburg will see you now. He's in the library." When Pali made no move, she added, "The library is just through that door and on the other side of the hall."

Pali walked across the hardwood floor, then over the worn, Oriental rug, savoring the textures on her bare feet. She knocked on the closed door.

"Come in," Ira Rodenburg said.

She opened the door and stood there.

"Come in," he said, "you must be the healer, Pali."

"I Pali, Medicine Woman of the Chicora Tribe, descended from long line of Medicine Women." She bowed slightly once again.

"Pali, do you receive any money for the services you perform here?"

"I get cloth to make clothes, food to eat, one pair of shoes every two years, but no money. No."

Ira shook his head, and, scratching his bearded chin, looked at her a long time.

"How does ten dollars a year sound to you? You will stay on here, won't you?"

"You pay me for work I do?"

"Yes. Yes, of course. You provide a valuable service here. How do you get medicinal supplies?"

"I make."

"But how?" he asked.

"From forest, swamp. Tree bark. Bushes. Flowers. Herbs. Plants. Roots. All good plants. Bad plants leave alone. Poison," Pali answered with a puzzled look on her face. Did the new owner not know how a medicine was made?

"I see," he said, just as puzzled. "So none of the medicine is bought? Is ten dollars okay with you?"

"Ten dollars good. I save for Saylee. She my girl. She learn to be Medicine Woman, too."

"Do you need any supplies for the treatment of the slaves? Any blankets? Are they clothed for the coming cold weather? Do they have enough food? Are any sick at the present time?"

"Zeke dying. He old and he sick. He die soon. Need sugar for teas and syrups. And it good for healing wounds. Always need blankets, cloth—ticking, you know, for making new beds. Shoes never last. We need shoes every year. You go see?"

Ira said, "No. I'll take your word for it. Well, maybe I will take a tour. Could you take me to see the cabins and meet the slaves? Maybe tonight?"

"Yes. I do that. It a good thing you do."

Ira Rodenburg smiled. He said, "I'm new at this. I have never owned another human being. I am a biographer by trade. And a pretty good tailor, too." He saw by her expression that she did not understand. "I write books about famous people. And I make clothes."

She nodded.

"Pali, I will see you before dark at your cabin. Is that all right with you?" She nodded again. He went back to his ledgers. Something caused him to glance up. Seeing her still standing just inside the door, he said, "Uh, you may go."

Aunt Mindy, by working in the dining room just across the hallway from the library, had managed to hear practically all of the conversation between the new owner and Pali. When Pali turned to go, Aunt Mindy motioned for her to come into the kitchen. She said, "Well, I never thought I'd see the day a slave owner talk like dat! What you think?"

Pali said, "He surprise me, too. Pay me for workin? You think he mean it?" Not waiting for an answer, she said, "I best be gettin' on. Don't want to rile nobody."

"Here a biscuit and a little piece of chicken. Ever since they come last week, Missus is had me working gettin' rid of all pig meats. I don't know if I can cook without my lard, but I guess I has to."

Pali accepted the biscuit and chicken, tucked it into her pocket for later, and whispered, "We talk more." She hurried back to her house wondering when the money would begin to be paid. Since Germahl died in late March, she had not allowed herself to think about her future and now it was approaching autumn.

She had seen the first yellow in the trees only that morning. She and Saylee and the slaves had suffered extreme hardship all three months after Robert Sinclair was shot and killed -- until his widow was packed up and moved upstate with her relatives.

They had thought *he* was hard and indifferent to their plight. The cold had lingered until mid April. Some had been reduced to eating grass and bark and clay to try to assuage their hunger. Mrs. Sinclair had kept everything under lock and key.

Mitilda Sinclair left on the last of June, taking everything edible with her.

They lived without supervision from the end of June until late in August when Ira Rodenburg and his wife showed up. They had not planted the usual cotton crop, but had planted corn, beans, squash, tomatoes, peas—in short any food seeds they could beg, borrow or steal.

The men hunted and fished. The nearby Black River teamed with crappie, catfish and bream. Opossum and squirrel were plentiful. Nat had killed a wild boar. In July they had picked blackberries. Saylee found a honeybee hive and they cooked the berries with honey and ate until they could pop.

Suddenly children had a shine to their eyes and a hop and a skip to their walk. Laughter rang out as they played in the dirt before their cabins.

The slaves kept a low profile. They were afraid of the patter rollers, men hired to patrol the countryside for slaves who might be out without a pass, or out after dark without good reason. In truth they were little more than hired thugs. They were encouraged to terrorize the slaves as a way of keeping them in line. The hierarchy of the those who dealt with slaves was: owner, overseer, slave trader, slave driver, and patter roller. Patter rollers were sometimes paid extra to mutilate a runaway slave, or to execute him to make an example of him. The slaves even feared the owners and overseers on neighboring plantations. The rule of survival was to go un-noticed.

Nobody bothered them because the plantation had been sold on the auction block in early June to the Rodenburgs. Everybody thought the slaves would all run away and the Rodenburgs be the laughingstock of the community. They didn't like having Jews living on a plantation. Jews were barely tolerated as tradesmen, but a planter? Well, it was not much of a plantation. But still.

Ira and Rose lived in New York City, and thinking the banker was looking out for his interest, he had not been worried when he had been unable to get down to South Carolina right away.

Pali found Nat repairing tools out in the barn and told him the strange behavior of the new owner. How he seemed really polite. She chose not to tell him that she would be getting paid to be the slave doctor.

"You spread word he want see everybody's cabin? You do that for me? I come with him. That good?"

"Huh," Nat said, "he be the first white man I ever seen that don't talk bad. Most of them think they shit don't stink. Um, Pali? When old Zeke gonna die? He mighty poorly."

"I know, but I not know when he die. When he get good and ready, uhn? Nat, how old is he?"

Nat scratched his head.

"Must be eighty years old if he a day. I been knowin' him goin' on twenty-five year, and he was old when I first started knowin' him. He was a hard workin' man, useta be."

"Well, I best be gettin' on back. I look in on Zeke.

Zeke rallied under the new regime. The Rodenburgs created a little dispensary for Pali. Food rations doubled and tripled and there was much more variety of food for the slaves. Ira Rodenburg learned a lot about farming and most of it he learned from the slaves. He bought more acreage and more slaves. He treated everybody like he or she was a valued employee. Though it was against the law, he taught them all to read and write. Saylee seemed to blossom under the new owners. Zeke died twelve years later when Saylee was twenty four years old.

The night after they buried Zeke, Saylee, her mama, and Aunt Mindy sat in the kitchen at the big house piecing a quilt for Saylee. Pali looked over at her daughter so tall and thin. She had the high cheek bones and the bronze skin coloring of her people, but she had Germahl's mouth and eyes. Her hair, jet black, hung in loose curls nearly to her waist.

So beautiful, but so strange.

Saylee said little. She was given to deep trances. She knew more about plants and roots than Pali. She knew all the black arts her father had known from Africa and she knew some that Pali didn't know about, nor from where she had learned them. Unless from the books. She read a lot. The Rodenburgs liked Saylee and gave her anything she wanted. They acted like grandparents to her.

"Who'd a thought Zeke would live another twelve years after old Masta Sinclair done died?" Aunt Mindy asked.

"Uhn, uhn, uhn," said Pali.

"Don't call him 'Master', Aunt Mindy. He not your master. Never was," Saylee said.

Mindy laughed. "You sho Lawd right child! I got one master. That the Lord Jesus. He my Masta for shore!"

Saylee got up, kissed her mama's cheek and Aunt Mindy's, and said she was going for a walk.

"At this hour?" Pali asked. "We hardly begun on your quilt. Don't you like the colors?" When she saw that Saylee was not to be stopped, she said, "It's cold out. Take your shawl."

She took her gathering basket and when she got home, it was nearly full. Aunt Mindy had gone to the big house and Pali was brushing her hair, getting ready for bed.

"Mama?" Saylee said, "Aunt Mindy will die tonight. Her heart, I think. I feel sad. Goodnight."

Pali knew better than to ask her how she knew. For even if asked, she couldn't, or wouldn't, say. Saylee shared most of her premonitions with her mama and as far as Pali knew she had never been wrong.

Pali said, "I be sad, too. She a good friend. Death come in threes. Who next?"

Saylee looked at her in a startled way and went to bed. Rose Rodenburg knocked on the door early the next morning and when Pali answered the knock, Rose was crying.

"Mindy's dead. Died in her sleep. Oh, Pali, I'll miss her so."

Pali turned from the door and went to the little back alcove to wake Saylee, but Saylee was already up and gone. This happened often. Saylee needed little sleep. She returned late in the morning with dirt under her fingernails and her arms all scratched up. Pali spoke only to tell her that Aunt Mindy was, indeed, dead.

"There will not be a third death," Saylee said, "not this time."

Saylee read some of the passages she had always read to Aunt Mindy from Psalms. She and old Nat conducted the funeral service for Aunt Mindy. The Rodenburgs stood quietly at the back of the crowd, Ira holding his hat over his heart. Rose cried all through the ceremony.

For years now Saylee had done almost everything for the slaves that needed to be done. Pali went with her sometimes, but Saylee knew everything Pali could teach her and then some. Pali had given up hope that Saylee would marry and bear her a grandchild. After making the beautiful double wedding ring quilt for Saylee's hope chest, Pali and Rose Rodenburg had embroidered table cloths and napkins, and many lovely nightgowns for her. Some of the slaves had tried to court Saylee, but most were respectful and a little fearful of her. She was gentle and loving, but pensive. She had a habit of going for days and not saying a word to anyone. Late in life, after her mother was laid to rest, Saylee would fall in love with a promising young black, only to have her heart broken. For now, she didn't seem interested in romance. She stayed busy reading and studying her craft. She became one of the best Medicine Woman her mother had ever heard about or seen. On days when she was in one of her trance-like states, if she heard someone talking to her, she gave no indication. Trance work became a regular part of her self-training.

Pali now spent long hours dreaming of her past, or talking with her daughter about things that happened years before. Reliving the days with her own people. The thirteen short years of happiness with Germahl. She was now in her late fifties. Sometimes she wondered where her own people could be. Strange they had never come back this way. Was her mother still alive? Where were the Chicora now? Would they perhaps return? One day would she wake up and hear the drums, signaling a big ceremony deep in the forests?

Most of all, she missed Germahl. She had never even considered another mate. Germahl was her one great love. Would she see him in Africa Land? Or must she go to her ancestors when she died?

"Where," she asked Saylee one day, "you think I go when I die?"

Saylee had just come in from foraging for plants and roots. She looked at her mother for a long time without answering.

"Where you want to go? To Africa Land? Or the Happy Hunting Lodge?"

"That no fair. You do that every time I ask you something important," her mother said.

Saylee saw that Pali was cross.

"You go," she said, without a moment's hesitation, "to Africa Land."

Pali smiled and nodded her head as if this confirmed her own belief.

In 1854, Pali died at the age of sixty from diphtheria. Saylee knew, but could not prevent it as she once had twenty-one years earlier. The night Zeke was buried and Aunt Mindy died, Saylee had seen a vision of her mother tripping over a root in the swamp and breaking her neck. She had gone to the swamp and found the root and dug it up with her bare hands. Performing a protection ritual deep in the swamp, she knew her mother would be safe. But this time, there was no black magic, nor any white magic to ward off death. Saylee worked around the clock taking care of her mother during her week-long illness, but in the end the grim reaper had had his way. She deeply grieved her mother's death.

Often her duties included taking care of Ira and Rose. Their only child, a son, had left after a few years to study medicine. He came to see them occasionally for a few days, but always hurried back to his practice in New York. They were getting up in years now, and with talk of the impending war between the North and the South, the Rodenburgs decided, in 1858, to free their slaves and return to New York City again. Most of the slaves stayed on the plantation, free

Negroes. Ira would not sell the place, and encouraged them to stay and work the land as though it were there own.

Shortly after the Civil War, Saylee went on one of her frequent foraging trips into the swamp and never returned. Over the years, she had begun staying in the swamp for longer and longer periods of time, always returning to the little cabin where she had grown up. This time she didn't come back. The freed slaves that remained on the place thought maybe she had been eaten by an alligator. One by one, most of them left, too.

Many thought the big house was haunted. Old Nat, now in his nineties, said Saylee's ghost lived in the big house. In 1870, Nat, well over a hundred years old, died in bed. His great, great, granddaughter found him when she came, like she did every day, bringing him his supper. The last two families had moved off the land two years before Nat died. The Union Presbyterian Church, built in 1860, stood across the highway from the old Rodenburg place. Vines grew up and over the big house, and folks said it was a disgrace. Some of the old slave cabins had fallen in on themselves. The Rodenburg land, situated not far from the Congaree Swamp, looked like it really might be haunted.

Saylee increasingly had visions of a daughter that was to be her own. A daughter with no legs, but other than this, no further information was forthcoming, try as she might to do trance work.

On Sunday mornings in the winter, when mists lay thick across the land, members of Union Presbyterian coming to the early service sometimes thought they saw a tall, thin woman, black and gray hair streaming down her back, and carrying a basket on her arm, going into the house. Sometimes late at night, folks thought they saw lights, like maybe a candle moving from room to room in the old, abandoned house. A few people knew the truth. And these few never talked about it. But most people stayed off the land, the sad-looking, desolate land where Root Woman was said to roam.

Chapter 4

Mamie's Mother, Lizzye

Wednesday's child is full of woe
Thursday's child has far to go
Oh precious child, God go with thee
And let thy load not heavy be

While visiting Mamie and Saylee, Isaiah asked Saylee to tell him what she knew about Mamie's past. Root Woman, a good storyteller, began at Mamie's birth.

"Lizzye used to read to me from her diary," Root Woman said, leaning back in her rocking chair. "Here's what I remember mostly."

Lizzye Manigault stood at the foot of the crib and cooed to her sleeping daughter. She marveled at the tiny fists. Her daughter, four months old today, weighed only thirteen pounds and three ounces.

Lizzye's mother popped her head in at the door and said, "Get the child up and dressed, or we'll be late."

Mamma has spoken, Lizzye thought, making a face at the departing back.

Lizzye's mother, a tiny Creole woman in her early forties, still beautiful, had never held the baby.

Both her father and mother had wanted her to abort the child when she found that she was expecting after being raped by the drunken Marino on her way home from classes at the Academy de Lyceum. In the aristocratic Creole society of New Orleans in 1866, this could perhaps be understood. Even in Catholic circles, it could be arranged. She had steadfastly refused and now neither of them acted like Mamie was in the world. Lizzye had finished her schooling over their protest. When the baby came, they had provided the base necessities of a layette. No celebration. No 'Oohing' and 'Ahhing' over this precious baby.

Except for today. Today, the last day in April, Mamie would be baptized at Holy Trinity Catholic Church with a reception following the baptism. The party would be here. Servants had been busy for days.

Lizzye heard her sister and her husband arrive with their two year old, Lacy. Lacy came running up the stairs to see her 'Auntie Lizzye'.

"Auntie Lizzye," she said, "I come to see you. Where is the baby? Where's Mamie?"

"Here," Lizzye called. "Here, Darling, here we are. How's my wonderful niece?"

Lacy seemed to love the baby. This endeared her to her aunt the more so. Her sister, Maryanne LaFont came up, too. They kissed and then Maryanne looked down at the still sleeping baby.

"Hello, Sleepyhead" she said,"Ma Cherrie? This is your big day. Rise and shine." Mamie stretched one tiny arm above her head and yawned, but did not wake up.

"She likes to sleep late in the mornings. She's up often at night, nursing." Lizzye then leaned over and whispered into her sister's ear, "My breasts are sore."

The two young women giggled like school girls. Maryanne was only four years older than Lizzye and they had always been close.

"Mine were, too," Maryanne said, "at first. By the way, Lacy is weaned. She drinks from her little silver cup that Papa gave her when she was born, and . . ." Realizing that Mamie had not received the same, she stopped, and, hugging her sister to her bosom in a fierce embrace, said, "Oh Darling, I am sorry. I shouldn't–"

"No, it's all right. Papa and Maman–"

" . . . are wrong! Mamie shall have the identical cup with her name and birth date engraved on it. Raule and I will see to it!"

Mamie woke up and began to cry. Maryanne picked her up, cooing to her in a soft sing-song. Lacy asked to hold her. Lizzye said, "Right after the ceremony, Lacy. Let me nurse her a little and then we'll dress her in the pretty, long christening gown that was mine when I was christened."

"This?" asked the little girl, trailing her fingers over the delicate silk with the intricate embroidery. "It's pretty," she said when Lizzye nodded.

The christening ceremony at church went off without a hitch, and the party, an elegant affair, lasted all day. Mamie slept and when she was awake, cooed and smiled at everyone. Lizzye's maman did not pay much attention to the baby, though all of her friends seemed charmed by the tiny infant.

Lizzye tried over the next four years to be as inconspicuous as possible and to keep the active, growing child out of the way, but a terrible rift developed between herself and her parents. The sad day arrived when Lizzye could stand it no more and she made plans to move away.

The day she and Mamie were scheduled to depart dawned cold and gray. Rain from a leaden sky pelted the rooftops, as a doleful wind whined and howled by turns blowing sodden leaves into the fences along St. Peters Street and up onto the wide verandahs. Maryanne packed the last of Lizzye's things and labeled the box. "Are you sure you want to do this? You and Mamie can come live with Raule and me. You can teach at the school where Lacy goes. You may get into . . ." Seeing the pained look on Lizzye's face she trailed off. "I'm sorry. Of course you are sure. I shall miss the two of you, that's all. It's a wonderful opportunity for you. You will be the whole school! How exciting! Do you know how many students you will have?"

Mamie, now four years old, sat on the floor drawing and coloring. Her cousin, Lacy, played with paper dolls. Mamie looked up and asked before her mother could answer, "Will I be your student?"

Both women smiled at her. Her mother said, "Of course, you'll always be my student." Turning her attention to her sister, she said, "The Freedman's Bureau indicated in their last letter to me that there would be about twenty all told. I will have adults and children. Many of the former slaves don't know how to read and write. I'll miss you and Lacy, too. And Raule. I guess I'll miss Maman and Papa, too." She hugged her sister, and both women gazed at each other through tear-shined eyes, but did not cry. The rain stopped and a weak sun played among the cumulus clouds piled high like puffy cathedrals in the sky.

Lizzye bade her parents farewell, believing that she would not see them again. They had not warmed toward Mamie as the child grew. Mamie was a difficult baby and an even more difficult toddler. She was often sick, and she had a temper. On top of that she was sullen and quiet.

Partly due to the hostile environment in this home.

Her father, descended from an African mother, and a French Creole father, was a physician and worked long hours. Her mother, whose mother was a beautiful Quadroon, and whose father was a French Creole man, was busy with various charities and social functions. Neither had time for the child. They pretty much left Mamie alone, and Mamie left them alone completely. They stood outside the big old house on St. Peters Street where Lizzye had lived all her life. Awkwardly they promised to write. Her father pressed a roll of money into her hand, hugged her and said, "If you need anything—anything at all . . . ."

Her mother stood stiffly, staring down at Mamie. "Mind your mama now. Try to be a good girl." Turning to Lizzye, she said, "Come back at Christmas time. You'll get some days off then, won't you?" Lizzye nodded not trusting her voice.

Rauel called from the Hanson cab, "Hurry Lizzye, we don't want you to miss your train."

Lizzye, relieved to be going, bolted across the sidewalk calling to her parents, "I'll write. Take care." She and Mamie got into the cab and they were off. She looked back to an empty sidewalk.

To her sister she said, "Typical. They have already gone back inside. And did you hear what Maman said to Mamie? She makes me so angry."

"No one can make you feel an emotion. It's up to you. You choose. Maman and Papa are the way they are. But you don't have to expend your energy hating. Remember the priest talked the other day about 'hate no man. Borrow God's love if you have to, but hate no man.' I believe that is good advice. I'm sorry they make over Lacy and not Mamie. It's not fair. Oh Sissy, I'll miss you so much."

At the station, they hugged and kissed promising to write at least once a week. Lizzye and Mamie boarded the train and began a journey into a world apart.

* * *

"So they came here when Mamie was just four years old?" Isaiah asked. "When did you first get to knowing them?"

"White boy, why you so curious 'bout all this, eh?" Root Woman asked, winking. "Cause you wants to know 'bout Mamie, or 'bout the cousin, Lacy?" Root Woman cackled. Isaiah blushed a deep crimson.

"Both," he said.

"Well, I pick up the story a short while back. No need to go through all the years, one by one!" Root Woman said. She began in Lizzye's voice:

"Mamie, come in now," Lizzye said. "You have lessons to do. School is not out for another week. Here sit down and let's eat. I made your favorite—shrimp gumbo."

"Mama, when Lacy commin'?"

"Honey, please try to speak correctly. When *is* Lacy coming? She will be here tomorrow evening. Her school lets out tomorrow. Maryanne and Lacy board the train at three o'clock in the afternoon and arrive here around ten tomorrow night. They will be very tired I imagine. The next day is Saturday so you go to sleep at your usual time tomorrow night and when you wake up, you and Lacy can play all day. Remember though, Lacy is two and a half years older than you. She may not want to play as much as she did in years past. It's been two years since we've seen them."

"Oh, she not be changed, I don't think. She is my best friend in all the world. De gumbo good, Mama!"

"Thank you, Dear. Remember to say 'the'."

"Sorry, Mama. I tryin'."

"All right, Sweetheart, go get your lessons done. If you need any help, just ask. I love you."

"Love you, too, Sweet, pretty Mama." Mamie gave her a quick peck on the cheek.

Lizzye cleared the table and thought how the child had blossomed since coming here to this little country settlement in South Carolina.

They lived in a tiny community called Balters. Balters lay to the Southeast of Brio which lay southeast of Kingstree. The Black River flowed into the Congaree River and both rivers fed into the Congaree Swamp, a place that was dark and mysterious. Balters backed up to the Congaree Swamp.

The year was 1876 and Mamie was ten and a half years old. Lizzye chuckled remembering how the doctor had said he'd give Mamie the benefit of the doubt and say she was born on Thursday, January 1, 1866. He had laughed and said she had straddled midnight, but this way she would always be a year younger. She had been too tired from the labor to understand his logic then. Even now it didn't quite make sense. Old Doctor Grimes had brought Maryanne and Lizzye into the world and had delivered both Lacy and Mamie. His eccentricities were the talk of New Orleans, but everybody loved him.

Lizzye tried to concentrate on her lesson plan for the last week of school, but kept thinking about seeing Maryanne and Lacy. Raule couldn't make it this time. He had a new shipment of fine guitars, violins, banjos and drums coming in. His music store, a thriving concern, kept him busy. He played guitar with a group of Negroes most weekends. They played a strange rhythm that Lizzye found absolutely beautiful. No one quite knew what to call the new music. For now they called it Be-bop.

She had seen her family briefly in 1874 at Christmas time. Her mother was as cool toward Mamie as ever, though she felt that her father made an effort to get to know the child. She said not a word to Maryanne, but determined to avoid her parents in the future. She didn't bear them a grudge, she just wanted Mamie to grow up without the contamination of their indifference.

Lizzye put her work away and checked on Mamie. The child had fallen asleep over her tablet doing her arithmetic. She lacked only one problem. Lizzye woke her up and put her to bed.

When Lizzye first came to Balters, she lived with a family with nine children. The following spring she hired a man to build her a house on Tamarack Road. She bought the plot of ground from a family who owned the adjacent property. They had planned to build for their son when he married, but he decided to move to New York City, and had been there for many years. They needed the money, so a deal was struck.

Lizzye's house consisted of a parlor, a kitchen, a dining room and two bedrooms. She had a deep well and a nice outhouse. In the parlor was a beautiful wood-burning fireplace with a thick walnut mantle over it. The floors, all hardwood, shone from the beeswax and hand polishing, and were covered with rag rugs that Lizzye hooked in her spare time. She had lovely flowers, trees and shrubs surrounding the property. Her front gate, topped by a wooden archway, supporting rambling, red roses, was the envy of her neighbors. She had hired an iron worker to craft a wrought iron gate like the gates in New Orleans. The gate, eight feet wide, opened onto a broad brick walkway leading up to her front steps—that'd be your papa, Saylee broke into her own story.

Isaiah nodded, so Saylee continued.

Six years she had lived in the house. The front porch, walkway, the rose-covered archway, and wrought iron gate always pleased her. She sat in the swing on her front porch in the moonlight enjoying the view. She sipped a glass of lemonade and thought about seeing her sister and niece.

She also thought about the group of white-sheeted riders who were terrorizing the Colored community. After the war, the freed slaves for the most part stayed on the land as farm laborers. Most of them share-cropped. Some were treated fairly, some not. A family had recently moved off the land of a former slave owner because every year they got deeper into debt with him. They moved in with relatives on another farm, also sharecroppers. The Ku Klux Klan burned a cross in front of their home and threatened the men with a lynching. Both families left in the middle of the night. Rumor had it they took off for a relative's house in Chicago.

Lord, so different from the sheltered life I led in New Orleans as a member of Creole society.

New Orleans boasted a large community of free Negroes, dating back to the early seventeen hundreds.

In those days, many of the original French settlers of Louisiana, the Creole men, saw no harm in choosing a mate of dark skin. These unions often produced offspring with outstanding qualities, both physical beauty and a superior intellect. Many of the female offspring, when they grew up, were courted and won by wealthy white business men. Some of these beautiful women were raised and schooled in the fine arts, gracious living, fashionable dress, the best cuisine, the best wines, how to appoint a fine table, how to smoothly manage a home.

Little by little, families were able to break away from this way of life and establish themselves in business—legitimate business—not the business of courtesans to wealthy white men. An aristocracy of mixed race Creoles was born. This coterie was fiercely proud and insular. The children found themselves leading the most sheltered of lives. Brought up in Catholic schools and raised in homes with servants to attend to their every need, they grew up surrounded by a society they knew little about.

Some of the parents were busy professionals, who trotted out their offspring to sing or play the piano, but failed miserably in the hands-on rearing of their own children. At least that was how Lizzye experienced her own childhood. She vowed anew that her child would grow up differently.

There were still Creole women who were courtesans. Both Maryanne and Lizzle knew of several. Quite discrete they were. They lived quietly in little town houses in New Orleans for part of the year at least. They traveled to Europe, the Bahamas, Mexico, New York, and Charleston. Usually these women were quadroon Creoles, or one quarter Negro.

Lizzye thought of Lacy who would be thirteen this year. Lacy had a governess, but Maryanne spent an enormous amount of time with her, too. They sat for hours embroidering together, sketching in the garden or the park, reading, painting with oils and water colors. Raule had built a studio, an add-on off the library. The studio captured the early morning light and was surrounded by a rose garden.

Maryanne taught French to her daughter and had since she was a baby. Lacy probably didn't need the French lessons anymore, but the lessons continued from long habit. Notwithstanding all this pampered treatment, Lacy seemed unassuming, a lovely creature, delicate of features and loving in nature.

Lizzye could not help but compare her own child with her sister's. Mamie often was cross for no reason that Lizzye could see. She threw temper tantrums regularly. She would not learn French, did not like to do fine needle work, had no interest in drawing or painting, and didn't like to read or to study.

Mamie had a yellow skin tone and kinky black hair not of good quality. Lizzye assumed it was from the drunken Marino that Mamie had inherited the kinky hair and yellow complexion. He was half

Spanish and half Negro. Mamie's hair broke easily. Lizzye had had to learn how to take care of the wiry, kinky hair of her child. She loved her dearly, but knew that she was no beauty.

Mamie had some good points, too. Lizzye smiled thinking about how Mamie took to the black community of Balters. She had been four years old when they moved here. Mamie was one with the entire community within a week. The few whites she came into contact with seemed to be no problem for her as well. In truth, Mamie was so ugly that most white people found her no threat and seemed to like her.

Mamie had recently discovered a general store over in Brio—your store, Saylee said.

Isaiah grinned.

It was little more than a stand by the side of the road. In fact Mamie had informed her that it had started out that way just a month ago. The young white boy who ran the store told Mamie that he had learned that people didn't have a need for fresh vegetables. He had added bolts of cloth, horehound candy, horse shoes and the like and a country store was born.

Lizzye awoke to a pounding on her front door. As she hurried to the door, wrapping her oversized shawl around her, she glanced at the tall grandfather clock. It was one o'clock in the morning. She peered out of her front window and seeing a small child, she let him in. He blurted out, "Mama say please come. She done sent fo the Root Woman and she not home. The mens come back and say her shack empty as a jay bird nest in winter. Mama's baby is comin'!"

"Your mama is Caroline over in Brio?"

The boy nodded and told her his name. "I called LeRoy." She got Mamie up and gathered a few towels and scissors, some twinc, and an old, soft sheet. They got the mule out of her cozy stall, hitched her to the wagon and hurried out Old Tamarack Road to the little Colored community in Brio. Lizzye wondered that a child as young as LeRoy could run all the way to her house in the dead of night.

"How old are you, LeRoy?"

"I twelve. I's little, but I twelve."

Lizzye smiled. Mamie, asleep next to her, was fifteen and shorter than the boy. She certainly knew about small children. "How many children has your mama had?"

The boy answered, "Dis un will make thirteen. Mama say that's bad luck. She say dat why the mens couldn't find Root Woman."

Lizzye said, "I know where Root Woman is living now. When we get to your house, I'll tell the men how to find her.

When they got to the boy's home, I was there already. I say, "How do, Lizzye? Baby come now. You help?"

"Why yes, Saylee, but how did you get here? I thought they couldn't find you."

"Spirit tell me. I come." Saylee turned back to the woman bathed in sweat lying on the double bed. There were pallets all over the floor with sleeping children curled into one another. A few men milled around on the front porch talking. Most smoked corn-cob pipes. A couple of children ran and squealed in the yard.

Lizzye checked the pot set to boil on the wood stove. The water was coming to a boil. She held the blades of the scissors in the boiling water for three minutes. There was no clock. She counted the time off silently. Next she dropped a length of the twine into the water and counted off the requisite three minutes.

She hurried back to the bed, and Saylee said, "Rub in circles up here on her stomach. Circles and down." Turning back to the panting woman, she said, "Now, push. Push!" Saylee reached both of her thin hands into the birth canal and turned the baby who was trying to present breach. She used her hands and arms to guide the baby out. A few more contractions and the baby slid out squalling. "No need to spank this un," Saylee said with the merest hint of a smile. As they were washing up, Saylee asked, "Where your girl?"

Lizzye replied, "She's curled up on the wagon seat, wrapped in my shawl and sound asleep. I declare that girl loves to sleep."

I met Lizzye when she first come to Balters to teach and a friendship had grown over the eleven years. I taught her about roots, bark, leaves. How to make teas and stronger concoctions. They foraged together and Lizzye learned how to identify plants and roots. They worked together in companionable silence. Finally Lizzye asked, "How've you been getting along, Saylee?"

"Fair to middlin'. I slowin' down some. Not so young anymore. How 'bout you? You havin' a good year at school?"

The two women chatted as they worked. I made the new mother comfortable. Gave her an herb tea to make her milk plentiful. Told her to rest a day or two if she could. Lizzye gave Saylee a ride to the edge of the swamp. "Saylee, why did you move to the other side of the swamp?"

"Had to get to higher ground. Swamps change, you know. That old place is most sunk into the swamp. 'Sides, I don't like to live in one place too long. Only a few peoples know how to find me. I finds them when they needs me. I gots ways of knowin."

Lizzye drove as far as she could and the two women said good-bye. On the way home, she wondered again how Root Woman could have known to come. Saylee had tried to teach her some of the magic, but Lizzye was uncomfortable with it. She told Saylee that it went against some of her religious beliefs. Saylee, from that day on, taught her only about medicine, never again broaching the subject of Voodoo.

On New Year's day, 1882, Lizzye gave Mamie a birthday party for her sixteenth birthday. Mamie was the life of the party. Six girls and five boys came. She laughed and joked with the boys as well as the girls. One boy, in particular, seemed taken with Mamie. His name was Rosco. Rosco came from a good family, but Lizzye thought he was too old for Mamie. Nineteen years old, he was polite, but too . . .? *Boisterous, he is so full of himself, she thought. Says please and thank you, though. Dresses nice.*

He and his mama went to the AME church where Lizzye had been going for several years now. She had not joined and she still said her rosary, but there was no Catholic Church for her to attend. Little by little, she had gotten used to the different style of worship, but she missed the stained glass of the cathedral in New Orleans, the ritual of the alter boys, the incense, the candles, and the formality.

She studied Rosco. She knew she had to be practical. She was no longer a rich, New Orleans Creole. The rules of society were different here.

Mamie is almost pretty tonight. She's growing up.

Coming out of her reverie, she realized it was nearly eight-thirty in the evening. The party had begun at three o'clock that afternoon.

"Children, may I have your attention, please? It's almost time to say goodnight. Ten more minutes, how does that sound?" There were groans of protest, but the youngsters took it in stride. Most of them had curfews and had to be home by nine or ten o'clock at night. "Does anyone live too far to walk home alone?" Eula Belle said she did, but Bessie May said her daddy and mama were coming to walk her home and she just knew they wouldn't mind walking Eula Belle home first. "Well, we'll ask them," Lizzye said.

Lizzye began putting away the leftovers. Little remained to put away. She and Mamie had cooked huge piles of fried chicken, a big pot of shrimp gumbo, dozens of little biscuits with home-churned butter and honey right out of the hive. She had baked a chocolate cake and had even found little candles to put on top. Saylee had come early in the day, bringing an intricately carved drum that she had made for Mamie. She had stayed only a short time, kissed Mamie on the cheek and left. Mamie was shy around Root Woman and no one else.

Oh well, I guess Saylee does seem a little weird to Mamie. I guess any child of sixteen would find a Root Woman a bit too much to joke around with like she seems able to do with everyone else.

By the time the last child was gone, Lizzye had the house in order. She sat with Mamie by her side and talked. "You like Rosco?"

"Yessum. He's nice. I think he likes me a lot. He kissed me on the cheek tonight. You see that?"

Lizzye smiled and answered, "Yes, I surely did see that. As he was leaving. He cut his eyes sideways at me. I pretended not to notice, but I saw him plant that kiss. How'd you feel about him kissing you?"

"I dunno, Mama! You alles ask me so many questions. I dunno!"

Lizzye wisely turned the conversation to more agreeable topics.

"Everybody seemed to enjoy the shrimp gumbo. Did you tell them that you made it all by yourself?"

"Yeah, that fat girl, Eula Belle, didn't believe me. I most draw back and knocked her head plumb off her shoulders."

"Mamie! I wo'tt tolerate such behavior. You know–"

"Aw, Mama. I said I *most* did that. I smile and say so sweet you wouldn't believe, 'Well, I did make it.'

She say, 'It shore taste *good*, too. You shore can cook, *Child*!' We still friends. You worry too much, Mama. I'm good. I'm alles good."

Mamie gave her mama a quick, impulsive kiss smack on the lips and they both laughed.

"Well," Lizzye said, "I'm so glad you are learning to control your temper. I'm happy that you and your friends had a good time. Do you want to draw with the new set of pencils and use the new sketch pad I bought you for your birthday present?" Mamie got them out and attempted a rose, but soon lost interest.

"Mama? What does it feel like to get a real kiss from a boy?"

Lizzye fought the impulse to lecture and answered calmly.

"I guess it would feel real good. I wouldn't know from personal experience. You know a little about my *ordeal,* but I've never told you much and you're not old enough even now to know all the sordid details of that experience. But just know this, I have never experienced even one kiss from a man that I liked and who liked me. I've never known love, although I'm sure that a real kiss would be wonderful." Her eyes were bright with tears. One slipped down her cheek and she hastily brushed it away.

"Mama? You cryin'. Don't cry. It be all right." Mamie awkwardly put her arm around her mother and they sat for a long time. "Mama? Maybe one of these days somebody will find you. You so beautiful. Not like me. I ugly. I know dat. But Rosco like me anyway."

"Oh, Honey. You are beautiful, too. In a different way. In a different way, that's all. I love you!" Lizzye hugged her.

"Now," Saylee said, "Isaiah, you know 'bout as much as I do. Time for you to go home and me to go to bed. Almost dark, now."

Isaiah left Saylee's house.

That was some story old Root Woman told. Feel like I've known 'em all my life. Especially *Lacy, Mamie's cousin. Hmmm.*

Chapter 5

Congaree Swamp

A foul deed done by the light of the moon
Out in the middle of the swamp
Never was brought to the light of day
The harm that was wroght? Who can say?
Good deeds, too, in that misty place, often go untold
Unsung unheralded, unknown though bold

In the fall of 1885, three years after Mamie lost her legs, her mother, and her home, she began the slow climb back into the world. And what a world she found. She looked around this autumn afternoon and saw plants and animals, birds and reptiles as though for the first time.

Saylee picked her way through the swamp, careful to avoid quicksand. Sink holes could suck a horse and rider under in less than ten minutes, or an old woman pulling a travois with the sleeping girl, in even less time. With all the beauty, there was the ever present sense of danger, mystery, intrigue.

They stopped at a quiet pool shaded by an ancient, moss-draped oak. Root Woman loosened the straps holding Mamie secure and lifted her off the travois. She sat with the young woman in her lap.

Light, through the thick canopy of leaves, gleamed with a golden-green, liquid quality. This liquid light seemed to soothe Mamie.

"This spot is your favorite, eh, daughter? Ah yes, the beauty of the swamp. So peaceful, so quiet. Just us and the animals and plants. A good place for healing."

Mamie nodded her head, but said nothing. She turned back toward the pool and began to sing and hum. Saylee remained quiet.

Root Woman stood up, holding Mamie around the waist with one arm, her long pole clutched in the other hand. She watched as a big alligator crept through the water toward them. When the reptile swam within two feet -- of the bank with only his eyes above water --Root Woman yelled and punched the pole down into the water, smacking the alligator on the head with a solid thump. The old reptile turned slowly away, seeking an easier prey.

Mamie chortled. Root Woman laughed, too.

"Don't do to get too easy out here in the swamp. No. Gotta watch out for snakes and gators, bears and wildcats. We best be getting on back 'fore dark, Child."

"No," Mamie said, "fish."

"Okay, but just for a little while."

Saylee baited their lines, and she and Mamie fished for a half hour. They caught two bream each, enough for supper. On the way home, Saylee sang a healing song.

Back in the cabin, Saylee lay Mamie down to change her diaper. Since the tragedy, Mamie had reverted to infancy in much that she did. She sucked her thumb and soiled herself.

Saylee finished diapering her, and placed her in her customary spot on an old quilt someone had long years before given her for birthing a baby. Then, she cooked the fish, along with wild greens and yam-like roots. They sat down to eat dinner at a short-legged table Saylee fashioned just for Mamie.

"Mamie the fellow who owns that general store, Isaiah his name, he come to see you earlier today while you sleeping. He brought lots of good stuff to eat. See the ham?"

She pointed to a home-cured ham that sat over on the dry sink. Mamie nodded her head.

"Ham," she said.

Often Mamie repeated a word. Saylee didn't know if she understood or just parroted what she heard.

"Mamie, we needs to un-lock those memories that are buried so deep. Let 'em out in the fresh air. Do you remember your mama? Your mama was killed the night you lost your legs. She—"

"Mama? Mama? Ai-y-e-e-e, nooo. Mama."

Mamie toppled over onto the floor.

Saylee jumped up and grabbed Mamie, who had fainted, hitting the side of her forehead. She took Mamie to the other side of the cabin and lay her on the low cot. Root Woman got the herb tea that she kept on hand for calming Mamie. She spooned the medicine into the unconscious woman's mouth, knowing full well that if she regained consciousness before the tea had time to take effect, Mamie would scream until she passed out again.

Mamie sputtered as the liquid went down her throat. She opened her eyes ten minutes later to Saylee singing softly to her. For a moment, Saylee thought it would be like other times. That Mamie would not remember what had just transpired, but this time she did.

"Mama is dead. Bad mens killed my mama. Oh-h-h-h, I scared. Go away. Leave me be."

Saylee paced back and forth with Mamie held as she would hold an infant. She sang to Mamie until finally the girl relaxed and went to sleep.

"You so like a tiny baby. My baby," Saylee said.

She lay the sleeping girl on her cot. Saylee cleaned up the supper dishes and then sat by the window. As a cloud drifted over the full moon, she realized that she could have told Isaiah when he visited earlier in the afternoon, about the impending death this night of his mother.

Wouldn't have changed anything, just made him sad before he needed to be.

She went into a trance to try to prevent the death she knew headed for Sadie Norris. She received a picture of a small woman with dark hair, faintly streaked with gray. A remarkably young-looking woman. Loving and full of passion for life. She probed deeper to see if she could somehow prevent this tragic event. Nothing.

Coming out of her trance. Saylee sat very still by the window, deep in thought.

There is a time for everything under the sun. It her time to die. Nothin' I can do. Aw Lord. Why some people die so young? Like my papa. Like my mama. I miss them both. And Isaiah gonna' miss his mama. So young to lose his mama! Soon now. Poor boy.

This cabin, the one Saylee began living in shortly before Mamie lost her mother and her legs, was a two-room, abandoned trapper's cabin. She had watched the deserted cabin for a whole year before taking up residence in it. She moved from time to time for one reason or another, but always stayed deep in the swamp. The swamp, home to more than alligators, snakes and frogs, proved a virtual cornucopia to those who knew where to gather and hunt.

Saylee made her security round, checking to make sure everything was all right. She kept animals to alert her to any approaching danger. These critters served as her pets in the day and alarms in the night. Until recently, her keen sense of alertness was enough, day or night. Now, she feared she would not hear approaching danger. Having the responsibility of Mamie caused Saylee to take extra precautions.

I know them Klans people would just love to get their hands on me. They's supposed to be disbanded, but I knows better. They held a meetin' just the other night. The low-down, white buckra! I fix them, they come messin' round here.

After *the incident,* as it was called, when Mamie lost her legs at the hands of the Klan, the Freedman's Bureau managed to get the Federal government involved in the investigation. After much dragging of the feet, no hard evidence ever came to light that the Klan caused the death of Lizzye Managualt or the loss of her daughter's legs. In truth, no one ever saw or talked to Mamie or to Root Woman.

I send them the bones from Mamie's legs, feet, and toes and they has their 'hard evidence'. I needs to bury them bones. Mamie ever see them, she might lapse into a worse state than she in now.

The Freedman's Bureau finally got a hearing, but not by the Federal Government, as they had hoped. A panel of local judges sat at the 'request' of the Federal Government.

Nobody testified against the Klan, except for the young boy, Isaiah Norris, and members of the local Freedman's Bureau.

"And where is the girl, now? Mamie is her name?" a judge asked Isaiah.

"Sir, I don't know where she is. This old woman who lives way out in the middle of Congaree Swamp took her," Isaiah said.

"This woman have a name? An address?"

"No sir," Isaiah muttered.

The judge smiled.

"You say you were a part of the Klan group who took the girl out to the swamp to scare her? Why didn't you stop them from tying her across the tracks? And you claim there was an engineer who stopped the train and dragged the girl out from under the tracks? What was his name? Where does he live?"

"I don't know, sir." Isaiah said. "But it did happen. Just exactly like I've told you. Judge Clayton and these other men know I'm telling the truth."

"Son, they all have iron-clad alibis for the night in question. November 14, 1882. Why, I might add, have you waited so long to come forward with this accusation? It is now almost three years after the incident supposedly happened."

"Why," Isaiah sputtered, "have we waited so long? The Freedman's Bureau has been trying ever since that night to get an investigation! God! Do you realize how hard it's been to get this hearing?"

"I wouldn't take that tone at this hearing if I were you, boy. This is a court of law and you used the Lord's name in vain. Do that again and I'll fine you for contempt."

After more questioning, some three hours, the hearing was over. No conclusive evidence. The Klan members were simply admonished to disband.

Root Woman had gone to the tracks to gather the severed limbs the day after Mamie lost her legs. Now the bones, picked cleaned by scavenger beetles, and bleached in the sun, lay protected in a wire cage. She kept the bones for the power she thought they brought to

Mamie. But as Mamie got better, Root Woman feared the sight might frighten Mamie and so she finally buried them, along with a powerful gris-gris, a cloth sack filled with herbs and cemetery dirt.

Saylee kept in her cabin a tall top hat, a man's shirt, a sharp-pointed spade, and a hoe. These object she arranged on top of an old coffin with a black cross painted on its lid. All this, the accoutrements of Baron Samedi, guardian spirit of cemeteries, she used in her Voodoo ceremonies.

She fashioned a snake out of white clay, painted it with plant dyes, and coiled it around a long pole. This she leaned in the corner behind the coffin. The snake represented Dambala the serpent god.

In addition to the coffin and the snake pole, Saylee kept various herbs and spices, animal parts and bones, and dirt from the old slave cemetery for mixing together in a special recipe for either white or black magic. She kept a number of jujus for good luck and mojos for bad luck. The formulas she placed in little sacks called gris-gris.

She placed several of these tiny sacks on various doorways in the town of Brio after Mamie's ordeal.

By the time of the hearing, Judge Clayton found himself in such poor health that he no longer served as a magistrate. He stopped holding or even attending Klan meetings. Many in the town and surrounding areas said he feared the curse the old Root Woman put him under.

"He scared to death he gonna' die. But dat ain't what she say."

"She shore Lawd did say he gonna' die! A terrible death."

"Naw, she ain't say he gonna' die. Least wise, not right off. She say he gonna suffer years and years and then die all alone without friends or money. Yes siree. She say dat! Um huh. And ain't he doin' jest dat? He done most lost he wife. She don't even sleep in the same room wid him, they cook told me."

"Uhn-uhn-uhn. You right. He payin' fo what he done!"

And so the talk went. It did seem that from that very night, the judge's health began to deteriorate. First his eyesight went bad. Then, because of the failing eyesight, he fell and broke his leg. The leg never healed right. After being re-broken and re-set twice, it still wasn't straight, but he lived with the withered, twisted leg.

The judge lost weight to the point of emaciation. His stomach hurt every time he tried to eat. He developed asthma. He became allergic to everything imaginable. His nerves were shot. He jumped at every noise or movement. He didn't sleep well. Bit by bit, he fell to pieces.

The Clayton's cook, Summey, brought news of the progression of his poor health to the colored community.

"I hear his wife tell him 'I ain sleepin' with you until you stop keepin' a loaded pistol under your pillow.' Well suh." Summey rolled her eyes, and when her audience could stand the suspense no longer, she continued, "He say 'you might not ever sleep with me again 'cause the pistol stays. No tellin' what that crazy old Root Woman might do,'"

"Naw, Lawd. He ain't dat scared, is he?" an old woman asked.

"He dat scared," Summey said, "and more. He keep a shotgun propped up right by the front door. Laws-a-me. That white man is scared shitless."

Judge Clayton's deteriorating health proved scant consolation for the loss of their beloved neighbor and teacher, Lizzye. Mamie was lost to them as surely as if she, too, had died. Saylee sent word every now and then as to how Mamie was getting along. Occasionally, people saw the child, but always they feared her.

"Mamie teched in the head. Them mens done took her mind plumb away. Poor thing. You hear the way she babble about 'the burning cross of Jesus'?"

"Yass, Lawd. And the way she stare at a body. I wonders does she know anything at all?"

When people saw Mamie on the occasions Saylee took her along at a birthing, they tried not to stare. Mamie's former friends now shunned her.

Saylee all but gave up practicing midwifery. That constituted another loss to the community. But with each new ailment Summey told about, Saylee's reputation as a Voodoo Queen grew.

Others who tortured Mamie that night met with one misfortune after another.

The consequences of that night ranged wide and far. Callie, Rosco's mama, died early in 1885, just two and a half years after her son left.

She died of a broken heart thinking her boy, Rosco be dead -- but he alive somewhere, thought Root Woman as she made her rounds tending to the sick in Balters.

There were many lives ruined by the evil of them Klans peoples. I glad I put the hex on them mens.

Except Isaiah, all of the men who took part that night experienced one thing or another that people attributed to Voodoo. Clem lost a leg. Hunting accident. Claude sliced a foot off chopping wood. All were afflicted in one way or another in the legs and feet. All but Judge Clayton. He suffered all over his body. Isaiah never had an illness, nor an accident.

Saylee thought of him now as she made sure of locks and alarms in the cabin.

I was right about that boy. He is good.

She remembered the ham he brought and cut herself a small piece and sat eating it looking again out the window at the moon. Saylee could now feel the pain of the grieving father and son, Robert and Isaiah, and so said a prayer of blessing for them both and went to bed.

Saylee worked with Mamie on through the fall and winter, trying to get her to walk, wearing shoes purchased at Ike's General. Saylee bought the smallest brogans.

Mamie lost her balance each time she tried to walk. Sometimes she could stand for short periods of time on her callused stumps, but a few steps, and she tumbled over backwards.

Always backwards. Why always backwards?

On the first day of spring, Mamie took the shoes off and threw them across the room. She sat and glared at Saylee.

"You win. You don't have to wear them."

In one of her famous shifts of mood, Mamie scooted over to where Saylee sat on the floor. She hugged her and called her Ma-Saylee, her special term of endearment. Saylee sat holding the child-woman.

I got to find a way. She is never gonna walk, less I can get shoes on her. How would I keep my balance if I had no feet? Toes help anchor a body to the floor. Hmmm! How?

Just as she dismayed of figuring out a way, Mamie crawled and scooted over to where the shoes had landed. She stuck them on the stumps of her legs, and stood up. The shoes were not laced up. Mamie took a step and one of the shoes fell off. Saylee jumped up and put the shoe back on, lacing both shoes. Mamie walked across the cabin without falling.

Saylee and Mamie grinned at each other. Mamie walked with a peculiar side-to-side gait, but she walked. Saylee picked her up and danced around the cabin with her.

"You smart, you know that? You solved the problem all by yourself. Put 'em on backwards, eh? It works. Girl, I'm happy."

Mamie practiced walking the rest of that day. She didn't want to take the shoes off at bedtime. Saylee sat up long into the night, fashioning goose down pads that fit over each of Mamie's leg stumps like a pair of socks.

Mamie worked hard learning to walk, and by her twentieth birthday, managed quite well.

Mamie acted normal for long periods of time, then she lapsed back to previous behavior; screaming, baby talk, nightmares, and temper tantrums. Saylee knew the temper tantrums were not altogether the aftermath of the accident. Several times before she died, Lizzye mentioned Mamie's temper. Saylee even witnessed a tantrum a few times while Mamie still lived at home with her mother.

I worries about the girl. I wants to get her to a place where she can live with a family in the community after I'm gone. Her grandparents ain't never gonna' take care of her. Where Lizzye's sister and her family gone, I don't know. They done move to Chicago, I think. Saylee walked outside.

How her sister can just turn her back on this child is more than I can understand. I think Maryanne scared of me. Folks from here told her 'bout me commin' outta the swamp glowin' all green. Puttin' the hex on them Klans people. She scared of me. Thinks I some Voodoo Queen. She don't know nothing 'bout Voodoo. If she did, she wouldn't be scared of it. Humph.

Saylee shook her head, thinking about the family.

Lizzye be so sad to see how her sister is toward the child. They were so close. The child ain't got nobody, but me. Them grandparents had a bad influence on Maryanne. Raule, too, I guess. Jes don't care 'bout Mamie, Uhn?

Isaiah came again the week before Christmas, a year and a few months following his first visit. He knocked on the cabin door late in the day.

Root Woman peered through the one window at the man standing on her front porch. He held a box, hugged to his chest as though heavy. She hurried to the door.

"Come. What is in the box? You bring more ham?" Root Woman asked.

She noticed that he had filled out and didn't look as much like a boy. He stared at her cougar who was penned inside a big chicken-wire cage.

"You like my cougar? I ride him to work and back," she said with a straight face.

"Where did you find such a big ole cat?" Isaiah laughed. A riotous, booming laugh.

Yes, the boy is gone. I like the man even better.

"How do you come to have a cougar? Not enough humans to treat? Branching out in your practice of medicine?"

"About two months ago, I come up on this poor soul. He layin' right in the path, with a paw most rotted off his leg. He musta got caught in a trap, but sprung the thing open. Anyway, he hurt bad, but he wouldn't let me anywhere near him. Bad as he hurt, he jump up to fight me." Root Woman paused, staring fondly at her caged cat.

"So," Isaiah asked, setting the box down, "how did you manage to get him here?"

"Well," Root Woman said, "I turn easy-like, come on back home, mix up a powerful sleepin' potion, soak a chicken leg in it overnight, and throw it to him the next morning. He sniff the leg, lick his chops, and growl at me. I leave him with the chicken leg, and when I come back an hour later, he sleepin peaceful. Here, come on in. Come in."

Isaiah picked up the box and followed her into the cabin, still laughing.

"So you tricked him so you could heal him, eh? Well, I imagine sometimes that's how you have to do it. With humans, too, would be my guess. How are you, Mamie?"

Mamie sat very still, staring at Isaiah.

"How'd you get that big a cougar here to the cabin?" Isaiah asked, setting the box down.

Saylee motioned him to a chair, as she inspected the things in the box.

"I pull him on a travois. Say 'hello', Mamie. You remember

Isaiah, don't you?" Turning back to Isaiah, she said, "I had that pen from years ago when I found a baby black bear orphaned by its mother. Good thing that pen stood ready for its latest occupant. When that cat come to, he mad! He snarl and claw up a storm, but he ain' do no damage to that chicken-wire cage! Pretty soon, he tame as a kitty cat. He my pet, now." She grinned, obviously enjoying her own story.

Mamie got up and walked toward Isaiah. Half way there, she stopped, veered away and continued on to Root Woman. She buried her face in Saylee's dress. Root Woman picked her up and held her on her lap.

"I walkin' now," Mamie said. "See my shoes?"

"Yes, I see," Isaiah said.

Don't stare at the stumps and the shoes turned backwards.

"Was it . . . was it hard to learn to walk?" he asked.

Mamie nodded, but didn't say anything. After an awkward pause, which Root Woman left lying there for the two of them to do with it what they would, Mamie ended the impass.

"You the boy with a store. How you do that? How you get a store?"

"I built it," Isaiah said. "I have a brand new store now. It's called 'Ike's General Emporium.' I hope you'll come to see me there. I have a whole showcase of penny candy. I'll give you some when you come. In fact . . . ." He got up, rummaged in the box, and brought out a paper sack. He handed it to Saylee. "If Saylee thinks it's all right, you can have a piece right now. Do you like peppermints?" Not waiting for an answer, he asked, "How'd you know I have a store?"

Mamie didn't answer, but stared at him as she sucked the peppermint stick. After another long pause that this time felt more comfortable, Isaiah said, "There's more stuff in the wagon. I left it—"

"--up in the clearing," Saylee said. "I know. Let me get a coat on Mamie and me. I'll pull her in the cart, and we'll go with you. You brought many things. You did not have to. Only if you wanted. From love, not guilt."

Isaiah looked at Saylee for a long moment. He wondered how she knew where he left the wagon, but he didn't ask. They pulled the cart to the spot and loaded a few of the soft parcels with Mamie. Isaiah heaved a large box onto his shoulders, while Saylee carried a shopping bag and used the other hand to pull the cart. Isaiah, after finding the balance on his shoulder, took over the pulling of the cart when they got to the rise of ground the cabin sat on

Back inside, they shivered and rubbed their hands together. As the sun sank lower in the winter sky, the thermometer dropped, and a brisk wind sprang up. Isaiah watched as Saylee began putting away the food. With Mamie's attention elsewhere, he motioned for Saylee to step near.

"Why," he asked in a low tone, "does Mamie talk with a broken English? She had such good schooling."

"Her mind," Saylee said, "never been the same. She doesn't remember much that she knew before. It is like starting all over for her."

Their eyes met and held.

I wish I could heal him from the guilt and shame he still carry, but that something he must do for himself. Time will do the rest of the healing for both Isaiah and Mamie. Or it won't.

"I—um, I'd best be going. I want to get out of the swamp before nightfall. It can be treacherous, you know. Merry Christmas. Come see my new store and be sure to bring Mamie. Bye Mamie."

Mamie said nothing.

"Isaiah," Saylee said, "I am sorry 'bout your mama dying. The ointment help your papa?"

"Thank you. Who told you my mama died?" When Saylee didn't answer, he said "Thank you, I miss her a lot. And yes, the stuff you sent Pa really works. I meant to mention that."

"I know," Saylee said, bringing her hand out from the deep apron pocket, "you don't smoke, but here's another gift for your papa. And, I have somethin' for you."

In her hand, she held a clay pipe, intricately carved with tiny birds reptiles, and animals.

"I make it," she smiled and said. "Now, don't be thinking I another of these womens who is sweet on your papa. But he likes to smoke and I do this for him. He can smoke his pipe and think of his Sadie."

They both laughed.

"Now, wait," she rummaged around in a small alcove, and came out holding a drum. "Keep this close to you. It was Mamie's. When she better, you may want to return it to her. Meanwhile, it yours! It will protect you."

After Isaiah left, Saylee let Mamie open up the packages. One contained a dress for Mamie. The dress dragged the floor, but Saylee could cut off the material and hem it up. The extra cloth she would use to make something else. The dress, made from a soft cotton with a little print, tiny roses all in lines, showed excellent work.

This material called dimity, I think. Somebody sew this that know what they's doin'.

"Look Mamie, a little cardigan sweater for you! Probably knit by one of Isaiah's aunts. Hmm," she said, fingering the sweater, "his Aunt Isabelle knit this. I'll have to ask him if his Aunt Isabelle sew the dress, too."

Saylee thought it strange that everybody couldn't do what she did. When she first began as a child to see and know, she thought that everybody knew things about other people like she did. Gradually, she learned that what she had was a gift. Or a curse. Her papa explained it was a blessing.

Isaiah had brought a long, warm coat for Saylee. She tried it on and it hung perfectly on her thin, tall frame. Made in a store or factory somewhere, the label read c-a-s-h-m-e-r-e. Saylee spelled it out, but didn't know the word. The green, the color of winter evergreens, complemented Saylee's bronze skin tone.

"I like this coat, Mamie. I'll wear it to his new store. Why you so quiet, Child?"

Saylee put away the rest of the groceries he brought, and with Mamie by her side, prepared for bed. Mamie sucked her thumb and had a far away look on her face.

As Isaiah rode back to town, he pondered the situation.

Can't believe how much I enjoyed this visit. With over a year gone by, I was afraid Root Woman might not welcome me, but she acted like it was the most natural thing in the world, me coming.

Nearly four years now since Mamie lost her legs—and her mother. She's walking good, but I wonder? Will she ever be her old, self-assured self? Root Woman is a treasure.

After his mother died, he kept busy; building, stocking, getting everything ready for his store. With the involvement of brothers, sister, uncles and aunts, the year sped by with new curtains for the store and even a hooked rag-rug. So he had let a whole year pass before returning to the swamp to see Saylee and Mamie.

Isaiah rode along, cautious in keeping the wagon centered in the narrow trail. Parents told children to keep out of the swamp, but they seldom did. He ventured in a few times as a child, but never to the heart of the swamp where Saylee and Mamie lived. He didn't even know there existed the little ponds, trails, and huge trees. A world apart.

He had looked for alligators all his life and saw two or three at most. They seemed to just lie there in the water, but he feared them. He didn't see any the last time out here or this time, but Saylee told him about the big one she called 'Mama Alli'. He wondered how anybody could stand to live where a gator or a snake might show up on their doorstep at any time. He had to admit, though, the swamp had a certain allure for him. It seemed so mysterious. Dark and mysterious. Like Root Woman.

What was it Root Woman said? 'In winter, the mist, along with the half-light of the slanting sun through bare branches, make a world of solitude. A world good for the soul to sort through pain and joy, sadness and wisdom. A wonderful place for healing.'

Lacy wants me to bring her to see Mamie. Next visit.

Sometimes it seems difficult to tell where the water ends and the air begins. The light really does look green, like the water. A liquid world, dark and dangerous. Mysterious and timeless.

The day after Isaiah left, Mamie regressed, screaming in terror all day. Root Woman finally drugged her, but still Mamie cried and moaned. Saylee sat and rocked Mamie, crooning the healing chant. Root Woman sang, over and over until her voice almost left her. In late afternoon, Mamie fell into a sleep that held her for two days and nights.

She awoke three days before Christmas and asked for food and ate like she was ravenous. Mamie seemed not to remember the screaming. Saylee decided, after fixing her a meal of scrambled eggs and ham, to bring it up.

"Mamie, you tell Ma-Saylee what happened? Why you scream the other day? Do you remember when you so scared?"

Mamie looked at her over a spoonful of scrambled eggs. She sat, spoonful of eggs poised midway from plate to mouth. Just when Saylee thought Mamie would not answer, she did.

"That man," Mamie said, "he was there. He there at the burning cross of Jesus. I scared of him." Her face crumpled, but she managed to control her tears. "Why he come here? I don't like him. This place safe. He hurt Mamie."

Mamie looked down at her stumps, then beyond them as though seeing her missing legs. She jumped down from the chair and came running to Saylee burying her face in Saylee's lap. She cried for a long time, but from sorrow, not from fear.

When her crying subsided somewhat, Saylee lifted the child-woman to her lap and turned the tear-streaked face up to hers.

"Listen Child, that man *was* at the burning cross, but he tried to help. He was just a boy, but he tried to stop the mens. That is the truth. Ma-Saylee not lie to you. You know that."

Mamie didn't answer, but sat sucking her thumb. She would not let Saylee put her down that whole, long day and night. At dawn, Saylee eased onto the cot with Mamie still in her arms. They slept until noon when Mamie woke up crying.

She had just stopped crying when Isaiah returned with Lacy the very next day. The visit lasted about an hour.

"Mamie, don't you remember me?" Lacy asked. "We played with dolls and paper dolls in New Orleans? I came to see you in Balters?"

Mamie stared solemnly at her beautiful cousin, but did not reply. She clung close to Root Woman and sucked her thumb.

Mamie retreated after seeing Isaiah and Lacy. On January 1, 1886, her twentieth birthday, she stopped talking altogether, and remained mute for a long, long time.

Saylee sent word for Isaiah not to come and told him why. Year in, year out Saylee tried to get Mamie to talk, to open up, but to no avail. She remained mute. From time to time Isaiah left good things to eat, or a special piece of clothing on her doorstep. She knew each time he came, but she never let on to Mamie.

Over the years, Mamie remained mostly mute, but gradually started talking again. A word or two at first, then more and more. Finally Saylee determined to test the waters with a visit to Isaiah's store. On a bright spring day in 1900, shortly after Mamie's thirty-fourth birthday, Saylee took her to Ike's General Emporium. When they entered, Mamie saw Isaiah for the first time in fourteen years. She smiled at him.

Isaiah, six feet four inches tall, a big barrel of a man, stooped and held out his arms to Mamie who stood beside Saylee. Mamie buried her face in Saylee's skirts, but didn't cry or scream. She peeped out at him and smiled.

"You the good boy?"

Isaiah stood up, nodding his head happily. He and Saylee laughed. Mamie laughed, too. Mamie said no more, but listened intently to Isaiah and Saylee as they talked.

"Isaiah, I'm sorry 'bout your wife dying two years ago. How your boy, Rob? He must be over two years old now. And you just got married again?"

"Thank you," Isaiah finally said as he continued to pack the groceries, "Jane died in childbirth. A fine woman. I miss her. I wish now you had attended her. And yes, I got married again just two months ago.

"Could be I couldn't have done better than the doctor. Some things meant to be. Who the wet nurse?"
"My Aunt Isabelle. Her son's just a couple of days older than Rob."

"Well, good. At least you got somebody in the family to take care of the baby. Lacy went back to New Orleans twelve years ago, hmmm? Back in 1888? You ever hear from her?"

The color drained from his face. Their eyes locked. Mamie stood with head cocked, listening.

"I—um, I . . .."

He lowered his eyes, then squared his shoulders and met her gaze again.

"I sometimes see Lacy. When I have business in New York. She's, um, she's in New York, now. Has been for about ten years. She wanted to come out to see Mamie, before she left, but we thought—"

"I know. With Mamie so scared and all. I know. So how she doin', Isaiah?"

Now his face flushed red.

"She—um, she owns an antique store. We correspond. I see her occasionally. She is a dear friend. She asks about you and Mamie."

"I know," Saylee said. "Well, I best be gettin' on back. Long way to go. Long way."

Isaiah got one of the men sitting on the front porch to watch the store and took Saylee and Mamie as far as he could with the horse and wagon.

"You can manage from here?"

Root Woman held his hand in both of hers.

"I can manage from here. Say 'good-bye,' Mamie."

"Good-bye, Isaiah," Mamie said.

Saylee walked the trail, Mamie at her side. She held Mamie's hand and carried the few parcels she'd purchased at Ike's General. The shopping bag bumped against her leg with every step. She thought about the swamp and about how long she had lived in this present cabin.

Three cabins existed in Congaree swamp. At one time or another, Saylee and Mamie lived in each. They moved every now and again to get to higher ground, or to stay hidden.

Some people, those Root Woman deemed safe, knew how to find them. Mostly they came troubled at heart, wanting to talk, or needing a birthing. Sometimes they came for her to cast a spell. Occasionally, if she thought the matter grave enough, or if a large reward was offered, she even held a Voodoo ceremony for them. More and more, her whereabouts came to be known.

"Mamie, you not scared of Isaiah? That good. He is a good man."

"I guess. I figure it in my mind. He not one of the bad mens."

Saylee had, over the years, continued to talk with Mamie about what happened that night so long ago when she lost her mother and her legs. She knew that if Mamie could unlock the terror bottled up inside and clearly remember what happened, she would get well.

Mamie shied away from horses, especially white ones. She talked about 'the burning cross of Jesus' and seemed to make up a whole theology all her own.

"Jesus, he done hung on a burning cross," she would say from time to time.

Over the years, she seemed to forget the night when the Klansmen took her away, and the train severed her legs, but she made up another history impossible to follow. In garbled fragments about that night, she mixed fact with fiction.

Maybe it her way of coming to terms with it. Well, finally she feeling safe again, but every Tom, Dick, and Harry knows how to find me. Judge Clayton ain't no threat, but all them mens got chil'ren commin' along every whip stitch. No tellin' what some of them might try. Not good, living here. Need another swamp altogether. We has lived all over this here swamp.

In 1902, Saylee managed to take Mamie to Charleston to see a doctor she had heard about. They rode the sixty-two miles in a borrowed, horse drawn wagon. They went first to Monks Corner, some thirty-five miles, where they stayed overnight with a relative of someone Saylee knew in Balters. They continued on to Charleston the next day. Thirty-five miles to Monks Corner and about twenty-seven miles on in to Charleston. They made the trip in four and a half hours and a little over three hours. Good time for the condition of the roads.

The doctor examined Mamie's stumps.

"Well, the doctor who took care of her must have known what he was doing. I've seldom seen amputee legs heal better than hers. How long ago you say this happened?"

"In 1882, when she just sixteen years old. I want to see can you make her shoes any better? She walk pretty good, but sometimes these brogans chafe her leg stumps pretty bad."

"Yes, I think I can special order some shoes for her. It will cost about ten dollars for the pair, though. I know that's a lot—"

"Yes sir, but we pay. I got the money. These new shoes go on backwards, too?" Saylee asked.

"Oh yes, I would think so. Whoever thought of this had an excellent idea. The toes give balance to the body, even more so that the feet. Without either, she does remarkably well. She walks by using the weight of her body as a counterbalance to the backward shoe. Intriguing. Very ingenious. Who has she been seeing all these years?"

Saylee answered his questions, always asking a few of her own. By the time the shoes were precisely fitted and they actually had them in hand, Mamie confided to Saylee that she loved going to Charleston.

On the next trip to Charleston, out of the blue, Mamie asked a question.

"Ma-Saylee? You know my boyfriend from long ago? He called Rosco. He is gone, but I don't know where. I ain't seen him since I saw the burning cross of Jesus. I liked him, too. He one fine fellow."

"No, Child I ain't knowed him. He in Chicago, I think. He thought the train killed you. He is all right. Don't worry about him.

He is not coming back. He long gone."

I likes him. He kiss me one time. On the lips. It felt good."

"Well," Saylee said, "that musta been nice for you. You remember him, uhn?"

After they got to the cabin, Saylee settled Mamie in bed for the night and took her customary seat by the window. Sitting with her cup of herb tea, she looked at the full moon.

Isaiah *in love with Lacy, always has been always will be. And jes cause she got a drop or two of colored blood in her, they couldn't get married? Uh-uh-uh-uh! And she look as white as he do! Uhn?*

Rob not his firstborn, but he don't know that. That is not good, but I don't know if I should tell him. Lacy must have good reason for not tellin' him. Hmmm.

She sat by the window long into the night, remembering her own lost love. Letting the sadness envelope her like a cloak, she allowed herself to remember.

Before slavery ended. I lived in the cabin on the old Sinclair plantation. Mama had died two years before. Amos. His folks lived in Kingstree, free persons of color. I birthed his sister's baby and he told me he would soon be a minister at his daddy's church. We courted for a whole year. He stop coming. I learn through the grapevine he done got this little slip of a girl big with Child. And her just seventeen. The only other free colored family around. A shotgun wedding? Maybe so, maybe not. It the way he treated me that hurt so much. Not a word to me. Just stop callin on me and leave me to find out from gossip! I turned forty-seven that year, but I cried like I was seventeen. Humph.

She got another cup of tea and sat back down.

I remember others before Amos. They all thought I was strange. Maybe I was. Maybe I am. I know Mama hoped for a grandchild. She shore wanted something to come of that — oh, what his name? Oh, the Simmons boy from Balters. Wonder what ever happened to him?

She chuckled, remembering him.

He sweet, but so dumb. I offer to teach him to read, and he say, 'No thank you,' like I offering him a cup of tea.

She laughed out loud, got up, and went to bed.

Chapter 6

The General Emporium

On September 2, 1886, one week before school opened, Isaiah invited the public to a 'Grand Opening' with balloons and a piece of peppermint candy for each person who passed through the door. Isaiah felt good. He was twenty, and the sole proprietor of a store that sold just about everything. He sold out of slate boards and chalk and had to order more from the manufacturer before closing time that day.

The people in the little town of Brio flocked to the store. Some came all the way from Kingstree, saying they didn't have anything near as big in Kingstree, even. His store bustled with folks from near and far, and he sold more each day than he used to sell in his other store in a month.

Isaiah's first dollar bill hung on the wall behind the gleaming glass counter where he displayed the penny candy. He framed it on opening day and hung it up to the cheers of the crowd.

The wide porch across the front with three white oak rocking chairs quickly became a favorite place for folks to sit and chat. The table in back by the stove, already in the first week, had a couple of regulars who played checkers there every day.

Isaiah made his own brine pickles with lots of garlic. The pickles caught on slowly. Folks around these parts seemed leery to try new things. He made the pickles for his own enjoyment and for the wonderful smell.

He turned from getting the last of the canned goods for Mrs. Miller, and saw his pa pull up to the hitching post and water trough at the front of the store. He tied up his horse and wagon and sauntered into the store.

He's aged in the year since Ma died.

"What else can I get for you, Mrs. Miller?"

That'll be all for today," she said, turning to look at his pa. "I declare this store is just too good to be true! I used to have to go all the way to Kingstree at least once a month to pick up things you didn't have at the old store, but now? Well! This is just wonderful!"

Isaiah carefully placed each item into her tote.

"Thank you," he said, "for your kind words. If there's ever anything Ike's General doesn't have, you let me know and I'll order it for you. That comes to two dollars and fourteen cents, by my figuring. Here, you want to double check me?"

On the way out, the woman spoke to Ike's pa coming into the store. The women of Brio, South Carolina, whether married, widowed, or single, competed to do for the newest widower in town. Some baked him pies, others brought over whole meals, still others knitted some little something, a scarf, a hat, a pair of gloves.

"Hello Pa, " Isaiah said, "what brings you in today? Do we need groceries again already?"

He noticed that Mrs. Miller fingered the material on a bolt of satin.

"Why Mrs. Miller, I'm sorry, I thought you'd left. What else can I get for you?"

Ignoring him, she walked around to the other side of the bolts of material.

"Mr. Norris, um-m-m, Mr. Norris, what do you think of this color for me? I've been told that I can wear red, seein' as how I'm tall and thin. Your dear wife, Sadie, was slight built, too, wasn't she? God rest her soul."

Isaiah noticed the fleeting pained expression that swept his father's face for an instant before he turned and moseyed over to the dry goods.

Isaiah heard the hum of their conversation. He saw a fly lazily circle Mrs. Miller's head and alight on her bun. The skin on the back of her neck looked like that on chicken feet, all cross hatched with wrinkles. The fly crawled across the bun and then flew away.

September and still there are flies. I'd better hang up more flypaper. Wonder what she's saying to Pa? He's got that tolerant smile on his face. Like he wants her to finish and go on about her business.

The volume of the voices came up a notch and he strained to hear the conversation between his father and Mrs. Miller.

"Well, thank you for advising me. I'll decide for sure on the color later on. I'm sewing a new frock for the Christmas party at church. You, um-m-m, you do plan to attend this year, don't you, Mr. Norris?"

"We'll see. We'll just have to see. Bye now. Oh, and come again."

The two men stood side by side as she departed the store. When she was safely out of the store and her carriage almost out of sight down the road, Isaiah started laughing.

"She's sweet on you Pa. You better run. She's a smallish woman all right, in a wrinkled sort of way. How you reckon she got so wrinkled?"

Robert cocked an eyebrow at his son.

"Your ma was just exceptionally unwrinkled. Most women of a certain age have wrinkles. Men too. Mind your tongue—and your manners."

He winked, but Isaiah knew he was trying to teach him a bit about how to treat his customers. Or people in general. His pa often didn't go at a thing head-on-all-at-once like his ma had.

"Yes sir, I'll remember that. I miss Ma a lot, Pa. You do too."

It was a statement, not a question. It lay there between them, getting heavier and heavier. When Isaiah thought he couldn't stand another minute, his pa spoke.

"What say we pack us a picnic basket and go down to the Black River and do a little fishing later this afternoon? Maybe swim some, too, if the water's not too cold."

Isaiah closed an hour early and they headed out to the river in the old farm wagon. They took fried chicken, pears, a jug of iced tea and an apple pie left the night before by Mrs. Grace Trobridge. Widowed for ten years or so, she remained a cipher to both Robert and Isaiah. Neither of them knew if she held aspirations of snagging the eligible

Mr. Norris, or if she acted out of kindness. Pretty enough in a reserved kind of way, she never smiled.

Although the water stung like ice, they stripped off their clothes and swam. Finally, the water felt just cool on their skin. His pa raced him across the river at its widest and beat him.

"I didn't know you were such a good swimmer, Pa. You're pretty strong for someone your age."

"Just how old do you think I am, you young pup?" he asked, "I'm not ancient, you know. Some of us 'oldsters' make it past a hundred. I'm, only fifty-one years old. But to answer your question, it's my working as a blacksmith that makes me a good swimmer. Strong arms, you know?"

His pa splashed him and he dunked his pa. They played and swam a little longer, yelping and hollering like little boys. When they started getting tired and cold, they got out and dried off.

Isaiah watched his pa as they got dressed.

Pa's laughing like he used to before Ma died.

They stretched out on the bank, their backs propped against gnarled trees and prepared to fish.

"Pa, what did Ma die of?"

Robert took his time adjusting his fishing line, pulling it up, checking the bait, throwing it back in.

"Her heart I reckon. Why do you ask?"

"Do you mind talking about her? You never say much? Isaiah asked, careful not to look at his pa.

"I, Well I . . . I guess I don't say much, do I? You don't either. We're a lot alike. You and me."

Robert reached over and tussled his boy's hair.

"Son, I was married to the woman since she was fourteen and I was twenty-two. Seems like my whole life. Your ma had been feelin' these squeezing pains in her chest for a few weeks before she died. When the doctor came out to pronounce her dead, I asked him and he said she probably had a heart attack.

"I . . . I tried to get her to go see the doctor when she first mentioned the pains, but she kept sayin' it was only indigestion. You know how she was about doctors."

Robert sat for a long moment before speaking again.

"Right after she died last year, I couldn't bear to think of life goin' on without her, but it does," he said, wiping his eyes.

He pulled a handkerchief out of the bib pocket of his overalls and blew his nose noisily.

"Yep, whether we're ready or not, life goes on. Kept feelin' like I'd turn a corner and see her. At night I could hear her singing." He carefully folded the handkerchief; put it back into his pocket.

"My eyes played tricks on me. One day I looked down the driveway to the mail box, and I glimpsed her gettin' mail outta the box." Robert shook his head.

"Then little by little . . . I dunno. I just kinda turned loose a little bit. Let go of some of the hurtin' . . . some of the tightness. Oh, I guess I'll always want her back, but . . .."

Isaiah waited for him to continue and when he didn't, Isaiah patted him awkwardly on the arm.

"I know what you mean. I miss her, too. Her quick smile, and strange to say, her quick temper. You remember how she had a way of blowing up over the least little slip of the tongue? What she thought was cussin'?"

They both laughed.

"Well," Robert said, "there's a ton of other things I remember about your ma. Her cool hand laid on a feverish brow, whether mine, or one of the younguns. Her fine sense of humor. I'll tell you a secret," Robert lowered his head and winked, "your ma enjoyed a good joke if it was told in private. And her singing. You remember the hymns she used to belt out? Lord, for a woman weighing just ninety-five pounds soaking wet, she shore had a powerful voice!"

"She did. She sure did have a good singing voice. I know how much you must grieve for her, Pa. I'm sorry. I wish there was something I could do to make it less—"

"Oh son. Oh son," Robert said.

He hugged his youngest son to him and choked on his words.

"You lost a mother, too. I know. And I know you want to do something for me, but things like this just take time. Ah, yes. Time."

Now, Isaiah cried in his father's arms. Cried unabashedly. Cried in great gut-wrenching sobs. When he had no more tears, Robert blew his own nose and then handed the handkerchief to Isaiah.

"Sorry, Pa. I don't know—"

"It's all right, son. We both needed to shed some tears. It's okay."

He patted Isaiah's shoulder. Then both men fished in silence for a long, long while.

"Pa," Isaiah said.

Robert jumped.

"Sorry, Pa. Didn't mean to startle you. Um-m-m, if someone had colored blood in them, but didn't look colored, uh, you know—um-m-m, maybe looked white—would folks think they were colored or white?"

Robert's line doubled over, and then Isaiah got a bite. They each landed a fish.

"Son," Robert said, after slowly taking the fish off the line, re-baiting his line and casting it back in, "to answer your question, they would be colored. Folks would think they was colored. Why do you ask?"

"How would folks even know? If they looked, you know, white—"

"Maybe that's why folks in the south always want to know everybody's background. Who their mama and daddy is. Where they come from. Who their grandpa and grandma is. Why you askin'? You know somebody who's passing for white?"

Isaiah answered his question with a question of his own.

"You mean there are some colored folks who 'pass' for white?"

"I reckon there are. None around here that I know of. That girl, Mamie, her mama looked as white as you or me, but she was colored, and folks treated her as such. Why in the world you askin'—?"

"Mamie's mama was an aristocrat. A Creole from Louisiana. You're right, she looked as white as you or me. She—"

"How you know that. And what do you mean 'an aristocrat'? I never heard of no colored aristocrats. Who's been puttin' those kind of notions into your head, son?"

"Mamie's cousin teaches school over in Balters. We talk, sometimes. And, yes sir, in Louisiana, there are colored people who are aristocrats. They even have a debutante ball. A coming out party. They get all dressed up and—"

"Son," Robert said, frowning at his line, "who is this cousin? What's her name? You talkin' nonsense, you hear! Folks hear you talkin' like that, they'd be scandalized. You seeing this cousin of Mamie's? You courting her?"

"No sir, we're just friends. That's all. Just friends. And I don't talk about this with anybody."

Robert sat, looking at Isaiah long and hard, his fishing pole forgotten. Finally, he broke the silence.

"Why you askin' all these questions 'bout whether somebody is white or colored? This woman thinkin' about passing for white?"

Isaiah stared at his pa in silence for a long time.

"No," he finally said. "No, she isn't. I was just curious, that's all."

Robert didn't say any more and neither did Isaiah, but a knowledge lay between them, uneasy, heavy, churning like a sky before a storm. Several times, Robert cleared his throat as though about to speak, but remained mute.

About an hour later, Robert shifted, pulled his line up, re-baited and sat looking at the far horizon.

"Son, you're young. You'll meet a suitable woman by and by."

He placed ever so slight an emphasis on the word 'suitable'. Robert held his son's gaze for long moments before continuing.

"Someone you can love, who will love you, too. Someone who will give you children.

Isaiah opened his mouth as though to speak, but closed it without saying a word. They fished in silence.

I should tell Pa everything, but I just can't. He would never understand! He once owned slaves. I don't think he ever mistreated any of them, but he was a slave owner! Born and bred in the south, with southern traditions, values, outlook. And I am, too!

Isaiah remembered his dream.

I'll be damned if I'm going to leave my store, my land, my family. If it hadn't been for Mamie, I never would have met . . . I'd never have met her. I'd never have fallen in love.

I can't imagine my life without Lacy. Heck, I can't imagine my life with Lacy. We will not marry. Can't even think of what a lonely life it will be without her, but I know . . ..

He threw his line out again. Robert fished, too. Isaiah didn't see his father sadly shake his head.

"You've bought land and built a store," Robert said after a while. "Your ma would be so proud of you. One day you will marry and raise a fine family. You'll see. One day you will grow into your manhood and assume your rightful place in the community."

Isaiah nodded, but said nothing. They each caught a dozen or so good-sized fish. After eating their picnic supper, they headed home. Conversation consisted of comments about the good food, the size of the fish, and the beautiful day. What they didn't say hung in the air, an almost palpable tension between them.

Pa's worried I'll get involved with Lacy, but I won't. I know I have made the right decision, but it hurts like hell! (Sorry, Ma.) Look at Pa. There he sits, so full of his own hurt, and here I am burdening him with my tale of woe.

"Pa? I won't be going to . . . I won't be goin' out much anymore. You don't have to worry about me. I'm all right."

But that very night he dreamed an awful dream. In his dream, he ran through a field of white daisies. Lacy ran ahead laughing, arms flung wide. White petals blew across his face caressing his checks, his eyes, his mouth. The petals became cold, changing to snow—fluffy flakes of snow, soft as goose down. He tried to brush them away and discovered tears—hot, scalding, salty tears. His tears tasted good. He tried to call to Lacy to wait for him, but she ran faster and faster, and soon disappeared in the whiteness of the snow.

He awoke, cold with the covers all kicked off. The open window let in a frigid wind. Hard rain pelted the roof. He went to the window and closed it. Crossing the room to his bed he wiped his face on the arm of his flannel pajamas. Rummaging in his dresser drawer, he pulled out a handkerchief and blew his nose.

He walked down the hall to his pa's bedroom and found him sound asleep. He went back to his room and put some clothes on. Tiptoeing down the stairs, he threw a rain slick over his head and ran for the outhouse.

Isaiah piled extra quilts on his bed and climbed back in, but could not go back to sleep. He tossed and turned for an hour or so, finally deciding to get up though the sky gave no hint of daylight.

He got dressed again, went down to the kitchen, and fixed himself a cup of hot cocoa. He took it back to his bedroom. Getting back into bed, he tried to read from the Bible as he sipped his hot drink. The words were just that, so many words and meaningless. He persisted, forcing his mind to comprehend. He turned to the story about David and the Philistines and read the story from beginning to end.

Still not able to sleep, he got out of bed, sat at his desk, and recorded his dream. He picked up the Bible again, and, sitting there at his desk began to read the story about Joseph and the dreams he interpreted while a captive in Egypt. Closing the Bible, he went back to bed and tried to pray. He finally dropped off to a fitful sleep, full of fleeting images that, upon awakening, he couldn't even remember in the bright, but cold, sunlight of that September morning.

Years and years would pass before Isaiah would even recall that he had told his father he would be all right, meaning that he would heed his veiled advice about marrying the right woman and not being involved with Lacy.

* * *

Isaiah dropped Lacy off and turned the wagon toward home. Their visit with Root Woman and Mamie had not been a spectacular success. Mamie had sulked the whole time.

I wonder why? Mamie seemed all right just the day before. Why would she seem to be so frightened this visit? Was it because I brought Lacy?

Shortly after the visit, Root Woman told him to stay away, and told him why. He, nevertheless, from time to time, left supplies on her doorstep. She knew each time he came, but she never said anything to Mamie.

Saylee many times over the years went into trance to probe the situation with Isaiah and Lacy.

* * *

After many years, on a bright spring day in 1900, shortly after Mamie's thirty fourth birthday, Saylee took Mamie to Ike's General Emporium. When they entered, Mamie saw Isaiah for the first time since she stopped talking. She smiled at him, then frowned.

Isaiah, six feet four inches tall, a big barrel of a man, stooped and held out his arms to Mamie who stood beside Saylee. Mamie buried her face in Saylee's skirts, but didn't cry. She peeped out at him.

"You the good boy?"

Isaiah stood up, nodding his head happily. He and Saylee laughed. Mamie said no more, but listened intently to Isaiah and Saylee as they talked.

"Isaiah, I am sorry 'bout your wife dying two years ago. How your boy, Rob? He must be over two years old now. And you just got married again?"

"Thank you," Isaiah finally said, as he continued to pack the groceries, "Jane died in childbirth. A fine woman. I miss her. I wish now you had attended her. And yes, I got married again only last month."

"Could be I couldn't have done better than the doctor. Some things meant to be. Who the wet nurse?"

"My Aunt Isabelle. Her son's just a couple of days older than Rob."

"Well, good. At least you got somebody in the family to take care of the baby. Lacy went back to New Orleans fifteen years ago, hm-m-m?? Back in 1885 or 86? You hear from her?"

"She is a dear friend. She asks about Mamie and you."

"Isaiah, she more than just a dear friend, eh? I understand. More than you know. I understand! Well, I best be gettin' on back."

That man is in love with Lacy, always has been, always will be. And jes cause she got a drop or two of colored blood in her, they couldn't get married? Uh-uh-uh-uh! And she look as white as he do! Uh-huh!

Rob, not his firstborn, either! He don't know that. That is not good, but I don't know if I should tell him. Lacy must have good reason for not tellin' him. Hm-m-m-m.

She sat by the window long into the night, remembering her own lost love. Letting the sadness envelope her like a cloak, she remembered.

Saylee got up and paced.

Mama shore wanted me to find a husband, but it never meant to be.

She got another cup of tea and sat back down by the window. She chuckled, remembering the Simmons boy.

He so dumb! He say, 'No thank you,' when I want to teach him to read. That shore Lawd the wrong thing to say to me! I love books. How can a body not care to learn to read?

She laughed out loud, got up and went to bed.

* * *

Isaiah thought about what Root Woman had said.

God, that woman knows everything. I know I have kept Lacy's and my involvement secret. How does she do it?

For a long time after Isaiah and Robert had their picnic and swim at the Black River, he had kept himself busy around the store or the house. He stayed close to home, reading, playing checkers with his pa and his customers, riding his mare on the farm and over his fifty acres. Often he opened his journal and read about his fateful dream.

But on a beautiful, warm Sunday in October, he rode to Balters. He and Lacy walked down to the Black River. Standing under an oak draped with Spanish moss, he kissed her. The moon and the sun fell out of the sky. The earth collided with the falling moon, the sun danced and whirled.

"Lacy," he breathed, "Oh, my love. Here I am kissing you, when what I intended to tell you is that we can't go on seeing each other."

She looked at him with liquid brown eyes that glistened with tears.

"I know," Lacy said. "We can't. We must end this foolishness. Now!"

His arms tightened around her waist.

"I don't think we can ever end this 'foolishness'. Lacy, I love you. I know you feel the same. We can't just—"

"Yes, we can. We must. Before it goes any farther! Oh Isaiah, I do love you. But you know how people feel about mixed marriages. Even up north we would have a hard time. Here it would be impossible. Are you prepared to leave home and family?"

She watched his face intensely.

"I thought not." She pulled out of his arms, shouting over her shoulder, "Leave me alone! Don't come back. Ever!"

* * *

For almost a year, the two young people didn't lay eyes on one another. Then one day the following September, Isaiah looked up from his ledger book behind the cash register to see Lacy pulling up to the hitching post in her smart, black rig. She wore a tailored gray suit. Her skirt fell to just above her leather boots. She got out of the carriage and Isaiah caught a glimpse of trim ankles. She walked into the store and asked for slate boards as though she had seen him only yesterday. No other customer was in the store. He came around the counter and took both her hands.

"Oh, Lacy! Come. Let's go into the office. Do you want a sarsaparilla? I've missed you so much! I thought I'd never see you again. Oh, my dear, my darling Lacy."

He backed toward the office, holding her hands and pulling her along with him. She resisted for just a moment, he put his arms around her and kissed her. She took a few more steps, and stopped.

"No. Isaiah, this was a mistake. I must go. I'm sorry. I just had to see you. I . . .."

She turned and fled.

Isaiah closed up the store. Certain moments in life are fixed in memory forever.

I'll never forget this moment. The moment she said, 'I just had to see you'. Oh, darling Lacy. My love, my life.

Rattling the door to make sure he had locked it, he walked out to his horse and headed to Balters.

Chapter 7

Good-bye Old Friend

By the dark of the moon on a windless night
Gris-gris made for a woman's flightBy Root Woman, gone now to Africa Land
The old woman died according to plan
Mamie took jujus, gris-gris, and charms
And left the comfort of Root Woman's arms

Mamie, you thirty-six years old, woman! When you gonna' learn to be pleasant? You so cross! Makes me outta' sorts, too! You been poutin' for three days, now. Enough!" Saylee said as she slammed the door behind her.

She left without Mamie.

As she entered Ike's General, she brushed past someone hanging on the arm of a younger woman.

"Saylee, how you doin', daughter? Where Mamie at? She walkin' good now, eh?"

"I doin' fair to middlin', and Mamie, too," Saylee said. "She just ornery as a ole mule. She been in a bad mood and I got tired of it and left her to home!" Saylee searched the woman's face.

"And how you gettin' along, Auntie?"

What her name? I knows her. Birthed her last youngun some sixty-odd years ago! Oh, Miz Effie Bell Rogers.

"You didn't seem too much older than Mamie last time I see'd that girl! She sho done aged a right smart bit since her legs got chopped off. Uhn-uhn-uhn! Dem Klans peoples ought to a been shot!" Effie whispered to Saylee.

"Miz Effie, you shore right! She done aged a lot! It good to see you so spry, Miz Effie," Saylee said.

"You ain't' remember my name, at first, is you? Well, no wonder! We gettin' on up there, Girl! I is one hundred and two years old! How old you is, now? Tell the truth!" She cackled.

"Why, Miz Effie," Saylee said, "you done caught me out! I shore ain't remember you, on first glance. I turned ninety-five my last birthday."

"Take care, and say 'hey' to the cranky little one," Effie said as she left the store.

"I'll tell her you said hello. And you take care of yourself, too," Saylee called.

Mamie walked everywhere, now. Root Woman thought she could no longer carry her, but discovered she could. In the middle of the night she heard a noise, grabbed Mamie, and fled. From a safe distance, she watched the cabin.

"Oh, Mamie, it just old Mr. Raccoon. He most as old as me! He done knock over the wire cage he suppose to sleep in! Let's get back to bed, Child."

At one time or another, Saylee and Mamie lived in each of the three cabins in Congaree Swamp. As Root Woman aged, she began talking to Mamie about moving away.

"Mamie, we needs to get plumb away. Isaiah told me he found out some mens in the Klan was asking where we live. Wouldn't do for those Klans people to come snooping around and find us," she said.

Only a few select people whom Root Woman deemed safe knew how to find her shack. Mostly they came troubled at heart, wanting to talk. Sometimes they came for her to cast a spell. Occasionally she even held a Voodoo ceremony for them—if she thought the matter grave enough, or if they offered enough money or trade for her efforts.

It was in 1902 when she took Mamie to Charleston to see a doctor she had heard about, that she hit on the perfect solution. They rode the fifty two miles in a horse drawn wagon. They traveled thirty-five miles to Monks Corner, going right by Hell Hole Swamp, and twenty-seven miles from there to Charleston. They made the trip in four and a half hours to Monks Corner, and a little over three hours on in to Charleston. Good time for the condition of the roads.

The doctor examined Mamie's stumps and was fascinated by the way she was able to walk with the brogans turned backwards. On the first trip, Saylee and Mamie talked on the way home, Saylee half-listening to Mamie.

"You know my boyfriend from long ago?" Mamie asked. "He called Rosco. He gone, but I don't know where. I ain't seen him since I saw the burning cross of Jesus. I liked him, too. He one fine fellow.

"No, Child," Saylee said, "I ain't knowed him. He in Chicago. He thought the train killed you. He all right. Don't worry about him. He not coming back. He long gone."

"I likes him. He kiss me one time. On the lips. It felt good."

"Well," Saylee said, "that musta been nice for you."

"I just this minute remember him. All these years I have not been remembering him, but I just did. Huh! So where is Chicago?"

"Way off, Child, way off," Saylee answered absent-mindedly.

Saylee pulled the wagon off the road. She sat at the little dirt road leading into the swamp. Past the bend, past all visible land, she allowed her mind to 'see' the murky darkness of Hell Hole Swamp.

She felt herself drifting over the grassy bogs, the endless waterways. Deeper and deeper she went. There an alligator, up ahead a flowering wild azalea. She smelled the honeysuckle of early summer. She tasted the blackberries, big as a man's thumb. The blackberries of June and July.

Dambala undulated over the waters beckoning her ever onward. Africa. Jungle. She heard the drum beats.

Now I know why the swamp always called to me. This be as close as I will ever come to being in Africa, the land of papa's peoples.

After that day, Saylee made a side trip into Hell Hole Swamp each time she went to Charleston and back home.

Look like ain't nobody ever lived in this place. I likes it, though. Bigger, darker, and more dangerous than Congaree Swamp. Suits me jes fine. A good place to hide.

Not finding a cabin in Hell Hole Swamp, Saylee drew out plans for a cabin just like the biggest one in Congaree Swamp. She hired a builder, using some of the money she had saved over a lifetime.

Three hundred dollars. A lot of money, but I need to get Mamie far away from the white scoundrels who did that to her so many years ago. They knows I'm gettin' on up in years now. They'll be layin' for a chance to get us both!

The carpenter, sworn to secrecy, delivered all the materials late one night in September on the full moon.

By the end of October, it was finished. As in the past, Saylee waited to occupy. She frequently borrowed a horse and wagon, driving the thirty-odd miles to Hell Hole, just to spy on the new site. Finally she felt safe, and, the next year, on June 1, 1904, Saylee left in the middle of the night, not telling anyone, except for the builder whom she again hired, this time to help them move. Before she left, she made a trip into Brio to tell Isaiah, but he was out of town on one of his frequent trips.

After moving, she and Mamie explored. Saylee showed Mamie the sink holes. She began teaching her about good plants to eat and for medicine, and the ones to leave alone.

She cautioned her about the bigger alligators. Saylee found one which she called 'Mama Alli'. The huge reptile lived in a recessed place on the bank of a slough. The cave, filled almost to the top with mud and water, made a great hiding place.

A casual traveler would not have seen the alligator. Only her eyes and snout rose above the mud as she lay submerged just inside the mouth of her den.

Saylee left Mamie in the cabin one morning in June, and walked to the slough where the scaly monster lived.

I wants to see you outta there on dry ground. Come to Saylee.

She poked her walking stick into the mud to entice the alligator out. At first, the reptile hardly moved. Then, she was out of the cave and at the side of the slough, mouth opened wide. She climbed out of the mud and water, hissing. Saylee almost fell over a tangle of roots as she turned and ran.

From a safe distance up the trail, Root Woman looked back as the alligator turned and crawled back to its den.

She's a big one. Must be twelve feet long. And mean. Hungry, too, from the way she attacked. She probably has a nest of eggs, or even little 'gators in that den with her.

Saylee hurried home and brought Mamie back to the slough.

"Mamie, you mark well where this spot is and stay away from it."

Mamie looked up at Saylee with a puzzled expression.

"Why you tell me that? I never go out in the swamp without you. You know that! I 'scared of them 'gators! I can't run as fast as you. One of them 'gators was to catch me, they'd eat me thinkin' I choice meat. Like a dog."

"Mamie, one of these days I will be gone. Gone to Africa Land under the sea. Remember the story I told you 'bout my papa? He died when I just a little girl. He is in Africa Land. My mama, too, I think. My mama's people got another place where the dead go, but I think she go to the place where my papa is."

"Who your mama's people?" Mamie asked. "They not like our people?"

"No, they Indians," Saylee said. "My mama come from the Chicora Tribe. Fact is, the Chicora hunted all around these parts. They was in a place called Winyaw Bay close to Charleston long years ago,"

Root Woman stopped on the trail with a distant, far away look in her eyes. After a few minutes, they started walking again.

"My papa's people come from Africa as slaves. Your mama was never a slave, 'cause she was a free colored in New Orleans. A Creole."

"What a Creole is?"

As they walked along gathering fruit and nuts, Saylee tried to explain.

"The Creole is a rich group of peoples who live in New Orleans—maybe other places, too. They are French, I think. With maybe some colored mixed in for seasoning. You know, kind of like when we add a nice piece of fatback to the greens to make 'um taste good? You a mix, too. You a mix of French, Colored, and Spanish."

"I am? I ain't never know that. I such a mix, I must be awful good!" Mamie grinned from ear to ear.

"Yes, Child. You the best in the whole wide world, and I love you.

Always remember that. Do you understand when I tells you that one of these days I be gone? To Africa Land?"

Mamie scowled at Root Woman. For a long time she walked along frowning.

"I don't want to think 'bout that," she said. "You don't have to die. Use some magic to make it so I die before you. Let's us just keep right on living till we both old. Please?"

Saylee smiled and patted her head, but didn't answer.

So like a child in so many ways. Does she not know I am old now? Surely she does.

"Mamie, how old you think I am?" Saylee asked.

"Don't know," Mamie said. "Older than me. How old I be?"

"Your birth date, I think, is January 1, 1866, so you would be, um-m-m, thirty-seven. You like that age?"

"I guess I does. I sho can't change it, now can I? How old was I when I come to live with you?"

"Sixteen, why?"

"Just wondered? We don't see the good boy anymore, huh?"

"No, we done lost touch with Isaiah. We should try to send word to him, but I just don't know anybody I can trust to deliver a secret message by. You miss him?"

"Sometimes. I sorta remember things from when I was real little. I remember playing with Lacy one time."

"You remember Lacy, huh? That's good. Try to remember more and more of your past. It will do you good."

Mamie's face took on a solemn look. She stopped in the trail.

"What the word 'bastard' mean?. I can hear a woman speaking inside my head. She short and pretty, and she speak with a funny accent. What that word mean, Ma-Saylee? She look angry wid me. She callin' me that name."

Mamie blurted out to Root Woman that she, Mamie, was three or four years old, playing on the floor with a doll. The woman was in an argument with someone who was standing behind Mamie.

"The short, pretty woman say, 'No, I don't love the child. She's a bastard and you should have had an abortion! You were raped for God's sake! She is not one of us, and never will be! If that upsets you, so be it. Leave if you want. I don't care!'

"I trying to get a picture of my mama," she said, screwing her eyes shut. She trembled with the tension of remembering.

"The woman who spoke stood right in front of the little girl, and spoke to a woman who stood behind the child," Mamie said. "The little girl who was me at three or four years old." Mamie shut her eyes.

"That woman hated me. Wish I was turned the other way so I could see my mama!" Mamie began to cry.

Root Woman, sat down on the trail, and held her until she stopped crying.

"Why you cryin' so?" she asked.

"I is the 'bastard' and that woman," Mamie said, "is my grandma. What abortion is?"

"You hear your grandma's voice say 'abortion'? Inside your head?"

"Yes, my grandmama inside my head. What it mean? And what 'raped' mean?"

"Raped is when a man hold a woman down and . . .. You know, do the thing with her, the pleasuring' thing. It ain't no pleasuring when it happen like that! 'Bastard' is a low-down word that should never be used. It what evil peoples call a child who come into the world when the mama and papa ain't never got married before the birth."

"Ma-Saylee I is just such a child. I is a bastard. Was my mama raped?"

"Your mama loved you better than bein' a rich, Creole aristocrat. Better than life itself. Yes, your mama was raped. By a drunken Marino. You may have heard yo grandmama say those words, but that don't mean . . .."

Mamie reached her arms up to be picked up, again. Saylee sat back down on the path and cradled her in her lap. Mamie dropped off to sleep, sucking her thumb.

My poor Child, Saylee thought, what kind of monster calls a sweet, little girl a bastard? I should hex the woman, but for Lizzye's sake, I won't.

When Mamie woke up, she had a glazed, far away look in her eyes. Again she lapsed into silence. She didn't talk for almost a month. Saylee went about her gathering and drying, cooking and cleaning. She talked to Mamie every day.

One day she brought a baby bird in to Mamie. She built a little cage from dried willow reeds for the bird. The bird, a wild canary, sang in its little cage right next to where Mamie sat most of the day. "I been gone, ain't I?" Mamie said one day. She smiled. "Bird is pretty. He yellow with a little bit of green. He my bird?"

Root Woman smiled at Mamie and sat down next to her.

"Yes, he your bird. I didn't name him. I waited for you to come back so you could do that. What you gonna call him?"

Mamie looked at the bird a long time as he sat there singing with his head cocked to one side.

"His name," she said, finally, "is Song-Singer! You like?"

"Song-Singer is a pretty name for a pretty bird. I am glad you back. I was lonely with you gone."

Saylee looked closely at Mamie.

She looks old at thirty-eight. That 'cause she sick in the mind. Poor baby, my poor baby.

One day Saylee, busy making a recipe for a spell, turned to ask Mamie to bring her something. No Mamie. She dropped everything and began looking for Mamie.

Not in the cabin.

After a thorough search, she noticed the missing bird cage.

Mamie in the garden back of the cabin.

Root Woman looked there first. No Mamie. She called to her. No answer. Heart hammering, she began to search in the swamp. Root Woman still walked like a much younger woman, not bent at all, and with a brisk stride. She found Mamie by a little pool, sitting with the empty cage and crying.

"What wrong, Sweet Thing? Where Song-Singer?"

"He gone. He flew off and didn't come back. I sorry. I let him out back of the cabin in the garden so he could fly around, but he didn't come back. I try to follow him, but he gone."

"It's okay, Sugar Plum. He need to be free. It bother me to see him always caged up. You did the right thing. He'll be happy now."

"He wasn't happy when he my bird? He sing like he happy."

Saylee sat with her feet dangling in the cold water. She pulled her feet up out of the water and wiggled her toes.

"Mamie," Root Woman said, "look at my toes. See how happy they is to be free from my moccasins. They happy with shoes on, but happier without. You understand?"

"Yes, I think so. He is happy to be free. Like slaves. Slaves were happy to be free. Song-Singer will find worms to eat? Nobody to dig he worms now. He have to work for a livin.' "

Saylee smiled, and said, "Yes, he'll have to work for a livin.' You smart woman! Let's go home. I make you a good dinner of 'possum and sweet taters, some cornbread and winter greens."

"Ma-Saylee?"

"Yes, Mamie?"

"Don't die."

Saylee pulled her close as they got to their feet.

"Mamie," she whispered, her voice choking, "one day I will die. You can bet on it. You be ready by then. God give you what you need then. You understand?"

Mamie nodded, but walked with a frown on her face and her lips out, in a pout. She wouldn't answer when Saylee tried to question her further. Saylee let the subject drop. That night Saylee worked late in the night after Mamie had gone to sleep.

She mixed a gris-gris for protection. She mixed one for courage and endurance. Finally she mixed one for all-around good luck. She got out her own juju, a rabbit's foot, and laid it on the old dresser with its cracked mirror. She searched high and low for her horseshoe, but couldn't find it. The next morning she went outside, stretched and suddenly remembered where she had put the horseshoe. It hung over the front door. She stood on an old wooden crate, and lifted it off the five nails. She went back inside and placed this good luck charm alongside the other, the rabbit's foot.

After breakfast, Root Woman asked Mamie to sit by her side.

"Mamie, I got somethin' important to say. You listen and remember what I tell you, you hear? I givin' you some things that gonna help you after I gone. I wants you to keep them with you at all times. At all times," she repeated.

"This is to go over your door. Your front door. Wherever you live. Hang it on nails so the shoe points up toward the sky. The rounded part always got to be toward the ground. You understand? If it fall, put it right back up, but if you balance it on five nails, it won't fall. Come outside. I show you."

Mamie followed her out the door. Root Woman hung the horseshoe up again' showing her how to position the nails just so. They went back inside and Saylee continued the lecture. Mamie sat with eyes as round as saucers.

"This a rabbit's foot, my own juju. It near as old as I is. Keep this in your pocket, or tied around your neck. These gris-gris keep in your pockets or tied around your neck, too. Don't lose them. These things keep you safe after I go to Africa Land."

"Thank you, Ma-Saylee," Mamie said, "but please just don't go today. I not ready yet. I try to get ready to let you go, but I not ready yet. You understand me?"

Saylee laughed softly.

"We making headway!" Saylee said. "You will do just fine. Just fine. You one smart woman, you know that? You smart!"

Mamie smiled and hugged her.

"I love you, Ma-Saylee, " she said.

All that day Mamie fingered the gris-gris, looked at the horseshoe and held the rabbit's foot. That night she slept with all of them in the bed with her. Saylee heard her talking to the objects during the night. She was telling them not to let Root Woman die. Not for a long, long time.

In the days that followed, Mamie always had the gris-gris, and the rabbit's foot with her. The horseshoe they decided to hang back up over the front door. Mamie made herself a little sack into which she put ten nails. At first she dropped in five nails, but explained to Saylee that she might bend some, or lose some by dropping them while she was trying to hammer them in.

"If it was to roll off somewhere, I might not have enough. Better have extra. But I will be careful."

She kept up with the hammer as if her life depended on it. If Saylee left the hammer laying on something outside the cabin, Mamie came right behind her and took it into the cabin. She kept the hammer right by the front door.

Good, she's takin' it to heart by keepin' all the good luck charms handy so she knows right where they are. That good.

Saylee caught a little alligator, skinned it for the leather, and cooked a nice alligator soup. After they ate, Saylee worked the leather until it was soft and pliable. From the leather, when she finished the curing, she made Mamie an alligator purse; a small purse with a draw string. Mamie loved the way it felt.

She asked Saylee to make her a large tote bag from alligator hide. Saylee agreed to look for a big alligator for a large tote, but knew that would not happen.

Saylee went out less and less over the next two years, sending Mamie to gather the nuts and fruit in the fall.

"Always test the ground for sink holes with your walkin' stick. Your hickory walkin' stick I made you last year."

"You done buy up so much from the boy's store before we move!" Mamie said. "We ain't never gonna run out of ooking stuff!"

All that fall, Saylee worried about Mamie, but Mamie always came back. She came back with lots of plants, nuts and fruit. She took the animals out of the traps, and even learned to bait and set the traps. They trapped swamp rats, animals more like pigs than rats, wild pigs, turtles, squirrels, rabbits, and occasionally a small bear.

One day Saylee heard an awful commotion. She roused from her nap and stood in the open door of the cabin. She saw Mamie coming through the swamp, pulling a stubborn cow.

"Hey, Ma-Saylee, I done found us a cow. I found her. She all tangled up in the brush. I got her loose from the thorny mess and bring her here for fresh milk."

"Be more work for you, daughter," Saylee said, shaking her head, "but shore will be good to have nice fresh milk. You know how to milk a cow?"

"No'm, but I can learn. The teats is low to the ground, so I knows I can reach 'em. You teach me how?" Mamie asked.

"Yes, I reckon I has to. It ain't easy, you know."

Mamie learned to milk. She kept them in food that summer and fall almost single-handedly. Lots of food stood in barrels, stock-piled against the day Saylee would not be able to provide for their needs.

They sat out the winter in relative comfort, talking, going for short walks on mild days, mending things.

Saylee looked one night at the sleeping Mamie.

My sacred trust for all these years. Soon now, Mamie. Africa Land calling me. Good-bye old friend. You almost ready to make it on your own. Tomorrow I start to find you a family. Tomorrow, or the next day for sure.

The next day dawned clear and cold and Saylee forgot her resolve. And so the days of that winter passed in happiness and peace with Mamie taking care of Saylee more and more.

"You so tired, ain't you?" Mamie asked one day. "I know you is. Jes rest here by the fire. Mamie take care of you, Ma Saylee."

Saylee smiled at her, but said nothing. She slept more and more that winter.

The very next year, on the first day in April of 1906, Saylee lay bathed in perspiration, too weak to get out of bed.

"Ma-Saylee, you hot. Here drink some water," Mamie said.

She lifted the woman's head and put the rim of the cup to her lips. Root Woman took a sip or two and waved it away. She moaned. Mamie stood by the bed and fanned Saylee, wiping her face with a damp cool cloth. By mid-afternoon, Root Woman rallied a bit.

Mamie brought her water and cooked for her. Mostly boiled eggs. She went out and gathered the eggs and then cooked them in the little pot on the wood stove without mishap.

Finally the fever broke, and Saylee was able to get up. After a few days of sitting in her rocker, she washed her face, got dressed and started to go outside, for it was a beautiful spring day.

She fell face down at the door. Mamie ran to her.

"Get up Ma-Saylee! Get up!"

Root Woman didn't move. Mamie turned her over, and pulled her by the ankles just a few feet away from the door.

"You will be all right in a minute or two. You rest here."

She ran to get a cool rag to wipe her face, but when she came back, she saw that something was wrong.

She staring at me like she don't know me.

"Ma-Saylee? What wrong? No, no! Not yet. Not yet, please!"

She ran to get the jujus and the gris-gris. She came back with Dambala tucked under one arm and handfuls of charms. She lit the candles and placed them in a circle on top of the coffin. She intoned the best Voodoo chants she knew. Finished, she went back to where Root Woman lay.

She looked into the open, staring eyes of the only woman she could remember as her mother. She knew Ma-Saylee was dead.

"Not yet, please Ma-Saylee. I am not ready yet!"

She sat cradling Root Woman's head, keening her sorrow, her tears falling onto Root Woman's staring, open eyes. Every now and then she got up, carefully placing Root Woman's head on the floor, and put a gris-gris on her chest. By late afternoon, she noticed that Root Woman's arms would not bend.

Maybe she gettin' some strength back? No, she dead. But why she gettin' stiff? Oh, Jesus on yo burnin' cross, help my Ma-Saylee come back to life. I be good from heah on out if you brings her back to life. I won't be cross no more. Ever! I promise!

Resuming her place, with Root Woman's head in her lap, Mamie intoned every magic chant she knew over the old woman. She pulled the coffin over to where she could rest her back against it, and still hold Saylee's head in her lap. Toward dawn, she dosed. When she awoke, the sun was far up in the sky. She eased Root Woman's head onto the floor and discovered that her limbs bent easily.

That strange. Now, she bends. What happening?

She put her ear on Root Woman's chest and listened. She pulled her mouth open and listened for breath. Hearing nothing, she resumed her vigil. She sat two days and nights, holding Root Woman's head and singing softly the songs Root Woman had so often sung to her. The healing songs. On the morning of the third day, she smelled the faint smell of death coming from this old woman, this woman who was dearer to her than anyone on earth.

Finally, accepting the fact that Root Woman died, Mamie got up, and began to pack. Mamie took her gris-gris, the rabbit's foot, and the little sack of nails. She climbed up on the steps she used to reach the table. She stretched for the horseshoe over the front door. Not tall enough, she got down and looked for something higher. Finally, placing a couple of old boards on top of the steps, she climbed back up, and was able to reach it. She packed the horseshoe.

She took Root Woman's clay pipe with the little, carved pictures on it. She took some of the dried herbs in little cotton sacks. These, too, would become her gris-gris over the years as she tried to practice Voodoo. She remembered to pack water, food, clothes, and money. She even hid the money in two separate places. She looked back at Saylee as she was leaving. She went back to the body, and gently covered it with a beautiful bedspread Isaiah had brought on one of his secret trips when they lived in Congaree.

She unhooked the gate and opened it wide where the animals were penned. She had to shoo the cow out into the swamp. The other little critters ambled away without a backward glance.

Good-bye ole cow. I ain't even named you, and you been so good, giving us milk for two years. Good-bye. Good-bye, old friend. Oh-h-h, Ma-Saylee, how is I ever gonna' get by without you?

With a heavy heart, she left the cabin. She didn't know where she would go, only that she must get away from this place.

She cried as she walked out the door. A thin, desolate cry of anguish. She left, thinking this the worse that would ever happen to her.

Chapter 8

Root Woman's Remains

With twists and turns beyond all rime
Isaiah loved Lacy through all time
Some loves are open, with friendship and laughter
Others haunt the heart forever after

In July of 1904, Isaiah rode into the swamp to visit Mamie and Root Woman. Finding their cabin deserted, he checked the other two cabins. Deserted. Puzzled, he headed back home.

I'*ve waited too long to make a visit. I haven't been here in three years now. I'll ask Nat where they are. He'll know if anybody knows.*

Nat came out of the back of the ice house. He'd been hosing down the newly made ice, and he dripped from the spray. Where he walked, puddles formed. The sun blazed and the temperature already climbed to over a hundred degrees though it was only eleven-thirty.

"Mr. Ike, do come on in where it cool. Set a spell? What brings you by? You want some ice?" Nat shouted.

I guess he thinks if he can't hear too good, then neither can I.

"Nat, how you getting on? I might get a chunk before I leave, but I came by special to see you. I want to ask you something about—"

"You wants to ask me somethin'? Well, okay, ask."

"Yes," Isaiah shouted, "do you know where Saylee moved to?"

"Who? Pali? She dead. Been dead a long, long time."

"No, not Pali. Root Woman. Pali's daughter. Saylee. Lived out in the middle of Congaree Swamp? She's not there anymore. Moved, I guess. Do you know where she moved?"

"Oh, I see, Saylee. It Saylee you is looking for," Nat shouted. Yes, I see," he said, scratching his grizzled head. "She probably just gone to another cabin. There is two or three of them old cabins out there."

He stood nodding his head.

"Yes, I do know that. I checked all three. She's nowhere to be found in the Congaree. Do you have any idea where she might have gone? She's getting pretty old. Maybe a relative?"

"Aw naw!" Nat said. He let out a gleeful yelp and dried his head with a frayed towel which he took off a peg. The muscles of his powerful arms rippled. "That old woman ain't got no kin. Leastwise I don't think so. I will ask around for you. Somebody bound to know where she is. I might have better luck findin' that out than most."

"I'd appreciate that so much. Come by the store and I'll give you a bag of tobacco for your trouble."

"No need. No need to do that. I'll try my best for you just because you a decent man. Jes because."

Isaiah rode home with a small chunk of ice slung over his shoulder. Martha sat on the front porch, two toddlers playing at her feet. She ran out to the hitching post, a big smile on her face. When he dismounted, she whispered in his ear.

"He didn't! You felt him kick? Honey, that's wonderful!

She glowed with the bloom of pregnancy. A pretty woman, with hazel eyes that sometimes seemed blue, sometimes gray, and once in a while green, she had beautiful strawberry blond hair and a full figure. A comfortable, gently rounded, uncomplicated woman who laughed easily.

Rob, his firstborn, still lived with Robert, and Isaiah knew that Rob kept his grandpa young. The old man doted on the young boy and the boy thought the sun rose and set in his grandpa. His living there started out as necessity, because Isabelle, his aunt, wet-nursed her great nephew. Over the years, Rob continued to live with his grandpa.

"You're so beautiful," he whispered to Martha.

"Why thank you, Mr. Norris, and I think you are handsome. We make a nice-looking couple. Well, couple and a half," she said, looking down at her expanding waistline.

After tucking the children in bed, they retired, too. Isaiah lay awake long after the last sleepy goodnight, thinking about Mamie and Root Woman. Whenever he thought about them, he inevitably thought about Lacy. Though he had just made tender, passionate love with his wife, he ached with longing for Lacy. He could feel her body, taste her lips. Drifting into a fitful sleep, he dreamed.

Root Woman spoke to him in his dream, trying to tell him something, but he couldn't quite hear her. He concentrated on her face and thought he understood her to say 'she had your baby'.

"Who?" he asked.

"She." Saylee said. "New York. Long time ago. Long time . . . ."

The dream faded. He struggled to get back into the dream, but couldn't. He woke up and looked at the clock by the bed. He struck a kitchen match and lit the candle, careful not to wake Martha. Three o'clock.

Well, you come to me in a dream at three o'clock in the morning. Lacy had a baby? Lacy Had A Baby.

The knowledge was in his mind. He didn't know how, but he knew. He wasn't guessing, he knew. He got dressed and went over to the store. Getting all his journals out, he fumbled through them until he found the one he wanted.

Entry date June 1, 1888. "Lacy has gone home to New Orleans. She wouldn't say why. Told me she never wants to see me again. This doesn't make sense."

Isaiah skipped over several entries about returned letters.

Entry date October 5, 1888. "Back from New Orleans. Maryanne and Raule wouldn't tell me where Lacy is. Only that she has decided to move to New York. I must find her. They say she doesn't want to see me."

January 10, 1889. "I'm sitting here at a table in a little restaurant here in New Orleans where Lacy and I have eaten so many times. Just came from Lacy's parents' home. They promised to tell Lacy that I have to see her. I go back there tomorrow."

January 11, 1889. "They told me Lacy said, 'not now, maybe in the summer'. Strange."

May 1, 1889. "Lacy has written and given me her address. I leave on the earliest train for New York. My love, I can't wait, but why did you leave like you did? Why the year-long separation? Did you really think we'd never see each other again?"

June 1, 1889. "We met. The stars fell out of the sky. Again. We each made a sacred vow never to separate. No matter what. We talked about getting married, but realized we just can't. We made a pact. We will always love each other, but live apart. Sad."

Isaiah slowly shut the journal.

Could she have kept such a secret from me? Was that the reason for the year-long separation? A boy, or a girl? Born when? December of '88, or January of '89 I bet. Where has she kept him over the years. I've never seen evidence of a baby or a child. Why did she not tell me?

How old would the child be now? Fifteen. God, almost grown.

Isaiah looked at the time. Five o'clock.

If I hurry, I can catch the cannonball express that makes one stop between Florida and New York. Charleston at 9 AM. God knows I've caught it often enough.

What will I tell Martha? I'll think of something.

He hurried back to the house and got there just as Martha got out of bed.

"You're up early," he said, giving her a kiss on the cheek.

"I got up to see about you. You're up early."

"I've got to pack. I need to meet with a food broker in New York tomorrow, and I plumb forgot about it."

"You want me to help?"

"No, I'm just going to throw a few things into my old valise. You make us some coffee and a bite of breakfast. I'll be right out."

At five-twenty, he saddled up the mare and rode off for the Charleston depot, hoping he could make the sixty or so miles in a little over three hours. It would be close, but he thought he could get old Turner at the depot to take the mare to the stables for him.

Isaiah got to the train station just as the train pulled in about ten minutes to nine. He bought his ticket, arranged with Turner to board his horse, and scrambled aboard just in time.

Lord, what am I doing? Am I suddenly touched in the head? Do I think I can know like Root Woman always could? But the dream was so real.

Where is Root Woman, anyway? Got to find her when I get back. Hope she's still alive.

By the time he arrived in New York, the strangeness of his dream had worn off.

What was I thinking? Probably a touch of indigestion! Oh well, I wanted to see Lacy, anyway. I've always wired or called before. Maybe this time I'll just surprise her. I'll walk the thirty blocks. I need some physical activity to get the stiffness out of my joints.

He could have used his key, but rang the bell. It was just after ten in the evening and he could see lamps lit all inside the brownstone that he and Lacy had called home all these years.

Lacy opened the door, and all the color drained from her face. A tall boy came into the foyer, and froze in his tracks.

"Come in, Isaiah. Moses, go to your room. No, I mean, stay right here."

The boy stood, staring at Isaiah. Recovering, Moses walked over to where Lacy still stood. He ranged almost six feet tall with a shock of sandy-colored, curly hair.

A good-looking boy, thought Isaiah, *my boy!*

The three of them stood like a tableau just inside the front door.

"Well, um, hello Isaiah," Lacy said. "This is a surprise. Come on into the sitting room. Can you guess who this is? You know. Ma-ma must have—"

"No, Lacy, and it wasn't Maryanne either. I had a dream last night. A strange dream. I don't know how, but Root Woman told me in a dream."

"Root Woman?" Lacy asked.

"Who's Root Woman? asked the boy.

"Son, sit down, there is much we have to tell you. Isaiah, I'm sorry I never told you. Moses knows who you are, don't you, Son?"

Moses nodded his head.

I don't know all that much, Moses thought. *I know he has brought you pain and joy over the years. And me? I feel . . . .*

". . . and then it just got more and more difficult to tell you," he heard his mother saying. "Isaiah, I knew how conflicted you would have felt if . . . . I knew we could never marry . . . ."

Heavens no. Marry a nigger? God forbid. Moses thought, as he eased out of the room.

"I knew . . . ." She broke down and cried, and Isaiah rushed to her side. He pulled out a handkerchief. It was crumpled and dirty.

"Moses," he said, thinking he was still present, "could you please get your mother a —"

"He's gone to his bedroom," she said. "Moses, please comc back in here."

He came, a scowl on his face.

"What, Ma-ma? What do you want?"

"Could you get your mother a handkerchief?" Isaiah asked.

Moses stood looking at his father a long moment, turned on his heel and returned with a white, lacy handkerchief. Isaiah sat, holding Lacy in his lap. Moses stood awkwardly by the chair, his hand on his mother's jerking shoulder. Lacy stopped crying and stood up.

"I hope," she said, facing her son, "you two can come to know each other. And love each other as I love each of you.

Isaiah reached up and patted Moses' hand. Moses jerked his hand away and walked across the room and sat down.

"Tell me about yourself, Son. That is if you feel comfortable talking to me. You probably have mixed emotions right now. I wouldn't blame you, if you," Isaiah blurted, "if you hated me."

I look so much like him. At least he seems to know how much I hate him. But he's right. I love him, too, Moses thought, feeling the hard knot in his chest ease. *He's easier to like than I always imagined. My father. Wow.*

"Isaiah, do you want something light to eat?"

"Light or heavy, I could eat a bite," Isaiah said.

Father and son talked. Haltingly. Shortly, Lacy brought in a tray containing a sandwich for Isaiah and some English tea biscuits and hot tea for everyone.

"Ummm, you make the best sandwiches. What's this? Oh, I see." He peeked inside the black Russian rye, sliced paper thin, to find cream cheese and black olives for filling.

"You'd love anything as long as it didn't bite you back," Lacy teased.

"I go to school in Trenton," Moses said. "I'm home only for a long week-end. Next year I enter the university to study art."

Isaiah, having just taken a bite, continued chewing, trying to digest what the boy had said.

"So you're that close to finishing high school? That's good.

"I'm in tenth grade and I graduate in the spring of next year. I go year round. It's a boarding school that has summer classes."

"I see," Isaiah said, "this sandwich is delicious, Lacy. How are your grades?"

"Ma-ma says with my grades, I can pick any college or university. Study comes easy for me." Isaiah noticed that he pronounced 'mama' with a French pronunciation.

And why not, he thought, *probably speaks French as easily as his mama. My boy. He's easy to like.*

"Moses dear," Lacy said, "why don't you show your father some of your sketches?" Looking back at Isaiah, she said, "He is a fine artist."

Moses left without a word, and came back with a thick sketch book. Isaiah took the book from his outstretched hands, and began looking at the drawings. Done mostly in charcoal with a scattering of pencil drawings, he saw that they were good. He turned a page and there before his eyes was a sketch of himself as a young boy of ten or eleven. He looked up at Moses.

"That's me about three years ago. I've filled out a little now."

"Son, that is the spittin' image of me as a boy."

As the three of them talked, Isaiah noticed that the boy was a little guarded, but he seemed to relax more and more as they continued to get to know each other.

He doesn't seem to want to know anything about my life in Brio. I think I can understand why, but I'm going to take the bull by the horns and broach that subject. If he accepts me, it's something he will have to deal with.

"Moses, you've never been to Brio, have you?"

"No sir. That's not a place I'm likely to ever go, either."

"Well, that's where I live and where your mama and I first met.

She stopped on her way to the schoolhouse in Balters to get directions. That was back in 1883!"

"Yes sir, a long time ago," Moses said. An awkward silence hung in the room.

Isaiah tried again, "Maybe, sometime you—"

"It's getting late, Moses. Back to school tomorrow. Better say goodnight now and get to bed."

Moses was on his feet and shouting.

"Say goodnight to the nice man and go to sleep for another fifteen years?" Turning to his father, he shouted, "How am I to visit you? As your man-servant? Your yard boy? I know what the South is like. I may look white, but I am a Negro. I am your nigger bastard—"

"Apologize." Lacy said. "To your father. To me. I'll not have you talking like that in my—"

"You can't stop me from saying the truth. And this is not my father." He spat the word out. "He may have sired me, but he is nothing but, nothing but—a white man with a, with a . . . you are his whore."

Lacy slapped him and he wheeled and left the room, sobbing. She stood, her back to Isaiah, trembling. He put his arms around her.

"The boy is just upset. Let me try to talk to him. I, I am so sorry. Oh Lacy, sh-h-h. Don't cry. There, there my Love."

Moses wouldn't open his door and Isaiah didn't push him. Isaiah and Lacy sat at the little table in the dinning room, talking.

"Each time we meet, it's like falling in love all over again," Isaiah said. "So you moved to New York, and had the baby all alone? Oh Lacy, if only I'd known."

"No, Ma-ma attended the birth and helped me some afterwards. Isaiah, I wanted to tell you, but I just couldn't. What would have changed? Our lives had already taken two separate courses, even before he was conceived. Do you remember that time when we went to the park there in New Orleans? The day you almost turned the little sail boat over?"

They smiled remembering. He nodded, holding her hand in both of his.

"That's the day," Lacy said, "I remember thinking 'it's never going to happen for us.'

"But—"

"Let me finish. That's also the day I got a kind of peace about us. I knew there would always be an 'us', but I knew we'd never marry."

"Never say never," Isaiah said. "I see those tears glistening in your eyes. I love you so much. You are my heart, my life. Oh Lacy, Moses is my firstborn."

"Yes, Isaiah, your firstborn," Lacy said.

"I have some old photographs of myself at that age. A traveling photographer came by our house when I was about eleven or twelve and took some pictures. I'll send you one of me sitting on a horse out by the barn. Moses looks just like me at that age. It's uncanny."

"I know," Lacy said. "Isaiah, have you seen Mamie and Root Woman lately?"

"Oh, I went out to their place just the other day. They are not in any of the cabins. You reckon they could have moved into town somewhere?"

"Oh, I don't think Root Woman would ever leave the swamp. Maybe there is another cabin that you don't know anything about?"

"I have Nat looking into it. He knows everybody and just about everything that goes on around Brio and Balters. He'll find out, I'm sure. I hope nothing's happened to them. Saylee is getting old, you know." Isaiah said, a worried frown creasing his forehead.

They talked until three o'clock in the morning. Nothing was settled about how to handle Moses. Isaiah told Lacy that he would, of course, keep in touch with the boy as much as Moses would allow. They made love in the third bedroom, a room Isaiah had never slept in before. At first light, Lacy crept into her own bedroom.

Isaiah and Lacy had bought this brownstone years ago when the price had been a steal. On the corner of Lexington and Fifteenth, it was prime real estate. Within walking distance of Central Park, it got good light in through the high windows. The ten-foot ceiling gave the place a spacious feel.

Lacy had, over the years,furnished the place with antiques. Antiques that gave comfort to the body and beauty for the soul. None of the little Louis XV chairs too fragile to sit on, nor any of the hard settees so in demand these days. Everything was massive and solid, yet light and airy in color.

A good blend of the masculine and feminine, thought Isaiah as he lay in the unfamiliar room. *Like Lacy and me. Now, if I can only figure out a way to achieve harmony and love between Moses and me.* He finally dropped off to sleep, and didn't hear the stirring of Lacy and Moses.

When Isaiah got up, the house was empty. A note on the dining room table said that Lacy had taken Moses to Grand Central and would be back shortly.

Telling the cab driver to wait, Lacy stood with her son in the awkward silence. He got his valise out. She handed him a sealed envelope.

"Read this, please. It's a letter from me to you. I wrote this when you were a baby. Your father will be writing to you. I gave him your address."

He nodded, pecked her cheek, mumbled that he was sorry for his outburst the night before, and headed into the station before she could respond.

On board the train, he got out the letter.

March 3, 1889

My dear, sweet Son,

One day you will be old enough to read this. I love a man who is dearer than life itself to me, but we can never marry. I am a Negro and he is white. We are connected in a way that even I don't understand, so maybe you won't either when you are older. Just know that we have 'une histoire d'amour' and a marriage in every sense of the meaning except the normal.

I love you and would spare you any hurt that I could. I pray that one day you will understand.

Love,

Your Ma-ma

Moses crumpled the letter and flung it down on the seat beside him. He sat there, breathing hard and crying.

Lucky for me this car is empty.

He picked up the letter and smoothed it out. He re-read it and laid it aside.

I can't deal with this right now. I'm so sleepy . . . .

Moses slept until the conductor awakened him as they pulled into Trenton. He crammed his mother's letter into his suit case and disembarked.

Isaiah left later that same day. Lacy took him to the station.

"I'm making a habit of this," she said, kissing him good-bye. "Oh Isaiah, I wish you could stay longer. Thank you for understanding about my keeping our son a secret from you for all these years. It's the hardest thing I ever did. I'm glad you finally know."

On the train ride home, Isaiah slept. Getting home after twelve o'clock at night, he slept again. He fell into bed without waking Martha and slept.

The next morning Isaiah slept in. Martha was in the garden when he came downstairs. He got a cup of coffee and walked out to the garden to drink it.

"Are you planting butter beans? You better be careful. Don't get too hot out here."

"How was your trip? Did you see the food broker? I'm so glad you're back. Can I fix you some breakfast? "No," Isaiah said, kissing her forehead. "I've got tons of work at the store. See you at lunch time."

Nat came into the store the day after Isaiah got back from seeing his son for the first time. Isaiah slipped a package of Prince Albert into Nat's pocket.

"I has talked to a carpenter over in Balters," Nat said, patting his pocket, and grinning from ear to ear. "He says he believes Root Woman in Hell Hole Swamp over near Monks Corner in Berkeley county."

Every eye in the store turned in their direction for while Nat thought he spoke in a confidential tone, he almost shouted.

"Well, that's good to know." Isaiah shouted back at him. "Thanks, Nat. Good work."

"Well, I'll be gettin' on back down to the ice house!" He left the store, pulling the package of Prince Albert out of his pocket on the way out. "And thanks for the tobacey," he shouted from the door.

Not until March of the following year did Isaiah find the time to really look for Root Woman and Mamie. Martha's pregnancy proved a difficult one, both children got sick, and his relationship with Moses was tenuous to say the least. He simply had too much to do. He found himself putting out one fire after another.

Then with Tense and William on the mend from diphtheria, Martha had a set of beautiful twin boys.

By and by, Moses started acting a little more accepting of him, his wife and children thrived, everything seemed to be settling down. He found that he had some time to look for Mamie and Root Woman.

He started by exploring the periphery of Hell Hole Swamp, going in just a short way. It was different from any swamp he'd ever seen.

It's scarier in here than in Congaree. I'm afraid I'll get lost.

By summer, he had not seen any trace of them. It got so hot that he abandoned the search until cooler weather. He tried to send Root Woman a message with his mind.

Maybe she's not listening, he thought with a grin.

He tried that fall and winter a few more times. In 1906, he got so busy with his growing family and the store, that he looked for them only once in the spring of that year.

It was in the fall of 1907, that he asked Nat to take him to see the carpenter over in Balters. They saw the man sitting on his front porch, and he walked out to the street to talk with them at the wagon.

He told them that yes, he thought Saylee had moved into Hell Hole Swamp about three or four years ago.

"And," he said, "I ain't goin' in that god-forsaken place again. No sir."

"So you've seen where they live?"

"Did I say I's been there? I didn't say that, nawsir, I shore Lawd didn't say that."

"No, of course, you didn't say that," Isaiah said, realizing his mistake. "But can you give me just an idea of how I might go into the swamp to run up on them?"

After eyeing Isaiah and Nat, the old man apparently decided that Isaiah might be trustworthy.

"If I was huntin' for their cabin, which I'm not, mind you, I'd go in from the old logging road. It cuts off from Highway fifty-two along about where that there big, old oak tree stands on the road. You know the one I mean?"

Isaiah nodded.

"That old logging road goes aways into the swamp. From the end of that road, I'd veer off to the left. Mind the sink holes. I'd take me a long walking stick to test for quicksand. A stout one, too, in case you has to bonk any 'gators over the head. I'd walk about a mile or two and start looking for the cabin on a rise just past a water oak. It's a big tree. You can't miss it." He walked back to his front porch, not waiting to be thanked.

Isaiah called from the street, "Much obliged." They drove back to Brio and as they neared the town, Isaiah asked, "Nat, you know anybody that would go with me to look for Saylee?"

"Well, I might. I just might. Let me know when you want them. You offering to pay them to search with you?"

"Yes, I'll pay them. Sure. I know it takes their time and all. The sooner, the better," Isaiah said. He looked over at Nat and grinned.

"See if you can find two or three good men, and we'll do it next week. Maybe we'll camp at the edge of the swamp if we don't find the cabin the first day. Tell 'em I'll pay 'em each a dollar a day. You think that carpenter told the truth about where to find her cabin?"

"I specks he did. I think he built it for her. She asked him not to tell anybody where she moved. Now he's told me and he's told you. I hopes she don't hex him. Or me!" Nat rolled his eyes, then said, "But at my age it don't much matter."

"How old are you Nat?" Isaiah laughed along with him.

"Don't rightly know. I was an old man before the war. Well, maybe not old, but old for a slave. Maybe forty-five, fifty, fifty-five. I had plenty gray hair."

"So, you could be gettin' on close to a hundred years old, or older!" Isaiah said. "You seem to be in good health. I'm glad that you are, old friend." He smiled at Nat and they rode on in comfortable silence.

It was late November, in 1907 that Isaiah found the cabin in Hell Hole Swamp. Following the carpenter's directions, he had come upon the rise. A little farther on, he found the huge water oak and then the cabin. No one ever found the time to help him search, even though he offered to pay them. He approached the cabin alone.

I got a bad feeling about this. Root Woman ain't here. That cabin has an abandoned look.

He found the remains of Root Woman. Wild animals had scavenged the body, dragging bones off. The skull, rib cage, pelvic girdle and leg bones still lay on the floor of the cabin. They had been picked clean by crabs and bugs. The remains of Root Woman lay forlorn with no arms or hands, no feet. Sad beyond words, Isaiah left, wondering where Mamie could be.

He returned the next day with some colored men. He had been able to hire them because he knew exactly where they were to go this time. He told them about finding Root Woman's skeleton, and that he needed them to help him bury her.

They carried a crude coffin and gave Saylee proper burial out behind the cabin. As they stood around the grave, the minister who had performed the ceremony left the group and walked back into the cabin. He came running out almost immediately.

"Oh, I say. Mista Ike, come quick. Look at what I done found."

In the direction he pointed toward with shaking finger, stood Saylee's old coffin. Half burned candles still stood on top range around small gray, cotton sacks. On the lid, the black cross was still discernible, though faded. The spade and hoe that had lain on top of the coffin, now lay on the floor, probably knocked off by some plundering, wild animal. The same one, no doubt, who had chewed the brim off the top hat.

"Owww. This here Voodoo stuff," one of the men said. "We done give her a Christian burial. I hope that don't hex us. You reckon?"

"I don't see how that could cause harm to any of us. We just did the right thing by her," Isaiah said. "She was a good woman. I saw this coffin years ago when she lived in Congaree Swamp. It was part of certain religious beliefs of hers."

"You always sees the good in people, but this Voodoo stuff . . .. I just don't know. It powerful," the minister said. "You has always tried to do the right thing by her, and by Mamie, ain't you?" He patted Isaiah's shoulder. "You a right charitable man, Sir. So she explained this here coffin and stuff to you?"

Isaiah answered absent-mindedly, "Well, some. Not in any great detail, but some."

Where is the pole with the snake coiled around it. She always put such stock in that pole. Called it 'Dambala'. I don't see it anywhere.

* * *

Later that night, back in town, the men sat in the home of the AME minister who had performed the burial service. They speculated as to the possible harm into which they had inadvertently placed themselves.

"That there Mr. Ike," John Talmage said, "he's a good man, but he don't know the half of it. Voodoo is real, and it powerful."

"Well, that's true. So true," said the minister, "but I don't think Root Woman would object to a nice Christian burial. You know I been knowin' she practice Voodoo, but I just wasn't thinkin'. She was spooky, but she was good to that poor Mamie that got her legs cut off. Wonder what ever become of that girl?"

"God only knows," said John, "but she ain't gonna' be able to make it on her own. Listen, what's done is done. Let's not tell the womens about this. They worry enough without more to worry 'bout. They get to thinkin' how she done hex old Judge Clayton, and they be fit to be tied. They likely worry themselves to death."

"You right 'bout that," said Joseph, "the womens don't need to hear any of this talk. That judge do poorly up to this present day. I declare she hexed him good. Reckon we should tell him she be dead, now?"

There was a long moment of silence, then, in unison, they said, "Naw. Let him keep on worrying what she be up to next."

They burst out laughing. They sat long into the night telling one story after another about Root Woman. As they talked, her reputation grew even bigger.

"Did y'all ever hear 'bout the time she held that Voodoo ceremony out by the crossroads on the yonder side of Balters?" They all avowed they had never heard, but in truth they had heard the story many times.

"Well," he began, "it was thundering and lightening to beat the band. They played the Congo drums with everybody standing round in a circle. A circle, mind you, that went all the way around the crossroads. At exactly midnight . . . ." He continued the story they all knew by heart, scaring them anew with the wonder of the supernatural.

"Yes, Lawd, they's power in crossroads. That's where you has to go at the stroke of midnight to summon the Devil," one of them said.

"I believe in jujus," another said. "I got me a rabbit's foot. Ain't y'all?" They all admitted they did, indeed, carry around a rabbit's foot. All except the preacher. He had one, but thought he'd better not let them know. They talked about hexes and witches and devils, wondering if they were the same in Voodoo beliefs as in Christian.

"Naw, Voodoo is a religious belief that is mixed all up with Christian beliefs, but it come out of African beliefs, I think," the minister said. "I hear Root Woman got some from her father and some from her Indian mother. No tellin' what her particular Voodoo beliefs were. We best call it a night. Y'all coming to church tomorrow, ain't you?"

They all assured him they would be there. And, in fact every one of them showed up and for many Sundays afterward. The death of Root Woman and the disappearance of Mamie seemed to have put the "fear of God" into them. Or maybe it was the fear of Voodoo. When they stopped worrying about Saylee hexing them from the grave, their attendance dropped off somewhat.

Isaiah, meanwhile, continued searching for Mamie. Everywhere he went he asked if anyone had seen her. He thought often of his dream about his son, Moses.

Root Woman, if you could tell me about Moses, why not tell me about Mamie? Maybe I'm losing my mind. I half believe she can hear me.

Isaiah continued, too, to balance his life and his time between his two families. He loved Martha. He loved Lacy. In different ways, but he loved both women.

One night, he settled in bed and dreamed about Mamie. Root Woman stood in her cabin door. "Mamie is gone. Not in the swamp anymore. You will see her againnnnn." She faded away. Isaiah tried to call her back, but she, too, was gone. He awoke, covered with sweat.

Chapter 9

Talk in a Small Town

Killed his Ma a'bornin' so goes the story grim
No one to sing, or laugh, or mourn
Wet-nursed by me, cuddled at my breast?
He sucked the last, the creamy rich, the best

I want to talk to you 'bout Isaiah
I hear tell he still sees that woman, Lacy
Poor orphaned boy; it just ain't right!
Rob's growin' up fast—and he sure is bright!

"That boy's a'growin' like a weed," Isabelle said as she plopped down on the rocker on the porch. "He's big for a nine year old. Killed his ma a'bornin', he was so big."

Rob played at the end of the porch. He listened. He'd heard the story before, but it always fascinated him. It was like a story in a book about someone else.

"Isabelle, I don't think—" Robert began to say.

"Yes Sir, I nursed him at my own breast for two whole years. Why, I love him like he's my own. I think the reason he grew so good was he got the best, creamiest milk, nursing after my own Charlie."

She laughed and leaned back in the rocker. Robert smiled at his sister's merriment. Rob continued to play.

"Grandpa, kin I go to see Pa?"

"I reckon you can if you promise to hightail it back here 'fore dark. And don't cut through the swamp. There's 'gators in there bigger'n you are. They might mistake you for a dog."

The boy grinned.

"Okay, I won't. Bye-bye!"

Skipping and running down the dirt road, he disappeared around a bend.

"Not a care in the world," his grandpa said.

When out of earshot, he sang, "Killed my ma a'bornin' . . . killed my ma a'bornin' . . . . killed my ma . . . ."

"Isabelle, would you like some iced tea? I got me a big hunk of ice this morning. Drove out at first light with the boy on the wagon seat. I let him play for a spell in the cool ice house while I visited with old Nat."

"How is Nat? He must be a hundred years old and still working at the ice house!"

"He's old, but I don't think he's quite a hundred. He's strong as a mule and seems healthy, too. He threw those blocks of ice around like they was cork wood. I got him talking about the old Cooper Plantation where he was a slave. He said there was an overseer named Mulkey way back about 1840 who whipped a young slave to death for stealing food."

Isabelle shook her head.

"Well, that was a long time ago, and them days is gone forever. Besides, you never mistreated any of your slaves, and me and Ben didn't own any slaves. No use dwelling on the hard times our poor old Coloreds had during slavery."

She rocked as she drank her tea, her big, round cheeks returning to their usual rosy hue. Her gray hair still contained a hint of red and curled in damp tendrils about her face and neck.

"Robert, how's Ike's family? That new baby doin' all right?"

"Reckon so. Went by there this morning to see if they wanted me to get them a chunk of ice, too. Martha was up and runnin'. Baby in a sling around her waist, and him only a couple weeks old. She was cooking breakfast for Ike and the other little door steps.

"I guess they're gonna' keep count of the years married by how many in their brood. They're a lively bunch, and seem happy as pigs in mud. Ike's store is growing, too."

He smiled, thinking of the name of the store. Ike's General Emporium.

"Folks 'round here sure have had a big time teasing him about the name he give that store. They don't know the meaning of Emporium or how to pronounce it." Robert laughed.

"Ummm, Robert? Uh, not changing the subject, and you can tell me to mind my own business if you want, but I gotta ask you. Is Isaiah involved with that woman who ustta teach school over in Balters? The one teaching at the colored school? She *is* colored, you know, though she looks as white as you or me! I hear-tell she left here and moved to New York?"

Robert cleared his throat, got out an old clay pipe with beautiful carvings on the bowl, took a long time lighting it, but finally looked over at Isabelle.

"Where did you hear that talk?"

"Old man Clayton, you know, the magistrate? Well, he supposedly told it to the fellow who cuts hair, and he told it to the banker, and the banker's wife brought it right into the Sunday school room last Sunday. Said the judge seen Isaiah and that colored woman in New York City at some fancy restaurant, holding hands."

Robert continued rocking and smoking his pipe. Isabelle looked at him for a comment. When he continued to stare off into the heat-shimmering distance, she continued.

"The one day I missed church in almost a year! Jewell dropped by to fill me in on the talk that very afternoon."

Again, she looked expectantly at her brother.

"Well? Is he, or isn't he? Robert *she is colored!* Another thing, I heard he was involved with her long before he married Jane, and after he married Martha. I declare, I hope you gonna tell me it ain't true!"

"Isabelle," Robert sighed, "I don't really know. Isaiah makes a lot a trips to New York. Business trips for the store, he says. That woman's been gone a long time now. I just don't know. He's a grown man. I reckon he can make up his own mind what's right and what's wrong. She's a pretty thing. And you're right. She looks as white as ever a woman on God's green earth. Still, she *is* colored. Just like old Judge Clayton to spread ugly rumors."

"Well," Isabelle continued to rock, "Isaiah's a good man. And Martha's a good woman. I just hope he don't bring shame on his family. Maybe it's all just idle talk. Ike seems happy in his marriage."

"Yes, he does," Robert said, "I thought he was gonna go off the deep end after Jane died. Especially during the two years before he married Martha. I'm glad Isaiah's been able to put Jane's death behind him. Speaking of Jane, I wish, Isabelle, you wouldn't mention Jane's death in front of the boy."

"Oh Robert, he don't pay no attention to that story. Still, uh, if you say so, I won't."

"Much obliged, and yes, I say so," he said.

He smiled and winked at his sister and she smiled her big, loving smile back at him.

Rob lit out through the swamp watching for alligators which he had never seen, but believed with all his heart were lurking in the water and waiting to eat him. Still singing his one-line song, he stopped singing, turned around, and headed back through the swamp to his and his grandpa's house. The words of his song slowly sank into his heart like pebbles thrown into the pond. Soon his body heaved with sobs.

He ran without seeing and tripped over a root landing in shallow water. He stopped crying and just lay there waiting to be eaten.

No alligator appeared, and, after about an hour, he set out for home like the Devil himself was after him.

He began crying again and was still crying when he reached the front porch. He could hear his grandpa and aunt talking in the kitchen, so he crawled up under the porch to hide. He didn't want them to see him crying, but he couldn't seem to stop.

"You ever hear," Isabelle asked, "any news about that girl the old Root Woman was raising? I hear the poor girl lost her mind from them Klans people messing her up like they did and killing her mama and all."

They walked out and heard sniffling. Guided by the sound,

they went to the end of the porch and Robert jumped off and Isabelle went to the steps, and around.

They saw Rob, wet and dirty, lying face down and crying. Robert called him out. Rob came out rubbing his eyes. Robert held him by the shoulders at arms length.

"You went through the swamp, didn't you? Did you see a 'gator? I don't believe the trouble you give one poor old Grandpa."

With this scolding, Rob started up afresh. "Ah, don't take on so. I'm not goin' to whup you. You just got scared out there in the swamp?'

He pulled him close and hugged him fiercely. His Aunt Isabelle patted his head as she said her good-byes. She left the two of them, arms wrapped around each other.

"Get the wash tub out from under the porch and put it yonder behind the mulberry thicket. We'll have us a nice cold bath so go draw some buckets of water. .

Rob pulled the tub out from under the low end of the porch, took the tub to their special spot and set it down. He began pumping water.

"Well, Boy, let's shuck these clothes and get clean. You know you're dirty as a pig."

Rob giggled and wrinkled his nose at his grandpa. They finished bathing, dumped the water, rinsed the tubs, put everything away, and went inside to eat.

As he finished his supper, Rob grinned at his grandpa. .

"Aunt Isabelle cooks good, huh, Grandpa?"

"Yes, Rob, she sure do," Robert nodded as he studied his grandson. He wondered what all the commotion had been about. He suspected it was a bit more than being afraid of alligators in the swamp. "Let's you and me tidy up the kitchen and then up to bed with you."

"Grandpa, when I get in bed will you tell me about the little woman with no legs? I saw her once in Pa's store. And tell me about the old witch she lives with. They live out in the middle of the swamp, don't they?"

Robert pulled the boy over. "Rob, did you see the little woman with no legs today? Is that why you got scared? Is that why you were crying?"

"Heck,no!" Rob paused. "Grandpa, did I really kill my mother getting borned?"

"Aw, Son, your mama died in childbirth, but that sure wasn't your fault. Giving birth can be risky. Sometimes women die. There can be complications. When you're older I can explain better. For now, just trust me. You didn't kill your mama."

He hugged the boy.

"Will you still tell me stories about my mama and daddy? And will you tell me about that woman with no legs? And the witch? I hear she put a curse on Judge Clayton and ever since he has been sick. Is that right?"

Robert ruffled the boy's hair.

"Son," he said, "that old woman is called 'Root Woman' not because of evil spells she can put on a person, but because she knows which roots and plants help make a person well. She is also an excellent midwife. You know, someone to help a baby get born."

"Did she help me get born?"

"No, maybe if—never mind. No, you were birthed by old Doctor Pritchard. He's dead now. He was real old when you were born. But getting back to Root Woman, she ain't no witch. She maybe practices a little Voodoo from what I hear, but I think she's a good woman. And she did a good deed, taking that girl in that lost her legs. Her name is Mamie."

Rob asked, "Does Root Woman have a name?"

"Yes, it's Saylee. Just Saylee. I don't know what her last name is."

"Grandpa, tell me about Mamie and how she lost her legs. Please? Tell me all about the Klan and the Root Woman and what Pa did—tell me everything. Make it like a ghost story. Well, not like a ghost story, but scary. I won't have bad dreams. I promise."

"Son, I don't have to do a thing to make it scary. It *is* scary."

"Make your voice scary!"

Robert smiled. The boy was tucked in. Just a little light showed from the kitchen below. Robert recounted the story ending by saying,"—and Root Woman took the girl deep into the swamp and nobody saw her for months and months."

"Is she still out there in the swamp?"

"No, I don't think so."

Rob said, "She died, huh?"

Robert scratched his chin and shifted his position a little. He said, "Yes, Root Woman died."

"What about Mamie? What ever happened to her?"

"Your pa ain't seen her. Nobody knows where she is. Your pa has been so busy what with getting married again and all you younguns.

When your pa found Root Woman's remains, there was no sign of Mamie."

"Grandpa, maybe she died out there in the swamp. Let's you and me go look for her skeleton. That would be real scary."

"And gruesome, too. You don't need to be thinking 'bout finding no skeleton just before going to sleep. I'll tell you a bedtime story about your mama and daddy courting. Would you like that? Hmmm?"

Rob snuggled under the sheet with his pillow bunched up under his cheek as he lay on his side, His eyes sparkled with love for his grandpa who was the best storyteller in the whole wide world. "Yeah, Grandpa. Tell me 'bout the time they met at the church picnic."

"All right, but you got to go to sleep after this story. Tomorrow morning we are going to town to buy you some clothes. And I need a new pair of pants. Is that a deal, young Whipper Snapper Norris?"

Grinning, Rob nodded his head, and his grandpa began.

"Once upon a time, there lived in our fair land a beautiful young woman. She was nineteen that summer day in 1897 when your pa happened by the spot at Black River where the church crowd had decided to have a picnic lunch. Your pa never was much for goin' to church regular like. He went occasionally, you know?"

Rob nodded, and grinned.

"Well," his grandpa continued, "the preacher spied him coming toward where they had the blankets all spread out. He saw your pa before your pa saw them. He had his fishing pole across his shoulders ready to go fishing. So the preacher called, 'Jane, could you come here for a moment, please?' Jane come runnin' over to where the preacher stood, close to the river bank, but still out of sight of your pa.

"Now the reason your pa couldn't see them? For one thing, they were mostly sitting down, and for another they were either eating or thinking about eating so there wasn't a lot of noise. Anyway, Isaiah looks up, sees them, starts to turn around, and the preacher steps out and says, 'Well, son I'm so glad you could join us. Let me introduce you to one of our newest members, Miss Jane Alder. Jane, this is Isaiah Norris, a fine young gentleman, the owner of 'Ike's General Emporium.'

"You see, the preacher was doin' a little fishin' himself, if you catch my drift." Robert paused for drama, with his eyebrow quirked up and a grin on his face.

"Your pa," he went on, "took one look at Jane, and decided to stay! They courted all that summer and fall, and he asked her to marry him in November. They got married in December, and you were born the following December. December 18, 1898 to be exact."

"And that's when she died? That's when my ma died? On December 18, 1898? "

"Yes, son. I'm sorry."

Almost asleep, he said, "Me too."

Robert brushed a kiss on his grandson's forehead and tiptoed out of the room.

Robert walked back into the parlor and thought about Jane, his daughter-in-law.

She had been a sweet young thing. Isaiah loved her, no doubt about it. But he never stopped loving . . ..

He paused as though a still picture had frozen his thoughts.

No need thinkin' about that. He's a grown man, and you'd think he'd know better. And maybe the thing with Lacy is all in the past. But I doubt it.

He thought about Sadie, dead now some twenty years. He could still feel her presence at times. He believed in ghosts and a few times he thought she was very near.

Like the time I was so sick. I had been burning up with fever when I was down with the influenza a few years back. I felt her cool hand on my brow. I smelled the lavender powder she always dusted on herself after a bath.

He sighed and eased into the rocking chair, leaning his head back.

Sadie, I wish you could have lived to grow old with me. To see this grandson, Rob. And the others that are coming along now. Hortense has your coloring, you know? Oh, not just Isaiah's children, but all of them. Of course, you know. You're still here.

At sixty-nine, he knew he would never remarry. He nodded off. He dreamed about Sadie. This dream was different from all the others he had dreamed over the years. She was older in this dream. The age she would have been had she not died back in 85.

She stepped up to him and kissed him full on the lips, her lithe body pressed close to his.

"Let's go to bed," she said. "I've got something for you."

He dreamed of making love to her. He tasted her soft skin. Felt the heat of their loving.

He woke with a start, his heart racing. He had slid down in the rocker, his long legs stretched straight out. He got up scratching his head.

That wasn't half bad for a dream. Sadie, we'll have to do this more often. I like the way you've aged, too.

He walked into the kitchen for a drink of water. He shook his head and wore a big smile on his face. He checked on Rob and went to bed.

He dreamed throughout the night. A jumble of images, not making much sense. All dreams evaporated like fog when he first opened his eyes. All except the dream about him and Sadie remained vivid.

He fixed grits,scrambled eggs and biscuits with a choice piece of country ham. Just as he finished setting the table, Rob came bounding down the stairs. "Hey Grandpa, I dreamed about Mamie and Root Woman last night, but it wasn't scary. Did you dream?"

"Wash up for breakfast. There's a basin full of fresh water on the back porch," Robert murmured.

Rob came back in and sat at the table.

"Smells good, Grandpa. Well? Did you?"

"Did I what?"

"Did you dream?"

"Oh, I dreamed some rigmarole, but I can't much remember it. Let's eat now so we can get on off to town. If I don't get you outfitted for school soon, it'll be startin' back up and you'll have to wear your old rags first day. And all the kids will laugh at you. Your pa gave me some money for your clothes yesterday when we stopped by there with the ice."

Rob yelped with laughter, forgetting about his question.

Chapter 10

Bound for Charleston

Jujus in pocket, Mamie trudged toward town
Stricken by grief, her head hung down
Beset by scoundrels along the way
Without the charms, who's to say

She could have gone to Africa Land
But a Good Samaritan lent a hand

Mamie plodded along the highway from Monks Corner to Goose Creek. She walked with head down, shoulders hunched. Though only April, the sun beat down on her head. She slowed her gait, rubbed her eyes, blinked and yawned.

I glad to be out of the swamp. I can go quicker now that I doesn't have to be on guard for snakes. Wonder how far I done come? Could I find a spot of shade, I'd rest for just a spell.

The day sparkled, birds sang, a cool breeze fanned her face. She sat down under a huge live oak tree alongside the roadway.

Soon she nodded off.

She awoke to the sound of a wagon rolling to a stop.

"Whoa, whoa, there. What have we here? Hello, little woman. You wanna ride?"

She looked up, rubbing her eyes. Three men, all of them black as coal tar, leered at her. Two sat on the wagon seat, the third peered at her over the side of the wagon. The fat one continued speaking as he chewed on a piece of straw.

"We'uns from the other side of Kingstree. We farmers, ain't dat right, boys? We goin' to Charleston. Where you headin'? We gives you a ride, far as we's going. Come on, get up here. We ain't gonna hurt you none. No way."

Mamie shifted and the bag--propped against her shoes-- fell over. The men stared at her brogans turned backward.

"What wrong wid yo legs?" one of the men asked. "You ain't' got much legs at all, has you?"

Mamie stood. She gathered up her stuff, glaring at the men as she walked past the wagon and horse. The fat man motioned with his head to the fellow sitting beside him, and he hopped down to the roadway. He put his hands on Mamie's shoulders and started to say something about not hurting her.

She jerked away and ran, but he caught her before she was out of arms' reach. He lifted the struggling woman to the wagon, and the man who was lying on a dirty, ragged quilt scrambled to his knees and held her down.

"I is Sojourner," the driver said, "cause I is on a journey, see? This here fellow go by the name Rufus. Jes Rufus. No last name. The one holdin' your mouth shut, is called 'Yum-yum' because he like to eat. We all like to eat, but he like to eat more'n the rest of us." They all laughed. "Give her a drink of that there white lightnin' Yum-yum."

"I can't," the man called Yum-Yum said, "hold her down and do dat, too. What you think, I got four arms?"

Sojourner motioned for Rufus to go into the back of the wagon. He hopped over the seat and held Mamie's arms pinned to her sides. In fighting to get loose, her dress hiked up and they saw that she wore no underwear. Yum-yum poured the raw whiskey down her throat and buried his mouth between her legs.

"Man, you crazy?" Rufus asked. "It broad open daylight. Somebody might see us. Sojourner, you know what he doin'?"

"That's enough, Yum-yum," Sojourner said. "You can wait. Give her some more whiskey. Time I finds a spot to pull this wagon off the road, I wants her to be drunk! Maybe she even enjoy my big dick. These tiny womens sometimes has big pussies. Uh-uh-uh! I gettin' excited jes thinkin' bout it. And another thing, I go fust! I the leader, you got that straight? You all can have a turn, but me fust!"

Mamie retreated into another world. She knew she was in danger, but she didn't care. Something about this present situation reminded her of another time, another place, but that was blocked from her mind for the moment.

She didn't struggle. She tried to swallow as the awful tasting stuff poured down her throat. Once or twice she choked. Her stomach heaved, but she didn't vomit.

Yum-yum held her with her back toward him so that he could fondle her breasts and between her legs.

Between Goose Creek and Charleston, in the twilight of the day the wagon pulled into some woods on a dirt road that was little more than a cow trail. Sojourner brought the wagon to a stop under some trees. He tied up the horse and told Rufus to feed and water the animal. He walked around to the back of the wagon. Mamie slept.

"Maybe I can wake the lady up."

He untied the rope that held his pants up, letting the pants fall to the ground. He, too, wore no underwear. He climbed, with considerable huffing and puffing, up onto the wagon. He had an erection before he even reached Mamie.

She opened her eyes and screamed when he knelt directly over her face.

"Here!" He thrust his penis at her closed mouth, but she moved her head from side to side.

"She ain't know whut I wants done. Kin you believe it?" he asked Rufus who stood watching.

He yanked her head up and pried her mouth open. Mamie started to bite down, but he jerked her head back. She yelped. He punched her, breaking one of her front teeth off at the root. She spat it out with a mouth full of blood.

He grabbed her and turned her over so that she lay face down. She scratched and bit, but he proceeded until he climaxed.

"Rufus, you next."

Watching quickened Rufus' appetite for the strange woman with no legs. His penis, not nearly as big as Sojourner's, stood straight up. Turning her onto her back, he tried to enter her, but couldn't. He pushed. She moaned. Sojourner held his hand over her mouth.

"Ram it in, you fool," Sojourner said. "What you waiting for?"

"Man, she too tight. She must be a virgin."

With one hard thrust, he penetrated the struggling woman. She managed to bite Sojourner's hand and he slapped her. She went limp.

Sojourner watched. He rubbed himself and shoved Rufus.

"Ain't you finished yet?" Sojourner asked. "I gettin' ready all over again. Hurry up."

"You nearly knock me off. Jes wait a minute, I almost there!"

Yum-yum said, "It my turn next."

Sojourner turned and looked at Yum-yum with a menacing smile.

"You can wait for Sojourner to get piece of that tight pussy, now can't you? Sojourner ain't had none of that yet!"

They all laughed.

"Besides there's plenty to go around. It just now gettin' dark and we can go all night."

Yum-yum nodded as he continued to rummage through her things. Sojourner saw the food, and before Yum-yum could eat it all, he told him to light the lantern. Sojourner searched her bags, taking what he wanted.

When the men became too drunk to rape the unconscious woman, they slept. At first light, they roused themselves, tied Mamie up, and got on the road again. She lay, bound, gagged, bruised and bleeding. As they neared the outskirts of Charleston, Rufus motioned toward the woman in the bed of the wagon.

"What we goin' to do with her?"

"We just let her out up the road aways," Sojourner said. "Ain't nobody goin' to find us. I don't want to kill her, and she too ugly to keep."

All three men laughed. After another mile or two, Sojourner stopped the wagon, untied Mamie and took the gag off. He gave her some water. They had eaten all her food and taken the money they had found hidden in the toe of one brogan.

"You can keep yo jug of water and the rest of your truck. See, I told you Uncle Sojourner be good to you. There a little community of colored folks right down this here side road. Don't send no police after us. You do, I'll find you when I gets out of jail, and next time, I kill you. You understand me?"

Mamie glared at him, but nodded her head. They laid her down in the middle of the dirt road.

"Good-bye now," Sojourner said, "enjoyed knowin' you."

They laughed as they drove off.

Mamie lay there afraid to move. She cursed the men with the little voodoo she knew. She ended the curse with the now familiar saying 'and so have you sealed your fate,' hoping she had gotten the words just right.

Praying for strength, she stood up, swaying in the early dawn breeze. As the sky got lighter, she summoned the energy and will to walk to the first house.

"Who dat knockin' on my door so early in the morning?" a woman's voice called. "I coming. Hold your horses."

A large, black woman opened the door. She looked at Mamie.

"Oh my God, who you is? Who done this to you? Come in, come in."

Mamie collapsed into the stranger's broad arms, sobbing. Mamie did not talk, did not cry out. The woman called her husband who was in the kitchen eating his breakfast.

"Jonah! Come quick. Help me, Jonah!"

He ran to his wife. There before him stood a woman two or three feet tall, battered, bruised, and bleeding. Her hair, a salt and pepper gray, held matted blood and dried dirt and trash. Her dress hung about her neck, useless for covering her nakedness. He saw what looked like bite marks on both breast, a scratch or cut on her stomach and both arms. She tried to pull the dress together in the front, and he quickly averted his eyes.

"I'll get the preacher. He'll know what to do. She in bad shape."

Jonah left through the front door, and Mamie began to tremble. She shook so hard, her teeth chattered. The woman noticed the broken tooth, the black eye, swollen almost shut.

"My name's Sukey. What's your name?" When Mamie didn't answer, she said, "Come to the kitchen. I will help you."

The woman started for the kitchen, but looking back, saw that Mamie stood in a puddle of blood. Sukey laid Mamie down right there by her front door and put a folded towel between the stumps of her legs. She tied them together with a sash from an apron. She pulled Mamie's dress back down, and, not knowing what else to do, sponged her face, neck and arms off with clear water.

"Who do this to you? Where you from? What happened to your legs? Poor thing. You can't tell me, can you? I Sukey. Sukey Thomas. I was a slave over on one of the islands, John's Island, I believe. I left that place soon as slavery was over. Ain't never been back either. I sixty one year old. How old you is?"

Getting no answers, she stopped the questioning, and sat down on the floor, next to Mamie. Mamie lifted her arms to be picked up. Sukey moved to a rocking chair with Mamie held like a baby in her arms.

"My own chil'ren all sold off. You seem like one of my lost little ones."

When her husband got back with the preacher, Mamie was sound asleep on Sukey's ample bosom. Reverend Tom shook his head.

"Do you know who she is or how this happened. Was she raped, or just beaten?"

Sukey whispered to her husband what she had seen when Mamie lifted her dress. Her husband motioned for the preacher to follow him out to the kitchen. Sukey heard the low murmur of their voices, and knew they would figure out what to do.

Sukey had to leave soon to go to work at Mrs. Banefield's house. She did her whole house and the ironing for three dollars. She worked there once a week. Each day she worked in another house. She went to the same houses every week on the same day.

When she was sure that Mamie was sound asleep, she laid her on a bed and tiptoed out to the kitchen, got some warm water, soap, the wash rag, and a towel.

How can anybody do this to another human being? Got no religion! I was to find somebody doing that to a po ole woman with no legs, I'd cut his thing plumb off!

"If you'uns will please stay here for awhile, I clean her up some more. The poor little thing."

She took the supplies into the living room.

"Honey? You awake? I's goin' to wash 'tween yo legs now. Make you feel better."

She laid a towel on the bed and moved Mamie onto it. When Sukey began to wash Mamie, she moaned, but didn't wake up. Mamie still bled.

Sukey surveyed the damage. Mamie was torn just like Sukey had seen women tear after birthing a baby. Her genitals were swollen, and her rectum was torn, too.

"You needs to see a doctor. You sho Lawd do! But what we goin' to tell the doctor? Can't you talk to me? Please? Wake up now, won't you?"

Just as Sukey turned to go back into the kitchen, Mamie started to shake in her sleep. She cried out and a gush of blood poured onto the towel.

"Help," Sukey called, "Jonah, Reverend Tom. Come quick. She rolled another towel, placed it between Mamie's stumps, and grabbed a belt to tie her legs together. Sukey told her husband to get a doctor.

"Jonah, do hurry. She worse off than we has thought. She bleedin' most to death."

Sukey hurried to the kitchen and chipped off a hunk of ice, hammered it in a towel to make crushed ice. She took this back into the other room and placed it on Mamie's stomach. Reverend Tom knelt by the bed holding Mamie's hand and praying that she would be all right.

Jonah ran up the dirt road to Old Meeting Street Road. With little trouble, he found the old white Doctor's house.

He found the doctor's house and pounded on the door until the sleepy doctor opened it.

"What in tarnation is wrong? You 'bout to break the door down, boy. Oh, Jonah, sorry. I didn't recognize you without my glasses. Sukey . . .?"

"No, it ain't Sukey. It some poor woman been raped and beaten. She most dead."

The doctor put his shoes on not bothering to tie them, found his glasses, grabbed his bag. and took off on his horse.

"Come along, on foot. It'll slow me down to ride double. I

know where your house is," he called over his shoulder.

When Jonah got home, Doctor Howard was just finishing his examination.

"She's torn up pretty bad. She needs surgery. Now. She kinfolk?"

"Nawsir," Sukey answered, "she just showed up at our door about dawn."

"I see. You all got a wagon, don't you? We need to get her to the hospital. And quick. Sukey, you did the right thing elevating her bottom and putting ice on her stomach."

"I kin take her to the hospital," Jonah said. "Sukey gots to get to work by a certain hour, but I works for myself."

"Jonah, I can go with you if you want. Doctor, I kin I help. I Reveren Tom."

"Sure can, Reverend. I can use all the help I can get. Let me give her a shot," Dr. Howard said, "this may make the ride more comfortable for her. You have an old quilt, Sukey? It's liable to be pretty soaked with blood time we get her there." Sukey nodded and left, returning presently with four quilts, tattered, but clean.

"I wish I could go, too. But God knows we needs this job. And if I don't show up, or if I come late, they have somebody else by next week."

"Pray God she's still alive, time we get to the hospital. Okay boys," he said, turning to the two colored men, "let's go. Jonah, how about you ride my horse so I can go in the wagon with the patient?" Jonah nodded, and the doctor said, "Good, Tom you drive the wagon. Let's go."

Sukey whispered to the unconscious woman, "You keep the faith. I be prayin' for you."

She watched as they left and waved good-bye from out in the street for as long as she could see them. She went back in shaking her head. That poor woman. That poor woman."

She got ready for work with a troubled heart, not expecting to see the woman alive again.

Ever since she witnessed a slave whipping, the sight of blood terrified Sukey. When they took down from the post, his back hung in quivering ribbons. Blood everywhere. Twelve years old when she witnessed this, she shuddered now, remembering.

Sukey continued to pray for the woman as she got dressed, as she walked the six miles to work, and all through the day.

The surgery repairing her rectum held, but the surgery in her vagina ruptured. The rape was so violent that her vagina tore all the way to the uterus.

Two weeks after the first surgery, Mamie had to be readmitted for the second. Dr. Howard arranged to have her admitted as an indigent for both surgeries.

Jonah and Sukey paid him at a mutually agreed upon, but greatly reduced fee.

About two months after Mamie's surgery, Sukey walked in one morning to begin her routine with Mamie.

"Well, child, you going to talk to me today? Do you know where you are?"

Mamie stared at the woman, and did not answer. She had not talked since coming to their house.

After a long time in the hospital and long weeks recovering at Jonah and Sukey's house, Mamie began to respond a little.

"Let me get you up, you can sit on this little, low stool Jonah done built for you. I make the bed, then you can eat some supper. You done most slept through the day. The doctor commin' to examine you later today. He say you gettin' along good as can be expected. Come on, Sugarplum, up we go."

Mamie smiled at this black, kind woman, and wondered who she was. It seemed like a long time now since she had known anything for sure.

"Who are you?" Mamie asked.

"I Sukey Thomas," she said trying not to show surprize. "What your name?"

"Mamie."

"So you is Mamie," Sukey said as she prepared to move Mamie. "That's a pretty name. Who your folks is? You from around here?"

Just as Sukey picked her up to move her, she cried out.

"Oh Jesus on yo burning cross, save me. Save me! I dying!"

Mamie screamed and didn't stop. Sukey thought she had hurt her.

She laid Mamie right back down on the bed.

"I so sorry. I leaves you right where you is. I don't have to make the bed. Why you still screaming? Oh please child, ain't nobody goin' to hurt you. Stop screamin.' Please?"

Jonah had left earlier to go to an afternoon men's Bible study class at Reverend Tom's house. Sukey prayed waiting for either Jonah or the doctor to come. Mamie still screamed when the doctor came an hour later. Sukey sat by the bed holding her hand. Doctor Howard rushed to the side of the bed.

"What's wrong?" he asked. "Is she bleeding again?"

"She not bleedin' far as I know. She been screamin' like this ever since she wake up. Maybe she remember what happened." Sukey reported all this in a hushed voice as though not wanting to disturb the screaming woman.

Doctor Howard clapped his hands together right in Mamie's face.

"Stop it," he said.

She stopped screaming, and looked at him.

"You the doctor, ain't you?" she asked.

He smiled and nodded.

"How are you feeling? I'm going to examine you, but only if you agree. Do you understand?"

Mamie nodded.

"I need to examine up inside of you. I'm going to put on these gloves, and then feel up inside your vagina and rectum. Sukey will stand right herd, won't you Sukey?"

Sukey nodded.

"Is it all right with you if I examine you now?"

Mamie nodded, but looked scared. Doctor Howard sat on a low stool by the bed and reached for Mamie's other hand.

"Can you tell me your name?"

"Mamie."

"Oh, Mamie, huh?" he asked. "Well, that's a pretty name. Mamie, do you remember what happened to you? Whoever did this to you ought to be shot. And what in God's name happened to your legs?"

He saw that she was becoming agitated.

"And don't," he said, "start screaming again. That won't help."

Mamie rolled her eyes then squeezed them shut. She took

several deep breaths and when she opened her eyes seemed to be in control of herself.

"I not remember good," she said in a barely audible voice. "I alles have trouble remembering. Root Woman say I don't have good memory. Evil mens do. Legs, too. Evil mens. Long time ago, I think."

The doctor patted her hand.

"This," he said, "is recent. It happened a short time ago. You were raped and beaten. You understand?"

Mamie nodded, her large, expressive eyes glued to the doctor's face.

"Your legs getting cut off?" he continued, "a long time ago. I would think ages ago. Twenty years or so, judging by the scars. I'm so sorry you were hurt. Now I'm going to drape this sheet over you, and examine your bottom. Is that okay with you?"

"You won't hurt me?"

"No. I will not hurt you, Mamie. Or, I should say I will *try* not to hurt you. If it starts to hurt, you tell me, and I will stop for a minute. I will be as gentle as I possibly can. Mamie, you are a brave woman. How old are you?"

He asked the question as much to take her mind off the examination as for knowledge.

She squeezed Sukey's hand.

"I don't know how old I is," she said, "but I believes I born in 1866. On the fust day of the year."

The doctor said, "I see. Where did you live before coming here? Do you have folks somewhere? A mama? A daddy? Brothers or sisters? Grandparents? Aunts? Uncles?"

She shook her head no to each question.

"You don't have anybody?" the doctor asked.

"No. Root Woman die."

"Who's 'Root Woman'?"

"She take care of me after. . . ."

Completing his exam, he straightened her clothes and removed the sheet.

"Go on. After what? You *can* remember. *Think.* Take your time."

To Sukey, he said, "She has healed. I didn't feel any

abnormalities. She can begin getting up and about."

"Have you remembered?" he asked, turning back to Mamie. "You said Root Woman took care of you after—what? After you lost your legs?"

Suddenly a torrent of words poured out.

"After the burning cross. After the train. Bad mens on white horses. Evil mens. I don't want to remember. Mama! Mama killed!" She continued, "Take me into swamp—the bad mens did. Root Woman came. She scary, but she a good woman. She took care of me many years."

Mamie shut her mouth and eyes, and moaned.

Doctor's exam hurt, even though he try not to. Don't want to even remember no more hurt!

Tears squeezed out from her tightly closed eyes and rolled down her cheeks.

The doctor placed the back of his hand on her cheek.

"I hope to God," he said as though reading her mind, "nobody ever hurts you again. God knows, you've endured enough. You are going to be well again. I promise. Do you understand? You are with good people here. We're going to help you all we can, but you have to help yourself, too."

He watched her intently, and when she nodded, he continued.

"I want you to start getting up and moving around. Don't lift anything heavy for another month or two. Walk some every day. And eat good, hearty meals. Get some flesh on your bones. Have you had an appetite?"

He realized Mamie didn't understand the last question, and amended it.

"Have you been hungry?"

Mamie opened her eyes. Suddenly she smiled, showing the missing tooth right in front.

"I's hungry now," Mamie said, looking from the doctor to her new friend, Sukey. "Yes, I am. I's hungry as a bear."

Doctor Howard laughed. Sukey laughed and immediately headed for the kitchen.

"That's a sure sign you're on the mend," the doctor said. "Eat hearty. See you in a week."

Sukey fixed her scrambled eggs and toast.

"I so glad to have you feelin' better." Sukey said. "I know it must be hard on you to remember those bad times, but I wants you to know somethin'. That day you come heah, Jonah—after he get you took care of in the hospital—he took off looking for those mens. The ones that done that to you. Lord knows what he was plannin' to do to them."

She sat down across from Mamie, with a worried frown on her face, shaking her head as though she still couldn't believe how badly hurt Mamie had been.

"Anyway," Sukey continued, "he found a wagon with three colored men turned over in the creek up the road aways. All three men had drowned."

Sukey watched Mamie closely as she stopped eating and her mouth dropped open. When she continued to sit mute, fork poised midway between plate and mouth, Sukey continued.

"He found some things that didn't seem to belong to them. This little cloth sack of money. These clothes. A clay pipe with strange carvings on it. These yourn?"

Mamie took the pipe, the clothes, and the bag of money. The money was even more than she had when she left the swamp. She began to cry, shaking her head over the pipe, remembering Saylee. She stopped crying and started laughing.

"I put a hex on them. I know Voodoo. Oh Sukey! I so happy. I really did the hex as I lay there in the road I seen the water come up and drown dem three mens. I learned Voodoo from Root Woman."

"Hush yo mouth, Child." Sukey scolded. "No Voodoo. Not in my house. Voodoo is bad. Tell me you don't know ,Voodoo."

Mamie smiled at Sukey. "Voodoo not bad. It *can* be evil. Or it can be used for good. I learned Voodoo from Root Woman. Ma-Saylee. She raised me after the burning cross. She a good woman, a healer. She say Voodoo from Africa. She say it our old religion! Dat's what she say. Say we should never give it up for the white man's religion."

"Well, I alles been scared of that stuff. I goes to the Baptist church myself. When you gets well enough, you can come, too, if you want. You knows our preacher. You remember him?"

Mamie nodded and continued eating.

"Did you," Sukey asked after a while, "really cause those mens to die?"

Mamie nodded.

"I guess I did it," she said, "I seen water rise up over them. To me it seem like the swamp swallow them three mens. I sho Lawd, did. But, I won't put no more hexes on nobody. 'Specially not in this house. You and Jonah is good folks."

Sukey patted her hand.

"Honey, don't you go puzzling on no Voodoo. Jes get well."

Mamie nodded her head. Sukey never saw the secret smile that flitted across Mamie's averted face.

Chapter 11

Charleston at Last

On the corner at Wentworth and King
She stood. Day after day, a thing
Old beyond reason, ugly and mean
She ruled her corner, a dwarf Queen
Mamie commandeered a spot on the street
Strange old woman, she had to compete

In Sukey, Mamie had found another mother. Sukey took care of her as though Mamie were one of her lost children. But, now that Mamie was better, the old spirit of contrary stubbornness cropped up in her. With Root Woman's death, faint stirrings of independence began to grow in Mamie.

Ever since she had discovered the ten dollar bill rolled up in Saylee's old pipe, she had been thinking about ways she could make money. As the bus rolled along, her mind was busy making plans. The pencil factory, located on Old Meeting Street Road, Mamie had discovered by accident.

She and Sukey had missed their regular stop on the bus because they were talking. They got off the bus right by the pencil factory.

The place seemed to draw Mamie. She insisted on going into the front office. She smiled now as she remembered Abraham and their conversation.

The colored man, sitting at an old work bench, piled high with paperwork and pencils, told her that she could buy pencils directly from the factory.

"Only ting, is, you hasta buy 'em by the gross. Does you know what a gross is?" he asked, smiling at Mamie.

"Nawsuh", she answered, "I can't say I does? How much a gross cost me? And how many is a gross anyway?"

"One dollar and twenty cents is what it costs. And a gross is a dozen dozen!" he said, solemnly.

"What is a dozen? Oh, I know. It twelve, ain't it? So, a gross is twelve times twelve? That a lot of pencils. And a lot of money, too. I'll think about this here thing and let you know. You here all the time?"

"Yep," he said, "been here every day since slavery ended. Name's Abraham. And your's?"

One day as Mamie accompanied Sukey on a shopping trip, the bus pulled to a stop and Sukey lifted Mamie and carried her onto the bus. Mamie stood next to Sukey's knees at the back of the bus, fuming. Sukey sat with her hands folded in her lap.

They got off the bus at Wentworth and Meeting Streets. Sukey again carried Mamie. This time, Mamie let out a yell.

"Girl, what wrong wid you? You make me embarrass to be near you when you act so," Sukey chided. "Please try to be nice. I ain't hurt you."

"Maybe I want to walk. Don't be always helpin' me," Mamie fussed. "Only if I ask you for help. Please?"

A sharp rebuke was on the tip of Sukey's tongue, but she noticed that Mamie's eyes were bright with unshed tears.

"Mamie, honey, don't cry. I know you wants to be independent. But it quicker to carry you on and off the bus. Don't you see?" she said, patting Mamie on the head.

Mamie jerked away, muttering under her breath. They crossed Meeting Street. Blacks and whites bustled about. The two of them ambled down Wentworth Street. A horse and wagon rumbled along the street as the driver, an old jet black man clicked to the horse and sang a *rag song*. People came out and placed boxes and bags at the curb which he picked up.

"What he singing?" asked Mamie.

"He saying 'Gimme yo rags. I come fo rags. Git yo rags picked. All sech as that," said Sukey.

"What he do with old rags?"

"Ain't just rags, Girl. It's old clothes and junk. He a junkman. He pick through the stuff and use what he can. I guess he throw the rest away. They's a old saying, 'she so poor, she take the leavings of de rag picker!' Now, that is some kind of poor." Sukey said.

She laughed and Mamie chuckled, too. A soft breeze cooled their faces and they smiled at each other, breathing in the scent of wisteria from the gardens behind the wrought iron fences along Wentworth Street.

Arriving at the curb at Wentworth and King Streets, Sukey took Mamie's hand. Mamie pulled her hand back and bolted across King Street. The ragman was just turning his tired old horse to head up King Street.

"Whoa. Whoa, there." he shouted, barely missing Mamie. He shook his head and scowled, first at Mamie, then at Sukey who raced to catch her.

"Is you crazy? You most got run over by that ole rag picker! Come along Mamie, we go in here to Kress Five and Ten Cent store. I guess I gonna buy you some ribbons for your hair. Less you don't want none. You so ornery, today."

"Red ones?" asked Mamie.

"Any color you like."

Sukey marched in. She looked down for Mamie. No Mamie. Sukey ran to the entrance of the store. There stood Mamie just outside, talking with a young black man. The youth, about seventeen years old, was twisted like a pretzel. He sold flypaper and shoelaces from a stand. Sukey listened as Mamie asked one question after another. He grunted his one-word answers, looking over his shoulder at Mamie.

Mamie saw her friend and joined her without a word to the twisted young man.

"Why you asking that man so many questions 'bout his begging? I wish you—"

"He ain't no beggar. And he ain't no man. He jes a boy. He sells things from his little stand. He say he make good money selling shoelaces and flypaper. Flypaper? I ain't know what that is. You?"

"It little strips of sticky paper," said Sukey, "to catch flies. Not changing the subject, but I want you to go to church with me tomorrow. You know, since Jonah died last year, I ain't been goin' to church as regular as I ought. I'm turning over a new leaf. As of tomorrow, I'm going every Sunday. That's a fact."

As she and Mamie walked into the colorful five and dime, Sukey thought of Johna. .

"Sukey, did you hear me? I say, I kin start sellin' my pencils—"

Sukey swiped at a tear. A clerk looked at the two women, but did not ask if she could help them.

"What the matter?" Mamie asked.

"Oh, nothing. Johna. Thas all. I's all right. What you say 'bout selling pencils?"

I say," Mamie replied, "I can sell pencils here on King Street right by Kress. I done found that pencil factory up Meeting Street where—"

"You going to buy something, or stand there talking all day?" the sales clerk asked.

Sukey and Mamie, keeping their eyes downcast, moved on to another spot in the store.

"I kin buy a dozen for a dime. 'Walkin' Stick' say it easy to get people to buy from a street person sellin' stuff. I gonna get started Monday. I gotta get me a stand—"

"Mamie, I ain't want to hear that right now."

They walked back to the ribbon counter, purchased ribbons and left the store. On the bus, Sukey sat on the back seat as usual. Mamie stood by her knees. As the bus rolled along, she thought about the idea of Mamie starting up a business.

"Mamie, with Jonah passed on, I ain't got nobody but you," Sukey said. "You is family to me. You don't know nobody in Charleston," she whispered. "Somethin' might happen to you. I ain't gonna let you do no sech thing.."

Mamie shook her head.

"I ain't a child. You can't always be bossing me. I still come to see you. You don't need to be workin' so hard, supporting both you and me. You getting old now. Maybe one day I help you. You can live with me when you gets too old to work, and I work for the both of us."

Sukey smiled at Mamie. She patted her head. Mamie jerked away, but remained silent.

"I 'preciate you wantin' to take care of me, but I don't think you can. You always got a home with me. Now, let's us just forget all about this nonsense."

Mamie nodded absently.

Sukey sat frowning at Mamie. Mamie, oblivious to Sukey's foul mood, continued thinking about making money selling pencils. Before their stop, Sukey broke her silence.

"What you sittin' there grinning at? You plottin' something, I know." Sukey snapped.

"What wrong wid you, Sukey? You must think I really am one of your lost chil'ren. Well, I a grown woman."

"Ain't nothing wrong wid me. What you was grinnin' about back there on the bus?" Sukey asked after they got off the bus.

"I was grinnin'," Mamie said, "'cause I been thinkin' about how I can buy me some pencils and make us some money. Come on. Don't be so mad. Please?"

Mamie held her peace all that week, but continued to plan out her strategy. On Monday morning of the following week, Mamie bought a gross of pencils. She sneaked out of the house while Sukey worked, walked to the pencil factory and made her purchase.

"Thank you, Mistuh Abraham."

"Just Abraham," he said, "and you welcome."

In July, a little over three years after coming to live with Sukey, Mamie moved to Charleston.

"Ain't no sense you moving out. You could live here wid me," Sukey said as she packed Mamie's things. Mamie said nothing.

Sukey cried as she packed the low stool Jonah had made for Mamie. Sukey rubbed the plain oak wood of the steps he had made so that Mamie could eat at the table with them. Now Sukey cried as she pulled Mamie's mattress into the front room.

"Don't cry, Sukey. I love you. I will visit," Mamie said.

Wiping tears, Sukey did not answer. She silently bundled up

kitchen utensils: pots and pans, dishes, an old blue-enameled cup, a tarnished silver cup that belonged to Mamie, and groceries.

At ten o'clock, Reverend Tom knocked. Sukey let him in.

"You all ready?" he asked.

"I guess we ready as we'll ever be," Sukey said as she swiped at a tear. "I sho hate to see my baby go. No tellin' what—"

"Now, now," Reverend Tom said, "she will be just fine. We'll look in on her from time to time. She'll be just fine," he repeated as if to reassure himself.

He helped Mamie get her things onto the wagon. When they had loaded everything, Mamie held up her arms to Sukey to be lifted onto the wagon.

"Here, let me do that."

He placed Mamie in the back of the wagon. Sukey sang an old spiritual. "Nobody knows the trouble I've seen. Nobody knows, but Je-sus." Tears ran unheeded and she didn't wipe them away.

Gone jes like my babies who was sold away during slavery times.

Reverend Tom patted Sukey's shoulder, then helped her up, too. Sukey and Mamie rode in the back with Mamie's belongings. Mamie scooted over and sat as close to Sukey as she could. Sukey hugged her.

At the house on Cedar Street that She had found advertised in the News and Courier, she learned that rent at one dollar a month needed to be paid in advance. Mamie peeled off a dollar bill and handed it to her landlord. Reverend Tom vouched for the gas and electric, and for the rent, too.

After getting Mamie settled, Reverend Tom and Sukey took their leave. It was a long painful leave taking. Mamie ran over to Sukey, threw her arms around the woman and hugged her.

"Don't you cry none. I'll be just fine." Mamie sounded, in that instant, so much like the Reverend Tom that all three of them laughed.

"Hold out your hand, Mamie," Sukey said, "here a little bit more money. Keep your money hidden. Don't tell nobody where you hide it. Don't trust nobody less you know 'em real good. You hear? Lock your door at night. All the time, in fact. Watch out for street cars. And horses and carriages — oh Mamie. How I gonna' get by without you? I miss you already, Sugarplum. Take care of your sweet self."

With that, Sukey almost ran from the house on Cedar Street.

Reverend Tom wrote his telephone number down on a calendar which he hung in the little kitchen area.

"If you ever need anything, you call this number, or get somebody to call it for you. You understand?"

Mamie nodded, and a tear slipped down her face. She hugged his knees. He knelt down on the floor and hugged her.

"Mamie, please be careful. Sukey is right. It might be dangerous for you living all alone."

"I'll be careful. Real careful. I'll call you even if I am not in trouble."

"Oh, certainly. Call from time to time. We'd love to hear from you. Mrs. Ashley has grown fond of you, too. So have our three boys. And Sukey would love to hear from you." He wrote the name of their street where he and his family lived, then he read it off to her, "Rosemount Road." Take the street-car marked "Old Meeting Street Road." He wrote that down, too.

I done lived right across the street from you'uns for three years. He must think I dumb, or something.

"I try to remember all you'uns done tell me," she said, trying not to smile. "I'll be careful. And I will come to visit—umm, maybe sometime anyway," she added. She smiled her rare smile, showing the missing tooth.

Sukey sat in the seat of the wagon with her head bowed and her eyes closed, her arms folded across her stomach. When she looked up, she smiled.

"I think Mamie will be okay. We'll see her from time to time. Not like she done gone for good," Sukey said.

He nodded and clucked to the horse.

As they traveled down the street, Sukey lapsed into a deep reverie. Tears again coursed down her cheeks. Staring straight ahead at the rump of the horse, she began to sing the same spiritual.

This the same old, faithful animal that was with Jonah when he was killed. Ah me, Jonah, I miss you. And I gonna miss my Mamie.

On Monday morning, a humid breeze blew the smell of magnolia blossoms toward her. Under the star-studded sky, Mamie walked, setting off for her spot on King Street. She traveled the seventeen blocks in the predawn dark. She took her stool, the pencils she had bought, a bologna sandwich, a coca cola, a cigar box, and the small silver cup all carefully packed in a tote slung over her shoulders. She arrived at daybreak.

Maybe I can't be no pencil seller. I might not be able to make change. I charge 'em a nickel for a pencil. If I sells ten pencils, I make fifty cents. I sell twenty pencils, I make a whole dollar. I guess I got out here way too early. Uh-oh, here come trouble!

"This the spot I alles has, Missus," said a young man as he came sidling up to her.

Mamie grabbed her cane and threatened him with it, waving it around her head with her face contorted in what she hoped was a fierce look. She took a step toward him and he backed away, grinning at her.

He was the young man who sold flypaper strips, matches, and shoelaces.

"You the one," he said, "was askin' me all dem questions one day, ain't you?" When Mamie didn't answer, he said, "Well, my name 'Walkin Stick'. I can go cross on the other side of King Street if you feel thataways. 'Scuse me. I goin' now."

She lowered her stick and nodded that she had understood him.

"Humph," she said to no one in particular, "It easier than I thought! Ain't taking nothing off nobody, no more. No, uh-uh!" She smiled. "Come on out now. Put money in Mamie's cup."

She looked up and down the street. Not a soul. It was only eight o'clock.

Shortly after nine o'clock that first morning, Mamie felt the urge to relieve herself. What to do? She simply looked straight ahead and let it go. She wore dresses that reached the ground and no underpants, so it didn't matter so much. She figured nobody would notice. She stood near the curb so the stream was not so noticeable.

I ain't plan ahead for this 'mergency situation! Uhn-huh! Deah you goes. Ain't nobody seen a thing.

As the day wore on, Mamie scrutinized every countenance, looking for a familiar face. She saw no one she knew.

Later that day, 'Walking Stick' came back across the street.

"Scuse me, please," Walking Stick said with big grin a spread across his face. "Why you so sot on this here spot? It been my place for a year now. If you don't mind tellin' me, that is. Does you want to be friends?"

"I has to be here by this store," Mamie said. I don't know why!

Because it here in front of Kress is why, I think. That spot across the street just as good as this'un. You go on back over there, now, and leave me be," Mamie said. "Please." she added.

She brushed a tear from her eye and rocked from one stump to the other in her nervousness.

"Okay, I guess," Walking Stick said. "You older than me, so I reckon I kin let you have this side of the street. Don't cry. I ain't gonna hurt you. You ain't say. Do you?"

"Do I what?" Mamie asked.

"Do you want to be friends?" he asked.

"Maybe," Mamie said, "but don't ask me to go to the other side of the street. I likes this side. Okay?"

"Okay." He stuck out his hand.

Mamie startled and he jerked backward, too. They laughed, and Mamie shook his hand. He ambled in his jerk-step-twist gait across the street.

Mamie, over the next few days would learn to sleep until eight, getting downtown by about nine or ten in the mornings. And so began fifty-two years of work for Mamie on King Street in Charleston. At the end of the day, she had sold two pencils and had collected a dollar and fifteen cents.

Most of the people don't even take a pencil. Well, I am selling pencils, if they don't want one, that ain't my problem. Pretty good way to make a livin' if you ask me!

People looked at her shoes turned backwards. They looked to see if maybe she was sitting on her legs and feet. A few asked her how she had lost her legs. She mumbled unintelligible words and phrases at them so that they would leave her alone, but she smiled at them so they would buy her pencils.

From her first day on the job, Mamie hit upon a tactic that would serve her well. Her weird behavior protected Mamie. The garbled, mumbled speech, mostly an act, caused people to put a nickel or a dime into her cup and quickly move on.

By Friday of that week, she had made three dollars and seventy five cents, and had established herself as 'that crazy old woman with no legs who walks with shoes turned backward'. Easily the most bizarre character sedate old Charleston ever saw.

Later that month, two women who worked for white families down on South Battery sat visiting, while their charges played in the grass on the strip known as White Point Gardens. Already the town buzzed with speculation as to who the newcomer could be.

"Who dat woman is wid no legs?" Tildy asked her friend. "I seed she on King Street when I done push the baby carriage downtown on my way to get missus some of that candy from the five and ten cent store. She sho act crazy! Growl at me and mumble somethin'. Shake she stick at me, too!"

"You know 'Chalk'? That nigger with the chalk white face and the red eyes 'n yallow hair? He done tol me he talk with she," Martha said, rolling her eyes. "She lost her legs long time ago out in the middle of the swamp. He say she didn't know 'xactly how she done lose 'em, but she babble about the burning cross of Jedus! That sound like the Klan to me. Po ole thing. How old you reckon she be?"

"Well, 'po ole thing' or not, she better watch she mouf! I give she the back of my hand she mess wid me!" Tildy answered. She pulled out a corn-cob pipe and lit it, inhaling deeply. She was thin and coughed as she smoked.

"Best give she a wide path. I hear she know Voodoo. Somebody done knowed some of she folks up near Kingstree," Martha said, laughing. "She ain't be like us Sea Island niggers. This here person say she live way out in the middle of the swamp with a witch woman. A conjure woman!"

Mamie tried to ride the streetcar, but she couldn't get her leg high enough for the steps, and she wouldn't let the streetcar driver help her. After fifteen minutes of struggle and an almost constant stream of strange mumbling and cursing, Mamie gave up and walked home. She was in a foul mood by the time she turned the corner of Cedar Street.

A group of little children ran up to her to ask her questions. They were dancing and running around. She cursed at them and waved her stick around in the air. They scattered. Parents watched from windows. A woman walked out into the street, introduced herself, and welcomed Mamie into the neighborhood. Mamie stopped, looked closely at the woman who had bent over in a deep bow in order to be on eye level with her. Mamie stuck out her hand.

"I glad," Mamie said, "to meet you. My name is Mamie."

The tall woman with a gold tooth in the front of her mouth, smiled, and stayed on eye level with Mamie.

"Well, Mamie, I live right across the street from you. I saw you moving in the other day. My husband and me been living here on Cedar Street for twenty-two years. Those your people helped you?"

"No, that was Reverend Tom and Sukey. They my friends. I has no family. What you say your name is?"

"Belle. Belle Washington. Belle is short for Isabelle. My husband's name is George. He's the colored barber. He cuts hair in our back room. He can do your hair, too."

"For how much?"

"Your first haircut," Belle grinned, "will be free. After that, I think he will charge you a dime. You can ask him when you get your free cut. I tell fortunes."

"How you do that? Are you a root woman?"

"No. I don't do root medicine. That can be dangerous if you don't know what you is doin.' I read tarot cards. You want me to tell your fortune?"

"How much you charge?"

"First reading is free. Then a quarter a reading."

"Well, I will see," Mamie said. "I be thinking 'bout doin' that. I got to go on home now." She walked away.

She seem friendly. Maybe too friendly

Mamie never did get her hair cut, nor her fortune read.

I wonder if that woman with the gold tooth is colored. She light skinned and wear a turban around her head. Big gold hoops in her ears. Alles barefooted and bright blouses and full skirts. I sees her peekin' at me from behind she window curtain.

A week later, the gypsy family packed up their colorful wagon and slipped out in the middle of the night. The neighbors learned the truth about the clever pair. Every house they had been in had money or something of value stolen. No one knew they were leaving or where they went. In less than ten days, they moved in, robbed almost everyone on the street, and slipped away.

Sukey came to see Mamie often. Sometimes she came by streetcar, sometimes with Reverend Tom in the wagon. The three of them were sitting at Mamie's kitchen table shortly after the gypsy family left.

"By the time them people gone from this street, they was seven different families got robbed by them, but not me! Dey moved in the day before I did. She done tell me she been livin' heah twenty-two years." Mamie grinned. "I didn't know they was gypsies. I jes knew that woman seem too friendly. They robbed the people who did business with them. If you got a haircut, she sneaked out to your house. If you got a fortune told, he did the thievin.' That a right smart plan, huh?" Mamie laughed out loud.

Seeing the looks on Sukey's and Reverend Tom's faces, she quickly added, "Not that it right. Stealin' wrong. I know that. But it a smart way to steal. And they children; lawd, they had a bunch of little ones running around. And alles dirty."

"I'm glad," Sukey said, shaking her head, "you had the good sense not to fall for their scheme."

"Besides," chimed in Reverend Tom, "Christians don't go in for fortune telling. I'm proud of you. So! A month and a half in Charleston. How does it feel to be out on your own?"

"I miss everybody, but I doin' all right. It gets real lonesome. I needs me a best friend. 'Walking Stick' is nice, but he too young. I needs a boyfriend." She said this with a straight face. There was a moment of stunned silence, then Sukey spoke up.

"Yes. You probably is lonely. But you be extra careful. Maybe a lady friend be better than a boyfriend." Mamie didn't argue. "Honey, we gots to get on back. Thank you for the tea. Come see us when you can."

Early one morning, about a year later, in pouring rain, 'Walking Stick' came over to where Mamie huddled under the overhang on Kress Five And Ten Cent store. He dragged a fat young man behind him.

"Mamie," Walking Stick said, "this here is Dorothy. Dorothy don't talk much."

The man grinned at Mamie, but said nothing. Mamie looked him over.

He look like he must be a little addled in the head.

His mouth hung open slightly when he finally stopped grinning and he had a blank expression.

"What wrong with you?" Mamie asked.

"Nothing wrong with me. What happen to your legs?"

Mamie made a cutting motion with her arm.

"Cut off," she said, "that's what."

Mamie turned her attention back to her pencil stand that she was trying to set up out of the rain. When she looked up again, 'Walking Stick' had left, but Dorothy still stood in the rain.

"Boy, get on outta here. Go on. Scram."

He stood his ground. She picked up her stick and waved it at him. He backed away with a puzzled look on his face, turned, and walked down the street. From that day on, he stopped by her stand every now and then for a minute or two. Sometimes they talked. Sometimes not. Mostly he just stood there for a little while and left without saying anything. She met his mother, an obese domineering woman. They disliked each other from the instant they met. As the months passed, Sukey tried to discourage Mamie's involvement with Dorothy. Sukey had met Dorothy months earlier at Mamie's stand on King Street. Dorothy came up and just stood around like he always did. Sukey leaned over.

"Who," she asked, "that big, fat fellow? What he want? He grinning at you to beat the band."

"Oh, that just Dorothy," Mamie said. "He alles does that. Dorothy, come on over here. This here's my friend, Sukey. Sukey this here's Dorothy. Say 'Hello' Dorothy."

Dorothy stretched out his hand. "Hello, Miz Sukey."

Polite, but touched in the head. Why he hanging around Mamie? I hasta warn her.

She stuck out her hand.

He hand limp like a dishrag!

"Your name is Dorothy?" Sukey asked, "that a woman's name, ain't it? You is a man, ain't you?"

"Well, yes. My name Dorrance. People just calls me Dorothy to make fun of me, I guess. I don't care what they calls me."

"You keeping company with' this boy?" Sukey asked when he left. "He a boyfriend?"

"Maybe so, maybe not," Mamie said. "Why? You doesn't like him, uhn? He all right. He just simple-minded. He is jes a friend."

"Mamie, he might hurt you."

"Naw, he won't hurt me. Everybody need a friend."

"Well, be careful who your friends are. Darlin.' I see you on Sunday?

You can come on out to the house on Saturday night if you wants."

"We'll see," Mamie said. "I might just do that. Now don't you worry none 'bout me. I doin' all right on my own. I loves you, Sukey."

After years of friendship, Dorothy came strolling down King Street one day with the biggest armful of roses Mamie had ever seen.

"These for you," he said.

She ignored him because there were people all around.

"These for you!" he said a little louder.

She grabbed his hand, pulling him off to one side.

"Take these roses," she hissed, "to 33 Cedar Street. Here my key. Put them in water and come on back here with my key. Don't you go bothering any of my stuff, either. You hear me?"

In about an hour he was back, grinning from ear to ear.

"I did it. I put them in a pot of water. I found the pot there by your stove and put them in the water. Here your key, too."

"Did you lock my door?"

"Yes Mam."

"Good. That good. You done good. Why you bring me flowers?"

"Because you is my woman. I loves you."

Mamie's mouth fell open. She stood there ready to laugh, but she didn't.

"I reckon you does, uhn? Well, I loves you, too. You knows I is as old as your mama?"

"Naw, you ain't that old. It don't matter if you is. I loves you anyway.

In the summer of 1911, Mamie stood in the hot noon-day sun, fanning her face with a church fan. She glimpsed an automobile.

That the boy who own that store back home.

She took a couple of running steps down King Street, then stopped.

What I thinkin'? He probably don't even remember me. What his name? Isaiah? Mr. Ike? Yeah, Isaiah.

At forty-five years old, Mamie looked fifty-five or sixty. She lived with a young man barely twenty-four years old. Dorothy had moved in with Mamie three years after they had first met. He just showed up at her door one day with a sack of clothes. He wouldn't say what had happened, but she learned that he and his mother had gotten into an argument about her and his mama had kicked him out. She thought back now to the conversation they had shortly after he moved into her house.

"Dorothy, why your mama doesn't like me? 'Course I doesn't like her either, but what her reason?"

"She say you old and ugly. That's why she don't like you. And because you a beggar. She say you a beggar."

"I ain't no beggar! I put a hex on that woman, she ain't careful. I would, too, 'cept she your mama, and I guess you loves her. She the mean, ugly one! She fatter than you, Dorothy. Her ass shake all over the place when she walk."

"Yeah, Baby, but you ain't got no ass to shake. You is purty, you ain't ugly. Come here let me give you a kiss."

That night, Mamie sat down by Dorothy and he kissed her and told her he loved her. They sat drinking beer and listening to a new radio they had just gotten.

"You know what?" Mamie asked. "I like your being fat, but I doesn't think it look as good on your mama. When you hold me close like this, I feels — I feels good! Like nothing bad is goin' to happen to me."

He, as fat as she was thin, hugged her close. His hair, a reddish, brown, complemented his sprinkling of freckles across his broad light-toned face. He grinned down at the little woman in his arms.

"I take good care of you, my Mamie. You my woman."

"I saw somebody the other day that I used to know. He own a store in Brio. You know where that is?"

"Naw, I ain't know. Where?" he asked as he took another swig of beer. "I likes the taste of this stuff."

He had never tasted beer before and neither had Mamie. They had bought their first quart at the liquor store on the way home.

"I does too. It taste bitter, but I likes it. This man I saw the other day is named Isaiah. That's a name from the Bible. He white. He used to come see Root Woman and me."

"Who Root Woman is?"

"Aw, Dorothy, you don't remember nothing I tells you? She dead. We lived way out in the swamp. She was my friend. She was real old. She died, and I came to Charleston. I told you about her."

"Oh, yes," Dorothy said. "I remember you said she do Voodoo spells and they was snakes and alligators out there in the swamp. She musta been scary. Wasn't you scared of her?"

Mamie got up and walked over to the door. She stood in the open door and looked up into the night sky.

"Naw, I wasn't scared of her. She was my friend."

"I your friend now. And Sukey is your friend." Dorothy had followed her to the door and stood with his hands on Mamie's shoulders. He felt her shiver.

"Is you cold?" he asked, turning her head a little so he could see her face. "Mamie, you is crying? What can I do to make you feel all better? Please don't cry. Don't cry."

Mamie said nothing. She stared out the door. Tears continued to stream down her cheeks.

She was the best friend a body could have. She was old. It was time. But oh, how I miss Root Woman. Wonder kin she see and hear me? Wonder if she is wid her mama and papa now? I hope she is in a good place with lots of swamp all around her. She told me one time, 'Mamie, I couldn't live anywhere, but way out heah in the middle of the swamp.' So, I hopes you is in the middle of a swamp somewhere.

"Yeah, Dorothy, you and Sukey my friends now. You's good friends, too. You is my sweet man, eh?"

"See, I done make you all better. I loves you, Mamie. You my sweet woman, too. Yes, you is. Does you love me?"

They were silent for a long time looking out the door. Not answering him, she shut the door, turned, and went to bed.

Chapter 12

A Gift From the Past

Dambala still coiled around the pole
Painted with plant dye, now faded, old
A snake and a rattle from long ago
Left from the past, a relic, you know
Under the house all mottled with mold
A gift from the past for Mamie to hold

"*Sure you won't go? It's an easy trip,*" *Isaiah said.*

Ida shook her head and murmured about 'her condition and pressing chores'. Married a year last month, she awaited the birth of their first child in March.

Well, she is probably a tad self conscious about the pregnancy. Not like she's in her twenties, or even thirties. Forty years old. And me? I'm pushing fifty! Who would have thought? At our age!

Isaiah grinned. His new Cadillac bumped over the ruts on the dirt road to Monks Corner. The sun sparkled. He turned onto the newly graveled road. The trees on both sides of the road were the wisteria's own trellises. This section of road got a write up in the Charleston News and Courier last spring as, 'the prettiest stretch of road anywhere hereabouts'. He smiled remembering driving with Ida to see the pretty wisteria last April.

First and only time Ida has ridden in the new Cadillac. Pa doesn't think much of it either. Oh well!

Gotta find that woman I spotted on King Street. My last trip to Charleston was just before I married Ida. I've got a perfect day for the drive. Shame Ida didn't want to come.

The gravel road gave way to a paved street. *He drove* on into the city of Charleston, and parked the car at King and Calhoun Streets in front of the Francis Marion Hotel. Walking down King Street toward South Battery, he passed the usual assortment of Saturday shoppers.

I saw that old woman somewhere on King Street.

As he approached Wentworth, he saw a few people gathered around the same old woman he'd seen on his previous trip.

Yep, that's the same woman I saw before*! But is that Mamie? Has to be! She's mumbling something. What's she doing?*

Isaiah moved closer to see and hear better. The old woman mumbled and waved her cane. She screwed up her face and started up an unintelligible sing-song dirge.

That is Mamie. She must be crazy.

He edged closer to see if he could make out what she was saying, or singing.

"Lee-me lone, eny? Gie on down the road! Go on now. Eny?"

She waved the cane around. She scrunched her face up in a fierce scowl. She looked at no one in particular. Isaiah watched for fifteen minutes or so.

Well, I'll be hog-swaggled! It's an act! By George, I'm glad to find her.

Isaiah slapped his thigh and his laugh mingled with the voices of the people all around him. Mamie looked in his direction, but went right back to her routine. He waited, and when the knot of people dispersed, he walked up to where she stood.

"Hello, Mamie." he boomed. "Do you remember me?" he asked, bending low.

Mamie drew back with a startled look, and waved her cane in his direction. He saw no spark of recognition. He tried again.

"Mamie, I'm Isaiah Norris. Root Woman and you used to come into my store in Brio. Don't you remember? I used to come to see you at Root Woman's house in the swamp."

No response.

He continued, "Saylee's house? You know me, don't you?"

"You the good boy? The one wid the store?"

"Yes, you know me!" Isaiah laughed at the old
term Mamie had used so many years ago.

"I am the good boy." He grabbed Mamie's hand.

She jerked her hand away and jumped back. He apologized for frightening her.

"You bring Mamie ham?" she asked from the far side of her stand.

His laugh bounced off the buildings on King Street.

"Well, well, you *do* remember me. Yes, I used to bring you ham. How you been? It's good to find you again. Where do you live? Can you leave work now and show me?"

"No, not a good time to visit. I go home when the day is over. People still on the street. Gotta make the good money. You go and come back when it starting to get dark. We'll drink some beer. I'll show you my house. I is glad to see you, too."

Isaiah left. He didn't know what he was to do for three hours, but he strolled down the street toward South Battery. The stately old buildings, housing the commercial establishment of Charleston, fronted either side of King Street. For a few blocks, he looked into store windows. He stopped at Berlin's Men's Store to buy some handkerchiefs. Leaving the store, he spotted a vendor selling hot, spicy, soft-shell crabs in little brown paper bags.

"How many crabs in a bag and how much you asking for 'em?" he asked. The man stopped his push cart, squinted at Isaiah as though figuring how much he would be willing to pay.

"Two tasty crabs for a quarter. For fifty cent, I throw in some tatters, and a Co-Cola, too!" He said.

"Tell you what, gimme' two bags of crabs, one of those biscuits, and a Coke for a dollar bill! You keep the change. How's that?" Isaiah asked.

"I kin do that, Gov'ner! You jest bought yoself the best soft shells in Charleston. From Crab-Man. Thankee kindly."

Isaiah bit into the warm crab, took a swig of his drink, and a bite of biscuit. He finished the lunch, and wiped his mouth with one of the brown paper bags. He stuffed the two crumpled bags, along with the empty, green, coke bottle into his pocket, and continued on his way.

Another block and he in the residential section, walking past wroght iron fences enclosing gardens bare of the daffodils and tulips, the irises and peonies that would perfume the air in a few more months.

Roses bloomed in gardens almost as old as the city. Winter roses with names like Aunt Caroline's Prize, or Southern Lady. Trees and shrubs showed the pale grayish-green hint of buds yet to open.

Now he saw the sparkling sea straight ahead, waves chopping from the wind. The water sparkled, and sea gulls circled just off the battery. Ships in the harbor sailed placidly. Sun played on the water and there was not a cloud in the azure sky.

He walked around High Battery from King Street to East Bay Street, drawing in deep breaths of the salty air.

Cold February wind whipped his beard and hair. He wished he had worn a hat. Coming back, Isaiah took a different route. He went down Meeting Street. He stopped at a stall on the corner of Broad and Meeting Streets.

"How much for this basket? You make it?" Isaiah asked an old woman sitting with her back propped against the courthouse wall.

"Yassa, shore did." Her skin gleamed black as ebony in the late afternoon sun. "It a sea-grass basket. Been makin' dese baskets since slavery ended. It a dollar."

"How much for this big one, too?" he asked.

"You gonna buy two? I make you a good price. Two baskets fo two dollars and fifty cent. De big'un cost two all be e'self, but I gie you a deal." She cackled

He bought the two baskets for Ida and sauntered away with the old basket woman still laughing.

He toured the old market place, but bought nothing. He crossed over to King Street by way of George Street.

Hhe still had an hour and a half to kill, he walked to his car, and drove to the Cadillac dealership on East Bay Street.

"You're driving a brand new Cadillac," a salesman said, "you thinking of trading it in for a different model?" He stuck out his hand and said, "Oh, by the way, name's Bob. Bob Lambert."

"Isaiah Norris. No, I have the Cadillac dealership in Brio up near Kingstree. In Williamsburg county, you know the area?"

"Oh yeah, up past Monks Corner? So you're just on a busman's holiday, huh? See how the Cadillac people do it here in Charleston?"

They talked shop for a while and then Bob introduced Isaiah to the owner. Isaiah got a couple of promotion ideas from him. They exchanged addresses and telephone numbers with a promise from the Charleston owner to visit.

He drove over to King Street and stopped at the curb. Mamie was just starting to pack up. She allowed him to help her into his car.

"I ain't never been in a car before. When did you get such a fancy car? This yourn?"

"Yes, it's mine. I own the Cadillac dealership in Brio."

"You don't own the store no more?"

"I've sold seventeen of these, not counting mine, but I still have the store, too."

Mamie rubbed her hand over the seat. "This is a pretty color. Blue my favorite color, 'cause it the color of the sky on a pretty day. I miss Root Woman. You know she die?"

Isaiah nodded.

"Yes, I found her remains. Years after she died."

"What you mean? What *remains* is?"

"I found her skeleton. Her bones. A sad day. I hunted for you. Didn't know if you —"

"No, I didn't die. The day she die, I cried and held her head. She real old, and ready to die."

They pulled up in front of Mamie's house.

"Mamie, how did you get here? How did you come to Charleston?" Isaiah asked.

"Bad mens rape me." Mamie looked away. She stared out the window of the car so long, Isaiah cleared his throat to speak, but she continued in a barely audible whisper. "I commin' outta de swamp, and sit down to rest. I fall asleep. Three colored mens come by in a old wagon." Her voice caught. "They most killed me!" She brushed away a tear.

Isaiah looked at Mamie, sitting there on the front seat of his car. Memories rushed in of Mamie in years past. It had been so long since he had seen her. She looked so different.

"Mamie, I am so sorry. Your life has been so hard for you, hasn't it?"

Mamie looked at Isaiah and shook her head.

"My life been—strange, but, not all bad. I wish I had my legs, but . . . I has lived a—a powerful lot. I put a hex on them mens and they drowned in a creek not more'n three miles from where they left me off." She stared out the window and then turned to Isaiah.

"My friend, Sukey, said her man, Jonah, found them dead. Sukey and Jonah helped me. They took care of me afterwards," Mamie's voice was sad. "See, I went to the first house I come to and it was Sukey and Jonah's house. Jonah found them mens' wagon turned over in the creek," Mamie slowly shook her head back and forth as though she could hardly believe it. "As they was driving away," she finished in a rush, "I saw flood waters. I thought it jes a picture pop in my mind from the swamp, but it was they death. You see? I know how to curse peoples. I do. I learned from Root Woman.

Mamie invited Isaiah in, motioned for him to have a seat a the low bench by the table, and fetched a beer for them both.

Dorothy, asleep on the mattress, woke up when he heard them talking. He jumped up off the mattress on the floor and stood with his hands on his fat hips.

"Mamie, who this white man is, sittin' here like he own the place?"

Mamie got up from her low stool at the table Isaiah, stood up, too.

"Oh, Dorothy, hush your mouth. This here is my friend from up home. He come all the way to Charleston just to see me," Mamie said, standing a little taller. "Dorothy this Isaiah. Isaiah this is Dorothy. Dorothy is my friend."

Isaiah set his beer on the table, and reached his hand out. Dorothy ignored it and went to the ice box to get a beer.

"Don't pay him no never mind," Mamie said. "He bein' ornery 'cause he done drink too much."

"I heard that. I ain't had nary a drink today. I been sleeping all day. 'Cept this mornin.' I worked for Mr. James over at the produce market on East Bay Street. I made two dollars. It in my pants pocket, you wants to see?"

"You kin give it to me. That the only seein' I wants to do."

"Yeah, so you kin stick it in your hiding place. You got more money than God, already. What you wants with more? You ain't gettin' this two dollars, I done give you all my money this week. This money is for me."

Mamie glared at him.

"Keep it, then," she shouted, "I don't care. You'll just drink it up, but I don't care. Worthless, that what you is. Jes worthless and shiftless,

Isaiah glanced from one to the other, a half smile on his face.

"Ummm, Mamie? You ever get up home?"

Mamie peered in Isaiah's direction, but then turned to Dorothy and said, "I gots more to say to you after I visits with my friend. You ain't goin' to disrespect me in my own home and get away scot free, ya'hear? You can count on it. We have a reckoning to do."

"I ain't," she said to Isaiah in a company voice, "never got the chance, but I would like to go there and see the house where Root Woman and me lived. I tried to find Dambala when I left, but I never did find him. I wants that snake for my Voodoo. Besides, I would just like to see the old place one more time."

"I could take you."

"Tonight?" Mamie brightened.

"No, I don't think it's a good idea to go into Hell Hole Swamp after dark. Too many sink holes. We'll plan to go within the next month or two. Maybe after it warms up a bit. How about in April?"

"You right. We go in April. How your wife? Last I knew anything about you, you had four or five children. You had any more?"

"Martha died two years ago. I have fourteen, no fifteen, children now."

Mamie laughed. "You gots so many children, you don't even keep the right count of 'em. Lawd have mercy. It must take a powerful lot of money to care for all them. You rich, eh?"

Isaiah laughed, "Well, the Lord has prospered me right good, Mamie. You know, that reminds me. I got a two-hour drive and it's already six-thirty or seven." He fished his pocket watch out and exclaimed, "It's seven-thirty. I'll have to say good-bye.

By the way, last year, right after New Year's day, Ida Cooper and I got married and we're having our first child next month."

A grin split Mamie's face.

She's almost toothless.

"So you gonna' have sixteen children soon? Goodness. That a lot of mouths to feed. Who Ida Cooper is?"

"She grew up right there in Brio. She never married. She's about nine years younger than me. Took care of her parents until their deaths. She's a good woman. Loves the children."

Mamie heaved herself up and stuck out her hand to Isaiah. He took her hand in both of his.

"I have enjoyed this visit. We'll go to Hell Hole Swamp when I come back. You want to go one Saturday?"

"Naw, Saturday is my good day. How about Sunday?"

"Let's say the Sunday after Easter Sunday. How does that sound? I'll come," Isaiah said, "about one or two o'clock in the afternoon. Good-bye, Mamie. Good-bye, Dorothy."

Dorothy stared sraight ahead, and Mamie walked with Isaiah out to the car. She waved from the curb until he turned the corner. Dorothy came out to the street. Mamie, without a word, punched him in his stomach.

"You jes had to show yo ass, didn't you? That man is my friend, and the next time he come you better be polite. I means it. I has spoken."

Dorothy held his stomach with both hands.

"Aw, why'd you have to go and hit me? You ain't that mad at me, is you?"

"No, I jes loves you acting so ignorant. Git in the house. The time to come out was when he was leaving, not now. Scat. Git on in. I ain't through with you yet, you low-down, worthless skunk. I ought to knock you down." She swung her cane at him, but he jumped sideways.

A tear trickled down Dorothy's cheek. Mamie saw this, and took him by the hand and walked with him to her house.

"Dorothy, try not to act up like that when my friend come back. I is hungry," she said. "You hungry? Let's have a meat sandwich with some cheese."

.

On a cold, rainy day shortly after Isaiah's reunion with Mamie, Ida went into labor. At three in the afternoon, she felt the first twinge of pain. The midwife worked throughout the night. Her contractions came strong and regular, and Ida seemed to know what to do.

Toward daybreak on February 14, 1913, the baby, a big boy, came squalling into the world. The midwife showed Ida how to nurse the lusty fellow, gathered up her things,and left. By the time Isaiah came into their bedroom, the baby nursed with gusto.

"Why, he's full grown already. I bet he weighs ten pounds if he weighs an ounce. Ida, he's beautiful."

"Yes, he is, isn't he? Oh Isaiah, I still can't believe it. He is the most beautiful baby I've ever seen."

"Easily the most beautiful," Isaiah agreed. Look at him nurse," Isaiah bent over the bed.

Ida's face turned bright red, and she looked away even though they were the only ones in the room.

He sat down on the edge of the bed and lifted the blanket a little to see better. She pulled the blanket back over her breast.

"Please, Mr. Ike. Leave us alone for a little while, won't you? I'm very tired."

Isaiah left the room, shutting the door behind him. Gall rose up in his throat as he thought of the difference between Martha and Ida.

Martha nursed right in front of the other children and she sure as hell nursed in front of me. I guess I shouldn't compare the two women.

Two months later he walked into the bedroom while she was nursing Louis. She adjusted the blanket to make sure nothing was exposed.

"Tomorrow I plan to ride into Charleston and take Mamie to Hell Hole Swamp. Do you want to come?"

"What on earth for? No, I do not wish to go. What would I do with little Louis?"

"I thought we could get Aunt Isabelle to look after him while we're gone. Tense could help her."

"Isaiah, Isabelle is too old and Tense is too young. Besides, I have no desire to go anywhere with that colored girl. I wish you would stop obsessing about her. I don't see why you ever looked her up. Leave well enough alone. Didn't you say she practices

Voodoo? Or thinks she can cast spells? Such things frighten me."

"Well, my dear, seems like everything scares you. I'm going and that's all there is to it. And stop acting as if sex is sinful. I want to make love. Tonight."

"Well, sounds to me like that is an order. What time shall I be ready? It's only been two months since the baby's birth, but so be it."

"Ida," Isaiah softened a bit, "I know you don't care much for lovemaking, but to me it's important. We've been married for over a year and you still act like it's the first time. Can't you relax and learn to enjoy it? Please?"

"Mr. Ike, women—or I should say *decent* women—don't enjoy that."

"Oh? Is that so?" His countenance changed. "Then I suppose I was never married to a decent woman before you."

He saw her face turn bright red. He turned without another word and left the room.

The Sunday after Easter dawned clear and bright. Isaiah headed for Charleston about noon. Isaiah drove, enjoying the warm spring day.

He passed a couple in a horse and buggy on the old Tamarack Road, leading to the main road. The horse, unaccustomed to the big noisy vehicle, shied a little. He saw no automobiles around Brio. As he neared Charleston, he saw a few cars.

Soon there will be cars and more cars.

On the outskirts of Charleston, he passed dozens of people, Negroes and Whites, on foot. They all craned their necks to see his Cadillac. The stench of the slaughter house at the city limits caused him to roll up his window. Sheep grazed on the pasture, seemingly oblivious to their fate.

About a mile past the city limits, he pulled up in front of Mamie's house.

Before he even opened the car door, Mamie bustled out wearing a red dress trimmed with black. In her hair, plaited tight to her scalp, little, brightly-colored beads peaked through.

She looks almost pretty.

"I been watchin' for you. I wondered if you would remember. Did your baby get borned? A boy or a girl?"

"Yes," Isaiah laughed, "a baby boy. And, of course, I remembered. I've been looking forward to this trip.

"Well, I figured you be scared to mess with Voodoo stuff," Mamie said, grinning. "You ain't afraid ole Dambala will get you?"

"Mamie, I wasn't afraid of Root Woman. Why would I be afraid of her snake? You know, I even looked for it when I went there and found her skeleton.

"Remember the coffin with the black cross painted on top? And the hoe and spade?" She nodded and he helped her into the car. "They," he continued, "were still there. Also the top hat, but I don't remember seeing the coat. Probably some animal dragged it off."

"Was she still covered with that pretty bedspread? The one you got her one Christmas? It had coconut trees on it. They were woven into the cloth. You remember it?

"No, I didn't see that either."

As they drove down the street, they heard Dorothy yelling. Isaiah stopped the car and they watched him trying to run to them. Isaiah backed up and Dorothy stopped running.

When they got to him, he was still panting.

"I wants," he said, trying to catch his breath, "to go with y'all. I wants to see the swamp."

"Naw," Mamie said, "there's alligators in the swamp, Child. Isaiah and me, we used to the swamp, but we has to be careful. If you was to go, you might git ate by a 'gator or step into quick sand. Then we has the devil of a time gettin' you out. And maybe we couldn't even get you out and you jes stay there and drown. Naw, you gots to stay here. Go see your mama."

Dorothy looked down at his feet, and then he brightened.

"I's sorry I showed my ass when you was here before. I wants to be your friend, too."

He stuck his fat hand in through the window of the car and Isaiah shook it, realizing for the first time how child-like the man was.

"That's fine by me, Dorothy. We can be friends. We'll see you later on. Bye-bye now." He released Dorothy's hand, and they waved good-bye as they drove off.

Isaiah got home well after dark. He parked in the garage he'd built at the end of the gravel driveway. Ida watched him as he walked to the porch.

"Hello, Mr. Ike. Have you eaten supper?"

"No, and I'm hungry as a bear. How was church today?"

Ida paused, and then continued on to the ice box to remove the pot roast.

"It was a good sermon," she said. "The children behaved well and seemed to enjoy it. Rob took Sunday dinner with us. So did your pa."

Isaiah came up behind her as she took out a portion of beef, potatoes and carrots to warm up on the still-hot wood stove. He put his arms around her and hugged. She tried to wiggle free, but couldn't. He turned her around and kissed her full on the mouth just as Tense came into the kitchen.

"Ida, I put the baby in his crib . . . oops. Hello, Pa, I didn't hear you come in. Excuse me."

She started to go, but Ida managed to push Isaiah away.

"Thank you, Tense. Here, help me get your pa something to eat."

Isaiah walked over to the table and sat down. They bustled about fixing his dinner. He sat straddled a chair, chin on crossed hands, wondering if Ida would ask him about the trip with Mamie.

Probably not. She'll chatter about everything, but what's important to me.

Ida sat with him while he ate, but Tense excused herself and went to bed.

"How was Pa feeling today? His arthritis still bothering him?" Isaiah asked.

"It didn't seem to be so bad today."

They sat in silence, Isaiah determined not to bring up his adventure with Mamie unless she asked him. She never did.

After dinner, he went over to the store. He got out his journal and began writing.

April 21, 1913. Went with Mamie to the old shack in Hell Hole Swamp, the last place Root Woman lived. It was so quiet. There was an eerie feeling about the whole area. I *could feel strange currents churning throughout the cabin,* and the surrounding swamp. Mamie was the first to notice it.

We found the "Dambala" still coiled around the pole. It was under the house. Maybe dragged there by a wild animal. Mamie sure was glad to have it back. Wonder what she plans to do with it? She says she knows how to practice Voodoo. I doubt it.

Ida is a good woman. A good mother to all the children. I just wish she was more . . ..

Isaiah looked up from his writing, searched for the right word, then continued.

. . . loving, Less inhibited when it comes to lovemaking. I wonder if she suspects that I see Lacy. No, how could she possibly know? If she knew, would she care?

That feeling out in the swamp was so strong. I could have sworn that the snake slithered toward me just before I moved it. Must have been the half-light up under the house.

I could feel Root Woman's presence. I half-expected her to materialize, or at least to talk to us. Wonder what happens to a person's soul when they die?

Do I believe in ghosts? No, probably not. I have never seen a ghost, so I guess they don't exist. What about when I dreamed that Lacy had a baby? That was like seeing a ghost, sort of . . . no, that doesn't count. Just a dream.

He saw a crecent moon out the window. He wanted to see Lacy. To hold her and make love to her. He wondered what Moses was doing. It had been three years since Isaiah last saw him; nine years since he first learned he was his son. He decided to go to New York to see them as soon as he could.

Moses. My son is now Father Moses, finished with seminary and a priest!

I hope he still sketches. He was good. So talented. I'll get him some art supplies.

Isaiah closed the journal, put it back in the safe along with the stocks and bonds, deeds, and ready cash. And then locked it up. He walked to the house.

Ida was sleeping or pretended to be when he crawled into bed.

Dorothy barged through the door.

"Look what I gots! A catfish for us. I been to the river fishing. Ain't he a beauty?"

The fish gaped, trying to breathe. It measured about eighteen inches long and probably weighed a good five pounds.

"That sho Lawd is a beauty, and we kin cook this fish right now. You help me get him cleaned? You want some cornbread? I ain't got no cabbage for coleslaw, but I got some onion for hush puppies. And look here, I got a tomato. And a can of turnip greens, too. Let's see if we can plant us some tomatoes and beans and okra this summer. What you think, Dorothy?"

Mamie set about cooking the fish and preparing a pan of cornbread.

"There ain't nothin'," she said, "I likes better than catfish fried in a pan with cornmeal breading. Look over yonder in the corner, Dorothy. That's 'Dambala.' He a serpent god. Root Woman made him a long time ago."

As they ate their supper, Mamie continued to look at Dambala.

"When Isaiah crawled up under the house to pull that snake out, I saw him move. He wiggled just a little."

Dorothy got up and walked over to the corner where the pole was propped. He started to take hold of it, but jumped back. The pole fell to the floor with a clatter.

"I didn't touch it. The snake jumped at me." Dorothy's eyes almost bugged out of his head. "Get rid of this, Mamie. I Scared. It's alive."

"Aw naw, you done knocked it over. It's not broke, though, and that's good. Don't mess with it," she added, propping it back up. "It won't hurt you. This only for me to touch. This for my Voodoo. Ya'hear me? Don't go messin' around with this heah snake. 'Cause next time it might hurt you. I'll put a good spell on you, and it won't hurt you long as you leave it be."

They went back to the table to finish their dinner. Dorothy kept glancing over his shoulder. Mamie had a secret smile on her face. She felt close to Root Woman.

After eating, they went to bed. She dreamed Root Woman walked along the path leading to the big alligator's nest.

"Dambala," Root Woman said, "heal your heart and mind. Isaiah's too."

Mamie called out to Root Woman to stay, but she began fading away. Mamie felt piercing loneliness and began to cry in her dream.

She opened her eyes and Dambala hovered over her as she lay

there in the bed. She got the feeling that the serpent god was there to protect her. When it undulated, she could see that it really was Root Woman. She blinked, and Dambala was gone. She looked around. Dambala still leaned in the corner.

I musta been dreaming.

Mamie went back to sleep with a profound feeling of peace and happiness.

The Monday after she and Isaiah went to the swamp, Mamie saw few shoppers. It rained and turned cold and windy. As she made her way home with only ninety-five cents to show for her labors, it cleared up, the sun came out and the wind died down.

Now you decide to be decent. Let me work all day in that miserable weather, and when it time to go on home, you clear up and turn into a pretty day! Humph!

When she turned the corner, it seemed to her that every child on that block was out playing in the street. Two skipped hop-scotch, three played jump rope, one rolled a wheel with a wire coat hanger, one hung upside down from a tree, and some played kick-the-can.

" . . .you missed, come turn the rope . . .no fair, you didn't count to one hundred, ...throw the ball . . .cin-der-ella-dressed-in-yellow-went . . . "

They saw her trudging down the street and stopped their play, freezing in place, wide-eyed. Then, getting up their nerve, they fell in behind her.

" . . . you's ugly. Short and little and old. We don't like you, and we ain't scared of you. You ain't nothing but a crazy, old beggar."

She shook her cane at them.

"Lee-me alone. Go home. Quit bothering me."

One of the boys, about eight or nine years old, ran up behind her and pushed her hard. She went down, sprawling on the dirt street. She skinned her hands and face on the cinders. She dropped her cane, but managed to get back up without it. The children all scattered to their homes. She yelled at them long after they were safely in their houses. She didn't realize that she was crying until, having retrieved her cane, she stumbled home. She leaned against the safety of her locked door, brushing away tears.

Mamie went to bed without eating. When Dorothy came in, she

was sound asleep. He didn't wake her. The next morning he saw blood on the white sheet and pillow case and saw her bruised and scraped hands and face.

"Who do this to you, Darlin'?" he asked.

"The children. They was all out in the street playin' they games when I come home last night. A boy pushed me down. Say I just a mean, ugly, old beggar. I ain't no beggar. I got Dambala inside me, and Root Woman, too."

"You gwine to put a hex on them?"

"Naw, they jes little children, Dorothy. I gonna' get to know them. Maybe I teach them a thing or two." Mamie grinned and winked at Dambala. The snake winked back at her.

Chapter 13

Dorothy

He drank his moon and danced around
When they fought, he lay on the ground
He was a cut up, a clown, a ham
Did he love Mamie? Or was he a sham?
He didn't fish, and he couldn't cut bait
But he waited for Mamie by the old wooden gate
They fit and fought all over the street
They cussed and fussed in a white-hot heat

"You," Mamie shouted, "get your ass outta here today, or I puts your stuff on the street tonight. You hear me? I not workin' for you no more! Get up. Go find yourself a job. You kin work like everybody else."

Dorothy lay on the mattress, watching Mamie get ready for work. Drunk since that night two weeks earlier when he had come in with the sack of fried chicken, he opened one eye and moaned. He watched Mamie getting dressed for work.

"Dorothy," she said, seeing that he was awake, "we both gets drunk a good bit. But I gets up and goes to work in the mornings.

You jest keeps on drinking! Get out of bed, I say." She glared at him as she prepared to leave.

He sprawled on the mattress. She whacked him with her walking stick. He came up off the mattress, rubbing his eyes.

"Stop it." he yelled, "I hears you. I go get some work. I gettin' up now."

Mamie stood by the bed, thinking.

"You," she said, "get a regular job, or you move out tonight. I mean it. I ain't supporting your worthless behind no more. I has spoken." She turned and left the house, slamming the door behind her.

She mumbled all the way downtown on the bus. People just looked at her.

At the end of the day, Mamie counted out three dollars and ten cents. This put her in an even fouler mood. She packed up and scowled at people right and left. On the way home, she stopped at the store.

"Gimme four quart bottles of beer, some canned pork'n beans, a fish, and some turnip greens," she said to Mr. Klaus behind the counter. Then, remembering her manners, she added, "Please."

The old gentleman packed up her groceries, figured up the amount on his little note paper, took her money and then said good-bye. He didn't even try for any small talk.

When she got on the bus, the driver started off before she got to the back of the bus. Someone reached to steady her.

"What you doing? Don't be grabbin' me!" she snarled. "Ornery, low-down, skunks. No-count . . .. "

She mumbled all the way to her stop. When she jumped down, she almost plowed right over the bus driver. He shook his head as he climbed out of the bus.

She got home and found Dorothy asleep on the mattress. She opened one of the bottles of beer and sucked it down in a few gulps. Throwing his things into a sack, she started on her second beer.

"Get up and get your ornery ass outta heah." she called to him.

She knew drinking on an empty stomach would make her drunk in a hurry, but she didn't care. The beer fueled her anger at Dorothy lying there while she worked all day.

Continuing to hunt for anything belonging to him, she glimpsed him still on the mattress and walked over. She nudged him with her brogan. Finishing the beer, she opened another and took a few slugs. She could smell the white lightening on his breath. He rolled over and kept on sleeping.

I want to dump water on you, but I don't want to sleep on no wet mattress. What can I do?

She stood fuming at the side of the mattress, then walked over to the little ice box. She took out a chunk of ice, chipped off a piece, wrapped it in a towel, hammered it, and dumped the crushed ice right in his face and into his wide-open mouth.

He sat up spitting out the frozen icy mess. Brushing ice off his face and neck, he rolled off the mattress and got to his feet staggering a bit. She pushed him toward the door.

"Out. You leavin' my house. I done told you this mornin' I ain't messin' with you no more."

He swiveled, a silly grin on his face, and held out his arms for Mamie. He couldn't believe she was throwing him out. Again. Two months before, she had done the same, and he stayed with his mama for a day or two until Mamie cooled off.

"Hit the street," she said as she kicked his shin. "This time you ain't gettin' back in my good heart. I means it. Git."

He walked out the door, took a few steps, turned and yelled, "I ain't want you either. You ugly, and you mean, and you yellow as a old mongre."

She came after him with the beer bottle raised as a weapon. Dorothy ran with Mamie giving chase. In the descending darkness, they fought under the street lamp.

Neighbors peaked out of their windows. Alice Turner, just over with a cake, stood on her neighbor's front porch. They watched from the railing. Others, all up and down the block, paid close attention to this latest fight.

"One of these days," Maud Simmons said, "they's goin' to kill each other. Sit here, Sister, while I get two glasses of cold milk from the kitchen." Back now with the milk, she asked, "Did she cut him cross the cheek with that broken beer bottle?"

"Yes, I believe she did."

"Look, he bleedin'. Oh, no, there go another one of her teeth."

They watched the fight while eating cake and drinking milk.

"He just landed a punch right in her mouth. See? She spittin' out teeth and blood. She ain't got too many teeth as it is, do she?" asked Alice.

"Oh, he down," Maude said. "She done knock him down, Child. That little woman kin sho nuff fight."

"Another piece of cake? This is so good. The cake, I mean," Alice said.

"I wouldn't want—Oh yes, thank you, another thin slice of cake—to get into it with her. No Siree," Maud said. "She got some powerful arms. You think it true that she practice Voodoo? She alles sayin' she puttin' a hex on somebody."

"Humph! She go to a Christian church, but it ain't no tellin'. She could do better," Alice said. "You know what? She pee right on the street in downtown Charleston. In broad open daylight. That the honest to God truth."

Alice, finished her cake, stood by the rail, her arms folded across her big bosom and her full, dark face set in a disapproving frown.

Maude, as thin as her friend was fat, maneuvered around the big woman and leaned against the rail.

"Well," she said, "I feels sorry for her. She ain't bad company when she not drinkin."

"When that is? When you catch her sober? Muss be the middle of the night when she asleep. I sees her over here from time to time. You bes be careful. I don't trust her. She dangerous."

"Oh, she is not. Well, let's have some more of this here cake you done baked. They liable to be at it till all hours of the night. Bless their hearts."

Alice looked at her friend like she thought she'd lost her mind.

"You mean you likes that fat slob she shack up with, too?" Alice asked, incredulity written all over her face.

Maude gathered up cake, plates and glasses, and suggested they move into her kitchen.

"Alice, that boy retarded. Mamie probably just take care of him. Now let's eat our cake and be happy. Don't always find the bad in people. Look for the good."

Alice, knowing Maude would always defend the underdog, let it drop and joined her friend for more cold milk and chocolate cake.

"This the best cake you is ever baked." Maude nibbled a little icing from her empty plate.

"You say that every time," Alice said, with a pinched smile. "How kin my cakes get better and better?"

"That," Maude said, "is just a sayin'. You even argue a compliment, Girl. You'd argue with a signpost, I do believe. I put it this way, 'this cake is good.' How that suit you?"

"Thank you." Alice smiled a real smile. "How come," she asked, "you so lovin' and nice to everybody? Don't you think Mamie got a bad temper? And she so ugly. My, my that is one ugly nigger."

"Maude," Alice said, "it easier to love than to hate. Did you know she been raped when she first come to Charleston? I done met her friend, Sukey. Sukey dead now. This been a while back." She shook her head.

"Naw, I didn't know that 'bout her."

"Sukey's the one told me 'bout that terrible time. Mamie showed up on her front doorstep early one mornin' most half-dead. And her legs. She think it had somethin' to do with the Ku Klux Klan. Mamie talk sometimes 'bout the burning cross of Jesus, and—"

"Oh yeah," Alice cut in, "I done heard her one day in church sayin' something about 'the burning cross of Jesus', but I figured it had to do with Voodoo."

The two women fell silent. After a while, with Maude still tasting small crumbs of cake off her plate, Alice continued talking.

"Yes, that could signify. Shore Lawd could."

Maude smiled and patted her friend's hand.

"Not to change the subject,but when I was waiting for the bus on Nassau Street the other day, I heard these mens tellin' some jokes. You want to hear a joke?"

"Now, Sister." Alice smiled. "You knows I likes a good joke. Speak, Child."

"Well," Maude began, "One man say, 'I knowed a man so ugly, when he die, the undertaker had to kiver him up, 'fore he could embalm him.' Another man say, 'That ain't' ugly, I knowed a man so ugly, he own mama wouldn't even kiss he cheek'. Next man say, 'Them boys was pretty mens, I knowed a man so ugly, they threw him in the Mississippi River and skimmed ugly fo six months.' "

"Honey, hush." Alice laughed until she had to wipe tears from her eyes.

They said goodnight, and Alice left to go next door. She crossed the back yards because Mamie and Dorothy were still out on the street fighting. It was mostly a verbal contest now. They were both tired having expended their energies swinging at each other and mostly missing.

Mamie worked on the last of the four beers, drinking slowly, deep in thought. Dorothy hadn't had a drop since about three that afternoon, and was almost sober, while Mamie was getting more and more inebriated. Many neighbors had long since wandered off. Maude watched from her front window, wondering if she should try to break it up.

Dorothy's face looked like it had a trickle of dried blood from eye to jawbone. She could see neighbors in several houses across the street, watching from their windows, or from their front porches.

She walked out and stood with her hands on the rail of her own front porch, breathing in the scent of her roses that climbed a string trellis at the end of the porch. Cooler in the evenings now, September gave respite, but the days blazed hot and humid.

Maude decided to turn in, thinking I hope Mamie and Dorothy winds down their fighting. Lord, bless us all.

It seemed she had just gone to sleep, when she heard a terrible ruckus. Jumping up, she grabbed a coat and went out onto her front porch.

The full moon cast an eerie light over the two figures sprawled in the street. A neighbor, a man, ran out to where they lay. She joined him. Dorothy was moaning with a big gash in his thigh. Mamie lay passed out. Dorothy's pant leg became soaked with blood as they looked.

Maude, the first to snap to life, said, "I'll get some scissors and bandages. I don't think we can move him. Stay here with him, won't you?"

The man nodded. Maude ran back into her house, gathering scissors, and cloth to cut into strips for bandages, iodine, and adhesive tape. She wondered if she should wash his leg, decided against it, and on impulse rummaged through a junk drawer for twine. Not finding any, she took an apron so she could use the ties as a tourniquet if the bleeding was too bad.

When she got back, Mamie still lay sprawled on her back. Dorothy lay on his side with the cut leg uppermost. Maude turned him onto his back and asked the man to hold him down.

"In case I hurt him," she said. "I wouldn't want this big bruiser swinging at me. He knock me plumb over to King Street and back."

She ripped the pant leg up from the ankle to past where the beer bottle lacerated the thigh. A long gash. Not too deep. Working quickly, she poured iodine over the wound and bandaged it, bringing the edges together as best she could. She put a folded piece of cotton square over the cut and adhesive tape over that, then bandaged the whole thigh to give it extra support.

"You think he need to see a doctor?" she asked the neighbor who helped her.

"No, you take care of it pretty damn good, look to me like. That iodine will kill any germs. He be all right. They alles fightin'. He used to it," he said.

Other neighbors lingered in the street. One woman came out of her house with two steaming cups of black coffee.

"Reckon, we can git them awake enough to drink this heah coffee?" the woman spoked to no one in particular.

"It sober them up some."

Mamie awoke and looked around at all the people staring down at her.

"What you all want? Leave me be. Oh, yeah. Dorothy. Where that worthless skunk? I skin him alive."

Someone had taken the broken beer bottle out of her hand when she lay passed out. She looked around for it. Then spotting Dorothy, all the anger seemed to drain out of her.

"Oh, Sugar, who do this to you? Wake up. Wake up, Baby."

"Here," the woman holding the coffee said, "drink this. It make you feel better. You the one do this to Dorothy. Don't you remember?"

Mamie sipped the steaming coffee. The neighbors began recounting the fight for Mamie. People laughed and slapped each other on the back. Each tried to outdo the other one in his telling of the fray.

"Yes, Sir. You one tough lady. I sho Gawd wouldn't want to tangle with you. No. Uhn? Uhn?" a coal-black, thin man with a bald head and a fuzzy little goatee said.

"That right," Mamie nodded. "I tear his ass up, he mess with me. I told him he better get himself a regular job. I tired of his trifling ways. I one tough broad."

She shook Dorothy. He groaned, opened one eye, then both eyes flew open.

"Don't cut me no more. Don't hit me, don't cut me." He held his arms up over his head.

"I ain't goin' to cut you no more, Dorothy," Mamie murmured, "you done bust out some of my teeth, too. My mouth hurt. You gots to get a steady job. You make me too mad. I just can't stand it when you lay up drunk while I out workin'. You think you can get yourself a steady job? Huh, Sweet Baby?"

The Remberts had watched them fight the night before from behind lace curtains. At the breakfast table, Reverend Rembert turned to his wife.

"Leslie," he said, "we need to talk to Mamie about her drinking. I think it's getting worse, don't you?"

"I believe you're right, dear. We certainly can't stand by and let them kill each other. She could just as easily have sliced into an artery. Let's pray for them, and then you talk to them. Maybe you can catch them when they not drinking."

"I'm not going to talk to both of them. That would seem like I sanction their union. I have never acknowledged their living together, you know."

"Oh, John! Talking to them both isn't saying you approve of their living together. But they each have a drinking problem. I wish you would talk to them as a couple. Please?"

Reverend Rembert didn't get a chance to talk with Mamie until the following Sunday morning. Dorothy was not on the premises, having left early to go see his mama. Mamie, expecting Leslie, opened the door to her minister, whom she seldom saw at her house.

"What the matter?" she asked. "Where Leslie? She not sick, is she?"

"Leslie will be back directly, but first I want to talk with you. May I come in?"

Mamie stepped back from the door and motioned him in.

"You want some milk?"

Reverent Rembert smiled at Mamie, trying to accustom his eyes to the dimly lit room.

"No, uh—no thank you. Mamie, I want to talk with you about a serious problem. Your drinking. It's gotten worse over the years.

What can we do to help you quit drinking?"

"Quit drinking? I likes my beer. It only beer I drink. None of that hard stuff. No Siree. None of that bad stuff for me."

"It doesn't have to be 'hard stuff' to be a problem. The other night when you and Dorothy got into it, you could have killed him. You could have—"

"Aw, naw, preacher, I loves Dorothy. He don't mean no harm. He just like a baby. Sometimes I gets mad at him for not workin', but—"

"That's just it. Sometimes you get mad. You could have cut one inch closer to the groin and cut through an artery. You know what an artery does?"

"Nawsir, I can't say I does. What a artery do?"

"Pumps blood from the heart."

"Way down in the leg?"

"All over the body. Mamie, the thing is, you need to quit drinking. For other reasons, too. It's not good for you. You're getting some years on you now. You need to take better care of yourself. And you a Christian woman, uhn? Christian women need to set an example for other women who are not so fortunate."

"Fortunate? What that mean?"

"Having fortune. Having good things happen to you."

"Well now, I is sho Lawd had a lot of 'fortune' in my lifetime, ain't I? Yes, Lawd. Everybody need to have such good luck. I still has my jujus. You want to see my rabbit's foot? You ever notice my horseshoe hung over my door?" Mamie, forgetting who she talked with, let her anger rise. With the anger, her voice rose.

"My friend give me those 'fore she die. She a famous Voodoo woman. She 'Root Woman'. Mix up any kind of spell a body might want. I got gris-gris, too. All them things done bring me 'fortune' here in Charleston, but 'fore I got them things, I had jes the other side of 'fortune'." Mamie sat down hard on her low stool and motioned for Reverend Rembert to sit on the chair. He did, and she continued.

"So, uh, 'scuse me for talkin' so blunt, but don't go talkin' to me 'bout me bein; so 'fortunate'. Humph."

"Mamie," he said, "you have had misfortune in your life. That's not to be denied. But, God loves you so much. God has kept you all these years since coming to Charleston in pretty good health. You earn a good living. You have friends that care about you. Please try to stop the drinking. That's all I'm asking. All right? Leslie wants you to quit drinking, too. Do it for Leslie? Uhn?"

Mamie scowled and stared at the floor. Just when he had thought she would not answer, she looked up smiling.

"I do it for the burning cross of Jesus. I maybe not quit all together, but I promise to quit gettin' drunk. That," she said, "I think I kin do."

Reverent Rembert walked, deep in thought, to his own house.

B*etter than nothing, I guess. We'll see. We'll just see.*

As he came into his front door, he passed Leslie who was gathering supplies for her weekly routine with Mamie.

"What did she say? Did you catch both of them at home? I thought I saw Dorothy headin' out the back way just as you left to go back there," Leslie said.

"She said she would try to cut down on her drinking. Said she would do it 'for the burning cross of Jesus'. Dorothy was gone. I'll talk with him, too. Later. We better hurry. Don't wash her hair this morning. That would take too much time, I think."

"I won't. Can you get Robert up and have him ready when I get back? I won't be long." Leslie thought about the problem as she headed back to Mamie's.

Cut down? I doubt it. She needs to stop all together. I'll work on her some, too.

She knocked and went on in when she heard Mamie say 'come in'. Mamie's face was tear-streaked.

"Mamie, what's wrong? What's wrong, Honey?"

"I shamed of my rowdy ways. Fightin' in the street and all. I goin' to quit drinkin'. No more beer for this woman. Nawsir. No more. Quit right out. Jes quit. You reckon I kin do it? I like it a powerful lot. It get rid of the anger build up in me. How I goin' to get rid of that anger if I quits?"

"You can ask Jesus to help you. He will, you know. He certainly will. Come here for a hug. I love you."

Mamie hugged her back. Leslie sat on the floor for this embrace. Mamie needed a bath. Bad.

"Mamie, do you take a bath every night? Or just sometimes?"

"Sometimes. Sometimes I forget. Sometimes I too tired. Why you ask? I stink, huh? Well, I goin to git a all-over bath soon's you do my hair."

"Mamie, I bet you miss Sukey, don't you? She been dead now how long? Do you know?"

"I don't know for sure. Maybe five or six years. I miss her. She was a good friend."

"Do you have another lady friend? Someone in the neighborhood, maybe?"

Mamie turned around so she could see Leslie's face.

"Why you ask? You tired of bein' my friend? You goin' away? You ain't goin' to die, is you?"

"Oh, no. You sweet thing, you. Seems like everybody who's ever been your friend has died, eh? Well, I'm not plannin' to die any time soon. I got to raise Robert and help John, now don't I? And you. I couldn't up and leave you." She hugged her. "I was just thinking that if you had a friend, it might make it easier to quit drinking."

"Thought you say Jesus help me with that?" Mamie looked sideways at Leslie.

"Well, of course, He will. But it never hurts to have a close friend to talk things over with. Like when you get angry, instead of drinking, you could tell your friend about how mad you are. In fact maybe you and the friend could even pray together."

Mamie thought a minute, her eyes squeezed tight shut.

"Naw, I ain't got no sich friend. I knows a woman in the neighborhood go to our church. Alice her name. She don't like me, and I don't like her. I sit by her one day in church and she jump up without a word and ain't never come back. She alles look at me funny, too."

"I think," Leslie said, "I know who you're talking about. I wouldn't worry about that. She probably went to the bathroom, or something. Or maybe she had to go home before the service ended."

"Huh, before it begin, you mean! There a woman across the street. Her name Maude. I don't know where she go to church, or if she do, but she awful sweet. We visits sometimes. She bring me dinner some nights. She alles make out like she cooks too much. But I know bet

But I know ter. She do it special for me. She a good woman. We not friends exactly, but we could be. We could be."

"Oh, yes, I know just who you mean. She's tall and thin like me?"

"Yep, that's the one all right. She work in one of them houses where Sukey always wanted to work. Down on the High Battery. I been down there one time, you know. They is beautiful houses. Look to me more like hotels than houses. Them peoples muss be some kind of rich."

"Yes," Leslie said, "I guess they are."

"I rich, too," Mamie said, brightening. "I gots money saved up. But don't tell Reverend John. He might raise my rent again. I ain't got that much saved up."

Leslie smiled and hugged Mamie again.

"All right, it be our little secret. Honey, he don't like to raise your rent. He probably never raise it again. It bother you a lot to have things change, don't it?"

Mamie smiled to herself. When she turned to look at Leslie, she had a solemn expression on her face.

"Yes, it bother me a lot. I needs my money. I don't like to spend it."

"Not changing the subject," Leslie said, "but I finished doin' your hair. Why don't you wash real quick. When you get dressed, walk across the street and invite Maude to go to church and have Sunday dinner with us. Tell her I invited you both to have dinner. That sound like a good idea to you?"

"I do that. I sho Lawd do that very thing. You has the best ideas sometimes. I likes to eat dinner with you and your family. Thank you."

When Mamie knocked on her door, Maude was just sitting down to a late breakfast. She went to the door thinking it might be Alice from next door come to borrow a cup of sugar or something.

"Why, Mamie. Come in. You want to have some breakfast with me? Or a cup of coffee?"

"I don't believes we have time for that," Mamie said. "Miz Leslie done invited both of us to dinner after church. Kin you come to church with us? We goes in a car! We goes to the AME church over on Meeting Street. Reverend Rembert is the minister. Oh, please say you wants to."

The women walked toward the kitchen as Mamie talked. Maude smiled down at her.

"Well, I attend the Baptist church when I go, but I reckon I could go. Let me eat just a bite and then I'll get myself ready. Tell Miz Rembert I be just a few minutes.

Mamie hurried across the street as excited as a little girl. When Maude came, Mamie sat right next to her new friend in the car, in church and later at dinner. After she and Mamie went home, John looked at his wife.

"Come here, you," he said.

He put his arms around her and kissed her.

"You make a better minister, sometimes," he nuzzled her neck.

"Oh, John, you old flatterer, you. Thank you."

"You welcome, young lady," he pulled her into his arms for a real kiss.

She melted against him.

"I love you," she said.

When Mamie lay down for her customary Sunday afternoon nap, Root Woman came toward her through swamp mists. "Drinking is no good for you. You stop. I help you, and Jesus help you, too," Saylee said.

Mamie asked in her dream about Maude helping her.

"She," Root Woman said, "be a big help to you. She is a good woman."

Saylee faded away with the mists. Mamie ran after her, but woke up with a start. The dream had been so real that Mamie looked all around in the bedroom to see if maybe Saylee sat perched somewhere working on a spell, or perhaps sewing. She felt happy and sad at the same time. She got up and ambled out through the yard to the street. She looked across at Maude's house. Seeing no sign of her new friend, Mamie went back inside and began reading her Bible.

Darkness settled around the house, but Dorothy had not returned. She walked around to the front of the house. Dorothy stood with his arms propped on the wooden gate. Bent nearly double, he cried softly.

"What wrong, Dorothy?" He didn't answer. "What wrong, Baby?"

She sniffed for fumes of whiskey on his breath, but found nothing.

Dorothy turned, drying his eyes with the back of his hand.

"Mama dead. She died today while we was eatin' dinner. She choked on a piece of ham. I tired to make her cough it up, but she couldn't. I slapped her back till I most knocked her over, but she never could cough it up. Doctor came and said 'she is dead, that is for sure.'" Dorothy began crying again. Then looking at Mamie, he sobbed, "She done choked to death on a piece of ham. I can't believe it."

"Come inside, Darlin'," Mamie said. "I goin' to get Reverend John. You needs to talk to a man of God at a time like this."

"Aw, naw. Don't get that preacher man. He don't like me."

Mamie led Dorothy by the hand into their home, made him sit down at the table, and left him with a sandwich and a glass of milk, while she fetched John. He perched on Mamie's low stool across from Dorothy.

Mamie fixed Reverend Rembert a glass of milk, but no sandwich because he said he wasn't hungry. Dorothy's sandwich sat untouched. She cleared it away and then went to the Rembert's house so they could talk.

When Reverend John came back home, he told Mamie to go be with Dorothy.

"He's hurting. He's lost a mother. I am glad you got me, Mamie. I think I helped."

From that day on, both Mamie and Dorothy changed. They stopped the drunkenness. Dorothy was able to get a steady job at the ice house. The only problem was that Dorothy began to eat more and more. Little by little, Mamie and Dorothy began to drink again, but the drunken brawls did not resume.

About a year after the drunken brawling stopped, Mamie saw a wagon and a crowd of people at the gate by the Rembert's house when she turned into her street.

What this all about?

Nearing the gate, she saw Reverend Rembert and some of the neighbors lift Dorothy from the back of a wagon. They tried to get him on their arms in a make-shift chair arrangement, but he couldn't seem to sit up. They laid him back down.

"We need a sturdy piece of plywood or something to carry him on," John Rembert said.

"What happened to Dorothy? Huh?" Mamie hurried over, "Somebody answer me. Dorothy? Sugar, what happened to you? You hurt?" Mamie asked.

"He's had a stroke, Mamie. He had a stroke at work. They got a doctor to him," Reverend Rembert said. "We are trying to get him inside. He's so heavy. Oh, here comes Maude. What's that she's got?"

Maude ran up with two sturdy brooms, a heavy piece of canvass cloth, and ten safety pins the size of her hand.

"We can make a stretcher to carry him on," she said.

The crude stretcher worked well. Dorothy's head hung off one end and his legs off the other, but they managed to get him inside with Mamie supporting his head with both her hands.

"Oh, Dorothy. You gonna' be all right. Mamie will take care of you," Mamie tried not to let him see her cry.

As the years passed, Mamie learned how to spoon chicken soup into his slack mouth. He ate soft food a little better, but never under his own hand. And so the tending of Dorothy became a chore of epic proportion. He tried to speak, but it came out all garbled.

"Hush now, don't try to talk," she said.

Mamie tended him with the help of Leslie and Maude.

Dorothy got a little better. His speech improved and he regained the use of his limbs. But, life took on a drudging pace. Exhausted from working all day and tending Dorothy all evening, Mamie one night gave it up and went to sleep early in the evening. Her two friends, Maude and Leslie, lingered in the next room, talking so as not to wake Dorothy and Mamie.

"And how is your friend, Alice?" Leslie asked.

"Sad," Maude said, "but, I don't see as much of Alice as I used to. She's been giving me the cold shoulder for a spell now. She kind of funny that way. She think if I be friends with other peoples, I can't be her friend. Poor soul. Don't she know friendship's not like a jar of jam. It don't get used up."

Both women laughed.

"That for sure," Leslie said. "I'm glad yo Mamie's friend.

And mine, too. How is your minister? I heard he been down with reumatism. He any better?"

"Yessum, he some better. His hands all gnarly now. His fingers bent so he can't straighten them out. His joints are all swollen. 'Cept they ain't swollen exactly. They is growed bigger, is all. It very painful, his wife tell me. I prays for him, and I wish you and the Reverend would, too," Maude said.

"Certainly, and for Mamie, too. She'll have a hard row to hoe, as the saying goes, with Dorothy so sick," Leslie shook her head.

"Yes, Lawd. Mamie, too. You know, Mamie ain't come to church with me but one time, but I goes with her every whip stitch. The last time I was in my own church, she come with me. My preacher tease me," Maude said.

Leslie nodded and smiled, getting up to tidy the little kitchen area.

"He say," Maude continued, "'you ain't join up with that AME church, has you? We been missin' you 'bout every other Sunday. What you is? Half Baptist and half AME?'" Both women laughed. "I laugh and say, 'I reckon I is.' He so sweet. He know I be Baptist till the day I die."

They locked the door and left the other two sound asleep. It was past midnight when Maude got into bed across the street.

Maude stuck close to Mamie and the Remberts. Maude helped Mamie, and Mamie helped her. After her drinking slowed to almost a stop, Mamie made friends with a few of the children on the street. These children of the children who had bedeviled her so many years ago got a chance to see Mamie in a better light. She reached out more to her neighbors after Dorothy's stroke.

I sometimes make seven dollars on a week day. Mrs. Buntley so sweet. She keep after me to put my money in bonds or in the bank to draw interest, but I don't want to change anything.

Ted Buntley ran the drug store now that his father was ailing. Mamie didn't like him and knew he didn't like her. She only went in when she saw Mrs. Buntley over there. And then only to turn over more of her money and to get a cup of coffee which she took across the street in a little paper cup.

With Dorothy sick and not drinkin' all these years, and the war making everything boom, I able to save most all my money. Even with Dorothy laid up not able to work. Not spending my money on beer help, too.

"Mamie, please let me open you a bank account," Mrs. Buntley pleaded, "or at least buy you some government bonds."

"No'am. Living with Dorothy so messed up is change enough for now. I miss him, you know," she said.

Months later at home, Mamie broached a subject with Leslie she had been thinking about for several weeks. "If anything happen to me," Mamie said as Leslie began to braid her hair, "if anything happen that I can't work no more, I got money over at the drugstore. Buntley's Drug Store." She craned her neck to look at Leslie. "You know the one? Over on King Street cross from where I work. If I gits where I can't work no more, will you and the Reverend take that money and keep me up?"

Leslie looked away, blinking her eyes.

"Yes, of course, but you're a tough little lady," she said with a catch in her voice as she looked back at Mamie, "and you're going to be able to work for many more years. I am so proud of you, my dear. So proud."

Leslie hugged her, fished a handkerchief out of her apron pocket, and blew her nose.

"How old are you, Mamie?" Leslie asked, "Do you know when you were born?"

"I ain't know for sure, but I thinks just after the war. That one between the North and the South? I thinks I born right after that war was over. When that?"

"My, my, that would have been 1865, or shortly thereafter."

"Oh, I remembers. It was 1866. Saylee tell me one time. She say she know. I born on New Year's Day, 1866. I split the time right at midnight. Could be I born on December 31, 1865. My mama told Saylee that the doctor sa*y* it 1866. He choose. Coulda been December 31, or January first. So it was January 1, 1866. How old that make me now?"

"Well, let's see, this coming January first, you'll be... eighty-three. I think. Let me figure it on paper. Yep. Eighty-three. We'll have to have a birthday party for you. Would you like that? Get presents and have a cake and ice cream?"

At breakfast the next morning, Leslie talked with her husband about Mamie's request. He had often wondered what they must do when the day came when Mamie could no longer work. He was relieved that Mamie had brought it up.

"That's good to know, Leslie," John said. "I don't think Mamie can work too much longer. Please pass the salt," He cut into his already salt-laden sausage. "She's been here—-my godness—these eggs are good—with us how long, now? Thirty years? Forty? I wonder how much longer?"

"Lord only knows. She sure puts great stock in working," Leslie said, gazing at her husband. "I wonder if people passing her on the street even notice her? Do they know her like we do? Or is she just 'a thing' to them?"

Chapter 14

Tough Times

Mamie ruled her corner like a queen
A Queen beggar, mean and lean
Drinking and age took their toll
More wild living as she grew old
Isaiah and Lacy, now living in France
Knew little of Mamie's mad dance

Mamie stared at the faded invitation in her hand. She put it down and picked up her pan of purple hull peas and began shelling again. Though invited to Isaiah's and Lacy's wedding, she had not gone so long ago.

"I wanted to go, but I couldn't stand the idea of coming back on the train by myself. He told me I'd be all right, but I was too afraid to go," Mamie tossed a handful of peas into the pan and shrugged at Leslie.

"Well, I wish you could've gone. It must be so exciting for them, living in France. You say Lacy is selling antiques?" Leslie asked.

Mamie nodded at Leslie. Although the wedding was years ago, on this hot, humid Sunday, she stewed about the injustice of wanting to go and not being able to conquer her fears.

At the last of the peas, Leslie stood, stretched and patted Mamie on the head.

"Well," Leslie said, "at least they write to you. I'd better go in now. I'll bring you a mess when I get them cooked.

The next day, Mamie sat propped against her stool, staring down at the pavement. She sat in a thin band of shade provided by the bus stop sign in front of Kress Five and Ten on King Street.

Humph. Dorothy starting to drink again now he most over his stroke. Least he working again. Ah, me. I misses Isaiah and Lacy. Why they livin' in France anyway? Bad enough he and Lacy go honeymoon clear cross the ocean. Den he and his wife had to decide to go live there?

Not realizing it, she lapsed into speaking out loud.

"Drat a body that do that to somebody. He suppose to be my friend."

Dorothy waited for her to look up.

"Woman, who you talking to? Who suppose to be your friend? Somebody done hurt you again? I knock him down and stomp on him!"

Mamie looked up and smiled.

"Oh, Dorothy," she said, "I didn't see you standing there. I just wish Mr. Ike was up in Brio like alles. Even though I ustta didn't see him all that much, still he lived here close by."

"Had umselves a nice little three-week honeymoon vacation over there in France. Uhn?" Mamie looked back down at the sidewalk and continued a monologue as though Dorothy wasn't even there. "Ain't back in New York but four months, when back to France they traipsed."

"Huh? You talking to me, Sugar?" Dorothy asked.

"No, Dorothy, go on home. I talkin' jest to hear myself talk. I talkin' to me." She looked up, and seeing his crestfallen face, she motioned for him to come close.

"I gots a postcard from Mr. Ike and Lacy just the other day." She reached the wrinkled card up so he could see it. "I liked goin' that one time in New York. Mr. Ike, he come carry me in his brand new white Cadillac."

"Well, you went one time on the train —"

"But, I *enjoyed* the trip in the Cadillac. Yeah, he back to Cadillac — wonder did he carry that car over to France with um?" When Dorothy didn't answer her, she continued talking to nobody in particular.

"Huh. That man sho is rich. Must be. I hear tell that Ida woman he was married to 'fore Lacy, she done got all his money. Humph, she must not of got all of it. He livin' pretty good from what I is able to pick up here and there."

She glanced at Dorothy.

"Dorothy, you still standin' round? Go on about your business. Why ain't you at work? You working today? You better not be hangin' round drunk when I gets home this evening. I ain't gonna put up with that. No more. Go on to work. Or go on home. One or the other. Scat. People don't want to put money in my cup with you hanging round." Dorothy dropped his head and shrugged his shoulders.

"Go on now," she said more gently. "I see you when I gets home tonight."

Dorothy lay drunk and passed out. Sprawled on the bed, he didn't even wake up when Mamie came home that night. She fixed herself a little supper and started to get into bed. Dorothy jumped up off the mattress.

"Hey, I ain't hear you come in. I get up and we can eat us a good meal. I hungry," he said.

Mamie put her hands on her hips and scowled at Dorothy.

"I done et," she said. "Fix yourself something if you want. I goin' to bed. I tired because I worked hard all day—like I does every day. Where you get the money for your shine?" When he started shaking his head to protest, she cut him off. "And how many beers you done bought? They's beer bottles all over the place."

"I bought me one little pint of moonshine and four quarts of beer. I sorry I ain't work today. Tomorrow I goin' in early and work all day."

"Yeah," Mamie mumbled, "if you still has a job, that is. Dorothy, where you get the money for your whiskey and beer if you ain't worked a lick today? Yesterday, I give you money for the block of ice when you say you flat broke."

Mamie pushed the mattress over and lifted the loose floor board. Her money was all gone from the mason jar. She ran around the mattress toward the startled man.

"I will kill you. You lazy, no-good bum!"

Dorothy bolted from the house, pulling on a pair of trousers as he ran. This time he didn't stop to fight. He ran down the street with Mamie in hot pursuit. She screamed for him to stop and fight like a man. She finally turned around and hobbled home, wiping away tears with the back of her hand.

She saw curtains parted all up and down the street. Some neighbors stood on their porches, talking and laughing.

Yeah, we putting on a show for the neighbors again. Humph! What I care what they think?

* * *

Dorothy stayed out all night. He still had not returned when she left for work the next day.

I guess I gots to do something bout Dorothy, but I don't know what.

The weather was hot and humid. Sitting on the scale at the drugstore later that morning, she drank her morning coffee and ate her boiled egg and toast. She mumbled just loud enough for people to catch a word or two here and there.

Ted Buntley, out of college several years now, worked behind the lunch counter. Eddie Fishburn leaned his pimply face over the counter and snickered in Ted's direction in a stage whisper.

"She's in rare form today, eh? Must be one of her bad days."

Ted shot him a nasty grin, and took a load of coffee cups and saucers into the back and told his mother about Mamie 'carrying on.'

"Oh, don't worry about Mamie," his mom said. "If she gets too loud, I'll speak a word or two to her. She'll be going on across the street in a moment, anyway."

"It's a disgrace," the boy said, "you letting her hang around in here. She's crazy and drives customers off. That's just not good business sense."

Mrs. Buntley smiled at her son, wagging her head back and forth.

"Well, College Boy-wonder," she said with a grin, "you let your father and me decide what is good for this business. Even though you managed this place when your father was so sick, you aren't running the show by yourself yet. Now go on back out there and wait on that new customer that just sat down. And don't say a word to Mamie!"

When he left, she chuckled.

He's grown up seeing that old woman in here. You'd think he would be more accepting of her.

She went out front and ambled to the end of the counter where the big scale stood.

"Mamie, how you feeling this morning? Might hot, ain't it?"

"Miz Buntley," Mamie said, "I got some money to put in your safe."

She handed Mrs. Buntley a paper sack full of change. "I worried that Dorothy might find my other hiding place. He cleaned out a pile yesterday."

"Took money?" Mrs. Buntley asked.

"Yeah, he got a whole mason jar most full. But, he ain't knowed 'bout this money, so I wants you to keep it up for me, please."

Mrs. Buntley handed the sack back to Mamie, walked to the back, and opened the safe. She got out the little book and returned to front. Taking the sack again from Mamie, she counted the money, putting the dimes in stacks of ten, the nickels in stacks of twenty, and so on. The pennies she left for last.

Mamie peered over the end of the counter as much as her height allowed. Ted Buntley watched the scenario and scowled at the little woman.

When Mrs. Buntley finished stacking the money, she entered each denomination in the little note book before changing the coins to bills for the safe. Mamie nodded in satisfaction.

"How much you get?" Mamie asked.

"Well, let's see. You got five dollars in dimes, eight in nickels, four in quarters. That's seventeen dollars. The pennies are in the sack. There are seventeen pennies. And here." She showed Mamie the amount she had written down in the little notebook — $17.00. Is that what you came up with?"

"No ma'am. I thought it was seventeen and two cents. I musta miscounted. How much I gots all together?"

"Seventeen dollars and seventeen cents," Mrs. Buntley said, puzzled that Mamie asked.

"No, ma'am. How much I got in your safe altogether?" Mamie asked.

Mrs. Buntley looked around, and seeing only her son near, leaned over the counter.

"Mamie," she whispered, "since beginning to save this money in 1913, you have accumulated eleven thousand, nine hundred and sixty dollars. You better let me—"

"Almost twelve thousand dollars?" Mamie asked. "I knowed I had over ten, but —"

"Mamie! Sh-h-h-h! Not so loud. You better let me set up an account at the bank for you. I want you to bring your notebook in and let's go over the numbers. You need to keep up with the amount, too."

Ted Buntley walked to the back of the store and looked over at the safe. It was locked.

As usual, the safe is locked! And no one knows the combination but Mama and Daddy.

Mamie put the seventeen cents in her pocket and folded the little paper bag up and stuck it in her tote. Gathering up her things, she grinned at Mrs. Buntley.

"I study on letting you set up a bank account for me," Mamie said as she started to leave the store, "but I don't think so. I don't trust the banks. Look what happen a few years back. Thank you, Ma'am." Looking over her shoulder, she continued as she got to the door, "You shore good to this poor ole woman. And I 'preciates it, yes I does. Bye now."

Walking across King Street, a wide grin split her face.

"That one honest woman. I knowed it was seventeen dollar and seventeen cents, but I keep thinking she might take a little tip for her trouble. She never do, though. She one good woman, I reckon."

She set up her stand right at nine o'clock and pulled the crumpled post card out of her pocket to read one more time. Isaiah had printed in rather large letters.

Dear Mamie—Lacy's antique shop is flourishing. He had scratched a line through 'flourishing' and had written 'doing well.' We live in a little flat on the left bank and enjoy Paris. We may come back home someday soon. Love, Your friend, Isaiah.

A tear welled in her eye. She swiped it away.

What I care for that old white man? He ain't nottin' to me even if he did marry my cousin. And she don't seem like no cousin. She jes about white. I thinks I do remembers her, though, when we was jes children. Seem like I useta play paper dolls with a little child who was older than me. But I can't remember much about her.

Mamie set up to sell her pencils and began singing and humming.

Later that morning, she went across the street and asked Mrs. Buntley if she could buy a post card. Mrs. Buntley showed her the rack and offered to get a few of them down for her.

"Naw, just pick out a pretty one that show the old houses down on the battery, please."

She paid for the card and left. Mrs. Buntley smiled at Mamie's departing back. She looked over at her son.

"I wonder who she's going to write to?"

"Who cares?" Ted mumbled. He went to the back and stared at the safe.

His mother, finally provoked to anger, followed him.

"Why are you in such a foul mood today? Are you still upset that your father and I choose to befriend that poor old woman?"

"She stinks most of the time," her son said, "she curses and acts crazy as a loon, she's colored, but does any of that matter to you? You treat her like royalty. I can't stand that worthless piece of junk! I wish she'd die and go to hell."

Mrs. Buntley raised her hand, but before she could reach him, he took off out the back door. She followed him shouting, "Don't you ever talk like that again in my presence, or, big and old as you are, I'll give you a whipping. You hear me?" she yelled as he rounded the corner at the end of the alley. She waited until her anger cooled. Shaking her head, she went back into the drugstore.

That night, Mamie wrote the post card to Isaiah. She got Leslie Rembert to help her spell the words. She wrote:

Dear Isaiah Norris, I got your card about a week ago. It is hot here. Be good. Say 'hey' to Lacy. Your friend, Mamie.

"And I," she said with pride, "ain't make a mistake. His card got a scratched out place. He musta spell a word wrong, or something. I ain't make a single scratch out on my card to him."

She showed the card to Leslie.

"Well, you're right," Leslie said. "You didn't make a single error. I'm proud of you. Your printing is neat, too. Isaiah will like hearing from you."

"Reckon if he write me back? I doesn't think so. That a one-time thing. He in France almost ten years. He's wrote me a few times over the years, but I alles lost the cards 'fore I could ever write him back.

Well, I did once 'bout five years back. I keep this card safe in my pocket and now I is going to ask Mrs. Buntley to put his card in her safe.

Mamie thought a minute and shook her head.

"No, I know," she said. "I'll find a new hiding place at home and keep it in the mason jar with my money."

Dorothy, after his last escapade, stayed away for two days. When the twelve dollars and some few cents he'd stolen from Mamie ran out, he came home. He walked in on Sunday afternoon, clean and sober. Expecting a fight, he edged through the door, eyes alert for a lunge from Mamie.

She sat at the table. Her lunch, which she had only picked at, lay cold now on her plate. She had been drinking the whole time Dorothy was gone. Her head hurt. She got up to get a drink of water.

"Mamie," Dorothy said, "I sorry for the way I behaves. I try to do better, eh?"

Mamie shook her head slowly back and forth.

"Dorothy, I ain't want to hear no more 'pologies from you. Jest come on in and eat, or do whatever you has to do and leave me be. We gonna come to a partin' of the ways, looks like. I ain't going to put up with you taking my money." She sat down heavily. "Oh, I knows you snitch a quarter here, a dollar there. But you done take twelve dollars and some change. I small, but I got book learning and I keep up with my money. I didn't know you knowed where that money was hid."

"I smart, too, Mamie. I see you hiding your money. You right, I ain't never take that much before. I won't do it again," he hung his head. "Please let me stay,. We could get ourselves married. What you say to that?"

"I say," Mamie snarled, "you must be crazier than I thought! I for shore ain't gonna marry up with you. Or anybody else, either."

Dorothy frowned, but said nothing. He got himself a plate and made a sandwich. Half under his breath, he mumbled, "Don't nobody else want to marry you."

Mamie came around the table and glared at the man.

"What you jest mutter under your breath, bad boy? You spoilin' for a fight? Or you just run away from me again? You not run as far this time, though 'cause your pocket ain't full of my money!"

She socked him in the left eye and went to bed.

He walked over to the bed and fished out two quarts of the ice cold beer.

"Here, have a beer, it'll improve your mood," he said.

She accepted the beer and sat on the mattress drinking the cold brew.

"We gotta stop all this drinking, Dorothy," she said. "We gettin' too old to be livin' like this."

"Aw, you ain't old, Sugar."

"Dorothy, on my next birthday, I be eighty-three years old. I feels old," she said. "I ain't been feeling too good lately. My stomach hurt jes about all the time."

"When you been to see the doctor last?" Dorothy asked. "I don't remember," Mamie shrugged. "I ain't studying' on goin' to see no doctor. I think my stomach hurt from all the drinking. I think I goin' to cut back on my drinkin' some. You should, too."

"I try, sweet thing, I try," Dorothy said. "Let's us go to sleep. Can I have a good night kiss?"

Dorothy kept his promise not to steal any large amounts of money again, but he continued to snitch small amounts here and there, and he continued to drink. Then it happened.

Mamie, on a crisp sunshiny day in November of 1949, sat watching the drugstore. She hadn't seen Mrs. Buntley for several days, maybe a week or two.

I guess I take my chance. I hasn't seen Miz Buntley for so long now. I go on over there and ask that son of hers where she at, or when she coming back. I hates to talk to that nit.

Choosing a time when only a few customers were at the counter, Mamie made her way to the drugstore. She stood at the end of the lunch counter for a long time. Finally, when he didn't ask what she wanted, she ended the stalemate.

"Mr. Buntley, sir. Excuse me, but could I just ask you when your mama will be back? I ain't seen her for a while now and I need to—"

"Why, if it isn't that strange little beggar-woman from across the street. What you mumbling about, old woman?"

"I say, 'where your mama at? I needs to—"

"My mother,' he said, "was killed a little over a week ago. Not that it's any of your business." His eyes were cold, staring. Mamie stood froze, mouth open.

"She was taking my father to the doctor's office, and their cab stalled on the railroad tracks," he continued. "The driver got out, but she and my father were killed. The story has been in the paper. I thought you knew. I thought that's why you were staying on your side of King Street. Now you go on about your business and don't think you can keep coming in here for your coffee, boiled egg and toast."

Looking at the one customer at the lunch counter, "My mother," he laughed, "was a saint. She fed this woman for years, not charging her a cent, even though she has driven away customers with her crazy behavior and body odor."

Looking back at Mamie, he roared, "Get on out of here," as though she were hard of hearing. "I don't want to see you anywhere near this lunch counter again. In fact, don't even come into my drugstore."

Tears streaming down her face, Mamie backed toward the door, but stopped; her eyes locked with his, she squared her shoulders.

"Could you please," she asked, trying not to cry anymore in front of him, "just get my money out of your safe?"

"What?" he shouted, then stared for a long time with his mouth hanging wide open. "What did you say?"

"You know what I say," Mamie bellowed right back at him. "My money. Your mama kept my money in her safe." She pointed toward the rear of the store.

"After my mother," he said, enunciating every work, "treated you so good for all those years, you have the nerve to come in here and say you have money in my safe? Are you crazy for sure? I always thought that was just a big act." Turning to his customer, he said, "Did you hear her? Wants me to get her money out of my safe? She must be having a bad day."

"I ain't crazy," Mamie said, "and you know my money is stacked up in your safe. Now, I wants it."

Two more customers had walked in. People snickered. Ted Buntley performed for his customers.

"Get on out of here, you crazy old coot, or I'll call the police."

At eleven in the morning, Mamie packed up her stand and headed for the bus stop, something she had not done in the thirty some odd years she had been on King Street.

Mamie got home well before noon and went to bed. Dorothy came home about three in the afternoon and found her sound asleep. She slept through the day and night, waving him off each time he tried to find out what was wrong.

On the third day, Mamie finally roused enough to tell Dorothy what had happened. He went to the house where the Remberts lived and knocked on their door. Leslie opened the door and asked him to come in.

""No'am, I best make this quick. Mamie, um, not feeling too good. Can I speak to Mista—I mean, Preacher Rembert? Please?"

"He's not home," Leslie said, "but I'll send him back as soon as he gets here." Seeing the look on Dorothy's face, she added, "Maybe I should come."

She hurried to Mamie's house.

"Mamie, you sick?" she asked.

Mamie sat up on the mattress, rubbing her eyes. She looked around her as though disoriented.

"I guess I is, Miz Leslie," she finally said. "Dorothy shouldn't a bothered you. I just feels like I goin' to die."

Leslie knelt by the bed and felt Mamie's forehead.

Hmm, no fever. At least she doesn't feel hot, but she sure looks sick.

Leslie hugged Mamie and rocked back and forth, patting her on the back.

"Mamie, what is wrong? Tell me, please!"

"My money," Mamie said, wonderingly, "all gone. I was scared of the banks, so I put it with Miz Buntley. Miz Buntley died—she been killed by a train. Her and Mr. Buntley, both. They done got theirself killed in a train wreck, and I, and they, that is . . ." She started to cry again in big gut-wrenching sobs.

"Whoever is handling their affairs will give you your money. Is the drugstore closed and boarded up? How did you find out about the train wreck?"

Mamie wiped her eyes with the back of her hand. Dorothy hovered. He handed Mamie a man's white andkerchief. She blew her nose and.

"They got a grown boy who runnin' the lunch counter now," Mamie said with a sigh of resignation. "Since Mr. Buntley been sick, he been doing more and more around there. That boy no good. He got my money, and he ain't gonna give it back, neither."

"How much money?" Leslie asked. "How much money are we talking about, Mamie?"

Mamie got up and pulled a notebook out from behind a loose board in the wall in the back of the closet. She opened it and turned the pages until there were no more figures.

"I has this amount," she jabbed a finger at the last figure. "Over twelve thousand dollars that I saved for about forty years. That counting the money old Root Woman saved and give to me. I started out with that money when I first come to Charleston in 1908. I started saving from the first day I had my business going on King Street."

Leslie's eyes widened

"Aw, no." she breathed. "You saved that much money in that woman's safe? Did she ever sign a receipt for the money?"

"A receipt?" Mamie asked.

"Mamie," Leslie asked, "did the lady who owned the drugstore ever write her name on any piece of paper showing the amount of money she was holding for you?"

Mamie shook her head and tears flowed again.

"She keep a book with the amount writ down. And I keep a book, too. She alles wanted me to open a bank account or buy gov'ment bonds. Oh, Lawd, I so hard-headed. I shoulda listened."

"Mamie, think," Leslie said. "Did she ever sign her name with maybe a date by her name in either her book or yours?"

"No."

"I'll send John back here as soon as he gets home. We'll try to help. Get out of bed and take a bath. I'll come back and do your hair. You'll feel better if you get up and get cleaned up. Try not to worry."

Mamie bathed.

Miz Leslie right. I does feel some better. A good hot bath is just the ticket. This just a little misunderstanding. That boy probably jes too upset about his mama and papa gettin' killed like that to remember about my money back there in his safe. He probably ain't never opened that safe up since they death. Reverend John will go find out what goin' on. That white boy will listen to a preacher.

Mamie resumed work the next day with lethargic movements. She watched as John Rembert went inside the drugstore.

"Who ever heard of somebody saving money in somebody else's safe? We're a drugstore, not a bank. And I don't want to see that crazy old woman's little notebook. You people are all alike. You think the world owes you a living. I never saw any money belonging to this woman in my safe. Before or after my parent's untimely deaths."

Mamie had come into the store and stood silently waiting by the scale. Turning his attention to Mamie, he glared at her.

"And you," he shouted, "I told you not to come back into my place of business. Ya'll get on out of here or I'll have you arrested. Go on. Git."

As they left, Mamie fished a little gray sack out of her pocket and dribbled graveyard dirt onto the floor at the entrance, on the sidewalk and halfway across King Street. Turning, she raised her arms above her head and whispered in an eerie voice.

"Damba-a-a-la? Oh-h-h, Dam-ba-a-a-la? Take him down, down to his death. By slow degree so he suffer much, take him down for me. And so it begin."

"Mamie," Reverend Rembert asked, "what was that all about?"

"That," said Mamie, "was a Voodoo curse. I done put a hex on that man. He be fairing poorly. Soon now."

When she saw his doubtful look, she added, "You'll see."

That night at the stroke of midnight, Mamie stood in front of Buntley's Drug Store. Dorothy, her unwilling accomplice, shifted from foot to foot, eyes bulging, perspiration beading his face. She took several small bags from her pocket and opened them. Sprinkling the contents on the door frame and all over the glass front of the drugstore, she uttered words Dorothy could only guess at. She next poured a trail of cemetery dirt from the drugstore to her spot on King Street. Retracing her steps, she stopped in the middle of the street and began a chant and a dance right in the same place she had hours ago uttered the curse.

Dorothy heard the clomp of the horse's hooves before he saw the policeman. He called to Mamie in a whisper.

"Mamie, police commin', let's hightail it outta heah."

"And so Dambala," she said, giving no indication that she had heard Dorothy, "send misery aplenty-" here she stopped, shook the clay replica of Dambala and turned round and round three times, shaking all over with the snake raised high overhead in the moonlight. "-brong this nit, Ted, to his death by slow, painful degree. And so it-"

"What do you think-"

"— is! I have spoken; it is done," Mamie said before acknowledging the policeman with, "Sir?"

"What do you think you are doing?"

"I is practicing Voodoo. You want me to do a spell for you?" Mamie asked, grinning.

"Your name Mamie?" he asked.

"Sho is. Sho Lawd is. Why you want to know?" Mamie asked.

"You get on home. You got quite a reputation for being, uh, shall we say, different. Anybody else, I'd take 'em in, but—just go long on home peaceful and I'll let you go."

"Okay, I was finished up here, anyway. Good-bye now," Mamie motioned for Dorothy to follow her.

"Hey, Murphey. Whacha know, man?" Joe Turner asked when John walked into the police station at two AM.

"Fun and games all night. Come on back and I'll tell you something you won't believe," John signed the duty roster to indicate that he had completed his shift. Two hundred and ten pounds and standing at five feet four inches tall, Murphey wheezed as he got a cup of coffee and sat down.

"So, what's up?" Joe sat, arms crossed over the back of the chair.

"You know that crazy old beggar who sells pencils outside Kress on King Street?"

"Oh, yeah. Everybody on the force knows that old coot. What —"

"She," Murphey said, "was down on King Street at midnight tonight spreading dirt all over the place, dancing, and yelling in the middle of the street."

"What? Maybe she was drunk." Joe scratched his head. "Was she all by herself?"

"Naw, there was a short, fat high-yellow with her. He just stood over on the sidewalk, and kept his mouth shut. She said she was doing some kind of Voodoo stuff!"

"Yeah, that's her 'boyfriend'. Ain't that a laugh? They were drunk. Didja run 'em off?" Joe asked.

"Yeah, but I don't think they had been drinking. She was dancing and shaking a pole with a snake wrapped around it, but I didn't smell any alcohol on them. Weird."

"A live snake?"

"No. Looked like it was made of wood. Like a prop in a play or something," Murphey said.

"Well, I wouldn't worry 'bout them two. They're both crazy or retarded—or both! Who knows? I'm going on home to the Missus before she sends the police to look for me. See ya, Buddy."

"Yeah, see ya. Uh, Joe?" Murphey asked as his fellow officer turned to go.

"Yeah, Fella? What'cha need? You ain't scared she put a Voodoo—"

"Ah, never mind, see ya tomorrow night," Murphey said.

Murphy stood by his locker recreating the scene on King Street.

Okay, I was tired, it was late, they scurried away down King Street toward Wentworth Street. I walked my mount down the Street, heading toward South Battery. I heard something. What? Don't know. I stopped, turned around in the saddle, looked back just in time to see their backs rounding the corner at Wentworth and King.

Murphy, now dressed in his civvies, sat back down with another cup of coffee.

I saw—or thought I saw—a snake crossing King Street on that trail of dirt she had poured. When I rode back, I saw no snake, but I did see the undulating *trail* of a snake. Naw. Could have been her dress dragging in the dirt. Yeah, right. In a perfect s-shaped curving trail like a snake would make.

Murphy shuttered. He looked at his hand shaking so much he sloshed hot coffee out onto the table and himself. He rose, rinsed the cup, put it away and splashed cold water on his face. He went home determined to put this out of his mind.

The next day Mamie, working as usual, watched as a crowd of people rushed in and out of the drugstore across the street. Moments later an ambulance screamed up King Street from Calhoun Street, lights flashing.

Mamie joined the onlookers in front of the store as medics brought Ted Buntley out on a stretcher.

"That rattlesnake came out of nowhere and bit me on the thigh as I reached into the safe," he screamed, eyes flashing wildly. "It must have been coiled up, ready to strike. Just sitting there on the counter by the safe," he said to nobody as he passed the crowd. He lay on the stretcher, craning his head. "My God," he shouted as he passed by Mamie without even seeing her, "how did a rattlesnake get into my drugstore?"

Leaning forward and stretching upward as far as she could, Mamie grinned at Ted Buntley face to face as he passed by on the stretcher.

"Dambala." she intoned, "Dambala has struck you. HEE-HEE-HEE!" her face contorted as she laughed.

"Get that crazy old woman away from me," he demanded. "What the hell is she muttering about, anyway?"

The medics hurried him into the back of the ambulance, closed the doors, and let their sirens blare as they bore him away to the hospital.

Three elderly colored men ambled down King Street after the fracas subsided. As the crowd began breaking up, one of them looked knowingly at the other two.

"I knowed a man name Jonah long years ago. He knew that old beggar-woman who work the street wid she pencil stand. He and his wife, Sukey—I believes she was called —anyway, this same beggar-woman ustta live with them folks." He scratched his ear and in a low, sing-song kind of voice, continued.

"Jonah tell me one day, 'this woman know some Voodoo'. Some even say she got a Dambala coiled round and round a long pole some old Root Woman made for her long years ago."

Another of the men, not to be outdone, joined in.

"You don't say?" he cackled, almost dancing his lithe body in excitement. He skipped around until he was between the two other men and added his wisdom to the pot. "I knows a little about Voodoo. That a powerful ting to have. If she really has a Dambala, that a powerful ting to have. She must be some kind of Voodoo Queen.

"Last night," the third man, a tall coal black man wearing a jaunty hat, spoke up, "Ransom worked the graveyard shift at the jail house, cleaning the empty cells and such. He was just getting off work when he passes outside the kitchen and overhears two of the police sitting there talking. They say she did a Voodoo ceremony right heah in the middle of King Street last night! In the light of the full moon.

"Ranson Jones?" asked the first man. "He say this?"

"That the man. Yes sir, yes, indeed."

They all agreed that it wouldn't do to get on her wrong side.

Isaiah and Lacy, home in New York, at last, visited family and friends in Brio at Christmas. Mamie told them about the loss of all her savings when they came to Charleston to see her the day after Christmas.

"Mamie, he kept *all* your money? All the money you had saved over the years? How much?" Isaiah asked.

"Yeah, he kept all of it, over twelve thousand dollars. I has it writ down in a little notebook. Reverend John tried to get him to give it back, but, he just laughed in our face. I fix him good, though. He still laid up from that snake bite."

After his visit with Mamie, Isaiah consulted his friend Bill Culver, his friend and attorney. Bill told him there was little they could do with no record of the transactions over the years. "A court of law would not take the word of an old, eccentric colored woman over that of a drugstore proprietor."

"She's got the notebook."

"That notebook is worthless."

"Okay, Bill," Isaiah said, "I'll lay low and try to come up with a scheme for getting her money. Right now, I can't think of a thing I can do."

He returned to Mamie's house where she and Lacy were catching up on news.

"Mamie," Isaiah said, "Lacy and I are leaving to go home to New York tomorrow. You know you can come and live with us whenever you want. I'll try to think of some way I can get that thieving skunk to cough up your money."

The drugstore stayed closed for the rest of that year and on into the spring of 1950. Even before the rattlesnake incident, customers had begun to go to the new Walgreen Drugstore. Speculation ran high about the closed drugstore.

"Well, if you ask me, the business had gone to hell in a hand basket long before the Buntleys' untimely death. Ted Buntley never seemed cut out for that sort of thing. Too impatient with people," said one former customer, sitting at the lunch counter down the street from the old Buntley place.

"Yeah, since his parents' deaths, the place hasn't been the same. They were the glue that held the drugstore together. Especially Mrs. Buntley," an old man sitting next to him said.

Ted Buntley reopened the drugstore in May of the following year. He was then and walked with a limp. The snakebite had become infected and he had undergone an operation on his thigh. The doctor had told him that he'd come close to losing his leg.

Almost all of the old regulars were used to the Walgreen's lunch counter and, to complicate matters, Woolworth Five and Ten now offered a really good menu of down-home cooking.

Ted Buntley seemed to make an attempt to rejuvenate the business. Every day he stared from his front window at the old woman across the street. When Mamie saw him, she shook a long pole with what looked like a snake wrapped around it. He had heard the talk of her Voodoo escapade the night before the rattler bit him. Day by day, she seemed to suck the determination out of him.

In the fall, he put the store on the market. Isaiah made a low bid, not expecting to have it accepted. Ted Buntley, using no real estate agent, came to him with a feeble counter offer. Isaiah said no, and Buntley accepted the pennies-on-the-dollar price. In town for the closing, Isaiah stayed for a few weeks to get his new toy up and running.

A week after the transaction, he called Ted Buntley.

"I found an old manila envelopecontaining something valuable. It was taped under the center drawer of the desk in the storeroom. Do you know anything about this?" Isaiah asked.

"What's in the envelope?"

"Cash," Isaiah said.

"Cash? How much cash?" Buntley asked.

"Oh, it's almost thirteen thousand dollars. Why?"

"Well, it's mine, that's why."

Isaiah laughed.

"What makes you think it's yours? I own the store now and everything in it."

"Well," Buntley stammered, "we'll ju-just see about that. I'm calling my lawyer." He hung up.

"Hey, Bill, I think he took the bait. Can you come down to Charleston tomorrow? Good, see you in the morning. Yeah, Lacy and I are staying in that monstrosity of Moorish architecture on High Battey. Sure, join us for breakfast. See you around eight then."

The next day, Isaiah stood behind the lunch counter serving customers. His attorney, Bill Culver, manned the grill. He saw Buntly and his lawyer's car pull up. The two men jumped out and hurried into the store.

"Gentlemen," Isaiah asked, "what will you have?"

In a low voice, the attorney said, "Could we have a word with you in private? I'm Henry Waddington. I'm Mr. Bentley's attorney. I understand you have some property that belongs to my client."

Mamie arrived as prearranged and sat on the scale.

"Step to this other end of the lunch counter," Isaiah said, "where the old woman is sitting on the scale. Quieter there, I believe."

They walked to the end of the counter. Ted Buntley glared at Mamie who was mumbling just loud enough to be heard about Dambala, the serpent god of Voodoo.

"Now, what were you saying, Sir?" Isaiah asked, a soft smile spread across his face. He looked over at Mamie, and winked.

"I have some of this man's property?" he asked. Loudly now. "I don't know what you're talking about. I'm running a drugstore and lunch counter, not a storage place."

The money," Ted Buntley said. "The money you found taped under the desk. The money in a manila envelope."

Isaiah's mouth dropped open.

"What in the world are you talking about? I never found any money taped under any desk. That's the most preposterous thing I've ever heard." Then, giving him an almost exact quote of what he'd said about Mamie, "You people are all alike. Think the world owes you a living." Again, a broad smile at Mamie. "How much money was I supposed to have found?" Isaiah's eyes twinkled, and he boomed out with his infectious laugh. That was Mamie's cue to make a scene.

"Thirteen thousand dollars, you said on the telephone," he began, just as Mamie got up and shouted to the people eating lunch, "Mr. Isaiah found the rest of my money. I alles kept half in one place and half in another place." She pulled an old-looking manila envelope out from under her coat and opened it just enough for Ted Buntley to see the stacks of money.

"Mamie, shhhh, don't say another word. Go on about your business, now." To the attorney and Ted Buntley he said, "She's crazy as a loon. Can't pay a bit of attention to anything she says.

Turning to Bill Carver who stood behind the counter wearing a spotless white apron, he smiled.

"Bill," he said, "I'm going to drive Mamie to the bank. She never trusted the bank before, but I think she does now. I'm going to help her set up her own account. Back after a while. Look after the place for me will you?"

"I thought," Waddington said, his jowls bouncing from indignation, "you said you never found any money. First you say she is crazy, then you confirm that she has the money

that you found. Now if that money was found in my client's store—ummm, his former store—then it clearly belongs—"

"To whoever found the damn money," Bill Culver said. "That is, if any money was found. Isaiah said he didn't find any money. Now, I would suggest that you two get on out of here. You are making a nuisance of yourselves."

Ted Buntley and the attorney asked in unison, "Who are you?"

Bill, enjoying himself immensely, pulled a business card from his wallet.

"My card, gentlemen," Bill tossed the card across the counter, "now good day."

He turned on his heel and went to the other end of the lunch counter. Mamie and Isaiah got into his white Cadillac and drove off.

Ted Buntley brought suit against Isaiah, but the courts threw the lawsuit out, calling it frivolous. Isaiah didn't even bother to come back to Charleston for the hearing. Bill handled everything.

Isaiah hired a manager for the drugstore, changed the menu to include country ham, red-eye gravy and grits, redesigned the pharmacy and store, added an ice cream parlor with tiny tables and wire-backed chairs, and, in short order, had the place booming again.

"Let's eat at the old drug store today," Mr. Kirston, the owner of a small stationery shop said to his wife.

"Yeah, let's," his wife agreed. "I hear that country ham and red-eye gravy over grits is mouth watering!"

"He serve that for lunch?" he asked. When she nodded, he said, "Man I like what's happened over there since that man from up in New York bought it."

"Well, you know," she said as they walked hand in hand down King Street, "he's originally from up around Kingstree."

Around two in the afternoon at a local high school, a young boy whispered to the prettiest girl in the school.

"Meet me around four at the new ice cream parlor, and I'll treat you to an ice-cream float."

"What new ice cream parlor?" she asked, dimpling.

"Oh, you know; the old Buntley place on King Street."

"All right," she said, "you're on. I didn't know they had a soda fountain in there. See you."

A year later, Isaiah made a tidy profit. He sold the place to his manager. He sat with Mamie after the sale at the counter in his previous drugstore. She sat on the scale and he at the end of the lunch counter.

From the profit, he reimbursed Mamie for the money Buntley had stolen from her. With that money, she repaid him the loan he made her to trick Ted Buntley.

"You didn't have to put that money in the bank for me, you know," Mamie said, as she counted out the money he had lent her.

"Oh, yes, I did. I just knew Ted Buntley would check it out at the bank to see if you really opened an account. Of course, they wouldn't tell him how much," Isaiah said, laughing. "But, in a small town like Charleston, when a colored woman opens an account of that size, word gets around. 'Mamie Managault' has a nice ring, eh?"

"And you had your spies," Mamie said, chuckling.

"And I had my spies," Isaiah agreed. "They told me he asked everybody he could think of until he finally got the nitty-gritty of it." He slapped his thigh, and continued before Mamie got a word in. "How I would have loved to have seen his face when old Mildred let it slip that you had actually opened the account with almost thirteen thousand dollars."

"Isaiah, I mean—Mr. Ike, you didn't have to give me fourteen thousand from the profits. He took just under thirteen thousand dollars. Why you give me fourteen?" Mamie asked.

"Because I made almost twenty thousand profit, after all the remodeling,paying Bill for that nuisance suit and the closing costs. And because I wanted to, now eat up and let's go. I got a train to catch."

Ted Buntley, hunting in the swamp the following year was bitten by a rattler. He ran right into quicksand and started sinking, but grabbed a tree branch and pulled himself out of the muck. By the time he got out, it was too late.

"He died in the parking lot of the hospital, Mamie," Isaiah said. "He died all alone, and his leg swelled up like a balloon. I kind of feel sorry for him."

"I don't," Mamie said. "Dambala."

She again heard of the death a few days later, from somebody else, and smiled a secret smile. That night she lit another candle in front of Dambala on its pole, and when she went to sleep, Root Woman came to her in a dream.

Appearing from the mists of the swamp, she smiled at Mamie.

"Tough times," she said in the dream, "not over yet, Daughter, but you will fare better by and by. Use Dambala only when you has to."

The dream faded and Mamie awoke with a start, her heart pounding. A nameless fear gripped her. She got up and lit another candle before Dambala.

"Dambala, I ain't want to cause no more harm to anybody with this Voodoo."

Then she prayed to Jesus on his burning cross. Finally she drifted off to a peaceful sleep, only to awaken hours later knowing something was terribly wrong. She got up, turned on the light and found her friend lying there in bed, too still, much too still.

"Dorothy," she whispered. "Dorothy?" She shook him. He didn't move. She lay back down on the mattress and cradled his lifeless body in her arms. "You done give it up, ain't you, Sugar?" Tears ran down her cheeks. "You done up and died, ain't you? My poor Baby. My poor sweet man."

Chapter 15

A Talent Long Dormant

She was there
Year after year
By Kress on King
Doing her thing!
That old indomitable citizen
That fussing fuming denizen
Through, smiles, tears, and pain
Through sunshine, cold, heat and rain
Storing up images of figures and faces
Colors, lines, angles and places

On May 15, 1959, Mamie stood in line at the Citizens and Southern Bank. She did not budge when the line moved up. The man next in line walked around her, looking straight ahead. She tried to take a step, but managed only to wobb leaning far over to one side. She righted her body, and then fell face-forward.

"Help, somebody help. I think she's dead," said the next person in line. The woman looked down at Mamie who lay on the cold marble floor.

Later in the hospital she opened her eyes.

"Hello? You awake now?" a short black woman inquired. Mamie's mouth felt like cotton and her head hurt. The nurse's aide continued when Mamie didn't answer. "You badly dehydrated," she said. She wiped Mamie's mouth with a lemon swab. "Who you wants us to call for you. You Mamie, ain't you?"

"Yes," Mamie's whole body trembled, "my name is M-Mamie. What dehy—de . . . wh-what you ca-call it?" She asked. "W-what tha-at m-means?"

"You is dehydrated, uh, you know, all dried out. You needs to get more liquids in you." The aide slipped a thermometer into Mamie's mouth and took Mamie's pulse. "We giving you fluids," she said, "through your veins. See the IV stand with the tubing that goes up to your arm. Keep your arm real still. It takes a long time to all go in you. Who you wants us to call for you?"

"Oh," Mamie answered, looking away from the needle in her arm. "Y-you c-can call, m-my pre—Can I have some water?"

"You kin have a sip," the smiling woman said, "here, just a sip or two. So," she asked, "who you wants us to call?"

"My preacher. Reverend John Rembert." When the woman did nothing, Mamie added, "I ain't know the number, but the operator give me they number one time. I is cold."

The nurse's aide piled two more cotton blankets on and left the ward. Mamie slept.

When Mamie awoke, she saw Leslie standing by her bed. John Rembert sat, reading the Bible.

"How long you been feelin' sick, Mamie?" Leslie asked, taking her hand.

"I don't know. A long time," Mamie said. She lay propped in bed with extra blankets piled on. Warm and re-hydrated somewhat, her teeth no longer chattered. "I got something wrong with my stomach. It hurt every time I eat most anything. So I don't eat too much. I guess I just forgot to drink, too."

"Do you want us to call your friends up in New York?" John asked.

"Naw, that long distance. He be down heah terectly. He come about every other month or so." Mamie motioned for the water, and with Leslie holding the glass, she drew in mouthfuls of the refreshing liquid through the glass straw. "It cost money to call New York. I ain't ever call them, but one time. That was when Dorothy had the stroke."

"Don't worry about the cost of the call. We'll pay for the call, won't we Leslie?" John asked. She nodded.

"I'm going to call him right now," he continued.

"You think I goin' to die," Mamie said. "The time not yet." Mamie searched their faces with troubled eyes. "I doesn't feel like I is goin' jes yet but you kin call him. He be wanting to know I is in the hospital I 'spects."

John patted her on the arm and left the room. He called Isaiah from a pay phone in the lobby. Isaiah answered the phone on the first ring.

"Hello?"

"Mr. Ike, this is Reverend John Rembert in Charleston. Mamie's minister? Yes, in Charleston."

"Oh," Isaiah said, "I thought you might be Lacy's doctor calling. She's in the hospital with a bad cold. Mamie all right?"

"Well sir, as a matter of fact, she in the hospital, too. Mamie got something wrong with her stomach, she says. Anyway, she passed out at the bank today. She seems to have a cold, too. At the hospital, they found out she is dehydrated," John said.

"How bad off is she, John? Isaiah asked.

"Well, they pretty much just making her comfortable and watching. I'm here at the hospital now. I talked with the doctor on the way in. He said he thought she would be all right, but at her age . . . ."

Isaiah allowed the silence to stretch to a thin, taunt line between them, and then burst out laughing in spite of himself.

"John, you don't have to pussy-foot around about our ages. I'm one year older than Mamie and Lacy is a year older than me. We're glad to be so old." Lowering his voice, he confided, "Means we haven't died young."

They both laughed.

"How long," John asked, "has your wife been in the hospital?"

"Just since yesterday. I'm hoping to bring her home today. The doctor wanted her in overnight, I think, just to run some test." Isaiah pulled the notepad closer and said, "Let me call you back. The number there?" He scribbled the number. "I'll call you when I know something about Lacy."

Isaiah called the hospital where Lacy was and asked for Dr. Morrisey. He came on the line almost at once.

"How is Lacy, Doctor?"

"The test came back just a few minutes ago. She looks fine. No pneumonia. Her lungs are clear as a bell. I'm going to let you take her on home. Bed rest for a few days and she should be good as new. It's just a nasty cold."

Relieved, Isaiah put down the receiver and immediately picked it up again. He called Moses.

The housekeeper, an Irish woman in her sixties, answered. Isaiah could barely understand her, but heard her call to Father Moses. He came on the line.

"Son, your mother is coming home today. Yeah. Real good news. She's just got a bad cold. But listen, Reverend Rembert in Charleston called. You know, you met him one time. He's Mamie's minister. Mamie is in the hospital, too. Also a cold. Don't that beat all?"

"How bad off is she, Papa?"

"Don't know, but the preacher sounded worried. You think you could pull loose and make a quick run down to Charleston for me? I'm not going to Charleston with Lacy sick, but Mamie could be—"

"Course I can go. Try not to worry until we know what's what. Okay?" Moses asked with concern in his voice. "I'll see you at the hospital."

Two days later, Mamie left the hospital. On the way home, she smelled the magnificent magnolias along Rutledge Avenue. With Father Moses by her side, she rode in the cab and inhaled the heady aroma of a spring day in Charleston. She noticed the blue of the sky, the birds singing, the other cars along the route the cab took.

I ain't never notice how beautiful the world is. Seems like I seein' color more bright and hearin' birds sing more beautiful. And oh, the smell of them magnolias.

"Mamie, you're getting too old to work," Moses said, "come back with me. Mama and Papa have plenty of room for you."

"I ain't want to be a burden. I be all right, but I might just pack it up and quit selling my pencils," she said, looking like a lost child. "I been on King Street too long. Too-o-o long," she added as though to herself.

"You know, Mamie, you're younger than Lacy and Papa," then rushing his next thoughts out as though building on an inspiration, he added, "my papa probably needs you to come and help him take care of Lacy. Remember, I told you Lacy had been in the hospital, too?" Moses turned to face Mamie and took both her hands in his. "Mamie, they really do want you to come live with them. And, in truth, you just might be a big help. Please say you'll think about it."

"I ain't know how to clean—"

"No, not to clean, Mamie." Moses said, "for company. Say you'll think about it?"

Mamie nodded and stared out the window of the taxicab. When they pulled into her street, she broke the silence.

"I'll think on it," she said.

After much discussion, Mamie agreed to the plan to move to New York. Moses stayed in Charleston, helping her get her affairs settled. For a week, he kept busy, helping Mamie pack, helping her to transfer her bank account, going with her as she made the rounds, saying good-bye to the people and the city that had been her life for fifty years.

On Saturday, he took her to the spot on King Street where she had sold her pencils. They got out of the cab and walked over to the corner by Kress Five and Dime.

Mamie heard a woman talking to her son.

"That's the woman I was telling you about. She used to sell pencils right there and she chased me half-way down the block when I was about your age, Michael."

Mamie stared at her departing back, remembering the little six-year old who had said, "Hi, Mamie" so long ago.

The woman's young son turned his head and looked back at Mamie. Mamie smiled at the boy.

Mamie took a few running steps toward the retreating backs. She watched them until they turned into a music store.

At the end of that week, the Remberts threw a party for her in the basement fellowship hall of the church. A red punch bowl graced the table as a centerpiece and little sandwiches filled two large platters. Red streamers hung overhead. Next to the sandwiches were assorted cookies and cakes. Little children ran through the hall as adults tried to make them sit.

Moses took a swallow of the red liquid and put it down on the table.

"What the matter wid the punch?" Mamie asked, seeing his face. She took a sip, then set her own cup down. "Too sweet, huh? Well, that's the way some folks likes it. It too sweet for me, too."

John Rembert asked them to bow their heads and asked a blessing.

After they'd eaten, the minister said a few words about Mamie leaving and how she would be missed. Tears running unimpeded down her cheeks, Mamie gave a little speech to the people gathered there to honor her.

"I been down-trodden, and I been up-lifted. I been blue and sad, and I been happy, but tonight I is overjoyed! Thank you all from the bottom of my heart."

She sat down to a round of applause and pleasant laughter. People filed by and shook her hand, and then they sang a few hymns and ate more cake and drank more punch, saying good-bye in all the different ways folks have for doing that sort of thing.

"I used to be scared of you," Alice Turner shook her head and laughed, "You sweet thing, you."

"Bye, Miz Mamie," Amos said, as even a few of the little children said their good-byes.

"I useta be scared of you 'fore I got to knowin' you, but-" He looked down at his feet, then back up at her, and whispered, "I sorry for the time us chil'rens pushed you down. I was in that crowd of roughnecks. I — I sorry."

Mamie hugged the boy.

The minister shook Mamie's hand and said, "Keep the faith, Sister. Jesus loves you and so do we."

"I'll miss you so much," Leslie said, crying, "don't forget to write."

Mamie hugged some of the people and smiled at each as they passed.

"I surprised," she said to Leslie as they sat in the back seat riding home, "that Alice woman come up to me and said what she did. I kin see some of the children bein' scared of me, but she a grown woman. I still don't much like her."

"Maybe," Leslie added, "now that you're leaving, she realizes how much she'll miss you. And maybe she misses her friend, Maude. I know I do, and I'll miss you."

"Me, too," Mamie brushed away a tear, "me, too."

Moses looked across the seat from the front and smiled at the two women.

Arriving in New York City twelve hours after leaving Charleston, they were met by Isaiah and Lacy at Grand Central Station and went directly home. In the cab, Mamie silently stared out the window.

"Not having second thoughts already, are you Mamie?" Isaiah asked.

She turned a big grin on him and shook her head.

"Aw, naw. I just lookin' at the sights. Been years since I was here visiting y'all. I alles love to see the streets in New York. And the smells. It different from Charleston, that for sure, humph."

Isaiah, Lacy and Moses exchanged looks, not knowing if the 'humph' meant 'good for New York' or 'I like Charleston better'. Nobody asked for clarification.

Lacy put her in the guest room. "We're getting Moses' old room ready for you," she said. They conspired to keep Mamie out of the house and busy.

The next day, Lacy persuaded Mamie to go shopping for some dresses. When they got back, a man with carpentry tools was just leaving.

"Mamie," Isaiah said, "we have a surprise for you. Close your eyes. Lacy will lead you."

"Mamie, this is to be your room," Lacy said. "Take a peek."

When Mamie opened her eyes, she stood in the doorway and grinned.

"If you think of anything you need, you let us know," Lacy said.

"Naw, Lacy," Mamie said, at last, "looks like you done thought of everything! How you make the furniture so short? The whole room is jes my size!"

"We're so happy to have you here with us," Lacy said. "I take it you like your bedroom?"

A child-sized, upholstered chair sat by a low-to-the-floor corner table. A straight-backed chair stood at the table, too. By the plush, rose-colored chair stood a small table with a beautiful lamp.

"How he build this so quick?"

"He has been working on the table and chairs for a week. He just didn't have them quite ready before you arrived yesterday, so," Isaiah said, "Lacy and I devised a way to keep you out of the house until he could get these delivered."

"I thought," Lacy said, "you were going to refuse to go shopping with me. You knew something was afoot, didn't you?"

"Naw," Mamie said, "I just didn't want to go out and spend any of my money. I didn't know you and Isaiah was paying for a couple of store-bought dresses for me." Mamie rocked from stump to stump and grinned. "When we got to that store, I like to have passed out at the price of them clothes. Miz Leslie make all my clothes for me back home. That sho is a good woman."

"Well, you have your own money, but Isaiah and I wanted your first few days with us to be special. You can decide if you want to find a seamstress to make your clothes in the future, or if you want to buy ready-made. What," Lacy asked, with a twinkle in her eyes, "did you think of Macy's?"

"That one fine store," Mamie said. "But I ain't buying no more dresses in that place. These two dresses cost more than I spends in a whole year." She cut her eyes at the two of them and they all laughed. "'Course you two payin' for these fine dresses. And I 'preciates it too, but no, sir. If I *do* buy ones already sewed in some factory—"

"There are stores where the prices are quite a bit lower. We'll go one day. Just to look," Lacy said.

"You sure," Mamie asked, running her hand in a caressing manner over the highly polished walnut end table, "you all don't want any rent from me?"

"No, you're family, Mamie," Lacy said. "You can live with us for as long as you like."

"How about," Mamie offered, fingering the frame of the heavy mirror, hung at eye level to Mamie's height, "I pays the electric and gas bill, then?"

"Ah, Mamie," Lacy said, looking around for Isaiah who had left the two women, and gone back to some other part of the house, "you'll have to take that up with Isaiah. I realize you want to do your part, but you really don't have to worry about any of that. You just buy your clothes and toiletries and anything else you might want."

After dinner, Mamie retired to her bedroom. Lacy and Isaiah sat in the alcove just off their bedroom reading some and talking over the day.

"Isaiah?" Lacy asked, breaking a long stretch of quiet.

Isaiah laid his book down, and looked over at Lacy.

"Hmmm?" he asked.

"Did Mamie talk with you about her paying the utilities here?"

"Yes," Isaiah smiled, "she sure did. I showed her a recent light bill. I thought her eyes would bug out of her head. I told her she didn't have to worry about paying any bills or anything." He scratched his scraggly beard and chuckled. "She's independent as a hog on ice and I think that's good. But you know, I could tell she was relieved as all get out." He got tickled and laughed. "Not to have to pay the light bill after seeing how much it was."

Lacy smiled at him, shaking her head.

"How much," Lacy asked, after a pause, "*was* it?"

"Not much by New York standards Fifteen dollars and something, I think. She's used to a light bill for a dollar or two, I bet. We are running a lot more electrical appliances than she was, plus the size of our place compared to hers." Isaiah continued to chuckle as he picked up his glass of wine, remembering Mamie's reaction. "You're not worried we can't pay the bills, are you?" he asked with a wink.

"No, dear," Lacy said, "but I wondered just how much it was. You spoil me, paying the bills and all." Lacy got up and walked behind Isaiah's chair. She massaged his neck and shoulders. "Don't know that I even remember how to write a check. How long have we been using checks, anyway?" When he just shrugged, she continued. "I remember when we paid everything by cash, and if you needed to pay someone that was out of town, you used a bank draft or a money order." Lacy returned to her chair spreading the soft afghan over her feet. After another hour of reading, she asked, "You about ready for bed?"

"Whenever you are," Isaiah stretched his long legs out in front of him and his arms high over his head. He dug his stocking-clad feet into the deep pile of the sheep skin rug. "How's your cough? I didn't hear you last night, or today."

"It's gone," Lacy said, "thank the good Lord. That's one cough I don't want to see again. Mamie seems all right, too. Glad she's over her bad spell."

"She's still not eating much," Isaiah noted.

"Well," Lacy gathered up her things, "I think her stomach bothers her because she can't chew. You think we could talk her into getting dentures?"

"No, not at her age," Isaiah said, scrunching up his forehead. "I think she's too old and set in her ways to want to bother with false teeth. Maybe we can fix food that's soft and doesn't require much chewing, though."

"You're probably right." Lacy headed to the bathroom. "I think I'll ask her all the same." Coming back with her hair freshly brushed, she called to Isaiah as he entered the bathroom, "Goodnight, dear heart."

Isaiah came back to the bedroom, crawled into the massive four poster bed and murmured, "Good night, my love. Give a little kiss?"

They kissed and held each other and then drifted off still in each other's arms.

After Mamie had settled in, she noticed Moses painting one day. She said, "I wish I could try that." He gave her some of his brushes and a canvas. Mamie took to painting like a duck to water. Isaiah's and Lacy's brownstone backed to a beautiful courtyard full of flowers. Beyond the courtyard, a mature garden thrived under their excellent care. The L shaped atrium overlooked this perfect gem of a garden. The sun, soft as April suns often are, came through the open skylights and floor-to-ceiling glass windows in palest gold. The light shone with a liquid quality as though the sun filtered through a fine mist, even though the rain, after three days in a row, had stopped earlier that morning. Moses and Mamie painted in the atrium; he at his full-sized easel, she at her child-sized one.

Mamie painted in sharp clear colors. Her characters took on a life of their own by the expressions on their faces and the positioning of their bodies.

"Mamie," Moses said, looking at her canvass, "your style is a unique blend of primitive and impressionist."

Mamie, finishing the leg on a little black boy, didn't answer him right away. She painted contentedly, thinking.

I love this house. This city. My life. The art galleries we go to. Eating in the restaurants. No segregation. I have even got more schoolin' in a manner of speakin'. Isaiah and Lacy teach me so much. And Moses. That boy is like my own son. That boy. He for sure a man. Big like his daddy. I loves him so much.

"What them two big words?" she finally asked, "What that means? I just paints."

"It means," Moses said, "that I like your painting style. That one," he pointed to an oil she had finished the week before, "of the people going into a little country church, dark skins, all white clothes . . . did you see such a scene when you were very young?" He walked over to the painting. "Their dress is the fashion of the late eighteen hundreds, I would guess. Just look at the smiles on those faces. Good? I should say so."

An easy camaraderie existed between them. Mamie painted on. Abruptly, she wiped a brush, grinned and looked at Moses. She waited until she caught his eye.

"Well if you should say so, then do."

Moses laughed. Mamie looked at him again.

"You the spittin' image of your daddy. You look like him. You sound like him. I likes to paint with you," Mamie said, smiling and cleaning her brushes. "I've learned a lot from you. I never knew I could paint."

"I've learned from you, too," Moses said. "You've been here for almost three years, now. You like living with Mama and Papa, don't you?"

"Moses," she said, as she slowly put tubes back in her paint box, "I do, but sometimes I gets lonely for Charleston. And even the swamp. I misses my old life, but it easy to live here."

Mamie cleaned the last brush and screwed the cap on the turpentine. While Moses worked, finishing his own painting, glancing at her from time to time, but not saying anything, she continued.

"I thought when I first come, we'd have to be visiting all the time, but they keeps busy and I does, too. And I like it that way. We visits and we lives our own lives."

"That's good," Moses said.

"And them television sets they bought last week! They got me one for my bedroom, too. Ain't that something? Dorothy used to take me to the picture show. Now I can see a show right in my bedroom any time I wants. I has lived to see modern times, I guess."

The maid came into the atrium, "Lunch will be ready in about twenty minutes. Mr. And Mrs. Norris are having their lunch in the bedroom, but I can set the table for the two of you."

"No, thank you, Marie," Moses said. "As a matter of fact, I've got to run, but if you would fix me a sandwich and wrap it in some wax paper, I'll eat it on the way to the parish. Think you could find me a couple of cookies, too?"

"Will do, Father," the maid said. "How about you, Miss Mamie? I fixed some nice homemade chicken noodle soup. Or I could make you something else? And I've got some pears soft as butter."

"The soup and pears will be good," Mamie said, "and I'll eat in my bedroom, too. And thanks."

The maid left after admiring their art work.

"I can't get over the way we lives," Mamie whispered to Moses. "A maid to wait on me. To tell you the truth, I feels kind of funny, having somebody doing for—"

"Mamie," Moses said, "you deserve it. Relax and get used to it. Enjoy the attention, you're almost a hundred years old."

"Naw," Mamie said, a toothless grin splitting her face, "it only 1962. I not a hundred until 1966."

"Well," Moses said, "you're right as usual. I stand corrected. You are over ninety-five years old, so kick back and take it easy. Let me run in and say bye to Mama and Papa. I'll see you later, sweetheart."

Mamie lifted her face for his customary kiss on her cheek.

He one fine man. Teach old Mamie to paint. My, my!

Mamie continued to paint, and over the next year, grew even more accomplished in her brushwork.

"Let's go to Central Park today to paint," Moses said.

"You go with me?" asked Mamie.

"Yes, of course, you don't think I'd let you go all alone, do you? I don't have any appointments this morning. Nothing until three in the afternoon. The light in Central Park will be a nice change for us."

They walked, Moses carrying easels and paint boxes for each of them. At the entrance on East Fifty-sixth Street, they passed a mime who drew a small crowd with his white-face and bright orange and red stripped stockings. Mamie's face took on a terrified look, and then relaxed as she realized he was no threat to them.

"Mamie," Moses asked when they reached a suitable spot from which to paint, "what happened back there at the entrance to the park? Did the mime frighten you?"

"Remind me of some mens from long ago, Moses. Long ago," she sighed.

"The Ku Klux Klan?" asked Moses.

"Yeah, for a long time anything white reminded me of that time. I better, now," she smiled up at him as she spoke.

"Yes, you certainly are," he said as he set up their easels. "You've come a long way, Mamie. How about we contact a friend of mine and see about having a show of your works?"

"Naw, I ain't want no show," Mamie said.

Moses let the matter drop. They painted all morning, had lunch from a street vendor, and got back about one in the afternoon. Moses prepared to leave, bending low to kiss Mamie's cheek.

"Moses?" Mamie asked.

"Yes, sweetheart? What do you need before I go?" Moses asked.

"You really think I should have a show? I that good?"

"Are you kidding? You're great. I mean it, Mamie," Moses assured her, picking up his briefcase, "just give it some thought. Bye, now."

"Bye-bye, Moses," Mamie said. "I loves you," she added, softly, grinning as she waved bye to him.

Chapter 16

Dambala Strikes Again

An easel, a paint box, a brush or two
Some red and brown, some white and blue
Wind on marsh grass by the Cooper River
A shrimp boat tossed like a toothpick sliver
Blacks on the dock bent double in wind
Pulling and hauling the small boat in
At the last, Dambala struck again
Then split down the middle in heavy rain

Mamie continued to paint. She, Isaiah, and Lacy often toured art galleries. On other days, Isaiah and Lacy accompanied Mamie to Central Park, sitting on a blanket, reading while Mamie executed deft strokes.

"She's got quite a talent, eh?" Isaiah asked in late fall.

"Yes," Lacy looked up from her book. "I've enjoyed seeing her grow as an artist. She and Moses. Have you noticed how close those two are? It's not just their art, either."

"Yeah, I know what you mean. Not changing the subject, but days like we've had are soon gone. It's already starting to get cold."

In late afternoon, Mamie packed her paint and canvass, and they left the park. Walking home, they planned supper.

The winter of 1963 in New York City was bitterly cold. The next April it warmed up with a false start. Then the rain came in driving, cold sheets for seven straight days. When spring finally arrived with soft breezes and beautiful warm days, a lot of people sniffed and wheezed.

Isaiah and Lacy, on a balmy day in May, got sick at the same time. Moses had them admitted to the hospital, and he moved into the house with Mamie.

Hortense VanCamp, one of Moses' sisters, arrived the day they were admitted. She and Moses talked. Tense's tea grew cold.

"Can I get you a fresh cup?" Moses asked.

She looked over at the teacup and shook her head.

"Moses, what do you think? Will Papa and Lacy pull through? I can't believe they are both in the hospital at the same time. Bronchitis?" She stood and began to pace. "They make it through the bitter cold and rain and get sick in May? It doesn't make sense, does it?" she asked with a catch in her voice.

Moses stared out the door of the study. It opened onto a garden filled with irises and roses. Lilac trees, ranging in color from lightest lavender to deepest magenta bordered the brick wall. The scent wafted through the French door. Moses tore his gaze from the garden and looked at his sister.

"Well, they *are* pushing one hundred. I wouldn't have thought they would come down sick in this warm weather, either, but I guess germs don't care how nice and balmy it is. They are," Moses said, pensively scratching his thick, curly beard, "getting the best of care. Want to walk out to the garden? Mamie just went in through the dining room door, so we'll have it all to ourselves. Want to?" Tense nodded, and they walked out to the far patio, and sat on the cushioned settee.

"Speaking of Mamie, how is she holding up?" Tense asked, as they settled themselves side by side on the outdoor couch. "She's older than they are, isn't she?"

"No," Moses said, his laugh so like his father's, booming out, filling the garden, "she is actually the youngest of the trio. By my reckoning,

Mamie is ninety-eight, Papa will be ninety-nine this fall, and Lacy is already one hundred as of March of this year."

"Yep, I remember," Tense said, "Papa's birthday is in September."

Moses nodded. Each sat quietly. Soft breezes caressed their faces, and the garden worked its magic.

"You know, Papa and Lacy," Tense said, "don't seem much older than — oh, say, seventy-five or eighty, while Mamie could easily pass for over a hundred years old. She seems just ancient. Is her health good?"

"Well, Papa persuaded her to go to the doctor way back when she first came here to live. You know, to see what ailed her stomach? She had stomach aches all the time, even with strained baby food." Moses stood, stretched, then sat back down. "The doctor found she had an ulcer, but it's cleared up now. She's got a little arthritis in her hands and elbows, but not bad."

"I see."

Moses got up and walked to the low table where the teapot sat in a cozy. He poured a cup for himself and offered one to Tense. She again refused. He returned and sat down.

"Over all, Mamie's in pretty good health. Of course her teeth being gone doesn't help her digestion, and she won't even consider false teeth," he laughed, recalling the row over whether or not she needed dentures. "She and Dorothy used to drink pretty heavily, from what I've heard, but that's been years ago, so I guess she's in no danger from that."

Tense moved over and sat closer to Moses. She laid her head over on his shoulder and he hugged her to him. She snuggled into his embrace.

"Say, when you saw Mama and Papa this morning, did you tell them I'd be there this afternoon?" Moses asked. "I hated to miss visiting them, but I just had to see this old fellow called 'Rabbit.' I think he's dying."

Tense smiled for the first time that morning.

"Rabbit? What a name. Yes, I told them you had an emergency call at dawn and had to go to the mission hospital. Tell me about this 'Rabbit.' How old is he and what's he got? You really think he's dying?"

"He's probably got pneumonia," Moses said, "he's much worse off than Papa and Mama, and yes, sad to say, I think he's dying." Moses ran his hands through his short, curly, gray hair.

"He started coming to mass about two years ago. I'd say he is over a hundred years old. He calls himself Rabbit. Why, I don't know."

"Interesting," Tense said. "Does he have family?"

"I doubt it. He showed up at the mission hospital this morning sick, running a high fever. They called me to see if they could admit him without his having a card. We issue cards to all the parishioners who use our clinic. You know it's a free clinic. Well, Rabbit didn't have a card because he is not a member of the church, but I told them to admit him anyway."

"I hope he's better soon, or at least that he doesn't suffer too much if this is it for him. I should be used to death by now, but I'm not. Not for Papa's. Not for Lacy's." She straightened up and fished in her pocket for a tissue. Moses patted her shoulder.

"So many of us have died over the years," she said. "You know I was eleven when my mother died. I miss her still." Moses drew her even closer into the crook of his arm. "And Ida. She was a good mother to all of us. When she died five years ago, I felt like I'd lost another mother. Even after the divorce, we kept in touch."

"I never knew Ida," Moses responded. "I heard through the grapevine that that divorce just about killed her. Split the family right down the middle, too, didn't it?."

"Yes. But, you know, Moses, she and Papa hadn't lived together as husband and wife for years before the divorce. Didn't even live in the same house, but she sure didn't want a divorce. Then, while they are fighting over whether or not to have a divorce, she put in to have the store. Why, I'll never know. She hardly ever set foot in that place." Tense shook her head. "Ida ended up bitter and divorced. She didn't, of course, get the store."

"Well," Moses said, "the store is dear to Papa's heart, even to this day. I imagine he fought her pretty hard on that point. She received a generous amount of cash and property in the settlement, though, didn't she?"

"She did get a goodly amount of cash, stocks and bonds. But she never seemed to enjoy a penny of it. So sad." Tense got up and led the way into the middle of the garden, breathing in the fragrance.

"Ida loved to garden, but after the divorce, she never seemed to care even about her lovely perennials. For years, she just sat on her front porch, rocking away in her old rocker. People would wave to her from the highway, but they said she never waved back." They returned to the settee and sat back down. Tense lay her head, again, on Moses' shoulder.

"How do you know so much about her after the divorce? You were off in Virginia with your family by then, weren't you?" Moses asked with a chuckle.

"Her friend, Jewel, wrote me all about her strange behavior. Said she even stopped seeing her oldest friends. That's when I doubled my efforts to bring her out of her bad mood. I made a point to write to her every week, and telephone her occasionally. She never seemed to respond to me as warmly after the divorce. I guess because I was still in contact with Papa."

"You were a good daughter to her. Probably the best friend she had during that time"

"Well, I knew she just couldn't seem to let go of the idea of getting the store. And I knew full well Papa would never turn loose."

"The store," Moses sighed. "Papa was talking about selling the store to the fellow who has run it all these years, but I don't think he ever will. I went with him a couple of years ago to see the place. It's nice. Still a real honest-to-goodness country store. Rocking chairs, pickle barrel, checkers and all."

"Hmmm," Tense said, "it's a part of Papa. And the community. It keeps Papa happy just knowing he still owns it, I think. You know he started that store when he was just thirteen years old?"

"Hard to imagine him being thirteen years old, eh?" Moses grinned. "To me he looks old and young at the same time. You know I was about that age when I first laid eyes on him."

Tense turned, and rested both of her hands on his chest.

"That," she said, "must have been hard for a teen-aged boy to go through."

"Well, I did have a bit of sorting out to do, but we got through it," he said, smiling at his sister.

"He's kept himself in good shape—and Lacy, too," Tense said.

"Yes, they exercise together. Papa holds her feet while she does sit ups. They *try* to do deep knee bends. I drop by sometimes early in the mornings and hear them giggling like a couple of school kids in their bedroom, doing their morning routine as they call it." Moses laughed. "Hey, let's walk around a bit. You feel like taking a stroll up this little stone path? I'll show you a hidden nook."

"They are like love birds," Tense said, as they ambled arm-in arm. "Always have been. I mean, well, ever since I've known them as a couple. Moses, doesn't it seem strange that they have always been together? Not together, but connected." She stopped talking and took in the sight of a small, hidden, garden-within-a-garden. There stood a statue of Saint Francis and a bird bath.

"Oh, it's beautiful," Tense breathed.

The statue depicted a monk bent over as though feeding three stone birds. Clumps of lemon grass gave it an almost Japanese look.

"Why, thank you," Moses said, "I gave this-the statue, the bird bath with the little birds-to Papa and Mama on their last wedding anniversary. You know, Papa told me one time that he fell in love with Mama when he was just eighteen years old. And she with him."

"Yes, he loved her all those years. Through three other marriages. I was there throughout his marriage to my mother, and throughout some of his marriage to Ida. I think he loved them, too. Though he and Ida had problems, in a strange way, I think he loved her."

"Yes," Moses said, "I believe Papa has a tremendous capacity for love. I think he loved even Ida. Too bad."

"You know, Moses, It's odd, that out of eighteen children born to Papa, only you, me, William and Philip are left. All the others died young. Too young. You think Papa and Lacy are going to die soon." It was not a question.

Moses cleared his throat as they sat back down. He looked at her steadily for a full minute or two without answering.

"Yes," he finally said, "I do. They are very sick. We will be all right, and they will be, too. Death is not a punishment, Tensie."

With a quick intake of breath, Tense took this in. "I know," she nodded, "we'll be all right. I never thought I could make it without my husband by my side, but life goes on." She stretched and said, "Moses, I think I'll skip lunch and just go on upstairs for a nap. You don't mind? I'm so tired."

Moses saw unshed tears glistening in her eyes, but chose not to mention the emotion they both felt.

He leaned over and felt her forehead.

"You go right ahead. You're not coming down with anything, are you?"

Tense shook her head.

"I'll be okay. Maybe I'll just see them this evening. I need time," she murmured.

Moses got up and walked behind his sister's chair. He began to massage her neck and shoulders.

"Sounds like a good idea to me. If I don't see you here, during the day, I'll see you at the hospital this evening. I'm going to make a quick visit with 'Rabbit', then head on over to the hospital. I love you, Sis."

He walked with her to the door of the guess bedroom, then proceeded on to his parents' bedroom where he was sleeping for the present. As he entered the familiar room, he shivered.

Wonder if I'll ever see the two of them in this room again?

Moses arrived at the mission hospital, a small storefront place just off thirty-third and Lexington. The smells of lunch permeated the front hall. Old carts rattled by with steaming bowls of hot vegetable soup.

He asked for a bowl of soup and some bread and took it into the little nurses' station with him. The doctor was busy with a patient so he ate his lunch while he waited to see the doctor. A nurse walked by just as Moses finished his lunch.

"Please bring me the chart for Rabbit if you don't mind," Moses said.

"Who?" she asked.

"He was just admitted this morning. He goes by the name 'Rabbit.' He's old, and I think he's pretty sick. Probably pneumonia."

"Oh, I bet you mean that old fellow in room sixteen. He told me his name is Rosco. I'll go get the chart for you."

Moses read through the chart as he waited for the doctor. He looked again at the chart.

Rosco, no last name. Presents with coughing, congestion, fever, x-rays reveal fluid in lungs, probable diagnosis, pneumonia, further test ordered. Nickname, Rabbit. Age, unknown. Address, The Exchange Hotel, room 120. Next of kin, niece in South Carolina.

Moses rubbed his nose and thought about the chart.

No, just coincidence. Of course he would be about the right age. No, too strange. Not a chance.

Doctor Kahn came bustling in.

"Father Moses, what are you doing reading that chart? Don't you know that's a 'Medico sin'? That's one of our ways to keep the non-doctors at bay, you know."

"Yes, well. I'm guilty as charged," Moses grinned. "What do you think? How sick is our friend, Rabbit?"

The doctor sat down and asked a nurse to bring him some soup and a sandwich and coffee.

"Father," he sighed, "I think he's a very sick man. I ordered a blood work-up and the results are not back yet, but his lungs are full of fluid. He's breathing with great difficulty. We are, in fact, giving him a breathing treatment as we speak. I just left his room. Is he a special friend of yours?" The doctor smiled and leaned forward. "Oh, I know, they're all your little lambs."

"He's a parishioner. Well, not a member of our church, but he's been coming for about two years or so. I get the feeling he's not a Catholic, even, but I can't be sure. Something about the way he genuflects. Not that it matters to me. But I just don't know him very well at all. He sits on the last pew and hurries out the door before I can speak to him."

The doctor began wolfing down his lunch and, between bites, managed to squeezed out a conversation.

"How's your mother and father? I heard from one of the nurses that you had them admitted to Presbyterian Hospital the other day. Bronchitis, I think she said. That seems to be going around."

"Well," Moses said, "they're both in the hospital. And yes, they're pretty sick. I am worried about them."

"Sorry to hear that," the doctor said, "let's hope for the best."

"Yes," Moses said, "let's. Well, I better get down to Rabbit's room if I'm going to visit with him and still have time to see my folks. No rest for the weary, eh? Good to see you, Jack. Take care of yourself."

Father Moses knocked on the door,which was ajar. A nurse nodded to him from within the room.

"Come in, Father," she said. "Look, Rosco, you have company. I'll just leave you two. Push this button right here if you need anything." She left, carrying a tray of equipment with her.

"Hello, Rabbit, how are you feeling now? Some better than this morning, eh?"

Rosco grinned, "How you doin,' Father? I ain't feelin' too bad right now. If I could just breath easier, I wouldn't be troublin' you none."

"And who said it is any trouble?" Moses asked, taking one of his frail hands between both of his.

"Oh," Rosco smiled, "that just a matter of speaking. Just a matter of speaking.".

"Rosco, you're from South Carolina? What part of the state you from?"

"Ah, I ain't lived there in eighty years," Rosco panted. "It a little old town up near Kingstree," he paused catching his breath. "A place called Balters."

The hair prickled at the back of Moses' neck.

"Tell me about it."

"Ain't nottin' to tell. I high-tailed it outta there back in 1882," he stopped again to catch his breath. "When I was just twenty years old. Ain't never been back there either. Well, I was back one time on the sly. Didn't see anybody. Just kind of sneaked in late one night and back out the next day. Learned that my mama had died. And my girlfriend . . .." He started coughing.

"What about your girlfriend?" Moses asked.

Rosco turned his eyes toward the wall. Moses waited for him to continue.

"Well, that was in 86 or 87." he cut his eyes up, thinking. "I don't remember 'xactly. No matter. Why you ask me about all that, anyway?"

"Well, I thought you might want us to call a relative for you,"

Moses said, knowing that was not the whole truth. "You know, Rosco, you are really sick. I don't want to alarm you, but-

"I know," Rosco squeezed Moses' hand. "I know I might be cashing in my chips. Well, I ain't skerred of dying. I ain't got nobody but a niece back home, and she don't know if I'm alive or dead." He grinned.

"As a matter of plain truth, she would be gettin' on up in years, too. She might not be still alive." He struggled with his breathing. After a few gasps for air, he continued. "No, I don't want anybody called. I got a room over at Miz Taylor's on 125th Street. The address is there on the stand." He burst into more coughing. "I got five hundred dollars in a manila envelope under the mattress. Maybe you can use that to bury me?" Rosco coughed until he almost lost his breath.

"I had a paid-up insurance policy and when I turned a hundred, they sent me a check for five hundred dollars. I beat the insurance company, by not dying before I turned a hundred, so they sent me the money. That's all I got. Think it enough?"

Moses cleared his throat and nodded, not trusting his voice

"Rosco," he finally said, "you mentioned high-tailing it out of Balters way back in the 1800's. I sense a story there. You want to tell me more?"

Rosco looked at Moses for a long time, then said, "No, it all happen so long ago. It a sad, sorry story and I too weak to go into all that now. I hope you understand?" Tears welled up in his rheumy eyes.

"It's all right," Moses said. "Rest. I'll be back later."

Moses walked the seventeen blocks to Presbyterian Hospital, hands shoved deep into his jean pockets. A taxi driver honked furiously at him as he crossed against the light.

A doctor and two nurses were tending to his father when Moses peeked into the room. His mother, down the hall, appeared to be asleep. He retreated to a small waiting room.

A nurse came into the waiting room shortly, and cleared her throat. Moses looked up.

"Sorry to awaken you, but you can see your father now."

Not bothering to explain that he wasn't sleeping, Moses

thanked the nurse and went in to see his father.

"How are you feeling?"

Isaiah opened his eyes and coughed.

"I have felt better. Is Tense with you?"

"No, Papa, she is taking the afternoon off to take a nap. Says she didn't sleep much last night."

"I hope she isn't coming down with this infernal virus. The doctor says it's hitting a lot of people. How is Lacy? I want her moved into this room. I don't see why she can't be in here."

Moses said he would take care of it and left the room. He came back with Isaiah's doctor and a nurse. The doctor ordered another hospital bed be put into Isaiah's room and Lacy was transferred within the hour. They smiled at each other, then up at Moses.

The two beds were jammed up against each other with the side rails down between the two beds. The doctor had made sure the wheels were locked so the beds would not separate.

"Papa, I think a man at the mission hospital might be Rosco from Mamie's past. He's bad off — dying, I think. I know it sounds too queer to be true, but he comes from Balters and he left in 1882. Some trouble which he wouldn't talk about. I couldn't get much else out of him."

"Oh?" Isaiah asked.

"Yes, my question is do I try to find out, and, if he is, do I tell Mamie?"

"Don't know, Son. Just can't say. Would it serve any purpose?"

Isaiah stared out of the window for long moments. Turning to his son, he asked, "You say he is dying?"

"I think he is not long for this world. His lungs are full of fluid. He has a high fever."

Isaiah said again, "I don't know." He lay as though asleep. Moses kissed his brow. Looking over at Lacy, he found her sleeping too, and tip-toed out of the room.

He went back to the mission hospital. Rosco lay on his back, sleeping with his mouth open, his breath sounding like a gurgling stream. Moses sat by the bed, praying and meditating for perhaps an hour. Suddenly, he opened his eyes and looked at Rosco.

I must have dozed off—something's not right.

He leaned forward. Rosco was not breathing. Moses called for the nurse with the signal by the head of the bed.

I'm glad I gave him last rites before I left earlier today and that I baptized him the day he was first admitted to hospital.

Laying a hand flat against Rosco's bony chest, Moses felt a tear slip down his face.

I'm *crying for more than Rosco's passing.*

Moses left, already planning in his mind how to do the funeral. Striding back to the parish, he thought it all out.

There are some funds in the parish for emergencies. Don't know how much. He rapidly figured the amounts he would need. *Probably not more than a thousand. Maybe not more than five hundred. We'll see.*

Moses returned home to find Mamie dressed and wanting to visit Isaiah and Lacy.

"Mamie, I have to get a shower and eat something. This has been a hard day for me."

"I know, for me, too," Mamie said. "I feels uneasy about your papa and mama. They gonna die soon. I know it in my bones. I wants to see them both before it too late. I has somethin' to say to them."

"I think you're right," Moses said. "I feel that the end is near for them. We'll go as soon as I can get ready. Is Tense still asleep?"

"Far as I know, she is."

"Let's let her sleep until I get through with showering. Ask Marie to fix supper a little early tonight. I won't need but about thirty minutes. I'll get Tense up in about fifteen."

The three of them arrived at the hospital about six o'clock, long before visiting hours. They were, nevertheless, allowed to go in to see Isaiah and Lacy.

Their dinner trays sat untouched. Tense tried to feed them some of the still warm broth, but neither of them felt like eating.

"How's Rabbit doing?" Isaiah asked.

"He died," Moses said into his father's ear, "I didn't tell Mamie anything.

"Probably for the best. Not to tell her."

"Not tell me what?" Mamie asked.

Isaiah laughed, or tried to laugh. He ended up coughing until he almost lost his breath.

"For someone your age," he said, when he could finally speak, "you hear remarkably well. Tell you that I'm feeling mighty poorly. That's what."

"Oh, I knows that. I ain't no fool, you know. I gots somethin' to say to the both of you."

Lacy and Isaiah looked perfectly at ease. They smiled at each other and then turned their attention to Mamie. Lacy, in a voice barely audible, asked, "What, Mamie? What do you want to tell both of us. Sounds important."

"Well, it is important. I loves you both."

Isaiah, mimicking Mamie's voice almost exactly, said, "Well, we know that. We are not fools, you know."

"I wasn't," Mamie said, grinning back at him, "finished. I got a heap of money saved up and nobody to leave it to, now that it looks like you two is gonna . . .." She stopped and hung her head. "What I sayin'? I just a old, confused woman. I—"

Lacy said, "Mamie, no need to avoid the subject. Isaiah and I— we know . . .."

" . . . that we are, um, how shall we say? We're failing fast. Yes, that's a good way of putting it. In short, we know we are dying. It's been a good life, but . . . ." Isaiah stopped, then asked, "Now, what were you about to say?"

Mamie stood by their beds on Isaiah's side, tears streaming down her cheeks. "I needs to know who you want to get my money? Moses? Tense? Or should I divide it up amongst the four children? I ain't got no other family that I know of."

"Mamie," Isaiah said, "you will know when the time comes. You will know."

Mamie buried her forehead against the edge of the mattress. Isaiah patted her head.

"Mamie, I'm glad you brought the subject up," Lacy said. "Isaiah and I were just talking about dying. It's hard to turn loose.

We'll miss you. Moses, come close, Son, I want-"

Philip burst through the door, with William right behind him.

"Hey guys, we got here as soon as we could. Papa? Lacy? We'd a been here sooner, but we just got the telegram when we got home last night. Moses—"

"Yes," Moses said, moving over to stand by his mother's side, "I tried calling you. Where have you been? We—"

"Ah, come here Sons," Isaiah whispered, "come close."

He hugged the two men, and Lacy wiggled her fingers at them and smiled.

"Mama," Moses asked, "what is it you need?" He bent down and kissed her cheek.

"You know how much I love you, and how proud of you I've always been. Try not to grieve too long, nor too hard."

"But, Mama, who says—"

"Moses," Isaiah said, his voice stronger than before, "we are dying. Now, you know where all our papers are kept. I asked Bill's son, William Jr., to update our will about six months ago. Moses-"

"Papa, don't—"

"Son," Isaiah wheezed, "let me finish. You will inherit the store, along with a strip of land all the way back to Rodenburg Pond. Tense, you get the house, along with ten acres." He stopped and rested.

"Papa," Tense said, "we don't—

"Please," Isaiah whispered, then continued, "William and Philip get stocks and bonds as well as some land." He stopped talking and took Lacy's hand, nodding to her in an unspoken message.

"Your father and I," Lacy said, "have specified what each of you are to have as to furniture and personal belongings. The old brownstone on Lexington goes to all five of you. You too, Mamie."

"Oh, Papa, Lacy, rest now, maybe you will get better. We love you so," Tense said, hurriedly leaving the room.

The children stayed at the hospital until late that night, taking turns sitting by their parents' beds. Isaiah and Lacy drifted in and out of sleep. The small reception area, at the end of the hall, afforded them a place to visit.

"So you and William were over in Aiken buying property and didn't get our telegram about the folks?"

We went to look at a parcel, but didn't buy it. Soon as we got back in town the phone began to ring."

"Thank God," Moses said, laughing, "for small towns, eh?"

They left around eleven o'clock, with Mamie staying the night, sleeping in a cot in their parents' hospital room.

Six hours after he'd left, Moses was back by his father's and mother's bed.

"How in this world," Moses asked, laughing in spite of himself, "did you manage this, Mamie?" he asked.

Isaiah and Lacy slept in Isaiah's bed, and Mamie in Lacy's. Mamie opened her eyes and grinned.

"I pushed that chair over here and climbed up here," Mamie said. "When the nurse come in, she near about had a fit. So I had one right back. I raised so much ruckus, she left me alone. I didn't like that lumpy, old cot. Besides, the bed plenty big enough for the two of them. Ain't that right, Lacy?"

Lacy nodded and smiled. Mamie got out of the bed with Moses' help. About ten o'clock, with Tense, Philip and William in attendance, Moses slipped out of the room. He took Mamie home to rest, and went to arrange Rosco's funeral for the next day.

Isaiah and Lacy's bronchitis now developed into pneumonia. Doctors came and went. Nurses tried to make their breathing less tortured with breathing treatments. At one point, the doctor wanted to put them back in separate rooms. Isaiah became so agitated that Moses prevailed on the doctor to leave the beds together.

Two days after Rosco was buried, Moses and Tense stood by Lacy's side of the bed. Moses held one hand, Isaiah the other.

"She's gone." Isaiah turned his face to the wall.

Isaiah could not attend her funeral. Moses consulted with him about all the details, and explained that the doctor didn't think it wise for him to try to leave the hospital. He did not protest. All the fight seemed to be gone from his big frame that was now just skin and bone.

In the limousine, coming back from Lacy's funeral, Mamie sat still and mute. Suddenly, she broke her silence.

"Root Woman always said, 'Death come in threes,' but it ain't my time yet, I don't think. Who next after Isaiah?"

Moses started to speak, but thought better of it, and looked sharply at Tense. He sat with a strange, puzzled look on his face.

"Rabbit," he finally murmured.

"What? What you say? Rabbit? I knowed someone call himself 'Rabbit.' It was a long, long time ago. What about Rabbit," Mamie asked.

"Oh, nothing," Moses said, "a rabbit just 'ran across my grave,' that's all."

"Oh," Mamie said, "I know that expression. Moses, is you ready to say good-bye to your papa? He goin' soon, now." They went directly to the hospital. Isaiah lay there, crying and wheezing. He wouldn't talk all the rest of that day.

The day after Lacy's funeral, Moses sat by his father's bed. He read from a missive, silently. Getting up, he moistened Isaiah's lips. He leaned over and gently kissed his forehead.

"Son," Isaiah whispered, "I want to tell you . . . ."

Moses heard the long shuddering breath. He waited for another. Nothing. Isaiah lay still, eyes wide open, a slight smile upon his face.

Moses gently closed his father's eyes and said a prayer.

Again, in the limousine, coming back from Isaiah's funeral, Mamie spoke of death coming in threes. When she again wondered aloud about who would be next, Moses looked at her with that strange, far away expression.

"You thinking," Mamie said, "it be me, that I gonna die next. I don't reckon to die jes yet. I believes it either someone close to me that gonna die, or somebody already died and I not know."

Moses didn't answer her. He hugged her to him in that fierce embrace so typical of Norris men.

Mamie took the deaths of Isaiah and Lacy better than Moses would ever have imagined. She grieved, but with great dignity. She seemed to be philosophical about it all.

Having buried their kin in late spring, Moses and Mamie

moved the next year, after Moses retired. They moved to Brio, South Carolina. Into the old home place next door to 'Ike's General.'

The man who rented the store had served as caretaker of the old house. He had lived alone in one of the bedrooms. When they came, he moved out to his own place.

Now, one of Mamie's paintings hung over the fireplace. The painting showed a young Isaiah and Lacy, standing under an oak tree on the bank of the Black River. It hung in the parlor, where so many children had played and quarreled, loved and grown up.

Mamie took Moses to the very tree. There, far up on the tree, for it had grown over the years, barely discernible, were the initials J. I. N. and L. L.

"Well, I'll be," Moses said, "Mamie, how did you know about this?

"Lacy told me that night I sleep in her bed. Said I was to show you. She tell me exactly how to get here, too." Mamie stood, craning her neck up at the tree. "My picture ain't quite like the tree, is it? Pretty close, though."

"How about us having an art show here at Ike's Emporium?" Moses asked.

"I study on it. Your paintings, too?"

"Yes, that's a great idea. I will, if you will."

Tense, after selling her house in Virginia, joined them. Tense, Moses and Mamie all lived in the old home place. Philip, divorced for the third time, came to live with them, too. Charming as ever, he was a card, even now that he was in his late fifties.

"Hey, Mamie, you painting today?" he asked as he came in to breakfast.

Looking at him over the rim of her coffee cup, she said, "Don't see why not. I paints every blessed day I is able. My arthritis ain't too bad this year, so I reckon I'll paint out on the front porch."

"Mamie," Moses said, "maybe it would be better to paint inside, or out back of the house. I don't know yet if there is any Klan activity around. I heard yesterday that there is a new group calling themselves White Supremacists who are going around trying to stir up trouble."

"I bet," Philip said, laughing, "they just love us all living here together. They come around here I'll give them supremacy. I'll give them a bullet right between the eyes."

"I hope you're kidding as usual," Moses said. "We don't want any trouble. Let's continue to keep everything low key. What do you say, Mamie?"

"Suits me. I ain't want no trouble from them Klans peoples. I paint inside, or out back. It warm for so early in the year, uhn?"

"I'm going shopping," Tense said. "Anybody need anything?"

"How about I come with you?" Philip asked.

"Sure," Tense said, "love to have the company."

Moses asked her to bring him a pair of white shoelaces.

"Long ones for high top tennis shoes, please?"

"Sure, Moses. Need anything, Mamie?" she asked. When Mamie shook her head, Tense and Philip headed for the kitchen door. Moses kissed Mamie's papery cheek and headed next door to the store.

"Paint me a butterfly, Mamie," Philip said. "I love that painting you did of the butterfly and the bee."

Mamie grinned up at him. He left the house with Tense.

"Mamie, don't forget to drink plenty of water. I'll be right next door," Moses said as he left.

Humming a happy little tune, Mamie carried her easel and paint box out to the back lot and set up to paint under a huge oak.

Maybe I will let Moses set me up in a show. Naw, too old to start showing off. Besides, he just like my paintings 'cause he like me.

Savoring the warm sun on her back and shoulders, she placed a blank canvass on the easel and began a simple country scene with tall hollyhocks and purple and yellow butterflies beside a sandy lane that curved away into distant trees. Some of the scene reflected what she saw, but most was imagined. Finished, she started a new painting of Blacks fighting to pull a small shrimp boat in to the dock. The scene showed a raging storm. She glanced at the sky. Dark clouds assembled and a wind whipped up.

She threw out a raucous burst of laughter from sheer pleasure.

Out beyond the fence, in the back field, two young boys, aged fifteen and sixteen, spied on Mamie. From the old apple tree at the edge of the property, they took turns with a pair of binoculars.

"That's that old nigger woman named Mamie used to live out in the middle of the swamp with the witch called Root Woman. Did you hear her cackling to herself? Root Woman was a witch. I bet she's a witch, too." The older boy handed the field glasses to his younger brother, Jonathan. "You don't know her, do you?" Jonathan steadied the glasses and looked at Mamie.

"Sure I do," Robert said, "the witch woman was the one put that Voodoo spell on great-grandpa, Clem. Caused him to blow his darn foot off in that hunting accident. I bet she taught Mamie how to be a witch, too."

"Aw, you don't know what you're talking about," Jonathan said. "You're just trying to scare me. I don't believe in witches. Hey, she ain't got no legs, is she?"

The older of the brothers continued studying Mamie. Finally he said, "Jonathan, I bet we could scare her. I'm gonna try something." He handed the binoculars to his brother and cupped his hands around his mouth. In a high-pitched voice, he called, "Mam-i-e-e-e? Ohhh, Mam-i-e-e-e."

Jonathan laughed, nearly falling out of the tree. The older one grabbed the binoculars back and looked. Mamie had stopped painting and was looking all around, her mouth dropped open in surprise, or fear. He tried again, this time tucking the binoculars under his arm. "Mam-i-e-e-e, this is Root Woman-n-n! I've com-e-e-e for you! Time to go-o-o-o."

He looked again, and saw Mamie walk toward the fence separating the two fields. The boys had a stash of small rocks in the fork of the tree for throwing into Rodenburg Pond.

"Watch this," Robert said. "I bet I can hit that tree half way between here and the fence where she is standing.
He threw a rock and it thudded against the tree with a solid whack. A five-foot-long snake that had been sunning itself along a lower branch, dropped head-first toward the ground, out of sight of the boys. Catching a branch with its tail, it hung upside down in plain view of Mamie and seemed to stare at her. Suddenly, a downpour. Rain pelted her face. She squinted to see through the sheets of rain.

"Dambala," she breathed, sagging against the fence and holding onto the top rail. Mamie watched as the snake slithered to the ground.

"Oh, it Root Woman! Or is that the light playing tricks wid my eyes? Oh-h-h, Ma-Saylee! I ready," she shouted.

Mamie raised both of her arms, and in a loud voice called, "Root Woman, Ma-Saylee," over and over, louder and louder.

Now both boys could plainly hear Mamie as she called Root Woman's name. Robert grabbed the binoculars from his brother and looked. He saw her arms slowly sink to the fence rail. She stood, arms resting over the rail and her chin on top of the rail. On her face was a peaceful smile. As he relinquished the glasses to his brother, he thought he saw another old woman, there by the fence, tall, thin, with a gnarled finger pointing toward the apple tree.

"Give me the glasses back a minute," Johnathan said, snatching at them.

"Give me," Robert said, "the damn things. Now!" He grabbed the glasses and almost fell out of the tree. He looked, then screamed.

"Get down, get down right now. Run." He scrambled down the tree, dropping the binoculars in his haste. His brother followed him. He pointed to a snake coming toward the apple tree, "Run", he screamed at his brother, "It's the witch. Snakes don't travel upright on their tails."

Jonathan took off running. When he looked back, he didn't see his brother anywhere. He ran and ran.

When he finally felt safe, he waited for Robert under the chinaberry tree in their front yard. About an hour later, he saw his brother, dragging toward him. He ran to meet him.

Midmorning, Moses found Mamie sagged against the fence. He felt for a pulse. It was a thread, but there. In the hospital, she talked disjointedly about seeing Root Woman and Dambala.

"It's not uncommon in someone her age," the doctor said, "to see things. I think she's suffered a stroke. Time will tell."

He walked out into the hall with the doctor. Coming back into the room, he heard voices. He looked all around. Seeing no one, he turned back toward Mamie who lay quietly.

"Who were you talking to, Mamie?"

"Root Woman," she breathed, drifting off into a deep, peaceful sleep. He heard a slight noise at the door, and looked up in time to see a thin, old woman slip out of the room. He ran after her. Down the corridor, he glimpsed a tall woman with long gray hair, hurrying away. He called to her. She kept a distance between him and her, and then seemed to just disappear. One moment she was there. The next, she was gone.

It was the light, he thought. *A trick of the way the light reflects off the shiny floor. But she seemed to shimmer with a green glow just before she disappeared. I'm just tired. I'll go back and see to Mamie.*

Mamie lay as he had left her, a peaceful smile on her face. She was gone. He knew it before he felt for a pulse.

Moses buried Mamie out by the fence where she had been when he found her. A few weeks after the funeral, he stood beneath the tree where the boys had hidden when they spied upon Mamie. He gazed out across Rodenburg Pond to the old Union Presbyterian Church.

Strange story that boy told. Can't believe he didn't die from the snake bite.

Moses, his back pressed against the rough bark of the apple tree, skimmed a rock toward Rodenburg Pond. He smiled when it actually plunked down into the water.

Strange, too, how I found the old clay snake. Cracked wide open from head to tail following each undulating curve of its five-foot length, it lay with mouth wide open and a fang broken off.

With his back against the old apple tree, he felt the warmth of the late October sun laid as a blessing across his shoulders.

The church is old, the tree ancient, the land permanent.

Moses tried to imagine his father here as a young man. A breeze fluttered the pale, faded letter with the strange spidery script. His mother's hand. He read it again.

March 3, 1899

Dear Isaiah,

Your recent visit has left me feeling more than ever that we must be together. I was so sorry to hear from your own sweet lips that Jane, your wife of little more than a year, had died in childbirth. When you visited me in February, you seemed to blame yourself. My Darling, I implore you to turn your thoughts away from self blame. This was not a punishment. We never hurt Jane. James Isaiah, don't you know tragedy just happens?

My heart goes out to you in your loss. I am, however,

gladdened by the fact that your son, Rob, is a big, strapping boy, and is thriving at the breast of his wet-nurse, his Aunt Isabelle. It is good that the two cousins were born only days apart. So for the time being he's living next door to his aunt and uncle with your father?

Dear Heart, sell the store, and come here to live. I don't think we could manage to live there in Brio or Balters. Considering what happened to Mamie, they would surely be out to get us. Say hello to Mamie for me when you see her. Isaiah, I would even 'pass' if you wanted it so, though that idea is distasteful to me. I love you.

Yours forever,
Lacy

Moses folded the letter and put it back into the fragile envelope. One letter. He stared at it.

I would have been eleven when she wrote this letter to Papa. He didn't know about me at that time. Are there other letters packed away in some forgotten box?

He kicked a spot on the ground where little pebbles lay scattered.

Ah, leave off with the old resentments. Why they did not marry then is none of my business. Stop trying to rewrite history. Things worked out as they were supposed to.

The bark of the apple tree felt rough against his hand as he leaned with his hand and arm behind him.

How had Mamie's Dambala, the clay snake made so long ago, gotten out by the apple tree? There on the ground, split down its length?

And the broken-off fang? The doctors found a piece of fang broken off and buried in that boy's leg. Hmmm. Too strange! I've got to stop thinking like this. I'm beginning to scare myself. Moses smiled and shrugged.

Union Presbyterian, bathed in late afternoon sunlight, was beautiful to behold. Leaves, all red and gold, carpeted the land. Pumpkins lay ripe in the field. He stretched and looked around.

Papa's land. My land, now. Everything's so beautiful. So peaceful.

The air, fragrant with the smell of apples, suddenly grew cold as a cloud obscured the sun. A chill wind blew; ruffling the thin pages of the letter he had taken back out and now held in his hand.

A pang of longing for Isaiah and Lacy hit him. And for Mamie.

I miss them.

He shivered as he turned, and headed back to the old home place. The old homestead that Isaiah Norris had carved out for his three wives and seventeen children.

The old home place where Mamie had lived out her days in peace and happiness. And where Moses, Tense, Philip, and William now called home.

Hearing his name called, he looked back toward the apple tree and Rodenburg Pond. He thought he saw an old woman, walking with Mamie. When he looked more closely, they vanished into the fading light.

Printed in the United States
92857LV00004B/280-297/A